WK 28
12
£249

From a young age ANTHONY JUDE MCGOWNE was an all-round sportsman, loving the fresh air. He found pleasure in football, tennis, golf, swimming and hill walking. Latterly, he has returned to music, art and writing, which he unfortunately discarded when young. He has always been fascinated by the power of steam locomotives and steam-propelled ships. He enjoys meeting people and travelling.

HIGHLAND ADVENTURES

HIGHLAND ADVENTURES

ANTHONY JUDE MCGOWNE

ATHENA PRESS
LONDON

HIGHLAND ADVENTURES
Copyright © Anthony Jude McGowne 2009

All Rights Reserved

ISBN 978 1 84748 454 3

First published 2009 by
ATHENA PRESS
Queen's House, 2 Holly Road
Twickenham TW1 4EG
United Kingdom

Printed for Athena Press

This book is dedicated to all youth leaders, charity workers and all who give their time for help of others without numeration.
To my loving wife Elaine who has been my inspiration.

Chapter One

I, Jamie Cameron, sixteen years of age, had asked my parents' permission to spend the whole of the summer holiday in the beautiful West Highlands of Scotland. It was 1964 and the world had come alive with music, travel and freedom for youth. I was a young, fit and healthy teenager who was about to embark on his first great adventure without parental control. Holidays would never be the same again. Life for me would change beyond recognition.

It was a bright sunny day when I left my Ayrshire home. The sky was soft blue with hints of white wispy clouds in the distance. My rucksack had been packed the previous evening with all the essentials for the journey. I was fully prepared and now it was the time to set off.

I met up with a long-standing school chum, Colin, who was a year or two older than I; he was also more experienced and less naive in the ways of the world. He is best described as a girl's dream boat – six foot in height, masculine build with blond wavy hair, blue eyes and a flawless complexion, a slight tan and shiny white teeth. I would fall into the small-to-medium category, with blue eyes, a fair complexion, and a sturdy athletic build.

We set out with the intention of reaching Glasgow by mid-afternoon at the latest. However, after we had walked at a leisurely pace and reached half the intended distance the road suddenly seemed endless. Then unexpectedly a pig farmer's van stopped and offered us a lift.

'I'm goin' to Glasgow if that's any good boys?' said the driver.

'That's where we're heading!' said Colin.

'Jump in and find a space then.'

Oh what a pong! I thought inwardly, is this what they mean when they say always take the lesser of two evils? The only consolation was that the windows of the vehicle remained open as the winders were broken. This allowed the stench to escape, along with the underarm odour of our sweat (from fear) as we hurtled round corners at breakneck speed.

Colin spoke to the driver about the road. 'Aye,' said he, 'this is a dangerous road even in the summer; mist can come doon onny tim' on Eaglesham Moor.'

Indeed this chap was a real character. One would have thought that we had stumbled on to a movie scene.

His dark coat was stained and moth-eaten with a clothes line rope tied round the middle of his large girth. He wore a large, chequered design 'Kilmarnock bonnet' tilted to one side. His breath had a stench of chewed tobacco, which tortured me every time I was faced with the exhalation of every outflowing word. He had bottom plate dentures which rattled against his own top teeth with every word he uttered. Two teeth were missing from the front middle, which gave a whistling effect as he stammered with every second syllable. I struggled to contain the mirth within as he addressed me.

I felt deep elation as he pulled into the kerb, as the odour had begun to overwhelm me.

'Thank you for the lift,' said Colin

'That was kind of you to stop,' I said

'Have a good holiday boys. Wish I had the time to take one!'

He then drove off.

'Phew, that's a relief!' I said.

'I couldn't take much more myself,' said Colin. 'I was relieved he was ending his journey in the city.'

'Not half as glad as I am, as I was closest to him,' I said.

We laughed all the way to the station.

Coming from a small town I had only been in such a large city very occasionally. The noise, hustle and bustle added more to the excitement.

The van had dropped us off on the south side of the river Clyde leaving us only ten minutes' walk to St Enoch's Station. It was absolute pandemonium. The rush hour had begun and we were right in the middle of it.

Colin told me we had to go to Queen Street Station, the departure point for trains north and west, where we would board a train to Balloch. He decided we should go by the underground train. This was a whole new experience for me. I could not believe there was a tunnel under the city by which we could be dropped off at a precise point. As we boarded the orange machine Colin looked at me with a grin on his face. Sensing my trepidation, he said, 'This is fun, enjoy it!'

My eyeballs were bulging as the train sped off. 'Everything OK?' Colin enquired.

I tried my best to look relaxed, wishing to put him at ease, while my mouth was dry and my stomach was churning.

'This is really exciting!' I exclaimed.

'It's funny, but fear sometimes can outweigh excitement, and the thing to remember, Jamie, is to enjoy the thrill of the moment and put those little negatives out of your mind,' said Colin.

On arrival at Queen Street Station we were unable to find the departure platform for Balloch. Never being shy of girls, Colin asked the most beautiful one he could find for assistance. With a cheerful smile and a gleam in her eye she pointed him in the right direction. All the while I stood amazed by my friend's ability to woo the opposite sex. Being a naturally shy person I hoped one day I could emulate his overwhelming confidence.

Platform one has a halt for commuter trains to its left further up the platform, which is the boarding point for Balloch and Helensburgh.

The train was due to arrive in five minutes so we hastily made our way towards the gate, producing our tickets for the collector to allow us to continue beyond the barrier. My excitement grew with every passing minute. It really dawned on me that I was travelling without my parents for the first time in my life.

A train trundled into the station as we were making our way forward and a group of girls on it spotted Colin. They began to wave furiously, thinking he was about to board the main train to Oban on the platform to the right. The incoming train came to a halt on our left and, seeing the sign for Balloch on it, we turned to board it.

The expressions on the girls' faces were priceless.

Colin, with a cheeky grin, entered their carriage and immediately indulged in conversation, enquiring where the girls had been and where they were bound for. Slightly embarrassed they told us

11

they had enjoyed a day's shopping and were now returning home. The first available train home meant coming in to the city to go back out again they explained.

'I get the picture,' said Colin.

In the blink of an eye he had them eating out of the palm of his hand. They asked where we were going and how long we planned to stay. Colin gladly filled them in with all the details.

'The whole summer!' they exclaimed

'Yes,' said Colin, 'aren't we lucky!'

Having waved farewell to our female companions at a previous station we arrived at Balloch. Walking to the bridge Colin pointed to the yachts and motor boats moored on the river. He also pointed out the paddle steamer *The Maid of the Loch*, which had an embarkation point further up the station at the head of the loch.

Light was fading fast with the shimmer of light bouncing off the still water but we were running late and had no time to waste, as delay could find us without a place to stay for the night.

We had walked twenty minutes or so when darkness began to descend quite rapidly. It was beginning to become rather spooky with rustling trees swaying in the fresh breeze. All at once a set of car lights appeared, casting large shadows. It was good just to have some inkling as to where we were going, as the road was now lit well into the distance.

The honk from the car slightly startled us. Then the loud and gruff voice hollered, 'Can I give you blokes a lift? I'm heading for Inverbeg if that's any good.'

Colin explained that we were making our way to the youth hostel, approximately two miles away on that route.

The lift was a welcome one as it had been a long day. The hostel closes its doors around 10 p.m. for walkers and we could not have made it in time had we not been given a lift. The kind gentleman delivered us straight to the hostel door after being told of our plight. Colin and I waved our goodbyes of gratitude to the kind stranger.

I said to Colin, 'I cannot believe that someone could go out their way for people they had never met before.'

'That was exceptional,' said Colin.

It heartened me to feel that there were kind individuals out there.

Chapter Two

The youth hostels in Scotland are set up a day's walking distance apart (this, of course, was in the 1960s and is no longer the case), which is approximately fourteen miles. Scottish hostels were a pioneer for the rest of the world, giving young people a chance to explore the Highlands and the rest of Scotland. The first youth hostel opened in the borders in Broadmeadows near Selkirk in 1931.

Loch Lomond hostel, where Colin and I are staying at present, is situated two miles north of Balloch. It is a Baronial-type mansion and was the divisional headquarters of the 12th anti-aircraft division, which protected the whole west coast of Scotland during the war. As far as I am led to believe, it was then gifted to the SYHA after hostilities ceased in 1945. The rooms here are set out with between four and eight bunks per room, which can be a hive of activity first thing in the morning. Inverbeg hostel boasts to be one of the earliest opened on record. It was only beaten by four months by Broadmeadows (to be accurate, it was the fifth one opened).

Hostelling is a marvellous way to spend one's summer holiday and every teenager should experience this at least once in their lifetime.

We arrived after ten o'clock and the main door was still open to my instant relief.

'What would we have done, Colin, if that chap hadn't given us a lift?'

'It doesn't deserve a second thought!' said Colin, pausing. 'Did we not get a lift?'

Colin's philosophy is transparent. If it's going to happen it will happen.

Some hostel wardens close doors to any late stragglers unless they have pre-booked. Luckily for us the warden was a really friendly guy and let us brew a cuppa and eat what was left of our packed lunch.

The room was filled with hikers and I was given the top bunk, which I was not looking forward to at all. I tucked my blankets in really tight as I had this vision of waking up in hospital, bandaged and plastered from head to toe, with an oxygen mask on my face. The warden, I felt, had almost sensed my trepidation and he smiled to Colin. 'Remember and tuck your wee brother in,' he chuckled, and winked at me.

Although I didn't look that young he had sensed that it was my first experience of hostel accommodation, or maybe noticed that my hostel card was brand new. I thought to myself, this chap has the power of empathy, probably through gaining experience of looking after teenagers and being able to put himself into their shoes by interpreting the feelings they are transmitting through body language. Well, whatever!

I needn't have worried as I went out like a light as soon as my head hit the pillow.

Waking with the noise and chatter in the room I quickly jumped to the floor and headed for the toilets for all the usual essentials. Fortunately for me I did not have a beard at that time and Colin, being very fair, was similarly clean-chinned. The water was freezing; boy did that wake you up when it hit your face. Life was at its most basic but it was great fun. I was starving and I knew my provisions were low, to say the least. When you're hiking you really only carry enough provisions for the day ahead.

The rucksack is ideal for this, with a light frame that rests on the hips and straps that neatly rest on one's shoulders. I won't go any further with that at the moment; my pangs of hunger have taken over. I headed for the hostel shop where all provisions can be purchased.

It's great that you are able to buy one or two eggs and not a box. I bought two eggs, a few rashers of bacon, four rolls plus a small packet of cornflakes. Tea was always on the stove so that would not be a problem.

Colin met me at the corner of the canteen door and, yes, he was chatting up the girls. A petite blonde spoke to me, saying, 'Is this what you're having for breakfast?'

'Yes!' I replied.

Without more ado I was relieved of my provisions and told to sit over in the corner where a young lady was sitting. I was naturally shy and found conversing with the opposite sex extremely difficult. I always got a 'reddie' – red cheeks to those who have no understanding of colloquial talk.

I sat down and introduced myself.

She replied, 'Pleased to meet you, I'm Bonnie.'

This was a beautiful girl I had nodded to in the corridor earlier. I couldn't believe my luck. Well, that name certainly matched what I was looking at, as I gazed into her dark hazel eyes. She was of slender figure with all the right bumps in proportion to her frame. Her calming demeanour put me at ease immediately, as she enquired where I came from and for how long I intended to be in the Highlands.

I told her this was my very first day living in hostel accommodation and that I was very excited about what lay ahead in the coming ten weeks.

'You are lucky – that's the whole summer!' said Bonnie. She went on to say she came from a small hamlet in the borders with no more than a few hundred people living in the community. 'Everyone knows what is happening as we sort of live on top of one another!' she said.

I smiled, as I felt that the same thing existed even in a town. I told her that life is much the same everywhere and all my neighbours and friends had wished me a happy and safe holiday.

We went from subject to subject as we became engrossed in one another. To the outside eye we could have been mistaken for a couple.

Colin now joined us at the table. 'You two are hitting it off well! I'm Colin, by the way,' he said, introducing himself to Bonnie and without hesitation he kissed her soft pink hands. Oh, how I wished I could have done that, as I was smitten by her beauty and for the first time I felt a tinge of jealousy. I pictured him in the moonlight, kissing and holding her gently in his muscular arms, then quickly put it out my head. Nonsense! I thought, I'm sure she likes me.

Heather and Lisa arrived at the table with a full breakfast for all except Bonnie, who had chosen scrambled eggs and toast. Famished, I set about my plate, gorging the contents.

Bonnie smiled and gestured for me to slow down, whispering in my ear, 'You will gain more nourishment by chewing your meal before swallowing.'

'Sorry,' I said, 'my dad is forever telling me the same!'

Heather told Colin to wash the pots and pans after we had finished breakfast. Lisa washed the crockery and cutlery, while Bonnie and I dried. I never knew drying dishes could be such fun or so flirtatious.

Clearing the tables of all food was the warden's allotted task for Colin and me. The girls were to follow behind, washing and cleaning up. This done, we were free for the day.

While doing our chores I took the liberty of asking Bonnie about her plans for the next few days. She told me, 'Heather, Lisa and I travelled north yesterday by car from the borders with a few stops in between. All three of us are heading for Skye to spend a few days at my aunt's cottage. Heather has an orange Volkswagen Beetle, a good sturdy little car, but it has little room for luggage, especially when three girls are on board.'

'Mmm... what about today?' I asked.

'O, we are spending another two nights here!'

My heart jumped; trying not to show too much elation at this news, I felt bemused at myself even thinking in this way.

'That sounds pretty good to me. I hope you have a wonderful time!' I said, wishing under my breath that I was going along with her.

I admitted that our programme was that of, whatever comes along we will take on board. Although I knew Colin would have planned a certain route and timetable for each day in advance.

She also intimated that in late July she was holidaying in the Inverness area. I enquired about the actual date. She smiled and looked at me, slightly surprised by the question. 'It's the last fortnight in July,' she responded, 'I will be staying with my aunt.'

'Well, you never know!' I said, with a vision in my head of meeting her on the banks of the river Ness, her hair blowing in the breeze. It was difficult to miss the dimples on her cheeks as she smiled at me during our little flirtation. 'I will be heading that way too,' I added.

'I'm sure you will like your stay,' she replied.

I had a quick word with Colin in the dormitory. 'What are the plans for today?' I asked him.

'Nothing set, Jamie boy! Let me guess, you want to spend the day with Bonnie. Am I right?'

'Spot on, how did you guess?'

'It was hard to miss all that billing and cooing.'

'I have arranged to meet Bonnie in ten minutes if that's all right by you.'

'Fine by me. Heather and Lisa want to walk up to Luss with me for lunch, so I intend making the day of it,' said Colin.

I took Bonnie's hand as she exited the hostel – a bit presumptuous of me, but I had made my mind up earlier to take the initiative.

She smiled, showing off her pearl-white teeth. Perfection indeed, I thought. This girl has it all, even a nature to match. I was indeed fortunate even to walk with her, never mind hold her hand.

The soft breeze brushed her shining chestnut hair as we meandered down the path towards the main road. 'We will have to walk single file for a short distance,' I told her, 'as there is no available footpath for quite a way.'

We walked facing the traffic, but she let her right arm tilt back so that I could still hold her hand.

At last a footpath was in sight. I was relieved, as the traffic was intense, especially with tourist coaches.

'Cross now!' I called to her.

She turned to face me and we sprinted across the busy road.

Clasping my hand tightly, Bonnie turned and said, 'I don't know what it is, but I seem to want to keep close to you.'

This made me feel like a knight in shining armour. Where's my white stallion? I thought. I smiled and said, 'I honestly feel the same way!'

We strolled into Balloch at a leisurely pace and I told her of my ambitions for the future. I felt sure my age was surely about to come into question so I volunteered it. 'I will be seventeen in August this year.'

'Oh, you're just a baby then... just teasing!' she said. 'I will be eighteen in August so that makes me a year older than you.'

I didn't know what to expect then. I could only hope she hadn't taken fright. My fears were allayed when she spoke.

'The girls will be jealous that I have found someone so young.'

I told her I was the second eldest in a family of five, with one brother older and one younger and two younger sisters. Bonnie responded by saying, 'I'm the youngest and the only girl. Both my big brothers are rugby players.'

'Rugby!' I said

'Yes, they are both well over six foot and built to match.'

My stomach began to churn. They will kill me, I thought. Oh, goodness they sound like giants! Will they take to me when they see me? I could only hope they were of the same gentle nature as Bonnie.

'Your brothers, Bonnie, are they single?' I asked.

'Yes, they are. My mum is always complaining about how much they eat. I have to help with the washing and ironing. With both playing rugby it's a never-ending stream of work.'

'My mum will heartily agree with you both, the washing machine is never off in our home,' I said.

By this time we had arrived in Balloch and a light shower began, forcing us to take shelter at a bus stop. She snuggled into me and, taking her short jacket off, placed it over both our heads.

'Let's go now!' I shouted, pulling my arm round her waist and then placing hers behind mine.

'This is cosy! Are you comfortable enough, Jamie?'

Comfortable! I was in a state of euphoria just holding her.

'As long as you feel OK then I'm good,' I said.

'You are so considerate,' she said with a tug at my waist and a smile towards me.

'Thank you. I always try to put others first, especially a girl like you.'

She stopped and kissed me and I went to heaven that very moment.

'I don't know what it is about you, but I have felt magnetically drawn to you from the first moment I set eyes on you,' said Bonnie.

'I can honestly say the same, since seeing you in the corridor last evening.'

She hugged me tightly and smiled once more into my eyes.

The drizzle had now stopped as we approached the level crossing gates in the town. 'We won't be long in drying,' I said, pulling the jacket from both our heads. 'I'll hold it for you,' I said.

Anything belonging to her was a treasure to me at this moment. The train pulled away and we moved towards the bridge over the river Leven. I had had little time to explore last evening.

'The views are even more stunning than I remembered, Bonnie.'

'Perhaps you were in such a hurry that you didn't have time to focus properly.'

'You're right. It's gorgeous, isn't it?' I said.

'Take me over the other side so that I can feed the swans, Jamie.' Clasping my hand even tighter she pulled me forward and started to run over the bridge. I felt like a ten year old with a new toy; the last toy to have given me such a thrill had been my train set.

We spent most of the afternoon on the banks of the river eating the sandwiches that Bonnie had provided.

'You came well prepared!' I said.

'Yes, I did. I did get a glimpse of your appetite this morning, though.'

We both broke into hysterical laughter simultaneously.

'I have no answer to that.'

We fed what little scraps were left (and I mean little!) to the swans and wild geese. Bonnie was about to take my picture as I prepared to throw my last two pieces of bread, when a duck caught my left hand with its beak and pulled me round. Bonnie was in fits of laughter at this. 'I've got that picture – now feed it,' she cried. 'I'll try to capture it on camera. Oh I do hope that one takes all right. It was a perfect shot!'

We asked a passer-by to take a couple of photos of us together and then it was time to leave.

If heaven is like this, I thought, then I would choose to hold this day for ever.

'Do you like fish?' Bonnie asked.

'Love it,' I said.

'Well, I'll cook us a meal in the hostel when we return.'

'Brilliant!' I said.

'There is a fishmonger's which also sells vegetables up the top of the hill. If you carry—'

'Carry you?' I said. 'Certainly.'

'Let me finish, Jamie!' said an amused Bonnie, slightly taken aback by my interruption. 'Again. If you carry… what I need, it would help! I will get enough for the five of us, as it's too expensive to eat out for us all,' said Bonnie.

Bonnie loaded me up with provisions, enough for two or three days. 'Will you be able to carry all this?' she asked, laughing.

'No problem!' I showed her my biceps as a proud male would do. And you too if need be, I thought.

'Well, if you're sure then!'

I loaded all the groceries into bags and then we set out for the hostel.

'I can't get away from what that duck got up to,' said Bonnie. 'It was as if it was saying, what about me?'

'I couldn't believe it either. I was startled at first. It is obviously quite tame as lots of people feed them here.'

'Thank you for my day, Jamie, I enjoyed it immensely' – and she kissed me once more.

I was glad to arrive at the hostel as the bags were starting to annoy me. Plastic bags tend to dig into one's skin after a while. I didn't want to show any signs of weakness on the way as Bonnie was enjoying the freedom to flirt with me. My feelings for her overcame the pain and I would gladly have walked back into town if she had asked me.

We had only just reached the kitchen with the provisions when Colin turned up with the girls. 'I hope you have enough for us all!' he shouted from the doorway.

'Nothing for you!' I said in response. 'We had to carry everything from town so go and get your own.' I got a little nudge from Bonnie which meant that was as far as I should go. I turned and smiled at her and said, 'He is forever winding me up so I like to get even now and again.'

She smiled that melting smile and said nothing.

'It's fresh haddock for the supper tonight,' I said.

'Mmm…' said Colin.

'Are you cooking?' I asked him.

This brought instant mirth from the girls who had now gathered round. 'We'll do it,' said Heather, 'you both can do the cleaning up as usual.'

It was after eight o' clock by the time we had eaten and cleared up so Colin suggested that we stay in and have a fun evening in the hostel lounge; everyone agreed. The lounge was busy. However, there was one table available with room for us all. It meant joining a chap who was sitting by himself though.

'Do you mind if we join you?' asked Colin.

'Not at all,' he replied.

'Where are you from?' asked Colin.

'Glasgow,' he replied.

Colin went on to introduce us all. 'I'm Colin from Ayrshire. Heather, Lisa and Bonnie are all from the Borders, and Jamie is also from Ayrshire.'

'Pleased to meet you all, I'm Derek,' he said, shaking everyone firmly by the hand. 'I come up here regularly, at least twice a month. I usually stay at Inverbeg hostel but I arrived too late to travel up there on Friday. I was held up at work as we had to finish a job before the weekend. I'm off till Tuesday now.'

'Well why don't you come with us to Ardlui tomorrow?' asked Lisa, who was totally captivated by this strikingly good-looking man.

'I have a Norton motorcycle if you care to come with me?' said Derek.

'Let anyone try and stop me!' said Lisa.

'That's settled then,' said Derek.

Colin went on to tell us of the fun day he and the two girls had had together. It was always funny the way Colin was able to relay his story. Perhaps he'll be a writer one day, I thought to myself.

Derek then produced a guitar. Oh, this was just what was needed. 'Magic!' I said, 'What do you play?'

'Folk mainly, but I put my hand to most of the new pop tunes,' he said.

'Colin will sing a ballad or two with me. You can join in if you can,' I said.

Join in! This guy was brilliant and the girls from all round the room merged round him, to the disconcertment of Lisa, who was feeling just a little vulnerable as a beautiful blonde pulled her chair close to him. Soon the whole body of the room was sitting round the table with Derek giving his rendition of an American folk song. This did not deter Colin, who was now up for the challenge.

'Derek, do you know any of the Everly Brothers numbers?'

'Sure do!' said Derek.

Colin turned to Heather and began to sing to her. 'Oh, I like this,' she said. 'That was wonderful,' she added, giving Colin a hug at the end of his rendition.

I wasn't going to be outdone, so started – 'Hey! Hey baby, I want to know if you'll be my girl' – while staring into Bonnie's eyes. She held out her hand to me as I continued, to the delight of everyone present. When I finished she whispered in my ear, 'Yes!'

Derek wasn't about to be beaten easily. He turned to Lisa and began to sing an Elvis number: 'Love Me Tender'.

She began whispering in his ear the second he finished the number.

I guess they will be seeing a lot of one and other from now on, I thought.

'Lights out!' was the call from the warden.

I kissed Bonnie in the corridor before the stairs and told her, 'I had the most wonderful day and I can't wait to see you again tomorrow.'

As far as I'm aware most of the others were speaking in similar vein as they returned to their dormitory.

Chapter Three

We were wakened early by the noise of trampling feet in the corridors. It would seem everyone was up and heading for either the washrooms or the kitchen. It was more like a stampede.

Our second day in Loch Lomond, and I was looking forward to going on a trip with Bonnie. On the night of our arrival in the corridor I had first become aware of Bonnie. She had a towel on her head and was singing as she made her way along to the dormitory. It was difficult not to notice such beauty even with so little to enhance her.

I hope I see her again, I had said to myself as she smiled walking past. Was I a lucky guy to have someone so beautiful even glance at me, never mind my going out with her the next day and then having her kiss me…

'Are you ready for breakfast?' I asked Colin.

'Certainly am!'

The dining room was almost filled to capacity. 'This *will* be fun!' I said to Colin.

'No worries, I'm sure the girls have everything in hand.'

Sure enough we were given a wave to come to the stoves to collect our breakfast which had already been prepared.

'I only hope you boys appreciate what we do for you,' said Lisa.

'Oh we do, we really do, you are marvellous cooks into the bargain!' said Colin.

'That's enough sucking up,' said Lisa. 'You can have your breakfast now.'

We hastened to a table after the departure of the previous occupants. You can't doddle about when a vacancy arises. I made a place for Bonnie beside me in the corner. We managed to get seats for all six of us as Derek had now joined the group. It was a little cramped but the girls don't mind being close.

Derek received his breakfast plate from a very attentive Lisa. Heather and Bonnie were not far behind.

'Excellent service in this establishment,' said Colin to Derek. 'I can highly recommend it, and of course the waiting staff are very pretty.'

'I'll second that,' said Derek, to the delight of Lisa.

After carrying out our chores, which included washing dishes of course, we were given the task of cleaning the toilets. Colin moaned, 'We must look like a couple of labourers!'

'Well, you will show off all those muscles,' I said. 'Come on, let's sing through it as you usually do.' The transformation was immediate as he burst into song and we sailed through the horrible task. 'We have to meet the girls outside at ten, so let's get a move on!' I said.

After the inspection met with the warden's approval, we departed hastily from the building just in case he found fault.

'What kept you?' enquired Heather.

'You don't want to know,' said Colin.

'Yes we do,' said Heather, 'don't we, girls!'

I'm sure I detected a chuckle in her voice. She knows we were cleaning the toilets, I thought to myself.

Derek had left earlier as he had been given only a light chore.

As we stood in the hostel grounds chatting, Derek came thundering round the corner on his gleaming Norton 500cc silver-grey motorcycle. He was clad all in black leather with matching helmet and gloves. I could see Lisa was in awe of both man and machine. It didn't take an artist to see the light in her eyes.

Taking off his helmet he called for Lisa to approach him and, reaching into his right-hand saddlebag, he produced a second crash helmet.

We all gathered round in admiration.

'Some machine!' I said.

All were in agreement.

Lisa said, 'I hope this helmet doesn't spoil my hair.'

Derek replied, 'It won't affect your beauty, nothing could.'

Jubilant at his comment Lisa quickly donned her newfound headwear. Heather and Bonnie were now just a little jealous as she mounted the cycle, maybe wishing they had been chosen instead.

Earlier we had discussed what we would take on our picnic. It was decided that we were short of supplies with the addition of Derek to our group. Derek offered to go into town for fresh provisions and of course Lisa volunteered to assist with the task. Derek told us to go ahead and he would meet us at Ardlui. Heather acknowledged him as she was our driver. 'We will meet you at the big car park close to the marina. You can't miss it,' she said.

Heather then went to the car park and brought her orange Beetle to the front of the hostel. Colin made for the left-hand passenger door, leaving the rear seats clear for Bonnie and me.

The traffic again was exceptionally busy on the narrow winding roads round Loch Lomond. As we were in no hurry we relaxed into the journey and just enjoyed the beautiful scenery, while I snuggled into Bonnie of course. It felt great to be close to her once more.

The VW Beetle narrows at the back, which is a boon to courting couples. It tends to tilt you into one another as it twists round bends, and there is no shortage of those on this road.

This brought Bonnie into fits of giggles every so often; so much so that it interrupted Colin's conversation with Heather, with whom he was totally engrossed, by the way.

'What's going on behind our backs?' Colin enquired. 'There's a lot of mischievous laughter coming over our way.'

'We are continually being thrown from side to side,' I said.

'Well, hold on to her more tightly,' said Colin.

After this intrusion Bonnie began removing her small chunky boots. When this was completed she whispered in my ear, 'Move over as far as you can so that I can sit longways on the seat and you can hold me in your arms.'

Only too willing to comply I duly obliged. 'Do you want me on the other side?' I asked.

'Why?' she enquired.

'Well, you will be able to see the view of the loch,' I said.

'The view I have is the one most important to me now, and I want to have it for as long as possible.'

She then pulled me down and kissed me.

I had only kissed one or two girls in my short life and they were at parties where you played those silly games – if you were trapped, you had to kiss the girl who was trapped with you. It had never worked out the way I wanted. It seemed as if I was destined to get nabbed by the big girls who crushed me in their arms, followed by a great slobbery kiss.

This kiss was like nothing I had imagined nor could have guessed was possible. To feel as close to someone had changed me in an inexplicable way. I held her face in my hand and caressed her like a child. I felt my masculinity was now coming to the fore as I cradled her head in my arms. I stroked her hair as she drifted further into my chest and she began to slumber softly, feeling safe.

The road was very busy owing to a large number of coach tours. We had thought it would take only around thirty minutes to get there, yet after that time we had only reached halfway.

Bonnie began to stir and pulled me down for a kiss a soon as she was fully awake. 'What did I do to deserve that?' I asked.

'Do I have to answer that?' she replied, with deep smile on her lips.

'No.'

'Oh, that reminds me,' said Bonnie, 'I phoned home last night to confirm the date my mother has arranged for me to stay at my aunt's in Inverness.'

'What date is it?'

'Patience, Jamie! It's the last week in July.'

'That's perfect!' I said. 'It means I will be able to spend a week with you.'

'Yes, I know and that's not all. She has arranged with my aunt as well for us to spend another two or three days in Skye.'

'So they are going to put me up as well?'

'Yes,' said Bonnie, 'and it won't cost us a penny if we do a few chores for them both. I told Mum you are very skilled.'

'I hope you didn't overdo it,' I said.

'You're too modest. Colin has sung your praises to me. He has been observing all the work you have undertaken at home.'

'Wait till I see him alone,' I said.

Heather handed over some sweets to us but Bonnie took only one from the packet. Colin said, 'You had better take more than that or you'll not get another chance with that gannet beside you.'

'We girls have to watch our figures,' she replied.

Turning into me she said, 'By the way I almost forgot. My two brothers are taking a youth group up to Oban for camp and they will be in Fort William for their second week. I have to ask you if you wish to meet up with them. They will pick you up near Glencoe.'

'Have they got a bus?' I asked.

'Yes. They also have two spare seats.'

'I'll check with Colin, but I'm up for it anyway.'

'They have sports days which will suit you and, of course, they will be spending a day climbing Ben Nevis, the highest peak in the UK,' said Bonnie.

'That will be something to brag about when I get back home,' I said, 'so I will definitely be going. When I phone you from Glencoe you can relay the meeting place and date.'

'I'll do that, darling. Wish I could come but it's strictly a lads' outing and boys don't like their wee sister tagging along,' said Bonnie.

It was beginning to get hot in the back as the sun became more intense. 'Thank goodness we are approaching Ardlui,' said Bonnie.

I was more than relieved myself as I had little room in which to move.

'Good. That's us here!' said Heather.

Heather made her way to the large car park to wait for the arrival of Derek and Lisa, which was only a matter of seconds later. Taking off her helmet Lisa called to us, 'That was my first time on a motorcycle, boy is it a thrill!' I'm quite sure she was trying to make Bonnie and Heather jealous, and I have to say she was succeeding. 'We just seemed to slip out of one bend and tilt the other way into another. I was clinging to Derek for dear life.'

There was a spontaneous response from Heather and Bonnie. 'Oh yes!'

Her cheeks were now red as Derek had removed his helmet and was now aware of the banter.

'Well, you know what I mean,' said Lisa, trying to hide her emotions.

Derek began to laugh and Lisa became more at ease. 'Hold the helmets, Lisa, and I will remove the groceries from the bike.'

Having gathered all our provisions together we shared them in a way that the entire group had a fair share of the groceries. The men carried the bulk of the heavy items which seemed only fair.

We made our way to a small secluded beach, close to the river which is the feeding source of the loch. The girls produced a small stove and quickly brewed a cup of tea, whereas the boys preferred a beer or a cola.

It was time for a bit of fun and Colin suggested the boys play the girls at rounders.

'We don't have bats or balls,' said one of the girls.

'No problem,' said Colin, 'Jamie will come up with something.'

'There's bound to be a branch we can use,' I said, 'not too thick so that the girls can't hold it.'

After a few minutes everyone had produced an item of wood they thought might do the trick. I selected the most appropriate piece and honed it into shape with a sharp rock.

'I never would have believed it if I hadn't seen it for myself,' said Derek.

'Told you so!' said Colin.

'You don't mind if we use your gloves for the girls?' I asked Derek. 'They won't forgive me if they get a splinter.'

'Not a problem,' said Derek.

'What about a ball?' the girls asked.

'Well, Jamie?' Colin asked.

I produced an old battered tennis ball I had found further up the beach.

'I don't believe it,' said Colin. 'We have a ball!' – shouting out loud for everyone to hear.

'Place a piece of clothing at each station and I'll mark the starting point with a delivering line.'

After a few mistakes we were all ready and excitement was building among the girls. Heather chose herself as the captain of the girls. Likewise Colin chose himself.

'Ball not above three feet,' insisted Heather, 'and must be delivered underhand,' she cried.

'Let the game commence,' shouted Colin.

Heather demanded that the girls go first. Derek was chosen by Colin to throw the first balls. Colin shouted, 'Just to remind you – you only have three chances to hit the ball. That's the rules I use.'

Colin then placed me in the boundaries, whereas he stood in the mid station so as to gain any advantage from a bad hit.

Derek commenced by throwing a gentle lob and to his astonishment Heather hit it a great whack. The ball flew over my head without any chance of my catching it. Dropping the bat and gloves she made for the first station, then second and third station, finally back to base. There was cheering and glee from the girls, jumping up and down in rapturous celebration.

Colin called Derek and me for a briefing.

'This is not funny any more; the girls are out to slaughter us. Lads, our reputation is seriously at stake. If they succeed we will never live it down. The reason I have called a meeting is that you, Derek, will want to throw little dainty balls to Lisa and the same goes for you, Jamie. This is all good and well if you want to lose, guys.

'Let battle commence,' said Colin.

Derek, not wishing to offend Colin, fired a fierce underhand shot towards Lisa, who was startled at the ferocity. She exclaimed, 'Oh, so that is your game.'

Colin shouted, 'Miss.'

Derek, having now recovered the ball, took aim. He then fired another fierce shot. This time, however, Lisa was more than a match for it and launched her bat at the oncoming missile. She struck it, almost parting Derek's hair in the process. He ducked rather late with fright at the venom in the strike.

Lisa, who was akin to a sprinter, reached all the stations and was back within seconds.

Colin, being annoyed at the outcome, took his temper out on me. 'Why are you not catching these balls?'

Obviously new tactics would need to be deployed. Colin gathered us all together once more.

'We need to divert the girls attention, boys. It is up to you, Derek, to divert Lisa's attention and the same goes for you, Jamie.'

We returned to our positions. Bonnie was next in line.

As Bonnie was of slight statue, I wondered if she could hit the ball at all. I didn't bother with Colin's tactics. Stepping up she stood firmly and faced Derek, who launched an even fiercer shot. To the total astonishment of us all, she hit a whopper and it went sailing over my head. *Oh no!* I thought, Colin is going to go berserk.

It was now Colin's round to throw the ball. Heather was back in position. From my vantage point I couldn't see Colin's face, but I felt sure he was making eyes at her or trying some other distraction. Colin aimed a shot keeping it rather low in the hope that Heather would miss it. However, Heather struck out and the ball went flashing past me and went bounding up the beach. I could see the amazed annoyance in his face.

Lisa was now in base and Colin let loose a flyer but Lisa totally missed it. Again he lined up to throw it low and she missed it for the second time. The third shot produced a determination on Lisa's face as she let swing. 'Miss! Miss!' She was run out. There were only two of them now.

It was now my turn to throw. Heather stood firm as I launched a shot low and hard. Yet again she cracked it over my head. However, this time it was caught by Derek, thrown to Colin and she was run out. The boys were now jubilant.

Bonnie was next, and I threw a little dinky one, to the horror of Colin. Bonnie met the shot full on, producing another great strike. She completed all the stations and returned to base.

With Lisa and Heather now both run out and only Bonnie remaining, it was my turn to throw, which I can say I faced with more than a little trepidation.

As I was about to throw she winked at me, as if to say go easy on me. I then threw the ball half heartedly and hoped that Colin would fail to notice. The little tigress hit it for six and giggled all the way round each station to return to base.

No more! I said to myself. She winked at me again but I wasn't falling for it this time. As she was still staring at me I threw a short, low but gentle delivery, hoping that she would sky the ball to the delight of Colin. I achieved my objective. Colin manoeuvred to catch it. He quickly threw the ball to me so that she was run out at base. 'Girls all out for five runs,' shouted Colin.

It was the lads' turn now. Heather, being the captain, chose to throw first. Colin was first in line. Heather thrust her first shot so close to him that he was unable to hit the oncoming ball. The second shot then came too high and he missed again.

'Foul!' he cried, but he was totally ignored.

Now he was disgusted. The third ball came low and caught him off balance, hitting the ground with the bat and missing the ball again completely.

'Out for a duck,' the girls shouted.

'That's not fair!' howled Colin. 'You're a bunch of cheats!'

'Colin's out!' cried all the girls.

Oh! He was not pleased at all. There was no consolation from Heather, who was now ecstatic at his demise.

Colin then called us all together. 'Well, you can see the tactics they're employing. All I can say is good luck.'

Derek stepped up to face Lisa, who had a facial expression full of mischief, as she ran up to throw her first shot. Sure enough her first delivery was too close to Derek for comfort. He had to dodge the ball. The second attempt was still too close, so he stepped sideways and took a lunge and a swipe at it, totally missing. He ended up in a spin, to the delight of Lisa. The third shot was a little easier to have a reasonable hit but he only managed to hit it to the side. Having had three attempts he was forced to run to the furthest station he could reach. He only made the middle station before the ball was retrieved, which left him stranded halfway.

It was now Bonnie's turn to throw and I wondered what she had up her sleeve. She started moving her hips in a seductive manner, then winked at me. She wiggled her body as she fired her first shot. This totally mesmerised me and I missed the shot completely without even swinging my bat.

It was left for me to salvage my pride, never mind the game. I tried to keep focus for the next ball thrown. This was not easy as Bonnie had diversified her playing style. She began wiggling her hips as she moved in to throw the shot. I was barely able to keep my eye on the delivery. I only managed to graze the ball, which landed but a few feet from me.

The third and final shot I felt I had to make contact with. It's now or never, I thought. So I gave it my all.

I lashed out and managed to hit the ball a fair distance, but the spritely Heather managed to retrieve it more quickly than I had envisaged.

Derek's attention had been drawn by Lisa, which diverted his concentration from the hit that had just taken place. By the time he had realised that the ball had been taken I was all but level. The cunning Lisa was standing over the base waiting for the throw of the ball from Heather. We made our dash almost together, but Lisa had caught the ball by this time. She promptly called, 'You're all out. Girls five, boys out for a duck.' There was an awful din and commotion.

Colin declared, 'I didn't expect to win as I knew they would use underhand tactics. However they even lowered that standard to downright dirtier ones.'

'There will be no living this down,' I said.

'OK! You win, girls. There was no beating that,' said Colin.

The girls were still cock-a-hoop with victory as we made our way back to our makeshift camp. I could feel my hunger pangs starting to bite. Hot water was first on the agenda. 'Anyone for tea or coffee?' asked Heather. We all placed our orders and soon the small kettle was ready.

Lisa by this time had emptied her plastic bag and produced a freshly cooked chicken.

'Mm... Oh, the aroma,' I said.

'Girls get first choice,' said Lisa. 'Leg or breast, Heather?'

'Breast!'

'Leg or breast, Bonnie?'

'Breast.'

'I guess I'll have a leg!' said Lisa. 'You can divide what's left among you boys.'

Although we didn't get much of the chicken the small portion we received was delicious. The girls provided us with various sandwiches and fruit enough to satisfy all our needs. We lay in the sun for an hour just relaxing and taking in the panoramic view.

A small discussion ensued between the girls about who should question Derek why he preferred to be alone. It would have to be

Bonnie or Heather. There wasn't a problem, as Heather volunteered immediately.

'May I be so bold as to ask! What's a good-looking guy like you doing up here by himself?' asked Heather.

'You don't have to answer that,' said Lisa, letting him know that she had no part of this enquiry into his personal affairs.

'I hope you don't think we're prying,' said Heather.

'Not at all,' said Derek, 'I'm quite happy to tell you now. A few months ago I would have probably walked away. There's not really that much to tell.'

'Do tell us please!' said Lisa.

Derek began to tell his story.

'I stay in the outskirts of Glasgow near Clarkston. I don't know whether you are familiar with the area. It's on the south side, very handy for travelling down to the Ayrshire coast.'

'Oh, we don't know where that is,' said Lisa. 'We are not too familiar with it; as you know, we are from the Borders.'

'Anyway, I'm a joiner by trade, which I do enjoy. I love building. Oh, and I'm twenty-four if you're interested.'

'Oh, I wouldn't have put you down for that age,' said Lisa.

I could see by the gleam in her eyes that she was captivated by his every word.

'Well, I knew a girl called Maria. We grew up together, same school, but it was the sort of I-love-to-hate-you attitude. I was better off, well my parents were. I think she resented that. Either that or she thought I was a snob.

'I was let down for the school dance. The girl I was going with decided on someone else so I went on my own. Maria was there on her own and I bumped into her at the lemonade stall. Before I knew it we were dancing away and our relationship continued. We had both made up stories of one and other without any foundation, which was totally wrong. I learnt a valuable lesson from that and took it on board.

'I was engaged and all set to be married last summer.'

'What happened?' interrupted Lisa.

'I'm afraid Maria, my fiancée, was diagnosed with leukaemia three months before the wedding was due to take place. She died in September last year.'

'How awful!' said one of the girls. 'So very sad.'

'Well, it's taken me all this time to get over it. I bought this bike in the spring and I've been doing a bit of hill walking most weekends.

'Lisa, you're the first girl I have really spoken with since last September.'

'Oh, that's nice! Thanks!'

'I told you there wasn't much to tell.'

Chapter Four

T he girls were now in a playful mood. They began to splash about in the water. There was a large rock about twenty yards out from the shore with stones protruding from the water in a line towards it.

'We can use them as stepping stones,' said Heather to Lisa.

They carefully placed each foot on one stone after another, keeping their feet dry all the while until they reached the rock.

'Be careful out there!' shouted Colin.

'Come and join us!' cried Heather

'Derek, you please come too,' said Lisa.

'How are we able to say no to that plea?' said Derek to Colin.

Colin and Derek made their precarious way out. Fearing they might fall in, Derek went first to test if the stones were stable enough to support his weight. As he was the lighter of the two it was a precaution that made sense. Colin followed close behind holding Derek's hand, much to the amusement of the girls.

'What are you pair like?' said Heather.

Derek retorted, 'I think you want us to fall in.'

'We do!' cried Lisa.

'Just wait till we get out there,' said Colin.

'I'd prefer to stay here, Jamie,' said Bonnie. She took my hand and said, 'Let's go for a walk along the shoreline.'

'OK,' I said. 'By the way, I've a bone to pick with you, lady!'

'What have I done?' enquired Bonnie, with an expression of innocence on her angelic face.

'Remember that little game, my naughty little girl?'

'What game was that?' asked Bonnie.

'Why, your antics during our game of rounders of course!'

'Are you saying I'm a naughty baby?'

'Since you put it like that, yes. From now on, Bonnie McKay, I'll call you my naughty baby.'

'I like it when you call me your baby. Especially the way you say it.'

She was flirting again. How does a guy deal with this?

I pulled her towards me, lifted her in my arms, and kissed her full on the lips. 'Naughty baby,' I said as we parted.

All at once there were screams of excitement from the rock. It wasn't immediately apparent what exactly had happened; afterwards, we discovered the full story. We had only restricted viewing where we were, as the girls were on the opposite side of the rock. Apparently the girls had led the boys to believe they had dropped a bracelet in the water. The boys fell for the bait, leaned over the rock at the deep end, and the girls had pushed them in. In retaliation, Colin and Derek had lifted them both up, all the while still in their wet clothes. Hence all the reason for screaming.

'I don't like the idea of someone lifting me with wet clothes on,' said Bonnie to Heather who was relating the story.

'It didn't stop there,' said Heather. 'They jumped into the water still holding us. It was freezing!'

'You don't mess about with Colin,' I said. 'He always wins.'

'I know that now,' said Heather.

Everyone had taken it in good part and we laughed and laughed. They all dressed themselves as best they could and then hastily returned to the car.

'I'm glad we are in the back,' I said.

'What's Lisa like in those leather trousers?' said Bonnie.

'They must be ten sizes too big for her!' I said.

'She had to change or she would catch her death on the back of the bicycle,' said Colin, still dripping wet, stripped to the waist showing off his meaty physique for the benefit of Heather.

'It's OK for you two in the back,' said Heather, who was down to her navy bra and shorts. Fortunately she kept a pair of shoes for driving in the car, which proved beneficial at the present moment.

'That should teach you not to play in water when you have no change of clothing, Heather, and you also, Colin,' said Bonnie.

That shut up the pair of them.

'I'm quite sure if we had been out there, Bonnie, we would be pulled in along with the rest of them,' I whispered in her ear. She smiled at me and nodded in agreement.

The roads were much quieter now, it being after six o'clock. We managed to get to the hostel pretty smartly. A quick change for everyone, with the exception of Bonnie and me, was the pressing requirement.

'Did you have as much fun as I had today, Jamie?'

'Yes, Bonnie, I did, or should I say naughty baby? Please be careful when you are in Skye and don't be doing anything outrageous or stupid.'

'Why? Are you worried? Do you care so much, Jamie?'

'Yes to both questions, Bonnie.'

'I promise!' she said. She kissed me in a way I will never forget. 'That's to remind you of me always!' She then ran into the hostel.

'Come on, Jamie, we had better lend a hand with the supper,' said Colin.

It was early beds for us all.

'Seven o'clock starts,' Heather said.

I made my way to the dormitory happy with my kiss but dreading tomorrow when I would have to say goodbye.

'Come on, Jamie boy, you'll see her again,' said Colin, reading my inner thoughts.

What about tomorrow? I thought to myself, I hate farewells.

Colin spoke before going to sleep. 'A new adventure tomorrow, Jamie boy! Are you looking forward to it?'

'Yes,' I said, with a tinge of sadness in my voice.

Although Heather and Colin had got on well together the chemistry wasn't there, as he put it. So I guess he was looking forward to moving on much more than I.

I fell asleep and morning came oh so quickly; heartbreak time had arrived all too soon.

I had to dash down to see her because of their early start. They had prepared all their gear the previous evening so that there would be no last-minute hitches. I held Bonnie in my arms for most of five minutes before saying goodbye. She gave me one of those special kisses once more.

'Remember this!' she said, 'It's from your naughty baby.'

'I will call you when I reach Glencoe so that I can meet up with Angus, Bonnie.'

'Call me as often as you want, Jamie, wherever and whenever you can. I only wish I could get on the bus. Angus will have none of it, but I promise you I will keep trying.'

I laughed and kissed her once more.

'Bye bye, Bonnie McKay.' The name had a ring to it and it sounded a bell in my heart.

She smiled and with that she made her way towards the car.

Lisa was now in the car crying, having said farewell to Derek earlier. Although the promise of continued contact had been given and sealed with a kiss, she was inconsolable.

Heather and Colin's plucky attitude was helping to make light of the situation. She tickled and hugged him and said, 'Don't break too many hearts, big man, before settling down.' She then started the car and set off down the driveway with Bonnie gesturing for me to phone as often as possible.

'Right Jamie boy, let's get packed up and head for Inverbeg,' said Colin.

We arrived later that afternoon after a few stops on the way. 'Inverbeg hostel. Oh, how I love it!' said Colin. 'What do you think, Jamie?'

'Secluded is the word I would use,' I said.

'We have the hotel next door on the main road. That should be good for entertainment.'

'Will I get in?' I asked.

'You only drink a cola, and it's a hotel, so I don't envisage any problem,' said Colin. He went on to say, 'The hostel is set neatly in the trees off the main trunk road to Fort William. If you are travelling by car it is easily missed. The River Douglas flows into Loch Lomond less than 100 yards from the hostel. Inver means a confluence or meeting of waters. Inverness and Inverclyde are other good examples.'

'You are a wealth of knowledge, Colin.'

'The very setting demands exploration from enthusiastic youths like us, Jamie boy.'

We signed in and I got a lower bunk, which pleased me immensely.

After an early night it was a cold morning wash at the sink – brrrr – then a stroll down to the caravan shop for fresh milk and rolls. Colin was already up and eagerly conversing with all the females in the hostel. It was fun, everybody lending each other a hand.

'Anyone for a spare egg?' was the cry, and Colin was at the stove before the last syllable was uttered. He was a big, hungry lad and still growing. Just what height he was going to be in maturity, goodness knows!

We didn't realise the cost of food and clothing at this stage in our lives. We just accepted that if we needed essentials they were purchased and provided for us. A hostel holiday is exceptionally good for learning how to cope on a low budget. It lets you appreciate how far your money goes. Colin had all the calculations worked out for us on our ten-week vacation. He also knew we would pick up some odd jobs in our travels.

After a hearty breakfast we were given a chore by the hostel warden. This was one of the rules for all residents at that time. I'm afraid we got the job of cleaning the large stove, which took us the best part of an hour.

After we passed the rigorous inspection, it was exploration time. I wanted to follow the path of the river that I could hear thundering down the hillside after late-night rainfall. Reluctantly Colin agreed. 'Now be careful,' were his last words to me before we ventured any further. 'Remember your folks said I was to be responsible for you.' I nodded OK.

His words would come to haunt me sooner rather than later.

The path along the river was damp and slippy and fresh leaves had fallen on the path during the heavy rain. It must have been pretty wild last night, I thought to myself.

'Sounds like thunder?' said Colin. 'The river must really be swollen.'

'I don't like the sound of it,' I said, 'the noise is quite frightening.'

As we walked further along the path the noise from the river became louder and louder, almost deafening. Colin gestured to me, pointing to higher ground, which I took to mean he was now unhappy with the direction of the path and was therefore intent on avoiding any danger which might be lurking further up the bank. Almost instantly I lost my footing and was slipping towards the riverbank. The ground felt greasy with nothing on which to grip. The thundering noise grew even louder and louder.

Was this to be the end? Misfortune at the very first part of my adventures? I thought.

'Help, Colin! Help!'

I could see Colin in the distance and glimpsed the agony on his face as he watched me heading for the precipice.

The roaring of water seemed intense. Would I be dashed against rocks? Would I break my neck in the fall? Or, horror of all horrors, would I drown? The chasm seemed to grow nearer. Was I going down into this cauldron? Everything filled my head, but the survival instinct took over at that very moment as disaster seemed imminent.

My film hero was Flash Gordon. As a youngster I loved the ABC Minors – Saturday Morning Pictures were another world. Flash never seemed to be out of danger, always trying to save the damsel from Ming. I recalled in an instant how he had managed to escape from a vat of water from which there seemed no possible outlet. Then I thought of Bonnie and how beautiful she was when we walked together. Oh what joy she had aroused in me.

I felt my body fill with renewed energy. Positive thoughts truly invigorated my whole being; an athlete would describe the moment as an adrenalin surge. My feet went over the bank, and as if by magic, a root from a tree appeared before me. Grasping it by one hand and then the other I held on to that piece of nature knowing my life depended on it. My body continued to fall and I prayed to my guardian angel for help.

I was now completely over the bank and I tried desperately to try to gain some sort of foothold. My prayers were answered! I felt some sort of root beneath my right foot. I put a little weight on it to try to take the strain off my hands, which felt as if they were red raw. Eventually I felt more secure but fear again started to play its part. I had to get rid of these demons, which I did simply by thinking of what had happened just a few seconds earlier. Positive, Jamie! Be positive!

By this time Colin had clambered down to try to assist me. If anyone could get me out of this mess, he could.

Reading his lips, as this was all I could do with the eternal din from the falls, I could make out the words, 'You can do it! Just hold tight!'

I dug my left foot into the soft bank in order to have both feet secure, which would allow less stress on my hands. He then left me for what felt like for ever. It was the loneliest part of my young life so far.

Going further downstream he had found a strong tree limb with small branches attached which were ideal for the plan he had in mind. Fortunately there was a young tree only three feet from me up the riverbank. Colin had arrived with his priceless lifesaver and signalled his intentions.

I could see him take off his belt. What I visualised was that he would tie his belt round the young tree; then the limb with the branch shoots would have to take the strain. How dodgy was this going to be?

I waited for the log to come over the bank and I knew that I would have to give him time to do what he had to do. 'Come on, Colin, make it secure!' I said to myself.

Time was up. It was now or never as I was growing tired. Colin had angled the log perfectly so that I could get a grip with both hands. How clever he was, I thought. He lodged the limb near to my left shoulder so that I could put my arm over it and pull myself on to the bank with my right arm.

With one hand I grabbed the log, still holding the root with the other, hanging on for dear life. Feeling it was secure enough to hold me I now pulled myself up with the root in my right hand, transferring most of the weight to the limb on the left as half my torso was now above the bank. I put both hands over the log and used my feet to clamber up the final leg. There is always a hitch though!

Yes! I had almost made it but I felt my right foot slip. I managed to transfer my weight instantly to my left and with a push and heave I was now clinging to the log and on the bank.

I rested for a few moments. I don't know whether I was shaking from the sheer physical effort or just plain fright. At that moment I didn't care. I was on solid ground and I mustered every grain of strength within me urging myself to move forward and out of danger.

I made my way crawling along the log to the small tree that had literally saved my life. Colin was waiting. He was astride the log holding it with all the strength and muscle power he had on his powerful frame. Once I had reached him I needed another short rest. He clasped my hand, saying, 'Well done, Jamie lad, I knew you would make it.'

Pointing to the slope he told me that I should go first up the incline, taking short steps, avoiding leaves, digging in with each boot step all the way. With every step I could feel my heart thumping on my chest till I finally made it. I gave Colin the thumbs-up sign and he followed tentatively towards me.

We lay on the soft fresh leaves for an hour without a word. Finally Colin spoke: 'Let that be a lesson to you, Jamie, I told you earlier to follow my instructions!'

Although he scolded me he made his point that one should learn from one's mistakes and that was the end of the matter.

'Fancy a bag of crisps and a coke, Jamie?'

Although I felt a little shaken, I took up Colin's offer of refreshment. 'I certainly do, pal.'

The hotel was only fifty yards away from the hostel, which was used by holidaymakers and climbers alike.

At eight in the evening the place was bursting at the seams with everyone intent on placing an order.

'I don't fancy our chances of getting refreshment tonight, Colin,' I said.

'You just watch me,' said Colin. I might have guessed there would be a pretty barmaid serving. He turned to me and smiled as he eased himself forward with those massive shoulders of his. He caught her eye and winked as she served the chap in front of him.

As if there was no one else in the room, she asked, 'What's your order sir?' He came back with a double round to save him the bother of reordering.

'Well, Jamie, what do you say to that?' I was speechless as he had cracked it again.

My first pint of cola slipped down easily as I had felt extremely thirsty.

'I think we were both in need of that, Colin,' I said as we put the first empty glasses on the table.

As we walked back to the hostel I thought of Bonnie and how beautiful she was. Colin left me with my thoughts. I guess he knew how dangerous my predicament had been earlier.

I awoke the next morning totally refreshed after a good night's sleep. Colin was already up and washed. When he saw me stir, he asked, 'Have you recovered yet, Jamie, after the drama of yesterday?'

'Just about,' I said. 'Didn't half get a scare, though!'

'The best thing is to leave it behind you and learn from the experience. We will take a stroll through Glen Douglas then climb to halfway up the hill opposite,' said Colin.

I didn't say a lot that day. I suppose you could say I was in some form of shock.

While strolling through the glen we crossed a grid meant to keep the cattle from straying on to the main road. A few hundred yards on we came in contact with some highland cattle. They were really friendly and unmistakable from any other cattle. With rusty, shaggy coat and big horns they make a perfect picture.

Seeing I had regained my composure and was laughing once more, Colin asked, 'Are you sure you are fit enough to climb after yesterday's episode?'

'I'm OK!' I replied.

'That's good. It should only take us an hour. I will follow behind you just in case you slip.'

Colin angled the climb in such a way that we didn't encourage danger at any point, which added time to the ascent. After forty-five minutes we reached a place where the full loch exposed its beauty from Balloch to the south and Ardlui to the north.

'Panoramic!' Colin said in a relaxed manner. 'That's Ben Lomond across from us over there and further down is Balmaha. 'Nothing like it!'

'Nothing I can compare it with,' I replied.

'We'll have to capture the picture in our minds,' said Colin.

'Without a camera?' I asked.

'Indeed,' Colin said.

We left in the bliss of this scenery with hardly a word spoken.

'Let's break out and have a meal at the hotel tonight. That'll brighten your spirits, Jamie,' Colin laughed.

'OK, that will be good,' I replied.

'Let's make our way down now,' Colin instructed.

We did so slowly so as not to encounter any danger.

The hotel was bustling but we managed to find a table eventually. I was a little perturbed at the cost of a meal but Colin assured me we would find some work along the way. After a lovely meal at the hotel we decided on an early night so that we would be fresh for travelling early in the morning.

Chapter Five

Having left Inverbeg, which had been our base for the last few days, we now headed back down to Balloch, on the route we had originally travelled. Our next adventure would be in the Trossachs, 'Rob Roy Country'.

The road down Loch Lomond's side is very dangerous for walkers so for hikers a lift is almost a necessity. After only a few minutes a lorry stopped and kindly offered to give us a lift to Glasgow.

'Only as far as Balloch!' Colin shouted to him.

'No bother, lads, jump in.'

He went on to tell us he had been delivering bottoming for a new road construction near Oban and he had to do two runs every day. How boring, I thought to myself. He explained however that he loved music and sang in clubs (welfare and working men's clubs). There was a heap of musical lyrics on his back seat. It was a way of keeping up to date with the pop tunes.

'I try to keep up with the charts,' he explained, 'because if you don't then no more bookings for you, boy, the old convenor would tell you. They want what's in the charts and expect to get it.'

There was a never-ending supply of singers and guitarists at that time so they could pick and choose and also keep the payment down. The club convenors were a law unto themselves and, oh how they loved to use their authority. The committees were only for guidance, the final say was theirs alone.

After his explanation of the ins and outs of working men's clubs, without any warning Jimmy burst into song: 'I love you oh my darling!'

'The Twelfth of Never' was a big favourite of the girls I knew at school.

As soon as Jimmy had given his full rendition, Colin burst into song: 'Just remember, darlin', remember you're mine.'

After Colin had given it his all he told Jimmy that we sang as a duo but had never asked for any fee. 'Jamie plays the piano and the accordion. I wondered if we could earn some money to sustain us over the summer.'

'Yes,' Jimmy told him, 'you'll both go down a bomb if you give them Scottish dance music and some of the modern stuff.'

He handed over some sandwiches to us as we pulled in at the junction for Balloch central. He told us to continue straight on the road ahead where we would see signs for Aberfoyle in about ten minutes. We wished him the best of luck. 'Hope to hear you in Glasgow sometime!' said Colin.

With a wave, Jimmy was off on another run. I could see his lips and throat move and almost hear him give a worthy performance.

I know I'll always carry the views from the bridge over the river Leven at Balloch with me. The scenery highlighted my first experience of the splendour of Loch Lomond. The view is spectacular. It had more than made up for the little time I had had to take in the vastness of it all on arrival. That day with Bonnie had let me see the full expanse of the area.

I just could not take in all this beauty. How I envied those who were able to live in such an environment. Maybe I'll be able to afford a boat one day, I thought.

The mountains reflecting in the water and the sound of wildfowl squawking as they fought for the scraps being thrown by youngsters; motorboats and rowing boats, all sorts of people messing about on the river; it was magical to be alive on days such as this.

Colin explained that to our right was Ben Lomond, near Inverbeg. The hostel was to the left, almost across from the Ben. At the head of the loch in the far distance was Ben More, which was close to Crianlarich. That is where the Glasgow train divides, one part going to Oban, the other to Fort William and Mallaig. This even today is one of the most beautiful of all rail journeys, called the West Highland Line. Oban is the gateway to most of the Western Islands, he went on to say.

Fort William is most famous for Ben Nevis, the highest mountain in Scotland, which stands at 4,406 feet. 'We will be climbing the Ben over the summer, thanks to Bonnie,' said Colin, 'when we meet up with your relations, in the shape of big Angus.' He tittered to himself. He was having his little dig at me.

He further related that Mallaig is where the West Highland Line ends and where you can catch the ferry to Skye. That's good to know, I thought, as Bonnie is heading up there today.

I often wondered where he had got all his information from. Of course, he was my hero, and I knew he had travelled in the Highlands many times. So I believed all he told me.

We stopped at a little cafe in Balloch where we had our flask filled. Further on we sat down at a little hedgerow about a mile or so out of town for lunch. The meat sandwiches that Jimmy had given us were a treat, along with a bag of crisps we had bought. Re-energised we were now ready to tackle the trek to Aberfoyle.

Colin had calculated that it would take us most of the day to reach the hostel if we failed to get a lift, which is not unknown on busy days such as this was. 'Too crowded today!' said Colin. 'I feel we are in for a good walk.'

'Isn't that what we came for?' I asked.

'Exactly that,' said Colin. 'With students all going in the same direction and all with the same intention, I just felt you should be prepared, that's all.'

'No problem! I'm enjoying every minute,' I said.

It was a winding road with trees on either side which obstructed the view – not my kind of walk. I much preferred the walk along Loch Lomond, even though it was dangerous. I hope Aberfoyle won't be disappointing, I thought. It's going to be a hard slog to reach Aberfoyle before tea time. I'll just think of Bonnie. With just the thought of her my whole mood lifted and my spirit revived.

It was almost dusk when we arrived at Loch Ard, having been given directions by a kind young lady whom Colin had spoken to earlier. The hostel was a mile or two from the town but it was worth the walk. Things had got much brighter with an array of firs going into hills and the sun glinting through trees casting silvery shadows on the loch.

I had never seen trees growing out of water before. It was indeed strange to me as I could not fathom how they would not just crumble and fall into the loch. The only reasonable explanation I could come up with was that the roots must be secured to some part of the bank. Perhaps I should have taken my nature studies more seriously.

Again it was quite late, around 9.30 p.m., when we arrived at the hostel. It was a large imposing white building with prevailing large windows looking over the loch. I thought to myself that the views must be stunning from the dwelling rooms.

'Hey, Colin this looks pretty good. Have you stayed at this one before?' I asked.

'First time, Jamie. I'm no wiser than you about it but I certainly like the look of it.'

We signed in and were fortunate to get a bed as the hostel was almost at capacity.

The dormitories are separated with the boys downstairs and the girls upstairs. This keeps a strict code of conduct for all hikers as rules must be obeyed. Anyone not adhering to the rules is automatically barred from the SYHA.

Lying on my bed and having secured a bottom bunk I still found that I was unable to sleep. I tried counting sheep but that didn't work so I went over all that had taken place that day.

While we were walking Colin had burst into song every so often, which took away the drudgery that occurs at times when you are on a hike. It had also been an opportunity for me to dwell on my thoughts of Bonnie and not indulge in frivolous conversation. That reminded me; when I had asked Bonnie to go for a walk I had said, 'May I take you for a walk, Bonnie?' It took me back to my English class teacher – I called him 'May I'.

At the age of fourteen I had asked permission to leave the room. He made such a fool of me in front of everyone when I said, 'Can I leave the room, sir?'

'You can jump out of the window, boy, if you like!' he replied.

I was so startled by his remark, that I repeated the question once more. Again he made a further fool of me in front of my class mates by saying, 'I'm told you are first in the class, boy. Is that true? The words you are looking for are "may I".'

With nowhere to hide my blushes I heard howls of derogatory laughter from my classmates.

I again asked permission to leave the room, by clearly saying, 'May I leave the room, sir?'

When I returned to class I found to my astonishment that my ordeal was not yet over. He asked me to stand up and give an adverbial clause of reason. I was flummoxed by the question and failed to give an answer. You could say I was caught out by the fact he made for me just after I had sat down.

'You could have given me a million answers to my question boy!'

He referred to me as being first in the class at most of my scholastic subjects. 'However, if you do not grasp and improve your standard of the English language you will end up going nowhere boy.' These words have haunted me ever since. I have tried, though I have found it an ordeal. It is easier for me to remember a number than a name.

Still awake…

Putting these thoughts out of my mind, my thoughts drifted back to Bonnie and her lovely figure. Those beautiful legs and her smart shorts with long boots and woollen stockings. I could almost feel her footsteps walking with me.

I told her how I loved art and music and that one or both of these would suit my career. I gave her a laugh about the art class teacher.

Art assignment:

'I want you all to draw a tree with charcoal. You have one hour to complete your drawing after which I will attempt to describe the character of every individual work in the class.'

One of the boys for a laugh put a noose on his tree. The teacher played along with his little ruse, saying, 'This boy will be heading west for adventure, where he will inevitably face the hangman for dastardly deeds.'

No names were written on the handiwork to ensure that the teacher did not know the name of the pupil he was describing. If you wished to claim your work you could do so, which everyone did, to my astonishment.

I wondered if I should claim my drawing. What would he say? I was amazed he could search out the character of a person by just analysing their drawing.

It came to my turn. I had drawn the mighty oak tree and a splendid one at that. He held it up to the class. 'Now!' he said, 'take notice. This young man is the biggest in the class. Whose drawing is this?' he enquired. 'Stand up if you wish.'

I stood up, all four foot ten of me. I think the howls of laughter must have been heard in the town centre. 'Ah!' he said, 'you may well laugh, but I am not talking about physical stature. I'm speaking about the strength of goal and willpower, along with aptitude, which he will prove at a future time in his life.

'You will be what you visualise and I hope you get what you deserve in life. You may think this a cruel speech, but it will come back, what I have said.'

These were his last words before retiring. I often think back on his words and wonder if I will be a success in life.

Zzzzz...

Chapter Six

This was our first day in Loch Ard. After a full breakfast it was time to explore. The weather had indeed been kind to us this summer – and what a perfect surrounding. The air was filled with a wonderful scent as Colin and I made our way along the loch towards Aberfoyle.

Whenever sunny days are in abundance in the west of Scotland everyone makes the most of it, usually by frequenting the beaches of Ayr, Prestwick, Barassie, Troon and Irvine.

'Colin, I feel as if I'm walking on air today. The fact we are not carrying our rucksack lets me stride at full pace unhandicapped.'

Colin nodded in agreement, singing, while I whistled and we marched side by side in unison.

'No plans for today. We'll just take on board whatever comes along,' said Colin with a cheerful smile. 'No women to tie us down, either.'

I'm quite sure he meant that for me, as he knew I had fallen deeply in love with Bonnie. Ah! The thought of her made me want to have her next to me.

Arriving in the small town centre we had a look at the array of Highland clothing in various shops. 'Fancy yourself in a kilt, Jamie boy?' said Colin, failing to withhold his mirth. He then held a kilt against me for size, knowing full well that I had short legs and a large trunk, which was not in proportion to my height.

The kilt is best displayed by round hips; tall and well filled at the rear is how I would put it (though I know full well the Scottish term) and of course long legs. Mind you I have seen small stout men in pipe bands banging the big drum to my amusement.

The carriage of the kilt is what the female is primarily looking for. I've seen how they are drawn to certain masculine manhood, especially at dances.

After an hour the smell of scones and fresh bakery attracted our attention. Counting our small kitty we decided that we could break out today and spend on non-essentials. Two currant scones each and a pot of tea for two was the order. The walk in had whetted our young, healthy appetites. The aroma, mmm... we could hardly wait to spread the butter and jam on the hot fresh bakery. I was not used to feeling so hungry as my mum always had at least two pots of soup ready to heat at any time.

The fresh-faced young girl glanced back at us after delivering the order to the table. She shook her head as she hastened back to the kitchen.

'She probably thinks we haven't eaten for a day or two,' I remarked to Colin.

'Either that, or she thinks we're a pair of gannets.'

Nevertheless we did not hesitate in devouring what lay in front of us, as we were the customers and the customer is always right.

Being fully satisfied we asked for the bill, which would be a few shillings. 'I'll get that, lads!' was a cry from a table near to the exit door.

'Are you sure?' Colin enquired.

'You look as if you needed that,' was the reply. 'What are your intentions for the rest of the day?'

'We have nothing actually planned,' Colin replied.

'Good! Do you wish to keep me company on a trip by car to Loch Katrine for the afternoon? I'll do the scenic route round the Trossachs if you're up for it. I have to book two tickets on the SS *Sir Walter Scott* for my wife Sarah and myself.'

Colin looked at me as he was good at reading my facial expressions. Turning to the gentleman he said, 'You're on, sir. It is a smashing day for a drive and neither of us has been in this area before.'

Which means 'yes' to those whose first language is English.

After paying the bill the man stepped outside with us and pointed to a two-tone Mercedes sports car. 'What do you think, lads?'

I took a step back and went 'Wow!' No other expression could be used to describe it, anyway I couldn't think of one. What a brilliant machine.

If I had had any misgivings before seeing our transport, then they had melted away instantaneously.

'Just where do you get the money to run a car like this?' I whispered to Colin.

'Jamie! My dad says someone who owns a car like this or is intent on buying one never asks the price. They simply know they can afford it.'

As we made our way to the car he inquired if we had any luggage to go along with us. 'No rucksacks with you, lads?'

'Just us!' Colin responded.

'Thank goodness for that, as there are only two upright seats with little boot space available. There is room for someone to lie across the back, though. Perhaps you should throw a coin to see who goes in the seat. On second thoughts, looking at the size of you I don't think that is feasible.'

'That'll be me up front then Jamie! You being of shorter stature, the position is made for you.'

Whether I liked it or not, if I was going on a tour of the Trossachs, it would have to be in the rear of this car. Colin would have been cramped in body and mind; most importantly his wit and art of conversation would have been restricted. We left town taking a steep incline with ease as the man throttled the powerful Merc forward.

I found my lack of knowledge quite alarming and inexcusable for a student going into fifth grade. What were the Trossachs, I thought? I asked Colin later and he told me it was Scotland's only national park, which I have to say meant very little to me.

'I'm Joseph Armadale, now that we are settled in, but please call me Joe.'

Colin accepted his offered hand and introduced me, 'This is my best friend, Jamie Cameron.'

'Pleased to meet you, Jamie!' He shook my hand with a strong grip, while holding on to the steering wheel with his left hand. This made me a little uncomfortable as I had trusted my intuition to lead us on this little excursion. Would it prove to be a fatal mistake after the near disastrous experience at Inverbeg? If this car was in a collision they would need a tin opener to get me out.

Colin provided his name with an air which always gave the

impression of someone who was well known, and that you really were privileged to be in his company. I envied that ambience which seemed to surround him.

After the necessaries were over, Colin was not long in finding out all about this smart, casually dressed gentleman. In my terms this guy was a real toff. He told us he was on holiday for the weekend with his wife and they had been dancing at the ceilidh in the hotel the previous night. Unfortunately she wasn't feeling too well this morning. Something hadn't agreed with her and her tummy was aching. As we would say, she must have had too much of the bottle, I thought to myself.

'Anyway she is sitting in the open lounge to the garden and has decided that's where she is going to remain for most of the day with a book and various other literatures. That's the reason I'm in town myself, lads!'

'This is some machine!' said Colin.

'She's a beauty. You just can't beat the Germans at engineering. Though I still like some of the small British sports cars.'

'How old is it?' I inquired.

'I have had her since new, for just over a year. She has only 12,000 on the clock.'

I could see the beam of pride on his face, and why not? I just hoped I would be able to afford such a machine some day.

'Talking of small cars, my wife has one of those Mini Coopers. It's her prized possession.'

My thoughts immediately transferred to Bonnie and Lisa with Heather driving. They were heading for Skye in that cramped Beetle. I wished I were in the back with her instead of where I am at present.

Colin was about to speak but I got in first: 'Two of my friends have Minis. I have been in them on short trips. What I found was that at 50 mph you feel as if you are going to take off. Being so low on the ground you get a real sense of speed,' I said.

Colin jumped in here with his tuppence worth. 'Not much leg room for me, Jamie!' he said, laughing heartily in the front seat.

Colin was inquisitive about the career of this refined, well-to-do young man. 'What type of work are you in, Joe?'

'I'm in the building and construction industry. I spent five years at a university taking an architectural degree.'

'That's pretty impressive.'

'Yes. I have been lucky in a way, too, as I managed to find a post with one of the largest builders in Scotland. They also provide a good salary with a lot of perks. Not bad for a twenty-eight year old. I met my wife at university. To me it worked out well for us both – no need to go to clubs and pubs in the hope of meeting the right partner. It also makes life simpler if you share hobbies and interests together.'

That is something I should take on board, I thought inwardly.

'I live just outside Edinburgh and I'm in the process of building a new home for us.' It just gets better, I thought.

Colin then asked, 'How do you find life in general, working in a city office?'

'Well seventy-five per cent of the time I'm on site, so the balance of both works for me. Enough of me. What are you boys about?'

Colin told him he was waiting on the results of his A levels, which would dictate his future path. I told him I would be sitting mine next year.

We gradually filled him in on where we came from and for how long we intended to stay as we travelled along this beautiful part of central Scotland.

'Oh by the way – that is a tent you are sitting on, Jamie. I hope it is the groundsheet you are sitting on and not the poles.'

Colin went into fits of laughter – so much so that Joe joined him.

Wait till I see him later! I thought, I'll tell him where to stick his poles. Joe then continued: 'I brought it along on the off chance that Sarah might just stay a night outdoors. However after how she feels today I'm sure that will be out of the question.'

Arriving at Loch Katrine Joe purchased two tickets from a kiosk for the next day's sailing.

'Sarah is looking forward to this trip. It's sort of her highlight of our short break.'

The afternoon sailing had just left but the ship was still clearly in view.

'She is a wonderful ship,' said Joe.

'I wouldn't mind sailing on her,' said Colin.

'I would love to as well,' I said.

'Make a point of doing it, then,' said Joe, 'Promise yourself you'll take your girl here one day. See it, believe it and it will happen. Well, that's that! How about lunch? I'm sure I can entice you. I've already witnessed the extent of your appetite.'

We both nodded appreciatively, finding it hard to believe we were in for another free meal.

We made our way through the winding tracks as hedgerows whizzed by. A smart hotel came into view on the next straight. 'That'll do us nicely!' exclaimed Joe. It was an old stone building with greenery covering most of the structure in an array of colour. Colin looked at me; I could read his mind from the facial expression. There was no way we ever could have afforded or even contemplated entering this establishment.

'Right lads, I fancy a ploughman's lunch with a little bit of everything.'

'Sounds great!' said Colin.

I nodded in agreement, gratefully.

Joe ordered from a young girl who was probably a working student, doing much what we were doing and earning at the same time. He wondered whether we would like a refreshment, 'Drinks, anyone?'

Colin immediately opted for a pint of heavy ale. I on the other hand preferred a cold Coca-Cola, especially from the bottle. The drinks were duly ordered along with a pint of shandy for Joe, which is a mixture of half beer and half lemonade.

The meal was served with all the trimmings on side plates filling the table space to capacity. Anyone seeing what was in front of us would have put it down to gluttony if we finished the contents. I have to say we ate the lot. We are a lot of greedy so-and-sos, I thought. The only thing I can say in our favour is that we all declined a sweet.

We moved to the back garden which had stunning views of the loch. 'This is the life!' Joe said. 'I'll bring Sarah back here tomorrow.'

Joe was in charge now and it felt good to be in his company.

'I would suggest that we dispense with conversation for a little while and take in this splendid scenery which we are so fortunate to be blessed with.'

Neither of us spoke for over fifteen minutes, which was an experience in itself. I had never enjoyed silence like this before as both Colin and I were chatterboxes.

Joe then turned to us and said, 'I lost my uncle in the D Day landings. He was the life and soul of our close-knit family. My dad was injured at the same time and recovered in a military hospital. He still has shrapnel in him as it proved to be inoperable at the time. My aunt never got over the death of Uncle Tom and died of a broken heart.

'In one respect they were fortunate that they had no time to start a family as they had only just married when the war started in 1939. My dad was forgiving. He told me that we should always pray for enemies. Dictators are usually bred from poverty and have often suffered beatings. Their instinct of survival has made them reach for power so that they can now control what once controlled them. There are plenty of examples around the world. It's everywhere at the moment.

'Greed is fundamental in most cases. Hostility over disputed ownership of land, though, has caused many wars as countries become jealous of the riches and minerals others may possess. Until there can be some compromise from both sides, hostility will never cease. Unless we take heed of the mistakes we have made in the past and consider the consequences then we are only heading for more turmoil.

'Enjoy what life has given you by God through his bounty. Wealth and prosperity don't make you happy. What you do for others will. Character building is relying totally on one another as in marriage or in the friendship you have with Colin. Trust, reliance and harmony should be your motto for life. With this you will be happy and your face will shine for all to see.'

With Joe away from the table I took the opportunity to speak to Colin. 'What a remarkable man. I could listen to him all day.'

'Perhaps we should take up philosophy when we return to our studies, Jamie,' said Colin.

After a coffee Joe mentioned a stroll around the loch. The fish were jumping out of the water trying to catch flies.

'It must be well stocked,' said Colin, who was a keen fisherman.

'Do you fish, Colin?' asked Joe.

'I go out with my two friends,' said Colin. 'We hire a boat on the small lochen (a small loch in the hills) not too far from home.'

'Catch much?' enquired Joe.

'We never come back empty-handed. We usually have at least a couple of trout each.'

Leaving Joe for a few minutes Colin and I had a game of throwing stones across the water. 'Skiffers', we call it; guess what, Colin won. I'm sure it was because of the power he had.

'I feel invigorated with our little nature ramble,' said Joe. 'I'm sure Sarah's head would have cleared much quicker if she had come along, but then again I would have missed out on the pleasure of your company for the day, lads. I think I will have to get back now, else she might think I'm enjoying being without her. You will have the pleasure of finding out how to handle a woman when you get married. You will find out that life doesn't come down to just yes and no. Right then, let's make a start.'

Colin and I laughed at his remarks. I think Colin in particular could relate to them.

Returning to the car I said, 'I can't thank you enough for your kind hospitality, Joe.'

'The pleasure is all mine. I would have been lost without your company today. I'll take the long way back giving you a full tour of the whole area. If that's OK with you both?'

'Perfect!' said Colin without waiting for my response.

We set out and all I can say is that the sights and colours were breathtaking. How lucky we were to be alive on such a day. The road narrowed at certain points, then we were faced with steep inclines and sharp bends. Having negotiated these with ease we hit a good straight run and Joe gave it a little throttle to add a little excitement to the day. This was only for a short duration then the inevitable bends were upon us once more.

Unfortunately there was not a sign for the next one, which was a double bend. The hedge was about five feet high so there was no way we could see what was coming. We were doing about 50 mph when we hit the first bend to our right. Swinging round again with ease we were hit with a hairpin bend with a slight gradient to our left. I closed my eyes. I felt there was no way we were going to make the turning. Oh no, I feared the worst! Would we make it?

Our back wheels skidded and caught the grass verge to our right, catapulting us to the left. We went straight up the banking (you could say we literally took off) and came to rest on top of the hedge.

An eerie silence ensued after the engine cut out. All we could hear was the spinning from the right front wheel which was free of any obstacles.

Joe spoke first. 'Everyone all right?'

'Yes!' Colin exclaimed.

I think I was in shock for a moment or two as I could not speak.

'Are you all right, Jamie?' Joe asked once more.

'Y-y-yes, I think so.'

'Well that's the most important thing. I apologise for my lack of thought and careless driving, lads. Colin, you can get out of the car first and drop into the field on the left. Do it slowly to see if we can maintain our position. We don't want the car toppling over,' said Joe.

Colin tentatively opened his door and, before leaping out, said, 'Move over and ease your whole body weight to the left, Jamie, to keep the correct balance.'

We were used to doing things in unison so my timing was spot on. There was hardly a movement when he dropped out of the car. He clambered through a hole in the hedgerow on to the road to survey the situation.

Joe opened his window to speak to him. 'How are we?'

'You will be OK in that position for the moment,' said Colin.

I knew immediately that Colin would hatch a plan to get the car back on the road. There was no obstacle or hurdle insurmountable to him. His attitude is that there is always a way. Being positive in nature always worked for him.

'Right, don't move,' he said with a Cheshire-cat grin on his cheeky face.

As if we could, I thought.

'I'm going into the woods to see what I can come up with. It's only about fifty yards back up the road,' said Colin.

Ten minutes later he returned carrying three tree limbs which had been left cut by forestry commission workers. The ten minutes would have seemed like an eternity had it not been for the calmness of Joe. In the situation we now found ourselves he told me that diverting my mind to other interesting thoughts would help relieve my tension. 'Travelling is a good example. Some people I know detest travelling by train and pass the time reading a book so the journey passes quickly.'

He also took time to tell me about friendships and how he had been let down by a close friend. 'You will find this will happen to you in one way or another when the bond is broken by a break of trust. The fundamental thing is not to hold a grudge. You must do what is right and walk away – let what will be happen.

'Remember, if they are wrong in what they have done the mere fact that your friendship has been destroyed through your friend's actions will haunt him until he says that he is sorry.' I hope you will remember that and always do what is right, Jamie.'

'I will, Joe.'

With this conversation I felt more relaxed and even more so when Colin gave us the thumbs-up sign, which meant he had a plan in his mind. Colin's plan was now to be delivered and would have to be carried out with precision and accuracy. He liked to be in charge.

'I need that tent out!' he bellowed. 'Ease it out your window, Joe, but you stay on the left, Jamie. OK!

'Is there a separate groundsheet?' he asked.

'Yes,' declared Joe.

'Great,' said Colin.

Once all the required attachments and of course the tent had been passed out the window he told me to climb over on to the front seat, slowly so as not to cause a jolt which would put the car in an unstable position. Adhering to his every word I obeyed his instructions, not wishing to incur his wrath. I made it over with a little sway to either side. The movement did not put us in any danger, though. It would have been impossible to make the manoeuvre without some sort of movement.

'Now I want you out so just ease yourself over even more gently. Open the door and come out gradually,' said Colin.

I finally made it into the field, feeling quite proud that I had not caused disturbance to the hedge.

'Right, the groundsheet has to be wrapped round one limb at a time. Then we will tie the guy ropes round the outer edges. After the first one is in position you go back into the field, Jamie.'

I nodded and proceeded with his instructions.

'I will push the limb through just under the back wheels,' said Colin.

I could now see what he was trying to achieve. The limb came through exactly in position. The problem now was to push the hedge down and get the groundsheet up on to the top level of the hedge where the car was resting. With a prod and tug and some sheer physical effort we finally managed it.

'Right, I'll push the next limb through,' said Colin. This was tough as the weight of the vehicle was resting in that area.

'As long as the sheet is over it then it won't do any harm,' shouted Colin. He then pushed the third limb through at the belly of the car. We managed to pull the sheet up and over, then tied the guy ropes, securing it to the limb. Colin then stopped for a breather to survey the situation. Satisfied with the progress made, he said, 'We need some logs now, Jamie! I saw two or three when I was in the forest, but I need a hand to fetch them.'

All the while Joe sat patiently listening to the radio, seeming to be oblivious to the peril of his pride and joy.

It took us twenty minutes to acquire all the material which Colin insisted was essential for the task in hand. Pointing to the groundsheet, Colin said, 'We need to follow the same procedure with the tent, Jamie. That should give us all-round stability.'

We were fortunate that the tent was wide enough to cover the area required. It just occurred to me that if this hedge had been less than six feet across, what would we have been able to do?

'Right, Jamie, same again, but make sure the guy ropes link up with the other limb securing both together,' Colin instructed. Again fortune favoured us as the banking rose up towards the front of the hedge. 'We need to make a ramp to run down to the road,' said Colin. Clearly he had the answer as he gave me more instructions: 'Help me tie these small logs and push them into the lower branches of the hedge. A pair on each side will give us a perfect run down.'

Checking everything was secure we were ready to try.

'Fingers crossed, Jamie, I hope this works. Right, Joe, we are ready when you are,' said Colin.

'Ready!' said Joe, starting the engine.

'Do it slowly now. Ease the clutch out but not full out. Give it high revs,' said Colin. 'You don't want it to stall. Just ride the clutch. If you have to brake, use your handbrake.'

Amazingly the car edged up on to the tent and logs till it started to tilt forward on to the front ramp, as we called it, and slowly down the slope and on to the road, taking only a few feet of soft turf from the bank.

I don't think anyone would believe what we had achieved that day unless they had seen it for themselves.

We wrapped up the tent, which was undamaged with the exception of a few tyre marks and some green fungus.

'That's how you get out of a mess,' I said to Joe.

'Colin certainly has the measure of situations and you are almost on par. I really am very grateful.'

I appreciated what Joe said and thanked him. All three of us carried the debris back into the forest. Having put nature right once more (in the words of the wise man, put everything back where it belongs) we now drove for Aberfoyle.

'I'll have plenty to tell Sarah when I get back to the hotel this evening,' said Joe. 'I'm quite sure I'll not be able to convince her of what happened as there is not a mark on the car after removing the mud.'

Chapter Seven

Joe drove a little slower after his encounter with a hedge. I think he got a little carried away on those narrow roads and was keen to make amends. He dropped us off at the hostel and shook our hands with a firm grip.

'I'm sure you won't forget this day in a hurry, lads. It's been an eventful one to say the least. I apologise once more. I was showing off and I got my just deserts. The main thing is no one was hurt. Here's my number in Edinburgh, if you want to meet up sometime,' said Joe. 'Or should you wish for any career advice, give me a call.'

'I will certainly do that,' said Colin.

'One other thing, do you want the tent?'

'Yes, please,' said Colin.

Colin was away ahead of me. While I was thinking of the physical effort involved his mind was on the savings and the freedom it would give.

'OK, it's yours. It's been a pleasure. May God go with you! Oh, here is five pounds. That should keep you going for a few days.'

'No, we can't take that!' I said.

'I insist!' said Joe. 'It could have cost me a lot more had you not been with me.'

'Thank you from both of us,' said Colin, accepting his gift.

'I wonder if we will ever meet again, Colin?' I asked.

'One thing is for sure, Jamie, I will never forget him!' said Colin.

'Bye lads, nice to have met you.'

As soon as he had gone Colin said, 'That brings our funds back to almost what we started with, Jamie. This has been an excellent day for our pocket.'

After our efforts of the day we were exhausted. We had a short nap and then a quick wash before heading towards the kitchen.

Luckily we still had some provisions left from the previous day.

The stoves were all busy and we were trying to push our way through to make a start on the supper. 'Not much room, Jamie boy!' said Colin. 'Everybody seems to be hungry at an inopportune moment.'

I laughed but said nothing. Colin picked up a tin opener then began shaking his head in bewilderment at the apparatus. A striking blonde came forward and, seeing his predicament, asked, 'Can I help you?'

'Yes please,' said Colin, 'I can't find a suitable tin opener to open my Fray Bentos steak pie.'

'Oh, that's one of those odd-shaped tins. You need to be very careful when opening that. I have had plenty of practice with them so I'll do it for you,' she said. 'By the way, my name is Janie.'

'Pleased to meet you, Janie. I'm Colin, and that's my young buddy Jamie looking a bit lost over there.'

Janie went on to say, 'There are a few potatoes spare in our pot if you want them.'

'Please!' he said. 'My pal and I have been out most of the day. We are ravenous and any scraps are most welcome.'

'If you wish to tidy up we will arrange everything for you. Your pie should be ready in thirty minutes,' said Janie.

'I can't thank you enough,' Colin said, taking advantage of the close proximity to her with what little room there was for manoeuvre. The charm never failed, he had her eating out of his hand.

With a wide smile she said, 'It's not a problem. We were late in arriving ourselves so we have permission to cook late. The warden is very nice here.'

We returned to the canteen after changing our shirts and there was our meal cooked and being dished out. The aroma – mmm. I could have eaten the plate the way my stomach felt. Just how does he do it? I thought.

There were two other girls in the party, both very nice and friendly. Janie, the leader, whom Colin had spoken to earlier, asked us if we would be interested in pony trekking the next day. 'We had booked a trek for five, but two of our friends were unable to come. Domestic problems have arisen and there are two spare places available should you wish to come.'

Without my being asked the answer resounded from beside me. 'Yes, that's brilliant!' said Colin. 'We'll look forward to that, won't we Jamie?'

Well, this is something new, I thought; the nearest I have come to riding a horse is a donkey ride on the beach as a child.

'Yes, I'll come along, Janie,' I said.

Janie then went on to introduce her two companions, Katie and Annie. We cleared our plates with the precision of a Hoover. Then we washed and dried our utensils.

There was little time for conviviality as lights were starting to go down.

'See you in the morning, girls,' said Colin

I heard a few giggles as they departed for the ladies dorm. Colin continued, 'They're talking about us, Jamie!'

It should be a fun day tomorrow, I thought. I think he is going to make up for lost time. A pony? I think it will be two horses for us. Colin will have a field day as they all make a play for him.'

The next morning, after our cold, fresh, customary wash we were up and off to the kitchen. Yes! There stood all three of the girls at the stoves. Janie spotted us and signalled for us to sit down at the table close to the stove. Colin acknowledged with a wave and duly led the way, turning to me with a twinkle in his eye. 'We've cracked it again, Jamie boy.'

Without any embarrassment we accepted the generous offerings on the plates laid before us. I thanked them all graciously and said, 'If we are able to do something for you, please don't hesitate!'

'Oh, I'm sure we'll think of something!' said Annie with a devilish grin.

'Right,' said Janie, 'we have to leave here in half an hour so pack what you need for the day.'

I could see that inner ego in Colin saying, 'All I need is myself.' After deciding on what to take with us we arranged to meet in the hall, then left together and strolled out to the car park. Janie began to approach a little Morris Minor. Surely we are not all going in that, I thought. The suspension will give way and we will all be crushed to death. I can almost bet Colin will sit beside Janie.

My fears were proved correct as the massive frame of Colin made for the front passenger seat. Three of us in the back of this! Oh boy, is this going to be a squeeze, I said to myself. I offered the open door to Annie but she insisted that I go in first as if some contrived arrangement had been plotted earlier. My instincts proved correct. The left rear door opened and in popped Katie. It looked as if I was the sandwich and one of them had opted for me on the menu.

Annie was what you would call pleasantly plump, a nice well-rounded girl. But in a car, especially a Morris Minor, things were going to be a little cramped. I was well built with wide-spread shoulders, which meant Katie would have to lean on me with her right shoulder. She turned to face me, snuggling closer. Uh-oh. I was now sure this was a set-up as Katie obviously had taken a shine to me with no prior eye contact or expression on my part. I was innocent.

Colin turned round to speak as we started out. 'Everyone nice and comfy in the back?' he asked, winking at me. He had that same devilish look that Janie had transmitted at breakfast. This now confirmed my suspicions – he was in on it, I thought. It looked as if Katie and Janie had set their minds on the two of us with Colin a willing participant.

'It's only forty minutes drive to the stables. We have to go back to the Drymen road to reach them,' said Janie.

Then Katie whispered in my ear, 'Have you ever been on a horse before, Jamie?'

'Never!' I said quite gruffly.

I turned to face her to see her reaction, almost kissing her in the process, as she seemed to have moved even closer to me.

As we journeyed on she began leaning in a way I found difficult to get away from. 'This more comfortable!' she said, squeezing her head under my arm. And guess what! Annie had transported her bottom further towards the middle so that this meant I was cuddling Katie without even trying.

She was really a beautiful wee girl, but no match for Bonnie. If she could see me now she would go ballistic. Oh goodness, what kind of day am I in for? I wondered.

I would have to play along for the day without taking advantage of Katie's feelings. I myself am of a sensitive nature and easily hurt. Therefore I had no intention of misbehaving. I tried to put myself in Katie's shoes. If Bonnie had rejected me quickly I would have been mortified to have shown my hand so quickly and then been abruptly dumped.

Turning to Katie I found her eyes were staring at me and continued to do so without blinking. I said, 'I hope I'm not crushing you against the door!'

'I don't mind,' said Katie.

Mmm, I thought.

No sooner had her words been uttered than we turned a sharp corner to the left; suddenly she was fully on top of me.

'I think I'll just stay here,' she said. 'This is much more comfortable.'

Maybe for her it was, but not for me. My lower extremities could not take the strain much longer.

'It's only a few minutes now,' said Janie.

Thank God! We have almost arrived! I thought.

Katie didn't seem to be in any hurry to get out of the car as we were now cheek to cheek. She squeezed herself back on to the seat while still holding on to my arm.

'That's us!' she whispered in my ear, then kissed it.

Presumptuous! That's what she is! I thought.

Annie and Katie both got out, giggling. My left leg was now asleep with severe cramp. I couldn't feel my left foot to stand on.

'I'll just be a minute!' I said, 'I've dropped my diary.'

I offered the first excuse that came to mind. I had to take the pressure off the limb to enable the blood to circulate again. Vigorously I worked my ankle, calf, then thigh. Finally circulation arrived and I hauled myself to my feet. I walked around the yard for a few minutes until I had made a full recovery.

We were greeted at the stables by a well-groomed lady, who introduced herself as Nancy. 'My stable lads will take care of you. I have given them five riding helmets, one for each of you. You cannot go riding without them!'

I put my helmet on and contemplated what the rest of the day might have in store for me. I shuddered to think. Dare I throw caution to the wind and play along? Or would this make things more difficult? No time for soul-searching.

I was guided to the stables to meet my mount Meg, for the day. She was a sturdy pony, light brown with a silky sheen to its coat. This will do nicely, I thought. It looked a good, quiet-natured beast.'

'Have you ridden before?'

'Yes!' I replied. What a porker! I said to myself, not wishing to look a fool. 'I was on one when I was younger,' I said, thinking of my one or two times at Blackpool beach on a donkey.

'That's good! Just remember not to put your full bottom weight on the saddle. Horses don't like that. Always lean forward and you won't have any problems.'

I couldn't wait to see what was provided for Colin. Yes, he got Dobbin! It was probably the only thing that could hold him comfortably. Fits of laughter from all quarters greeted him as he led his mount from the stables. 'Want a hand up?' I asked.

'I'll manage fine, thank you very much,' said Colin, a little dismayed by his steed.

We all managed to engage our mounts with ease with the exception of Annie, who needed a punt on to the saddle with the help of the stable lad. I had a good titter to myself at her first vain attempts.

We trotted along a meadow. Upon reaching the far side our guide dismounted and opened a gate to the Forestry Commission track. After closing the gate, when all the ponies were through, Nancy once more took the lead and broke her mount into a canter. Tall and slim, she rode a lovely chestnut stallion which towered above everyone else giving her an air of supremacy. She certainly knew the area and was positive in all her instructions. I felt good with the breeze on my face and I was fairly excited as I had never ventured into unknown territory on a pony.

The track was constructed of soft clay, which was easy footing for the ponies.

'Pass the word back,' our guide shouted to Colin. 'We will go into a gallop for the next mile!'

My heart began to give a little flutter as I leaned forward. Meg just went into her stride, following the leaders without any encouragement from me. Now this was exhilarating – however, I just hoped I didn't fall off and break my neck.

The straight mile track was covered in a matter of seconds. Well, it felt like that. We then slowed down to a trot. I have to say I really enjoyed the gallop.

'All right, dismount and walk your pony,' was the next instruction.

No sooner had I dismounted than Katie was alongside me.

'That was fun, Jamie!'

'Sure was!' I answered.

Gathering us all in a circle, Nancy said, 'The routine is pretty straightforward. We will walk, then canter for the next half hour, then we will take a break when we reach the forest above Loch Ard.'

Colin joined me and said, 'It looks like we are heading for the east side of Loch Lomond, which is used by trekkers walking through to the Highlands (later to become known as the West Highland Way). It's a route chosen by most walkers, including those of a more mature age, though it's one I have not yet undertaken,' said Colin.

He also mentioned, 'We are straight across from Inverbeg on the opposite bank of the loch. Remember? I pointed out Balmaha to you when we were up the hill.'

'How could I forget, Colin? After my life-threatening experience.'

Colin went on to say, 'The track is just down there.'

The track Colin pointed out leads from Drymen through Balmaha, Rowardennan and Inversnaid. The only road on the east bank is from the Trossachs to Inversnaid. From Rowardennan climbers take to the peak of Ben Lomond. Anyway, wherever we were it just seemed to get better.

After an hour or so we stopped for lunch in a clearing in the forest. Feeding the ponies was the first priority as they were our main means of transport. In other words, take care of it and it will take care of you.

Colin was snuggling up to Janie as I watched her bring goodies and a flask from a small rucksack. As usual we had nothing to offer. I could see Colin giving her the sad eyes – he was an expert in expressions. I always found it amazing how feelings characterise one's face – a scowl, a grin and so on, not forgetting the poker face.

A voice from behind me piped up. 'You'll be wanting my company now,' said Katie, as she produced a pack of various sandwiches and a flask of tea. 'Do you take sugar and milk?'

'No. Black tea please,' I said.

Handing me the first cup was kind of her. 'You go first,' I said, 'I can wait.'

'No you first! I have brothers and I know how hungry they become.'

Maybe I'm wrong about her, I thought. I have never met anyone so predictable though.

Colin and I had lived our early years through rationing and also both of us came from large families. It had been a difficult period in our lives as our parents did without and unselfishly provided all our needs. Neither of us therefore had what we call a 'sweet tooth'.

Katie told me the other girls each had just one sibling at home. 'Having two older brothers means extra chores for me,' she said.

She handed a plastic cup and three rolls to me and was almost on my knee again. The log was twenty foot long and Annie had sat close to me on the left. They're definitely together in this! If it is just for fun then it is good fun. I'll play along, I thought to myself.

'Not much room in the forest for a seat,' I said.

There were plenty of giggles but no reply to my statement.

Having drunk my tea and devoured the sandwiches I now felt I needed to go to the wee boys' room. I made my excuses as best as possible with the silly girls tittering as I left. I'm never going to win with this duo out to get me! Here I was, talking to myself again.

I found a secluded spot and did my necessaries. I had just managed to get my zip up and was about to head towards the track when I was pushed from the rear. I lost my balance and found myself hitting a clump of heather with soft spongy moss beneath me. Surprised, I turned quickly, only to see Annie laughing as she ran off.

Before I could say anything Katie was full on top of me, slobbering me with kisses. 'You owe me for lunch. It's payback time.' I tried my best but she was wriggling and was hard to dislodge.

If Bonnie saw me now or, even worse, if someone took a snap of this – Oh stop thinking, Jamie, action is needed, my boy.

I grabbed her just above the waist to see if she was tickly. Sure enough she went into hysterical fits of laughter and fell to the ground, defenceless. I got myself on to my knees but before I could rise to my feet she put both her arms round my legs and pulled me down on top of her again.

Our lips crashed together as we met after a long hug. She whispered to me, 'I'll bet you will have more fun with me than that stuck-up Bonnie.'

I immediately thought of the film *Calamity Jane*. Life would never be dull with someone like her!

'I'm sorry, Katie, but if things don't work out with Bonnie I will come for you. I won't be getting married till I'm at least twenty-six. Some big hunk will sweep you off your feet long before that. Let's just enjoy what we have today.'

I hope she accepts my lame excuse, I thought inwardly.

'That's what I'm doing!' she said.

She really is a fun-loving, good-natured girl, I thought.

As we appeared from the clearing, Colin, never one to miss a bit of fun, called, 'Hey, Jamie! What caused all that hilarity in the woods?'

He knew full well the position I had been put in.

With all the commotion I hadn't managed to indulge in much conversation with Colin. To put this right I called him over as all three females were having a parley.

There were ten of us in the group but because of my circumstances it felt like only three.

'How are you and Janie getting along?' I asked Colin.

'She is a wonderful person, a little older than the rest of us although she doesn't look a day over sixteen. She is studying economics at a university in Glasgow. I just love them all,' said Colin.

I often wondered if he would ever settle down; could one

woman be enough for him and stop him from straying?

'I hope you are going to tell Bonnie about all your shenanigans today,' said Colin.

I declared, 'I have nothing to hide!' blushing to a bright red and pink glow which was very difficult to hide.

Before I could turn Janie was leaning over his left shoulder. She bent down and kissed him. The rest of this party will be thinking we're sex maniacs, I thought impulsively.

Nancy now called for us to mount as it was time to make for the stables. We took in the views as we cleared the forest. It just gets better and better! I kept thinking. With every new scene came an array of beauty different from the previous one.

As we made our way back my legs, especially my thighs, began to feel heavy. I made the mistake of letting my full buttocks rest on the saddle. After a few minutes Meg, my pony, turned as if to bite me and gave a little kick up of the hind quarters. I got the message. If Meg hadn't had a bridle on I'm sure she would have nipped me.

I leaned forward immediately, taking the weight off the saddle and gave her a clap. All was well with her now.

On returning to the stables, our duties included removing the bridle and saddle, then giving the ponies a full groom. I have to say these chores are quite a task after a day's trek.

I dismounted and first removed the saddle. I then went round to face Meg, telling her I was sorry for putting too much weight on her, clapping her all the while. Then I sang softly into her ear. Meg really seemed to be enjoying it; either that or she liked my strong hands on her coat.

After all our tasks were completed each pony was put in its own stable housing. I led Meg in and made sure she was comfortable. Just as I was about to leave the stable I was pushed from behind and landed flat on my face. Luckily I went straight into a new batch of hay which had just been freshly laid. It could only have been Annie, as Katie weighed only eight stone, whereas I'm twelve, I thought. I turned round quickly but the stable door closed, blocking my vision of the culprit.

The next thing I knew Katie was on my back pulling me round so that I was on top of her. 'You didn't think you were getting out of here without a roll in the hay, did you Jamie?' She pulled me down by my head, forcing me to kiss her. She was enjoying every minute of this 'bit of fun' as she called it, teasing me something awful. I must confess if I hadn't met Bonnie I probably would have savoured the moment quite happily.

'Had enough?' I said.

'One more good squeeze and I'll let you go,' came the reply.

Boy did she make the most of it.

Having her way, she finally let me go and smiled. Dusting ourselves down, we sauntered out of the stables like a pair of innocent lambs.

Colin grabbed me. 'Well, what was going on in there?' he enquired.

'You don't want to know, big man,' I said.

Janie kissed Colin before going into the car. I was next to enter the car as I thought I could outmanoeuvre the deadly duo. I made for the passenger seat behind Colin this time, all the while thinking that I had managed to outflank Annie. However, Annie was more tenacious than I gave her credit for. She followed me to the door and all she did was push me over into the middle seat – and before I could move over to the far side, Katie entered, grinning from ear to ear.

It was the same sequence of events on the journey back. At the first bend she landed fully on top of me with arms clinging to my neck. Her full weight was on top of my knee. She proceeded to press her lips against mine. 'Oh this is so good!' said Katie, now nibbling my ear. Katie finally let go of me when the car became stationary.

'Well I think that was a fantastic day. The weather could not have been better with a nice fresh breeze which kept the flies and midges at bay,' said Janie.

'Hear! Hear!' was the cry from us all.

It may have kept the airborne menace at bay but it had done nothing to deter the human predator in the form of Katie from attaching herself to me, ably assisted by the ingenuity of Annie.

Katie had suddenly become melancholy. I sensed that she liked me immensely. My impending departure from her company would soon be upon her.

Janie suggested that the girls should take us into town for a bar supper and a drink. 'All agreed, girls?'

'Yes!'

Colin said to me, 'How can we refuse an invitation such as this?'

I could only agree.

We spruced ourselves up and headed to the pub. I was pleasantly surprised that the journey only took us ten minutes. As we all got out of the car Colin and I eyed up the girls and he commented to me that they looked pretty in their short dresses.

The girls were of well-to-do families and offered to pay for the meal.

'Steak pie and chips for Jamie and a Coca-Cola. I'll have chicken breast in a sweet sauce,' said Colin.

The girls opted for different courses.

We had hardly spent any of our money in over a week so we offered to pay for our own meal. Janie would have none of it as she knew we were hiking for the entire summer. Could this luck hold out? I wondered.

After we had finished our meal Annie was the first to speak. It turned out she was at university and studying to be a maths teacher. She was a very happy person, always looking to the funny side of every situation. Nothing seemed to fluster her at all. When she dropped her fork, another was requested.

Katie was the youngest and was a close next-door neighbour to Annie who had more or less taken her under her wing. Frivolous would be the best word to describe Katie, well so I thought! Though her attributes were overwhelming, her desire to have a man at all costs overshadowed her beauty.

I have to say they all blended well together, taking each others' part if any flak went towards them. Janie showed maturity in decision-making, with Katie and Annie happy to go along with her judgement. Annie cracked a few jokes which had us all falling into fits of laughter. What a girl! I would have loved to ask her if she had set me up with Katie but I didn't wish to create any disharmony or offend.

It was time to go, after a lengthy fact-finding session on each other. We exchanged telephone numbers and addresses and agreed to meet up at a future date. I would not forget those last few days, especially the fun... ever!

We stepped outside and as we made our way to the car I found myself in the arms of Katie. 'I love you!' she said. 'I have had these feelings from the first moment I saw you. I'll see to it that you won't forget me. I'm the girl for you not Bonnie!' said Katie. 'Please call me as I won't call you. I have made it perfectly clear how I feel about you, Jamie.'

I was about to speak but she put her hand over my mouth. When she took her hand away, she pressed her lips to mine and gave me a lingering kiss.

Turning toward the car I could see she was crying. Had I misread the signals? Maybe I had misjudged her! Only time would tell. I would have plenty of time to discuss the situation with Colin over the coming week. Maybe she was right. I was still young and perhaps I shouldn't commit myself to a steady girl. However, she wanted me now, the very same with Bonnie. Oh, hell. I'm too young and immature for all this.

Colin was now in the full throes of a passionate kiss with Janie and unable to move his head. Conversation is going to be really interesting over the campfire in the next few days, I thought.

'It's time to go, Katie!' Janie shouted. 'I don't wish to sleep with the four of you in a tent.'

Meaning we had better run lest we are locked out of the hostel. Katie had made her way to the car first and was sitting against the right-hand door. Annie stopped me from going in before her, leaving me last to enter and positioned against the left door.

'Leave her to herself, Jamie, she likes you too much for her own good.'

Annie then told me she had a boyfriend who lived in Glasgow. 'He is a big lad, big and cuddly,' she said.

Yes, I bet he is, he'll need to be to have half a chance with Annie, I thought. She could be best described as having the three Bs: Big Boobs, Big Belly, and Big Bottom. I was glad she had someone as she was an exceptional person. Humour was her delight. It had been a pleasure meeting her. She was alive and lit up every room she entered.

'Your boyfriend is a lucky guy to have you,' I said.

'Thank you, Jamie, that's very kind of you.'

She leaned into me and gave me a kiss. 'I'll tell him I was kissing another man now,' she said, giggling away.

Katie never spoke and ran into the hostel without speaking.

'She'll be all right in a few days,' Annie said, giving me a hug. 'Bye, Jamie.'

I shook Janie's hand but she also wanted a hug. Her eyes met Colin's as we parted. If I were to have guessed her thoughts I would have surmised she was saying, 'Look Colin, I can have any guy I want. No problem! So go and break someone else's heart.'

'Bye, girls!' I said as they were leaving at seven-thirty in the morning. We didn't see them again. My thoughts were still with Katie and I only hoped that I hadn't hurt her. She had certainly left me with many unanswered questions to turn over in my head. It was time to move on, though, once more.

Chapter Eight

It was another glorious day as we left the hostel. We turned left towards Aberfoyle.

'Peaceful here, Colin, isn't it.'

'Aye, Jamie! We'll be back sometime soon.'

I was over-conscious of the extra weight I was now carrying.

'Well, Jamie boy, how do you feel about spending a few nights under canvas?' asked Colin.

'I don't mind at all as long as the weather remains dry.'

'I can't promise that, but we will save a few pounds on expenses,' said Colin.

'How are you coping with the extra load, Colin?'

'No problem at all. It's having to swivel round to see you gives me a pain in the neck.'

'Ha! Ha! I'm pleased that you said you've a pain in the neck as I have the same annoyance.'

We were quiet for a while, taking in the beauty of the loch for the last time. After picking up some provisions in the town we headed towards Stirling. We had walked for only a short distance when a Land Rover pulled up alongside, offering us a lift.

'Stirling, then on to Callander if that's any good for you?' the driver called.

'Callander is where we are heading,' said Colin. 'Via Stirling is perfect.'

Colin put both rucksacks on the back seat and I climbed in beside them, still with room to spare. The gentleman was obviously some sort of businessman or traveller, as his jacket was on a hanger beside me, blocking the view from the window. We shook hands and exchanged the usual formalities as he introduced himself as Bill.

'You may wonder why I stopped for you.'

'Indeed we did,' said Colin.

'I have hiked all over Scotland. Camping is my preference as it allows me to be alone and at one with nature. I take youngsters on courses and let them bond. Also it tests their skills. It can bring out the best in them through their overcoming weakness. One day I hope they will follow my example. We need to rely on each other in this small planet that is why I have based my life on trust.'

'That's exactly how I feel,' said Colin.

'Self-reliance is a wonderful thing. It will help you with your chosen profession later in life, especially in leadership. But trust and love and the ability to show you care are fundamental in bringing up a family. Unfortunately family life is falling apart at the seams at this moment,' said Bill.

This is going to be an interesting journey, I thought. I'm overwhelmed by his speech in the past few minutes alone.

'You will probably know that we are in Rob Roy country, and will I be right in saying you know very little of the man?'

'Correct!' said Colin.

'We are in the Trossachs National Park which has to be preserved for the nation. I personally believe that one should find out more about one's own country's history. It broadens the mind and imparts knowledge. I can honestly say I was caught out while over in Europe on holiday. The courier asked all about the island of Skye and I was forced to say I'd never been. She was astounded; here was I touring Europe and yet I had not visited Skye. My face still gets red every time I think about it.

'The first thing I did when I returned was to visit Skye, which I thoroughly recommend to you. I also say that a good book should always leave you wanting more. One should automatically spring to mind!'

The Thirty-Nine Steps by John Buchan was my first thought – it has danger, espionage, murder, deceit and intrigue and it was set in the Western Highlands, I thought.

'Well didn't that journey fly!' exclaimed Bill.

We had arrived at the Wallace Monument and he finally gave us an insight into what he was about. 'I work for the Government as a civil servant, which entitles me to free entry. I'll give you both a pass to visit if you wish?'

'Yes please!' said Colin, without giving me a chance to respond.

As Bill stepped out of the car I was amazed at the perfection of the man's appearance. I could have cut my hand on the crease of his trousers. His shirt was whiter than white, showing gold cufflinks with a matching watch and rings. His tie sat in place, which is unusual for someone that is driving. He had light-tanned skin with brown hair, moustache and pearly white teeth.

As we entered the monument Colin commented, 'That guy looks as if he came out of Fraser's Stores window.'

'I couldn't have put it better myself,' I replied.

Bill informed us briefly of the history of the monument, saying, 'The idea for a monument to one of Scotland's national heroes came on a tide of Scottish nationalism. I suggest you purchase one of the booklets. You will find it good reading.'

Nationalism! I immediately I thought of my forefathers.

There had been little work for my great-great-grandfather and he had brought up his family with a meagre existence. His two sons were forced to seek work in Glasgow or go abroad. Around 1870 they chose Glasgow. Not being used to city life they decided to go down to an industrial town in Ayrshire two years later, where they remained all their life.

Interrupting my daydreaming, Colin said, 'Come on, Jamie, let's go in. I'm sure it's worth a visit and it's free.'

We took Jim up on his offer and proceeded in to the building. As we entered one of the main chambers Colin pointed to the sword that Wallace used in battle.

'Do you see the size of the sword, Colin?'

'Aye, Jamie, he would have to have been around six foot eight in height to wield it.'

'Was that his real height?' I asked.

'Aye, Jamie, it was!' said Colin.

'No wonder the English were afraid of him.'

We made our way up to the 220-foot tower by way of the spiral stone stairway. The tower sits on Abbey Craig, which commands a view of the Forth valley and surrounding district. With hills to the north and Stirling Castle to the west it certainly was a perfect spot for such a historic monument. We picked up a leaflet on the history of the area including the battle at Stirling Bridge and of course Bannockburn.

'Hey, Jamie, we could have a whole history lesson in this area alone,' said Colin.

'Aye, and an exam to test us on our knowledge,' I said.

We spent an hour at the top taking in the view from all angles. The Forth winds it way through the lush meadows in all shades of green all the way to Edinburgh.

'My mum used to say that the River Forth spells its own name, and this can be visualised from the Wallace tower where we are.' I tried but I couldn't see it. I picked out an 'O' though.

'If your mum says that then I believe her,' said Colin.

'We had better get back down. Bill said he would only be an hour.'

'OK, Jamie, I'm right behind you.'

He was being funny of course as there was only room on the steps for single file.

When we met up with Bill in the courtyard he said, 'I have very little time to spare! I can only afford a five minute stop at Stirling Castle. It is well worth a visit and if you wish I can drop you there.'

'The short stop will suit us fine,' said Colin not wishing to lose the lift to Callander. Colin, being more interested in history than I, decided to purchase a booklet and sent me as the errand boy, saying I would be much quicker. He was right and as Bill was in a hurry I readily agreed.

The booklet had a picture of the castle that displayed its massive structure to perfection. It was obvious for all to see why the castle had been built in this particular area.

Stirling Castle is the grandest of Scotland's castles and was built on an extinct volcano. Stirling became the strategic military key to the kingdom during the thirteenth- and fourteenth-century Wars of Independence and was the favourite royal residence of many of the Stuart monarchs. Many important events from Scotland's past took place at Stirling Castle, including the violent murder of the eighth Earl of Douglas by James II in 1452. Stirling Castle played an important role in the life of Mary Queen of Scots. She spent her childhood in the castle and Mary's coronation took place in the Chapel Royal in 1543.

The vast Great Hall, which dates from the end of the Middle

Ages, was built by James IV in 1503, and converted to a four-storey military barracks in the nineteenth century. The Royal Palace, built 1540–42, is the finest Renaissance building in Scotland. It is a three-storey building with an ornate facade of tall windows and niches which contain a selection of grotesque carved figures and Renaissance sculptures.

The King's Old Buildings house the regimental museum of the Argyll and Sutherland Highlanders. In the Crimea in 1854, the Sutherland Highlanders earned the nickname of 'the Thin Red Line', when they repelled repeated attacks from the Russian cavalry.

In 1854, the 91st Argyllshire Highlanders were amalgamated with the 93rd Sutherland Highlanders. They won six Victoria Crosses at the Relief of Lucknow in 1857 and throughout the twentieth century were involved in conflicts all over the world.

Bill took us round the west side of the castle as promised and Colin said, 'I don't think anyone would try and take the castle from this side.'

Bill laughed and said, 'Highly improbable', while emphasising the word 'highly'.

Both Colin and I promised ourselves that we would return and visit the castle as it had so much Scottish history to offer.

Bill dropped us off on the outskirts of Callander. We bade him farewell and headed for the small town centre. We had been fortunate indeed over the past few days to have been provided with transport to all the locations on our itinerary.

'It's time to stock up with provisions, Jamie.'

Not too many, I thought, as where would we put them?

'We're camping tonight, Jamie boy! It's time for the big outdoors. We've been pampered long enough,' said Colin.

We found a small grocer's which could fulfil all our needs and Colin duly placed the order.

'A loaf, two tins of cold meat with those cut-your-finger openers, some fruit, crisps and four tins of soup,' was the main order. 'Oh, and tea and a tin of stew,' he told the elderly assistant.

Turning to me, he said, 'We'll use the tins to drink out of and also boil the potatoes with, Jamie.'

I wasn't sure what we were about but I trusted Colin.

We followed the road out of Callander to Loch Lubnaig in the Strathyre forest. There are set camping sites in the forest but I was quite sure Colin had no intention of using them. We found a nice little spot where a small stream ran into the loch. I was scared about starting a fire with all these trees around. Colin put me at ease by telling me what would be done.

'First things first, Jamie. Let's get the tent pitched on a wee bit higher ground away from the stream. It will only take a few minutes.'

A five-minute job? I don't think so, I thought to myself. I was skilled in self-builds, but I knew there was no such thing as a five-minute job. It didn't help without instructions, either.

'I will etch each aluminium pole with a number so that we will be more proficient at our next camp, Colin.'

An hour later we had everything shipshape. Just as well, as hunger pangs began to take hold.

'Let's get the fire built now,' said Colin. 'You get some dry wood and I will fetch some stones from the burn.'

When I returned with sticks and a small log he was well ahead with his building work. A trench a foot wide and six inches deep had been hacked out the soft bank. He had hand-picked stones, mostly large ones; then he filled in the centre with dry grass and twigs. It looked like a small kiln when complete. The gaps in the stones would act like a small furnace and the small trench would catch all the ash produced.

I was impressed. 'How are we going to light it?' I asked.

He drew a cigarette lighter from his pocket and set light to the dry grass.

'Very good, Colin! Is that how they did it in the olden days?'

Colin never spoke, only grinned from ear to ear, which told its own story.

'It'll take about five minutes to give it a good glow so let's prepare what we have.'

'Let's have the soup first,' I said, 'that will allow us tins to use when we're finished.'

'Good thinking, Jamie! We'll do just that.'

Included in our kit from when we had first set out were a knife, fork, spoon, plastic plate and not forgetting a tin-opener.

Tomato soup you can take cold so I proceeded to eat half of it before heating the rest. Colin was intent on catching a fish but I was so hungry I couldn't wait.

'Is it OK to fish?' I asked Colin.

'Who is going to catch us?' Colin replied.

He had brought along a small reel of gut and two or three hooks for the purpose of fishing. Talk about being prepared; he will be going for the top fisherman's award this year at this rate. He dug up some worms while I looked for a piece of branch, which only took me a minute. Attaching the worms to two small hooks he let his line drift in the stream.

We settled down to our hot soup, sitting by our little fire on a log washed downstream by Mother Nature. Before we had finished, Colin was interrupted by a pull on his line. He grabbed the staff which had been resting between his legs.

'Feels good!' said Colin. 'Oh! Oh!' Colin felt an even sharper tug the second time. 'I hope the line holds,' said Colin, 'I'm sure I have two on now.'

I couldn't believe it. I had been convinced the line on a branch would be a waste of time.

'Hold on to the branch and walk with it away from the bank, Jamie. Gently does it. I don't want to lose them now,' said Colin.

I carried out his instructions carefully as I did not wish to incur his wrath.

'Stop!' shouted Colin. 'I'll get my hands underneath them now and throw them on to the bank.'

Colin used so much energy that the fish landed a good twenty feet up the bank. In his overeagerness he had miscalculated his strength.

'Your reactions took over there,' I said.

'Well, just a little,' said Colin. 'I didn't want to lose them as that was our one and only chance.'

Having retrieved the trout from the grass Colin immediately started gutting them. We finished the remainder of our soup and put the potatoes into the tins to boil. After twelve minutes they were ready. We then put the fish in with the potatoes and awaited the result.

'Perfect, Colin,' I said, 'you will make someone a great wife!' I ducked a fourpenny one on the ear.

We had purchased half a dozen rolls earlier. These, along with the meal, would suffice for the evening. Finishing, we kept our tins for the tea. 'This will wash everything down nicely,' said Colin, holding up his cuppa.

'That was a fabulous meal,' I said. 'I could go the same again.'

'Greed, Jamie, it would just be greed.'

After our meal we relaxed on the bank watching the sun go down, with the hills in the background.

'Time for a swim, Jamie.'

'The midges are beginning to bite, Colin,' I said.

'Well, let's get out of their way then. And it's a good way of washing your underwear when you have only one change,' said Colin. 'No women to do your washing here.'

'I wouldn't ask any girl to wash my underwear unless it was my mother or sister.'

'You will get no argument from me on that one, Jamie boy.'

'Come on, let's go for it then,' I said.

The water was chilly but you get used to it; it's better to acclimatise your body to the temperature rather than dive in. Many people have lost their lives through heart failure or have experienced shock to the system and have drowned by not adhering to the rules.

This was Colin's second dip and my first. It would be one of many in the coming weeks.

After a most enjoyable swim we dried ourselves off in the night air with not a fig leaf in sight. Hanging out our wets over the tent we retired for the night.

Colin was already out and about when I awoke. I had slept like a baby. It was my first night sleeping in the great outdoors though I had slept in a tent in the back garden like most youngsters do.

'I've walked halfway round the loch and back, plus I have lit the fire, and you're not even up yet,' said Colin.

I had to believe him as the fire was lit and the tea ready. There had been four rolls available between us for the morning but only three remained which proved he had been up early. I wasn't about to quibble about it as I was famished.

We had now only a bag of crisps left between us which would have to sustain us till we got to Lochearnhead.

'Time to break camp, Jamie. You take care of the tent and I'll hide any evidence of us being here.'

He painstakingly put all the stones back in the river, dousing the ashes with water from the cans. On the completion of this he replaced the divots of turf, treading on them until they blended and matched the bank surface.

'Perfect, Jamie. I don't think anyone will track us or find any evidence of a fire.'

I had to agree on checking the bank. 'Well done, Colin, you have convinced me.'

Oh-oh. I spoke too soon. As we finished packing and were about to finalise tying the tent to our rucksacks, a man wearing a deerstalker and wellingtons, carrying a gun, appeared from nowhere.

'Don't panic, Jamie I'll deal with him.'

As he approached within hailing distance, the man shouted, 'Camping here is prohibited, this is private land!'

'We were late on the road last evening and only set up camp as it was getting dark and we were totally exhausted,' said Colin.

'You should have checked where to camp before you started hiking,' he replied in a gruff voice. 'There are hostels and designated camping sites within walking distance. By the way, I hope you didn't start any fires!'

'No, not us,' said Colin, with an air of a saintly halo on his head.

That was close, I thought. Colin had been clever enough to cover our tracks before breaking camp and we were a good distance away from where we had lit the fire; which was either fortunate or cunning on the part of Colin.

'That's OK then. I'll let you off this time. I could report the matter to the police. As you're on your way I'll let you off with a caution.'

I was happy that Colin had taken the fish cuttings and dumped them when we were swimming.

'That was clever of you to have the fire a few hundred yards down stream, Colin. He only checked the ground round the tent and the nearest part of the bank. Have you ever done this before?' I asked.

'The truth is I read in a journal that when hunters are out in the wild they never cook a meal near their camp as it's a sure way to attract bears. Then you become the meal of the day. I only applied the same basic rule – our predator being the game keeper.'

'I would not have set up camp here if I had known what I know now, Colin.'

'That's why I didn't tell you, Jamie.'

The gamekeeper pointed us on the correct route to Lochearn-head. I'm not quite sure he was totally convinced by Colin's explanation as he followed us to the roadside and waved us off. We then headed along the road towards our next destination.

Chapter Nine

I t had become misty as we went through the lovely area of Strathyre. I felt a small spot of rain on my thigh – were the heavens about to open? I wondered. As long as it didn't get too heavy it would be welcome and refreshing.

I was disappointed at not being able to view Ben Vorlich as the weather deteriorated.

One of my favourite records had been a seventy-eight speed recording of 'Bonnie Strathyre' by Robert Wilson. Unfortunately the record was now damaged owing to carelessness on my part. I had sat on it and it broke in two. The new records of today are made of a more flexible material which is made for people like me.

The mist began to clear after a few miles and there was little traffic on the road so a lift was most unlikely. Coming round a sharp turn I glimpsed what looked like a car in the bushes. If I had been driving a car I would never have spotted it.

As we approached two people appeared: a man in his late fifties with silvery hair and fair complexion, and a fresh-faced young lady. They had just exited the car on our arrival at the scene.

'Thank goodness!' said the gentleman, 'I hoped someone would come along. I hope you can help us,' he said, 'I had a flat tyre and lost control on the tight bend. It only happened a few minutes ago and I'm still in a bit of a shock. As you can see my daughter has still not been able to deal with it – she is inconsolable.'

The young girl was sobbing but managed to utter a few words at a time. It turned out she was more distraught about her circumstances than the crash.

'I'm bridesmaid at my cousin Lorna's wedding and I have to be there by one o'clock, in order to get changed for the service.'

Colin, with his enthusiasm for any task that would give his

ego a boost, offered to help. This especially allowed him to show prowess and physical strength to a good-looking, impressionable young girl.

'We'll have you out of there in a jiffy!' said Colin. 'Get in the driving seat and steer while we do the rest.'

'I can't drive! I hurt my hand while trying to push it myself.'

'Jean, you will have to do it lass!'

'I haven't passed my test yet, Dad,' the young girl explained.'

'You can manage, darling, just do your best.'

'Put the car in neutral,' I said to Jean, who was now in control. 'Take the handbrake off and put it back on when I tell you.'

'OK,' said Jean timorously, leaning out the window.

'Right, Jamie we'll rock it first then give it one mighty heave and keep it going when it's on the move,' said Colin. 'The main thing is to watch your footing. We don't want any twisted or broken ankles at the start of our holiday.'

'OK!' I said.

'When I say now you give it your all… Now!'

We broke free of the slight ditch through the bushes and on to the road in one sweep. The determination of Colin was written on his face. His eyes were bulging and biceps rippling.

'Now brake, Jean!' I said.

She responded immediately and the car came to a halt.

Jean was now smiling and instantly became aware of the strong specimen of manhood that stood before her, probably for the first time in her young life. Her eyes met Colin's and I thought to myself, here we go again, she has succumbed to his charms in an instant.

'That was wonderful,' Jean exhaled.

I might as well have been on the moon, so impressive was her gallant knight. I could read her mind; it went something like this: 'What a handsome hero to come to my rescue in my hour of need. I'm his damsel in distress.'

Yuck. A damsel with raging hormones, I thought to myself.

'Oh, you have grazed your arm. Let me clean it with my handkerchief and a little water,' she said to Colin.

I was sure any excuse would suffice to hold his hand. I needed a hanky to gag my mouth. Oh stop thinking, Jamie!

'Jamie will change your tyre,' said Colin, 'He's an expert on cars, Jean. Seven minutes is all he'll take.'

'Jean, you'll have to drive,' said the elderly gentleman, who was Jean's dad and had introduced himself earlier to us as Tom Johnston. 'I'll put the L plates up, sweet,' he said.

I had the wheel changed in under seven minutes with the assistance of Colin, whom I pressed for support after his unwanted compliment.

'Oh that's wonderful of you, Colin, to have it ready so quickly,' said Jean.

How much have I to take of this nonsense? I thought.

Hurriedly we set off for Lochearnhead as a bride was in search of a bridesmaid. We arrived in plenty of time at the bride's house, only to find that mass hysteria reigned. Reason and logic had gone out the window; panic and noise had taken residence, only interrupted by Margaret giving gasps of, 'Thank God you have made it, we had all but given up! What happened!? Oh, never mind, you're here, that's all that matters,' answering her own question. 'We've your hair to fix and a thousand other things, so get up the stairs now!'

'Who are these two blokes in khaki shorts?' Margaret enquired. Margaret, who was Tom's sister and Lorna's mother, didn't give him time to reply and went on to say, 'Both Lorna and I have been worried sick; your timekeeping was always suspect, honestly man!'

He was under fire from all directions before he could explain what happened. Colin immediately came to the poor man's defence, setting the record straight.

Tom said, 'If it hadn't been for these two boys we wouldn't have been here at all. Oh yes and we have another problem. I can't play the accordion at the reception.'

'Oh, just great!' bleated Margaret. 'How are we going to get someone to provide the music at this late stage?'

'This is indeed your lucky day. Colin is a first-rate singer and I can play the accordion,' I explained.

'You're definitely a godsend!' said Margaret.

'We have one big problem though. I am sure you will not want us at your wedding dressed in these khaki shorts and T-shirts.'

Tom looked at me. 'You're about the same height and build as I am, Jamie. I have a spare kilt and jacket hanging in the wardrobe, which I'm sure will fit you. I use it when I am out with the band. You, Colin, on the other hand are a different story – proportion-wise that is! I'll have to put on my thinking cap. Mmm...'

Jean gave a loud laugh at Tom's comments while staring at Colin's massive shoulders, before scurrying upstairs, obviously taken by his stature.

I could see Tom was deep in thought. 'I've got it, big man,' he said. 'The brickie! Let's go, Colin,' Tom said, 'we have little time to spare. Have you or Jamie got a driver's licence?'

'Jamie sits his test in a few months,' said Colin.

'Great!' said Tom. 'I'll keep the plates up then.'

Following Tom's directions we finally reached Big Dan's house. Tom knocked on the door and a man similar in stature to Colin appeared at the door. He was more rugged and weather-beaten, though, with a little pot belly which one would expect of a builder. He was an amiable chap, grinning from ear to ear at the predicament we had found ourselves in.

'Has your sister been harassing you to death, Tom?' asked Dan.

Tom informed him of the problem. Dan then quickly responded, 'Come up the stairs, Colin, and see what you like and it's yours; with the exception of the usher's suit, of course, hanging on the bedroom door.'

Colin wasn't long in selecting a kilt and jacket from the wardrobe. 'This will keep Jamie and me dressed alike,' he said.

We could only dream of owning such attire. It was of the best material and obviously bought at a top tailor's. A matching white shirt, shoes and socks, were also produced from a cupboard.

We were soon off again, thanking Dan for his generosity and benevolence.

'See you at the church. Remember to be on time!' said Tom.

'Sure thing!' Dan replied.

Tom went on to tell us of the changing arrangements. 'We have to go to my other sister's house to get washed and changed. I had already arranged this with her before all this hullaballoo. She won't be expecting three of us though.'

Doreen and Bob's house was also in turmoil, with herself, her husband and two young daughters at odds with one another. The dispute was over the toilet facilities. Everyone wanted use of the toilet at the one time and the girls were taking too long, having gone in first. The two girls, Emma and Maria, were squabbling in the washroom as we were escorted into a bedroom to change. 'In here, lads,' said Bob. 'I'll bang the door and try and get these two out of the toilet.'

'Right, out you lot!' we heard him say, 'we have guests and they need the facilities. You have been in there long enough!'

Following the outburst from Bob there was a distinct silence from the washroom. Then only whispers, as it is with girls.

Next, words were heard: 'I wonder who it can be? We are not expecting anyone, are we?'

'No!' said the other voice. Silence… then, 'We will be out in a minute,' which took about ten. Then the door finally opened.

Out popped two fifteen year olds, scantily dressed.

Colin scrambled in the door first, leaving me to deal with trouble in the shape of identical twins. A parent's nightmare by all accounts; mischief was written all over their faces. I faced a grilling by them, as they wanted an explanation of our chance meeting with Tom and Jean. I gave them an account of what happened as briefly as possible. With such inquisitive teenagers a detailed picture of the events was demanded. Satisfied my explanation was plausible they now made for their bedroom, to put on some clothes, hopefully.

Thank goodness for that, I thought. I had been beginning to feel a little hot and awkward.

I could hear a little whisper now and again from the next room. Plotting the downfall of Colin and me, no doubt.'

'Come on, Colin!' I shouted, then knocked on the door.

'I'm coming.' He opened the door, saying, 'I have left a towel for you – and the shower is brilliant, by the way.'

I dashed for the toilet and had a quick shower in case my semi-clad inquisitors returned. By the time I had finished Colin was almost ready. I had to admit he looked good in the kilt but I didn't want to give him any encouragement for his ego was already enlarged without further praise.

'What do you think?' Colin asked.

'Not bad at all! You'll have all the women chasing you at the drops of brandy,' I replied.

'Jean will be falling all over me in this rig-out!' Colin sighed.

Of course she had already done that when he was in his shorts, so I had to agree. 'Yes, I'll second that, Colin.'

Tom's kilt was a perfect fit for me. Luckily he had a spare one for playing with the band.

I dressed as quickly as I could then turned to face the mirror. Not bad, I thought. Mmm, you look dashing, Jamie Cameron.

Colin had to help with my bow tie as I had never worn one before. The shoes were a size too big but thicker socks compensated. We descended the stairs to be greeted with huge wolf whistles from the girls.

'Hurry, Colin! We don't have a minute to spare as you will be the usher along with Big Daniel,' said Tom.

Colin nodded and made a dash for the car.

'You will have to drive, Jamie. I'll go into the front along with you. Girls, you'll need to squeeze in with your mother and Colin!' said Tom. This brought an immediate sound of tittering and whispers from the twins, who were obviously looking forward to some mischief in the cramped space of the back seat.

Yes, you've guessed it. Mum first, the one twin, then Colin, then the other twin. Right again… no room for movement!

Emma was sitting on Colin's kilt in the cramped space. As a result the kilt crept halfway up his thigh to almost the top of his legs. Result, a male miniskirt!

As there were plenty of bends in the road the girls made the most of every opportunity to grab hold of Colin's legs, claiming that they needed to grasp something or part of him to stop themselves from falling on to his lap. How Colin was managing to hang on to his dignity remained a guess.

At last we reached the church car park, to be greeted by the skirl of the pipes as we spilled out of the car. Tom was trying to tell me something which unfortunately was lost in the din.

Doreen pulled me to her left along with Tom, then asked, 'Has Ted the photographer arrived? I can't see him!'

Having pointed out the photographer to the exasperated

Doreen and after separating the deadly duo from Colin, Tom was able to tell us what we were supposed to be doing. 'Colin, you'll take my place as the usher for the bride's family and Big Dan will be for the grooms. You don't mind covering for me, lads, my hand is really hurting now. I'll be glad when it's all over so that I can have a wee half. They say this the happiest day of your life – maybe for the bride and groom it is,' said Tom.

'Oh, will you sit with the twins, Jamie, please?'

'Yes, Tom.' Oh, what a nightmare, I thought.

I was at last able to speak to Colin, who burst into a fit of laughter when he heard these two monsters were to sit beside me.

'Those two wee monkeys had their hands all over me. I was nearly minus a kilt. A good spanking is what they need! I will rephrase that. A clip round the ear hole would suffice. Wait till I tell Jean. She will sort them out when she is finished with her duties,' said Colin.

Tom grabbed me by the neck. 'Quick, I forgot, you'll have to play the organ. I forgot to mention it with all the commotion.'

'No problem,' I said, 'As long as I have a small rehearsal!'

Oh, sweet relief, I'm spared from these two terrors, I thought.

'You won't have to sit with the twins after all then, Jamie,' said Tom. He must have spotted the relief on my face as he went on to say, 'That will be my penance for the day!'

I received the signal to play the wedding march. It wasn't until after Lorna had taken her veil off that I noticed the bride was a beautiful, striking blonde, the type Colin would have gone for; but at the precise moment his full attention was taken by Jean.

Everything went well at the service. Clockwork would be the term used. I was thanked by the vicar for my rendition. I also got two pounds fifty from the groom, which I greatly appreciated. This is going to be a profitable day for me, I thought.

As we congregated outside Jean took Colin's arm while the twins grabbed me, one on each arm, for the family photos. I heard Colin faintly talking to Jean, no doubt referring to the mischievous twins. 'Wait till I get my chance, I will give them a good cuff round their ears!' said Jean. Colin was laughing once again. I think he had undergone enough and was beginning to see the light-hearted side of the situation.

The meal was wonderful and of course free. We were treated to as many helpings as we could eat, which was a lot. At this rate, Colin and I will be able to enjoy the summer break without overworking, I thought.

The groom gave a resounding speech and finished by praising us. 'These two lads from Ayrshire – what would we have done without them? There might not have been a wedding! There would have been no usher, no organist, and no bridesmaid. They are going to be part of the band for this evening, so a toast to Colin and Jamie. Cheers! Oh, and if they can sing as well as they can eat, all I can say is we are in for a fantastic evening.'

There was a rapturous applause after he sat down.

'I hope it was for us!' said Colin.

'Your big head again. It was the speech, you clown,' I said. 'If we get paid for this evening that will be worth more than any applause, do you agree?' I added.

'I'll concede defeat on that one,' said Colin.

The tables were cleared of debris and the room was rearranged to suit the dancing. Most importantly the bar was now open and was besieged by the male guests, with in addition the odd lady trying desperately to attract the attention of a serving waiter.

The band called for the bride and groom followed by the best man and the flower girl, and of course the gallant Colin, who had persuaded the best man to relinquish the first dance to him. The parents of both families took to the floor next, followed by the terror twins, one with Bob and one with Tom.

Billy was on drums and Big Dan was on bass guitar. I was between accordion and piano, depending on the piece of music being played. It turned out to be a fabulous night with reels and waltzes and a good mixture of music. This gave Colin the opportunity to dance with Jean. He liked close dances, which were few, although sometimes during them he was needed for singing. We gave them some of the Beatles and Rolling Stone numbers along with the Twist.

The young ones, including the twins, were having a ball. Windows were now hurriedly opening and emergency doors pushed ajar as the temperature began to rise. I was feeling the strain of the kilt. The weight and the density of the material was causing me to sweat profusely. I did not know how Dan was holding up as there had to be a puddle of sweat below him with the continual drip exuding from his brow. He had also consumed eight pints of beer already – and these were just the ones I'd seen.

For the last two numbers Colin asked if I would sing and play the piano. I played a Perry Como song and a Sinatra number. I could see Jean clinging to Colin as they slowly moved round the floor. She kissed him at the end of both songs.

I wondered to myself, if Colin met someone (and that someone being Jean) would she be the girl who could finally get him to settle down? I recalled our experiences of a few days earlier with Heather and the girls. Heather's words were still in my head: 'Colin, try not to break too many hearts!'

That is why she had never given him hers.

I was grabbed unceremoniously by the twins for 'Auld Lang Syne' which Dan had offered to sing. I received hugs and kisses from the twosome as they snuggled into me. They knew how to enjoy themselves. This gave Colin the opportunity to have the final dance with Jean.

'Three cheers for the bride and groom. Hip, hip…!'

The best man came up to pay the band and told us to share the fifteen pounds sum between us. Dan handed me four pounds and Colin two, while keeping the rest for Billy and himself. 'I think that is about fair,' said Dan. Colin agreed, as I had done more than him. 'Jamie deserves the extra pounds. He has been giving it his all,' said Colin.

Whoopee! I thought, this is turning out brilliant.

It didn't end there, however; the groom's father, in appreciation of our efforts, told us he had booked a room for Colin and me at a hotel nearby for the night. I had wondered where we were going to sleep. I had entertained visions of waking up in the night with the terrible twins pulling off our bedding, leaving us exposed.

Brilliant, I thought, a hotel for the night; but it was heart-breaking time again. Parting is such sweet sorrow! Jean couldn't hold the tears back as Colin said goodbye.

'Stop crying, I'll see you in the morning,' said Colin.

Tom consoled her and took her to the taxi where Doreen was already waiting.

We were given a lift to our lodging by the groom's mother, Debbie. Her husband was well out of it. 'He'll sleep it off tomorrow,' said Debbie. 'He is a good husband, George, but he does like the malt.'

She dropped us off at a quiet country boarding house where the proprietor was expecting two late guests. Debbie waved farewell and thanked us for all we had done.

'Oh, thank you!' said Colin. 'Neither of us has ever slept in a hotel before so we are going to make the most of it. Bye-bye!'

Chapter Ten

I slept like a log and didn't stir till well after 9 a.m. Breakfast had been specially arranged for ten o'clock so there was no rush. Colin wasn't even up, which was very unusual.

After a leisurely meal which was generous in portions we sat and discussed all the events of yesterday.

'What about Jean? Will you ever see her again?' I enquired of Colin.

'She really is something else. I can't say I don't have feelings for her, but the trouble with Jean and girls like her is they want to get married young and have kids. I have about five or six years of study ahead of me, as you do if you remain at school. I don't want to get married right after I get my degree. I want to see the world, Jamie!'

I reminded him of the words Heather had said when she said farewell at Loch Ard. ' "Don't break too many hearts, Colin." Remember?'

'How can I forget? She was right, I find it difficult to commit.'

Big Dan arrived to take us back to see Tom and Doreen before leaving for Killin. 'No headaches, Colin?' asked Dan.

'No,' said Colin, 'only heartaches.'

'Ah, yes, the bonnie Jean,' said Dan.

'Aye. It's going to be difficult to say goodbye,' said Colin.

We stopped outside Doreen's house and the door opened with Jean in the doorway. She was a beautiful girl. The only thing spoiling her was the sadness in her eyes.

The twins brought our rucksacks out to the car and Tom followed behind, once again thanking us for our help the previous day. The two monsters grabbed me once more and kissed me from each side. I was afraid to struggle in case I might hurt them. I am sure they realised this and took full advantage of my situation.

'That's enough, you two! Inside with you! You've had your fun for today,' said Doreen.

Thank God for that! I thought.

Jean asked Colin if he minded her coming along for the run as she didn't wish to say goodbye from here. We waved our farewells once more and promised to return and see them soon. I took the front seat along with Dan, who cracked jokes the length of the journey. Indeed, I liked this guy. I would miss him and I am sure Colin would too. His company would be great on Friday night at the pub.

In my mirror I could see Jean snuggling into Colin. This is going to be tough, I thought, the waterworks are about to start any time. At that Colin called to Dan to stop. 'I want to walk along the river.' He wanted to see the Falls of Dochart, which flow into Loch Tay.

Dan fetched the rucksacks from the boot and I kissed Jean goodbye. Her tears were uncontrollable now as she kissed Colin. Dan shook both our hands with a mighty grip, the sign of friendship.

'Remember your kilt, Colin,' said Dan.

'Thanks, Dan. I hope to make good use of it in the coming weeks.'

'Bye, Dan! Bye, Jean!' said Colin, blowing her a kiss.

The car drove off and I couldn't bear to look at the expression on Jean's face. Colin's silence said it all.

It was hard to take in what had transpired over the past few days. Perhaps Colin just wanted the tranquillity of this peaceful setting to find an answer to the dilemma he found himself in. Anyway, I walked on the rocks along the riverbank leaving him with his thoughts. We had certainly plenty to discuss over the campfire.

I had been given a cover calendar picture photograph of the Falls of Dochart a few years before. It was a place I had always wanted to visit. To view the falls at their best you need a lot of rain but you also want sunshine to enjoy the area; unfortunately you can't have both. The weather in the area had been dry in the previous week but it was now clouding over. But I was not complaining as the holiday had been great until then.

The river was reduced to a small stream, which left me disappointed that the scene I faced in no way matched my expectations. The vision I had imprinted in my head featured thundering water leaping over jagged rocks and spouting towards the bridge, crushing through the arch from the south into the deep chasm below facing north.

The mist of the previous two days had now suddenly disappeared. The sun had its hat on once more and was beating down on us. Colin had little to say so I continued admiring this beautiful riverbank, searching for signs of movement.

After a short while he called me over. 'Fancy a dip?' Colin asked, breaking the silence between us.

'Is it safe?' I enquired. Colin was an expert swimmer so I would always take his judgement as being sound.

'The water is only flowing gently through the bridge, but I'll check there is no undercurrent or shelf, that could pull us under.'

In his plimsolls he worked his way down to the edge, checking the water was safe and there were no jagged edges which would cause lacerations or other nasty injuries. He swam round in circles then dived, each time surfacing at a different spot.

He came towards me, saying, 'It's nice and warm, not what I expected. The water has obviously been warmed up in the shallows further up stream.'

'The pool is pretty murky. It's an artist's paint colour of burnt umber. That is the best description I can give,' I said.

'I have checked the middle and it's more than twenty feet deep, Jamie. I know you are desperate to dive so go for it.'

My local swimming pool had a top diving board which was blocked off by a door. We would take turns to keep an eye on the attendant lifeguard. As soon as his attention was drawn elsewhere we gave a signal to whoever was on the board at the time to dive, which was stupid and against pool regulations. Just my luck! I was caught and given a verbal warning and told by the lifeguard never to attempt that again.

'That was foolhardy you stupid boy! The shelf is too close for anyone to dive off the top board. If I ever catch you attempting that again you will be barred from this pool!'

It seems someone had hit the bottom when diving from that board a year earlier and had been badly hurt as a consequence.

The high board was deemed unsafe after this incident, hence the reason for the new regulations.

Before diving I tested the river edge myself then surface dived. It was pitch black as Colin had said, and I was unable to reach the riverbed bottom. Therefore it had to be deeper than fifteen feet, which was perfect for diving. I had dived into the pool on the east side of the river, swimming through an arch as close to the small spout of water as I could. Nothing was found so I said to Colin that I felt comfortable to dive off the bridge. 'I'm sure there will be some by-law prohibiting me from doing that,' I said.

'Oh, bother regulations!' said Colin.

'OK then, come up with me and watch for any traffic.'

We made our way up the east bank to the bridge. Reaching the road we sat on the wall admiring the view. Looking over, Colin said, 'It's a fair dive, Jamie boy.'

'I have dived from higher than this,' I said.

'Are you ready then? The road is clear now. Get up on the wall and just go for it.'

I took a deep breath and leapt from the parapet of the bridge. What a sensation. The excitement got me in the pit of my stomach. So thrilling – I felt as if I were flying like an eagle. The daredevil came out in me, knowing my parents would be livid if they had any inkling of what I was up to. I knew now what lack of parental control really meant. My dad would have had a fit and I would have been grounded had I been caught, even at my age.

By the time I had surfaced Colin was making his way back down the embankment. He then dived in to meet me.

'Well, I bet that made your day!'

'What a feeling!' I said. 'Don't tell anyone I did this. You never know the repercussions.'

'I won't tell anyone,' said Colin, 'just savour the moment.'

I think the excitement of the moment will always be with me; the fact that I know that I achieved the dive. I must confess to being an exhibitionist where diving is concerned. I would have preferred an audience but I was satisfied with exhilaration of the feat. Pleased with myself I lay on the bank enjoying the fresh air.

Colin decided it was time to move on. 'Right, Jamie, you've had your fun for the day. It's time to go.'

Gathering our pack together we headed into the small town centre. Our earnings, our new-found wealth, would enable us to stock up with the necessary provisions and, most importantly, lunch. We found a medium-sized restaurant in the small square. 'This will do nicely,' said Colin.

A cute little waitress in a short skirt approached us, smiling enthusiastically at Colin. Producing a menu she pointed to the special of the day. 'Give me a call when you have decided,' she said.

Colin was totally unaware of the special attention that she was paying him. I could see his problem clearly; however, he hadn't worked out in his mind what to do. It is difficult to have a serious relationship when you have alternative goals in life and one of them is to see the world before settling down. The combination is out of the question unless the girl gives you time and space. I could not see an answer and I knew he was in no mood for dialogue but he had to snap out of it. So I said, 'Wake up! What do you want, another Jean?' If that didn't give him a shake then it might rile him.

The very mention of the name Jean made him jump. Startled, he said, 'What about Jean?'

'Nothing at all. I was trying to get you to select from the menu. I have decided on steak pie.'

'I'll have the same,' he growled.

I signalled to the waitress, who in response turned her head away.

'Colin, I'm getting the cold shoulder here. It's time for you to buck up and use your charms.'

Colin looked up and caught the eye of the waitress without a signal. She was at the table in a jiffy. A few words of flattery and she melted. 'What can I get you today, boys?'

'Two large steak pies... portions, that is.' This had her tittering. A follow-up line had her laughing even louder. I never found out what he said. He only put his finger to his nose, which of course meant it was none of my business.

'She's very nice and friendly. Look at those legs... mmm, and black stockings,' said Colin.

'Yes,' I replied. When she wants to and whom she chooses.

The pretentious little flirt, I thought to myself. Anyway, it's good to have him back, even though he is a charmer.

A jug of water filled with ice was first brought to us with a drinking glass. I poured one quickly, as I was parched. The meal came a few minutes later. Colin's plate was filled to capacity, with no room for potatoes. She produced another side plate for him, obviously thinking, this guy will have a ferocious appetite.

My plate arrived only when she was satisfied that Colin's wishes had been met. I received only one plate, the portions being measured to the size of the dish. The meal was excellent, and Colin said, 'They give you a fair portion here.' He had not seen my plate, else he would not have mentioned it. Never mind, the meal was good as he had said.

I tried to lift his spirits, even if it was with spirits. 'Why don't we find a nice country hotel along the riverbank, near Loch Tay?'

'That's a great idea! I could go a pint or two. Maybe they will let us put up our tent in the back garden,' said Colin.

'I don't think so Colin.'

After a little flirting with the waitress we paid the bill, with a tip of course for her extra attention.

'Thank you! Please do come back!'

This remark was directed at Colin, of course. With a cheerio we were off and on the road once more.

The main road to Loch Tay is darkened with the many trees along the side of the road forming a canopy keeping out the sunlight. Not a road to be walking in the dark, I thought to myself. After about three miles it started to brighten, allowing more sunlight to break through.

At last we arrived at a small hotel in the clearing with lovely views to the loch where you could have a couple of pints of beer in their garden.

'This will do nicely,' said Colin.

Someone happened to be mowing the lawn on the right of the hotel as we approached.

'Well, do you think it's time I polished up my brass neck, Jamie boy?'

'You'll have to! There is no way I'm going to ask to pitch a tent in his back garden.'

'This is a perfect opportunity to have a word with him. With a bit of luck he'll be the proprietor.'

Colin strode up the drive, leaving his rucksack with me. All I could hear was a faint greeting from Colin and the offer of a handshake. I could see by the body language of the person mowing that an arrangement of some sort was being thrashed out. Finally, before returning to me, Colin shook the gentleman's hand once more. Whatever Colin had said obviously met with approval. Typical, I thought, he has worked out a deal with this chap without consulting me.

Colin relayed what had transpired. 'Right, we can pitch the tent at the rear of the hotel for the night,' said Colin.

'What's the catch?' I enquired, keen to know what was in store for us in the way of obligation.

'Well, in return for doing a few chores we get free camping and meals. What's the matter with that?' asked Colin.

'I'll keep my judgement till later,' I said.

'The bonus is we stay in the hotel midweek as he has a room yet unbooked. So now what do you think?'

Mmm... I wonder what he's got us into, I thought. I have always trusted him so I'll go along with it. This time, though, it looks too good to be true.

'Let's pitch the tent first, then we can see what's what,' said Colin.

Has he signed us up for something, yet he's pretending he doesn't know, I wondered?

With our tent in place it was time to report for duty, which I had deep reservations about.

'Any good at joinery Jamie? It is Jamie, is it not?'

'Yes, it is Jamie, and I am pretty fair at woodwork,' I responded.

'I'm Jack, the owner. Pleased to meet you.'

'Likewise!' I said.

Colin jumped in on the conversation. 'He's an expert at joinery. He is more polished than I!'

'That's just what I want to hear. I desperately need the back porch fixed quickly. I have had to shut it off to guests this week and it's losing me a lot of money,' said Jack. 'I need the surround painted white and Colin has volunteered to help me with that. Come with me, Jamie, and see what you think has to be done.'

On inspection I found that six of the surface planks of wood had deteriorated beyond repair and would have to be replaced. Jack took me to his large double garage where I was pleasantly surprised to find all the material and tools I required.

'I just can't find the time to repair it myself and they charge an arm and leg round here because I'm out the way.'

'I'll have to remove most of the surface area to find out what needs to be replaced, Jack.'

'How long do think you will take?' asked Jack. 'I would like it up and running for the weekend.'

'I reckon it should only take three days at most if I get started right away.'

'I'll leave you to it then,' said Jack.

I spent most of the next hour stripping the offending planks from the deck and eased a few others to check the main structure below. It was six o'clock when Jack came out to inform us that a meal had been set for us in the staff kitchen diner.

Jack's wife, Ann, greeted us and showed us to their washroom where we could freshen up before eating. Ann was probably only in her late thirties but looked slightly older due to her plumpness, which I guess was down to the fact she was the chef and food taster.

The washroom had an electric shower and, would you believe it, Colin had dashed in ahead of me. 'Elders first, Jamie boy!' said Colin. An electric shower was a luxury. I knew of only one person to have one: my aunt, who you would say was 'well-to-do'.

'This is the life!' said Colin.

'Oh, now I can go in after you're served!'

'Patience, Jamie, patience.'

I'll bet he's off to the table for his starter of soup, the rotter, I thought.

A quick wash and I felt great. I found when I reached the kitchen he had been winding me up again, and in fact had asked the young waitress to wait till I was ready. I had barely sat down when a large bowl of soup was placed before me. It was thick Scottish broth, my favourite. Yes, this is the life, I thought. A second bowl came courtesy of the nice young waitress, who had fallen under the endearing charms of Colin. The main meal followed, with lamb chops, local potatoes and vegetables. The sweet was ignored by both of us, as we liked to keep in shape.

Colin thanked the waitress for her attentive service and I could see now the old Colin was back and on the mend after leaving his lovely Jean behind. Heartache now nearly over, he began to discuss the options we had now we had the tent.

The bar was now open and Colin was in need of a good Scottish pint of Younger's Tartan. I had a Coca-Cola; being underage disallowed me from taking alcohol.

I asked Jack if I could play the piano and without hesitation he said, 'I'd be delighted if you would, it might bring in more custom. Guests are always looking for entertainment.'

I sat down to play and before long the lounge was filled to capacity. Colin decided it was time for him to join me; taking the microphone, he announced a few numbers which he was about to sing. He called us the Dynamic Duo, 'And if there is anyone out there with that name, then I'm not about to copy you,' said Colin.

The night went quickly with one or two singers requesting a spot as the alcohol took effect. All in all it turned out a very pleasant evening.

Jack approached us after he closed the bar. 'I have been busier tonight than all last week, thanks to you lads. Are you sure you don't want to stay here for the summer? It would be in the best interests for us all.'

Colin and I laughed. 'Maybe when we need some money next year for our studies. As it is, we have lots to do and see this year. Thanks for the offer though,' said Colin.

It was bed time, or should I say tent time, as our hotel accommodation was unavailable until tomorrow. If you have slept in a tent with just a groundsheet and your muscles are aching, you'll just know how uncomfortable trying to sleep can be. Morning came slowly as I was awake half the night.

Chapter Eleven

After a big breakfast it was back to work for Colin and me. Having assessed the situation I was pleasantly surprised to find rotting timber only on the south west side of the porch, which was open to prevailing wind and rain. I then set about tearing all the decaying wood from the frame leaving the structure totally bare. This took the bulk of the day as nails in awkward places proved to be difficult to remove. After measuring the material, I set about sawing all the pieces of wood in order of need. This would mean I would have everything to hand for construction.

One thing I was good at was precision; my pet hate was the possibility I'd have to alter things as I went along. I don't know where the expertise came from; I found working with wood came naturally to me. I had fitted a loft ladder just a few days earlier for my dad before I had left for this summer vacation in the Highlands.

Lunch! Then back to work.

With the wood all cut I needed Colin to give me a hand to lift and lay. He was an excellent mate. He knew what was required next by inspection without instructions.

Three days I had said. I'd done it in a day and a half! Even Colin was amazed and acknowledged the feat. Colin had almost completed his task as the paintwork only needed freshening up with one coat. So that just left the floor to be treated with a waterproof stain.

Jack came along to check up on how we were progressing and was amazed at how much work had been achieved in such a short period.

'You have been very smart!' said Jack. 'Oh, to be in my teens again!'

I told him, 'We'll be finished tomorrow, Jack.'

'I'm delighted at the prospect of serving coffees and drinks in a day or two. It will bring in extra business.'

After an early start both Colin and I were determined to finish at one o'clock that afternoon. The paintwork on the gable end was high but Jack had a good ladder for the job. He held the ladder for the full morning, securing it for Colin, who went about the job with ease. This left only the rails round the deck to paint after I had finished my task. I made sure the framework wood was all sealed with water-seal paint then I laid the deck planks to finalise. Another hour of paint seal on the surface and the job was complete.

We finished the tasks about one o'clock and that was that. Two and a half days, job done, and everyone happy – a fair achievement.

After lunch Jack offered us a small rowing boat with a fishing rod for the rest of the day. 'If you catch anything we can have it for supper,' said Jack.

Now having the comfort of a hotel bed, I felt really refreshed, even after our morning's work. That soft bed and snug duvet had done the trick. It proves that if you have talent and use it to full advantage, this type of holiday, albeit tough, pays its own dividends.

The boat was chained on a small jetty and could only be released by the key which we were holding. Once the chain was removed then the oars became available.

Colin decided he would row as it was good muscle training for his massive frame. I was much more at home carrying the fishing rod and tackle. Boy how he could row, and how he did, with sheer strength and determination. We were in the middle of the loch in no time at all.

The breeze had caused a small swell; therefore I had to set my bait on the rod sitting down. I let the line drift while Colin tried to find a way of lying full out on the boat. In no time he was asleep.

It was about an hour, after various attempts, that I felt a tug on the line. With the jerky movement of the boat Colin awoke from his slumber, startled at first, but he quickly got to grips with the situation. He lowered the net into the water as I reeled in my catch. As I pulled it closer to the boat, Colin leaned over and netted the fish.

Yes I had caught a beautiful trout, about a pound in weight.

No sooner than he had landed the fish when we heard shouts for help, from the east bank of the loch. Colin grabbed the oars and rowed as if his life depended on it. As we got closer I could see a young boy waving and shouting, pointing to the water. Without warning Colin was up and into the loch, leaving me to fumble for the oars. He obviously felt he could reach the casualty quicker by swimming. I would never argue that point, having seen him swim. He had also taken a first aid course this final year at school, which was about to prove beneficial to the casualty.

It was extremely difficult to look over my shoulder to see just what was happening. I edged the boat sideways so that I caught at least a glimpse of the drama unfolding. Colin had reached someone in the water and had decided to swim with the person towards the shore. About a minute later I arrived at the small cruiser with the young occupant on board. He was traumatised by the whole situation. I told him to climb on board the rowing boat as I inched alongside. As soon as he scrambled on to the boat I rowed as fast as I could for the shore, all the while trying to calm the distressed young man.

Colin had already administered the kiss of life to the gentleman as he could not feel a pulse. After a few attempts the casualty came round, spluttering water from his mouth and gasping for air. It took a minute for the gentleman to recover his faculties.

An onlooker had phoned the local doctor, who arrived on the scene within a few minutes. 'I'll take him to hospital to have him checked over,' said the doctor to Colin. 'You lads did a grand job!'

With these words he sped off.

'Let's go!' said Colin. 'We don't want anybody fussing over what we did. Anyone would have jumped to the rescue.' He was being very modest, as you would need to be brave and indeed to be an extraordinary swimmer to save someone in a cold loch.

We proceeded to row across the loch with the sun now glistening on the water after the sky's being cloudy for most of the day. It felt good just to relax and take it easy after the commotion was over.

I explained to Colin what had happened as we lay resting. The young boy, Bobby, had been watching his father trying to start the outboard motor on the vessel. After a few failed attempts it had burst into life and caught him unawares. He had fallen forward, striking his head, and as a consequence toppled into the freezing water. The youngster had been helpless so he had begun shouting for help.

He had told me how heartening it was, after his initial hysterics, to see someone making the effort to save his father. 'He asked me to thank you, Colin, for saving his life.' Colin just shrugged his shoulders and said nothing.

'Well, we have two lovely trout for dinner!' said Colin as he reeled in the second catch of the day. 'Let's go over to the west shore now. Start rowing, Jamie boy,' said Colin.

Though it had been an eventful day Colin insisted we say nothing of our afternoon. 'Not even of the fruitful catch of the day for our meal?' I asked. I had to duck a swipe for that remark.

We moored the boat and headed for the hotel kitchen and asked for the fish to be cooked for our tea. We then headed to our own twin room which was marvellous.

Cleaned up and famished we returned for our private corner table. Our fish had been cooked in a sweet sauce served with a large portion of potatoes and all the trimmings as one would expect of this type of establishment. Having had our fill we headed for the lounge bar which was quite busy.

A voice was heard saying, 'It seems two lads in a rowing boat saved Sam Anderson's life out on the loch today. He's OK now but got a bit of a fright. He had his young nipper of twelve with him whom they brought to shore suffering from shock. Not only that, they didn't take any credit for it. The lads just rowed away! I thought it a bit strange, but maybe the boys didn't even bother and just didn't want any fuss.'

Jack looked over in our direction from the bar. 'Did you see anything when you were fishing, boys?'

'We were too busy trying to catch fish,' Colin replied. 'A pint of heavy and a Coca-Cola when you have a minute, Jack,' said Colin.

I played a few soft tunes on the piano before retiring early. Whether the excitement or the fresh air got to me I don't know, but I felt exhausted.

Colin had only the railing to paint around the deck so I gave him a hand as it would take nearly all day to complete. With two sets of hands the job was finished just before tea. Taking a few steps backwards I could see that the white railing really brought quality to the building. It's amazing how a little transformation can enhance the character of a place.

Jack came out to inspect the job and was well pleased. 'It will be an hour before tea so I suggest you take Samson for a walk and get some fresh air into your lungs.'

Samson was a boxer and the most petted dog I have ever known – and most definitely the stupidest. When you threw a ball for him he didn't retrieve it, he just jumped on it as if he were trying to burst or bury it. What a lovely creature he was; although when he greeted you he put his paws on your shoulders and proceeded to lick your face as one would do with an ice cream.

'Time for dinner!' Jack called.

A large pot roast was on the menu. Mmm… the aroma, I swear I can still smell it! Delicious!

This was our last evening and Jack thanked us for the completion of the tasks. 'Well,' he said, 'you should have had two nights' dinner, bed and breakfast plus free ground rental for your tent.'

I had wondered if he had been going to say, 'You'll have to do some more work to pay for your privileges.'

'So, lads, what I am going to do is give you ten pounds each for the work plus another five pounds for entertainment. My lounge bar has been busier these past three nights than it has been for days on end. I think it is only fair that I give you a bonus.'

We thanked him for his generosity as he could have passed on any extras, simply by taking into consideration the luxury accommodation and the best of food we had been given.

The whole exercise was going to plan and at this rate we would have enough money to keep us through the summer term without having to return home early.

After a sound sleep and a full breakfast we bade farewell to all our friends, not forgetting Samson. Jack shook our hands and wished us good fortune.

'If you lads are ever in need of references don't hesitate to give me a call. Also, I know you will need more money next year. I'm always looking for staff to do the chores on the building during the summer months – and entertainers! The maintenance is never-ending and paintwork has to be kept smart.'

'We'll keep that in mind,' said Colin as we loaded our rucksacks.

It was difficult to be on the march again, having tasted the comforts of a small, plush hotel. It certainly weakens the morale, facing the prospect of tent life once more.

Chapter Twelve

We had been on the road for a short distance when I felt a tingle on my face, arms and legs. Fine rain or Scots' mist (as we call it) was descending upon us. I thought about digging in to my rucksack for my Mac but chose my bonnet instead as I didn't fancy a rummage through it. I was pleased at my decision as the rain cleared as quickly as it came.

Colin, meantime, had taken off his shirt to keep it dry and let the air dry his body. Typical of him – he would always do things differently.

Ben Lawers towers above the main trunk road to Kenmore and was clearly visible to us now the mist had gone. We stopped after a four-hour walk for our first break of the day. The packed lunch prepared by Beth, the young waitress, was absolute perfection and now urgently needed.

Beth – another lovely girl who had succumbed to his charms.

'Is that not a first-class picnic lunch, Jamie? Just what you would expect from a professional establishment,' said Colin.

I was waiting on the next sentence but it didn't transpire. 'I agree with you. I would find it difficult to surpass such a packed lunch.'

We set off once more with sun now blazing down on us. We felt contentment that we had not sought a lift, as we were enjoying the freedom which hiking brings. Stretching our legs after the rigour of crouching in a confined area gave me a sense of release.

The weather became very humid as the breeze had dropped completely.

'I fancy a dip, Jamie!' said Colin.

'I do too Colin.'

We put on our plimsolls to protect our feet. Colin had insisted that I must protect my feet at all costs, especially when needing them for walking. He told me about an incident regarding one of his friends who had failed to take precautions and ended up in hospital with a large blister that had to be drained. He had bought a new pair of boots and had not broken them in. After two days he was forced to see a doctor, who sent him straight to hospital. If he had taken the precaution of using Vaseline he could have prevented his injury.

We descended towards the loch and found a small sheltered spot with a beach. After our thirty-minute frolic in cold water it was time to look for a campsite for the night. We managed to find a quiet space at the campsite near to the loch – not too close, though, as we didn't wish to incur the wrath of the midges. The hats we wore had kept them off our brow, the wee monsters.

We were starting to feel peckish once more and there were all sorts of aromas from various quarters of the camp. We had two tins of corned beef and a tin of spam, one roll, and our usual beverage, tea.

Colin decided a stroll round the site would do no harm at all. But on second thoughts he said, 'I think you should wait and keep an eye on the equipment while I survey our options.'

I knew of course that he was in search of female company, a girl who would fall helplessly for his charms. Even better if she could rustle up a nice meal for a poor backpacker. Surely she would see his plight and come to his aid. I needed my hankie again. Colin was now fully restored to his former self, I was sure of that.

Twenty minutes later Colin returned, brimming with excitement.

'Well,' I enquired, 'what's making you so happy?'

'I have just met a family from Yorkshire. They are up touring for the week in their camper van.'

'Do they have a daughter?' I asked.

'As it turns out, yes, they do have a sixteen-year-old daughter.'

'I knew it!'

'Don't worry. I won't be the one making the advances!' That meant nothing as I was finding out that the modern girls were more likely to make the first move. 'They have offered to make us a meal,' said Colin.

'What's the catch?' I asked him.

'I've told them you will have a look at the water tap in the van. They have turned on the tap and nothing is coming through. Before you ask, the tank has just been filled.'

'I'll have a look at it but I'm promising nothing.'

'Oh, I've taken the liberty of telling them you're a genius with plumbing.'

'Thanks a bunch!' I was grateful that a meal was looming on the horizon, which is an incentive itself.

'Come on, let's get started. The sooner we finish, the sooner we eat. I'll be your mate!'

'OK, keep your hair on,' I said.

Colin led the way to the van and as we arrived the young girl came to greet us. She introduced herself as Thelma. Colin then introduced me. 'This is Jamie, my young friend,' said Colin.

Thelma took my hand, then leaned forward and kissed me on the cheek, saying, 'Very pleased to meet you, Jamie!'

Thelma went quickly to the van to tell her mum and dad that we had arrived. After the introductions I found that they were a very amiable family. George, Thelma's dad, said, 'I haven't got a clue as far as plumbing is concerned, Jamie. My wife, Marg, and daughter have tried without success.' Thelma said to me, 'Jamie, the tap is turning but no water is flowing out.'

'Have you got a screwdriver, George?' I should have asked Thelma, as she hurriedly opened a drawer and produced one in a second.

'That's what I call a mate! I'll use you as an example for Colin in the future, if you don't mind?'

'Not at all, I like to be an assistant,' said Thelma, smiling.

Thelma was a beautiful girl as I had first suspected, which proved my theory correct. Colin's attraction to the opposite sex was always his downfall.

I popped off the top of the cold tap to check if the screw was loose. The screw only becomes visible after removing the blue cover. The screw was secure so that was one fault ruled out. I then unscrewed the screw and took off the full tap handle, or grip. It has to be the plastic tap itself, it's the only thing it can be, I thought to myself. It looks a cheap part, anyway.

On examination I found that the whole handle was cracked.

As the handle is shaped to fit the tap head it must have a full grip on the head. The tap had been turned off too tightly and the handle was turning without gripping the head turning the spigot on. I had very few options open, as a spare was out of the question.

'Have you any plastic insulating tape? Even a roll of Elastoplast will do,' I asked George.

'I'm sure I can manage that,' he replied.

A minute later Thelma held out a roll of black tape. 'Is this what you want?' she asked, with a childish twinkle in her eye.

'That will do the job nicely,' I said.

I compressed the tap handle to its original shape and placed it back on the spigot head after applying the tape. I turned the handle and water flowed, to the delight of everyone.

I put some more tape on to make it as secure as possible before replacing the screw, then the cap. The job was done.

'Now, don't turn the tap off too tightly. Be gentle with it and it should last the week. If it does go you have seen what I have done.'

'I know what to do!' said Thelma.

George turned the tap for himself and was satisfied. 'That will hold till I get home and order a replacement. Thank you, Jamie.'

Marg summoned us to the table. 'I'll bet you lads are hungry, so sit yourselves down and Thelma and I will attend to you.'

Waitress service with good company – who could ask for anything more?

My appetite! Was it the fresh air? Was it the food? Was it that I was burning too much energy? Who knows! All I knew was I was forever hungry!

Huge portions were the order of the day. 'I'm sure you boys will manage the little extra,' said Marg.

'No problem!' said Colin.

We had light-hearted conversation during the meal and Colin filled in George about all our exploits over the past weeks.

'Sounds as if you've had some wonderful experiences,' said George. 'Wish I were young again!'

Marg jumped into the conversation from where she and Thelma were sitting, which was outside on the deckchairs.

'I've known you since you were a lad, Georgie, and the longest walk you ever took was to the game and then the pub.'

'Talking of pub, that's where I'm going shortly,' said George. 'You want to come along, lads?'

Colin responded by saying, 'It's certainly a nice evening for a walk!'

'So we're all going then?' asked George.

'Ladies will go first to be getting a wash and change as the lads are doin' dishes!' said Marg.

'I'll wash and Colin can dry as Jamie has already done his bit.'

Afterwards Colin and I joined up with the happy Yorkshire family for a walk to the pub. Thelma walked alongside me, asking questions about my skills. I explained that my dad did most of the plumbing and joinery work in the house and had taught me all I knew.

'It is always good for a wife to be able to rely on a husband to fix the simple problems that occur in a home. It also saves a lot of hard-earned cash. My mother preferred that I should put more into my studies especially my music and art. So it was a battle of wills,' I told her.

Thelma, still deeply interested, was intent on finding out more of my plans for the future. 'What career have you chosen? Or are you still in a quandary?' she asked.

'I have another year at school yet so I'm concentrating on maths, music and art, still leaving my options open though.'

'What about Colin?'

'Well he will definitely travel the globe! History is his subject. He likes to be in tune with how people lived long ago.'

'It's good to meet some company,' said Thelma. 'I wasn't looking forward to spending evenings with my mum and dad.'

'Well, you have us now whether you like it or not.'

'Oh, I like it!' said Thelma with a twinkle in her eye.

'Enough about me. What are your ambitions for the future, Thelma?'

'Oh, I'm going to be a vet.'

She came straight out with it. Oh, how I admired this positive nature in a person. They know exactly what they want and how to achieve it.

'I'm sure you will be a wonderful vet,' I said.

'I love animals so very much that I want to dedicate my life to helping them.'

I laughed. My dad had always said that vets were smarter than doctors. They have to be, as the animals, be it a cat or a dog or whatever, are unable to tell them where the pain is coming from.

'What are you laughing at?' she said.

'It was just a thought that crossed my mind, a saying my dad used.'

'What is it?' I had to concede, and I told her what he had said as I didn't wish to offend her.

She laughed. 'I hope I meet with his approval.'

Mmm, strange thing to say when we have just met, I thought.

The lounge bar was really busy, with seats at a premium. While George and Colin were jostling for an order a table with seating for four became available. We did not stand on ceremony and made directly for it.

After about ten minutes George and Colin arrived at the table with drinks. 'That was good timing,' said George.

'Pity you hadn't got a table for five,' Colin said.

With that, Thelma promptly jumped up and perched herself on my knees. I was slightly taken aback but didn't feel awkward with it as she was such a pleasant little creature, petite blonde with light blue eyes and a warming smile that portrayed her inner warmth of goodness.

I could almost read Colin's mind again: Jamie boy will soon be as bad as me at breaking women's hearts.

Marg told us they came from a small market town outside of Leeds. Otley it was called.

'If you're ever down our way drop in for a cuppa!' Marg said.

The evening wore on with deep laughter from George as he began telling stories of his youth. He became even more boisterous as he drank more of the local ale.

'I'm enjoying this break. It's our first in a long time but not our last, eh Marg, dear.'

'Oh, we'll be back all right, the scenery is wonderful, so different from the moors – which I do love as they possess an enchantment of their own.'

'Last orders!'

'Time for a quick one, George!' said Colin.

'As long as he behaves,' said Marg.

It was still light even at ten-thirty in the evening, with a hint left by the sun going down.

'How far is it?' asked Marg.

'It's a good half hour's walk back,' I replied.

'Colin, will you take one side of him and I'll take the other.'

'I've only had six pints!' said George.

'Yes, before you lost count!' said Marg. 'I don't want you falling and hurting yourself as you're the only one that can drive.'

He was just a little annoyed to be sort of told off in front of newfound friends, but after a few seconds he was back to his jolly self when the message got through to his brain.

I strolled behind with Thelma and as it got a little darker she got closer and asked if she could take my hand. I pulled her in nearer, hugging her. 'Come on, lass, let's be having you!'

'What about the boyfriend?' I enquired.

'Oh, I have never had one. I never seem to be able to talk with them, I become flustered,' she said.

'Well, you don't seem to have a problem with me then!'

'I know. You seem such a natural person and always have the right answer for every situation. I bet you have lots of girls running after you back home!' said Thelma.

'I don't have anyone back home. I never seemed to be able to communicate with them, either. I have met two girls while on my travels, though.'

'So you really have a girl then – someone close?' said Thelma with insistence.

'Well, there is one girl I'm meeting up with in a month's time.'

'Where?'

'Inverness,' I replied.

Thelma was silent and I noticed a hint of disappointment at the news.

I went on to tell her my age. 'I'm only coming up on seventeen, so I can have no long-term commitment to anyone. I can't even decide which career to pursue, never mind settle down with a girl. My plans are on hold and I take each day as it comes. I think that is the best way for the moment.'

'Then there still might be a chance for me!' said Thelma.

'You will have all the young vets running after you, and if I were around I would only be jealous.'

'Would you be jealous?' she enquired.

'Of course I would! With a heartbreaker like you.'

'You're not just making fun, are you?'

'No, Thelma, I'm quite serious.'

With that she pulled me to her and kissed me forcefully till my breath gave out.

Staring into my eyes after her long kiss with me she said, 'That is just a sample of how much love I can give, Jamie.'

This is becoming a nightmare, I thought. So far I have two girls who have literally thrown themselves at me and one that I am besotted with. *Am I now a replica of Colin?* I had to ask myself.

I kissed her forehead. 'Write down your address and phone number for me, just in case I'm in your area and I want to get in touch,' I said.

'Well, just in case,' she said.

I could see that her eyes began to sparkle, transmitting a glow of happiness. Obviously she is desperate to see me again, I thought.

I had plenty to ponder over as I lay in the tent, especially the teasing I had from Colin before retiring. I could not make up my mind whether his taunts were only fun or whether they were a dig at my newfound power of magnetism.

Chapter Thirteen

We awoke to a bright new morning with the sun glistening on the water. A quick jog was the first thing on both our minds.

'This will do the trick,' said Colin, taking a plunge into the cold water.

I don't believe him, I thought. I'm not that daft. It's just a little early for a cold bath and I'm definitely not for joining him.

I sprinted away from the scene as I was unsure of his intentions. For I knew once he started splashing about I might be tempted to get in on the horseplay.

'Chicken! Chicken!' Colin shouted as emerged from the water dripping wet. He started sprinting after me, taking his top off as he ran. When he finally caught up with me I asked, 'Why didn't you take your shirt off first, you daft gawk? And you know the routine – no diving into cold water without your body becoming acclimatised. *Your rules!*'

'Completely went out my head,' said Colin. 'You are so practical, Jamie, that would be the first thing you would think of.'

I laughed heartily out loud and Colin joined in. We shook hands and started running. 'I'll be dry by the time I get back to camp,' said Colin.

After about forty minutes we returned to our tent. We were met by Thelma who was patiently waiting on our return to the tent. 'Breakfast is ready. If you're hungry?'

'If we're hungry?' I said.

She was smiling proudly, knowing full well we both had a ferocious appetite.

'Just give us five minutes to freshen up – or get dry, in Colin's case – and we'll be there.'

'Whenever you're ready!' said Thelma. 'I'll have it on the table for you when you get there.'

Mmm. Crispy pancakes, double egg, sausage and four rashers

of bacon. Indeed, I thought to myself, how lucky we are, forever falling on our feet.

'This is very good of you,' I said.

'We have enjoyed your company, so that's a little show of gratitude from us all,' said Marg.

I told them we had been fortunate indeed with the people we had met over the past few weeks.

'Where are you off to now?' asked George.

Colin responded immediately. 'We aim to stay in Aberfeldy, then on to Pitlochry before heading further north.'

'We can give you a lift to Aberfeldy. It will be a bit of a squeeze though,' said George. 'It's on our way to Pitlochry, is that right, Colin?'

'You're spot on, George,' said Colin.

'If you are ready in half an hour we'll get underway.'

'We will get our kit together right now,' said Colin.

Thelma came with me to lend a hand. I didn't refuse her help as women are much tidier and good at packing. I was sure the rucksack space would be more economically set out for starters. When she had finished I was even more amazed. 'I can't believe you have got everything in the rucksack. There seems to be much more room!'

She made fun of me in that rather taking Yorkshire accent.

'What about me?' asked Colin. 'Am I to be left to my own devices?'

I'm sure he was not used to this lack of consideration, hence the outburst. He was more used to being the main focus of attention. His ego was usually being enhanced by female admiration rather than being totally ignored.

I myself had never been lavished with kindness from relative strangers before and I was somewhat bemused by it all. Nevertheless I decided to make the most of it.

We only just managed to get our gear in the van as space was fairly limited. As you can imagine the manoeuvring area was almost non-existent. George suggested that we keep rucksacks on the dining table as it was only about an hour's drive to Aberfeldy. 'Hold on to them tightly. I don't want them flying towards the back of my neck and hurtling through the front windscreen,' said George, laughing loudly as he started up the engine.

'Never mind what's going on in the back, you keep an eye on the road,' said Marg.

Thelma sat close to me, holding my hand below the table so that it was out of the view of Colin. She was a private person and didn't like to show everyone all her feelings.

It was indeed a short journey and I felt my heart sink as we bade our farewells. This one was proving to be the most difficult, since leaving Bonnie in Balloch. Parting is such sweet sorrow, as Shakespeare would say.

Thelma shook Colin by the hand. He gave her a hug and a kiss on the cheek and wished her well. He stepped out of the van where I handed out the rucksacks individually to him. I then stepped out, quickly followed by Thelma. Without warning both her arms were round my neck; she could hold back no longer. Her inhibitions were flung to the side as she now knew this could be a final goodbye.

Reality can do strange things to people when they are faced with a crisis. Friends departing for a new life come into this category. I have seen grown men cry in such situations. Yes, here I was again in the arms of a lovely girl. I was enjoying it but I still felt guilty in a way.

She let me go as quick as she had grabbed me and ran back to the van in an instant. 'You have my number and my address!' she said.

'You never know!' I said.

With that she closed the door and I was left with a wave from George and Marg as the van moved away.

We were becoming pretty good at finding out the history of the towns, and Aberfeldy proved to be no exception. Colin read from his booklet as we sat on the banks of the Tay. He was a good orator and enjoyed speaking in public.

' "Aberfeldy is situated in the heart of Scotland and sits on the banks of the river Tay which happens to be Scotland's longest river. It's also famous for salmon, and fishermen from all over the world come for the catch. Most stretches of the river are owned privately and huge amounts are charged for the privilege of fishing.

' "Aberfeldy grew up around Wade's Bridge, the first bridge to be built across the upper Tay in 1733 by the English general who subjugated the highlands after Bonnie Prince Charlie's rebellion in 1745. It's also famous for the poem by Robert Burns, who was so taken by the area it inspired him to write of the falls of Moness and the surrounding birch trees.

> The braes ascend like lofty wa's
> The foaming stream deep roarin'
> O'erhung wi' fragrant spreading
> The Birks of Aberfeldy

' "With so much to see the tourist has found this retreat; yet it still remains unspoiled. There is a sense of quiet in the area which is difficult to explain and must be a haven for those who seek peace and tranquillity." '

'That was interesting, was it not Jamie?' said Colin.

'You almost put me to sleep.'

I had to duck another swipe from him, for my cheek.

I felt a little sad as Colin and I made our way further down the Tay. It was difficult to part company from friends whom you might never see again. People come and go from one's life, I thought, and I guess I'm the only one who can deal with it. I suppose that is what they call growing up.

'This is a quiet place by the water's edge, Jamie, we can swim from here later.'

I agreed, and lay on the soft, lush grass for an hour just relaxing with my thoughts. We never spoke, Colin nor I, for the whole hour. Colin would be thinking of Janie and Jean, while I was trying to make heads or tails out of my tangled love life. I thought of Bonnie first and finally Thelma, who was a lovely girl, tender and caring; I liked the fact she intended to be a vet.

The picture most prominent became clear in the shape of Bonnie as my heart began to recall all the beauty and goodness that was her. Perhaps I had been weak and should have been stronger against the advances of lovely girls. Ach, I thought, I'm only human after all, and I've enjoyed the experiences.

Colin decided it was time for a swim. He dived in to determine whether it was safe for me to join in. He was in charge once more and was proud of it. I'm sure he liked the responsibility and was capable of carrying it, else my parents would not have consented to my Highland holiday. Although I was a strong swimmer I was the first to admit that I was no match for the bold Colin.

He returned to the bank with his findings. 'The current is very strong in the middle of the river. It's between five and seven feet in certain parts. I have swum the full breadth and there are no reeds to get tangled in. The water is not as warm as I anticipated so I suggest you acclimatise in the usual manner by dipping your toe in the shallows and throwing water on your torso,' said Colin.

'OK, big man! I'll do what I'm told.'

'No diving off bridges today. It's far too dangerous!' said Colin.

I waded in till I was comfortable enough to start swimming. It was a strong current as I felt myself swept off my feet. I quickly started swimming against the current. As I made my way across, although I still found myself going downstream, as I passed the middle it became less powerful. I was in control once more as I neared the far bank.

I became more confident as I got used to the force of the water. The river was as clear as crystal and I could see fish near to the bank as I approached.

After an hour my energy levels were sapping. I called Colin to say 'I'm going out as I'm feeling tired.'

'That's fine. I'm all in myself,' said Colin, 'I wouldn't recommend a dip here for weak swimmers! You don't swim in rivers full stop unless you have qualified instructors like me with you. Even then it's better to have at least two.' I nodded in agreement.

'I felt tired and I didn't want any more mishaps such as the one at Inverbeg, Colin.'

'I understand perfectly where you are coming from. There is no sense in taking risks. Chances are they will turn out for the worst,' said Colin.

We had taken the precaution of one of us being on the bank while the other was swimming. This was to ensure that our belongings were safe as well as keeping an eye out in case of any accidents.

Before we had left, an uncle of mine had come up with an ingenious method for keeping our money safe. This ruse was unique as far as I'm led to believe. He stitched a hollow tongue in our boots with a zip fastener below, which blended perfectly with the style of the boot. This acted as a wallet which held all our money. 'They will have to steal your boots to get your money,' my uncle said. Hence we were taking turns to look after them.

This innovation was to pay dividends in the next few days.

We loaded up once more and headed for a place to have lunch. After our meal we stepped out on the road to Pitlochry, where our friends from Yorkshire were. We found a place to camp on the outskirts of town and set up camp for the night.

Having had an early start this morning we decided on an early night. Nine o'clock and I was in bed – my mother would never believe it. Perhaps things were just catching up with us and our bodies were telling us to rest. I slept like a baby.

Breakfast consisted of an assortment of filled rolls purchased at a convenient store the previous day. It was a four-hour walk to Pitlochry according to Colin so we expected to arrive by one o'clock in time for lunch.

I wondered why Colin had only accepted the lift to Aberfeldy. It had me puzzled but I didn't want to make a lot of it. Colin could never be described as a team player. He preferred to be guided by instinct rather than play to the rules of another.

It was a scenic route to Pitlochry along the Tay and I was happy after a really good night's sleep. It crossed my mind that Thelma would be in Pitlochry, but I was reluctant to mention it to Colin in case he scolded me for taking advantage of a reserved girl.

We stopped for a break around twelve o'clock after walking for over three hours. The provisions consisted of two bags of crisps and a chocolate biscuit. Not a lot for two large human gannets.

Colin decided that we should march on as we were only a short distance away from Pitlochry. 'That's us on the banks of the Tummel. Not far to go now, Jamie,' he said, pointing to our position on the map. 'By my reckoning we have about five miles to cover.'

I disagreed for once. I felt we had walked far enough as my

feet were beginning to burn. 'I want to bathe my feet in the river for an hour and relax. There is no hurry, is there?' I said.

'None at all. You know what I'm like, though, I set out with an objective, I aim for it and always achieve it.'

'I don't doubt it for one moment and I have always admired your positive spirit. But this time I think the practical Jamie should win as his feet hurt!'

'Oh well, I have to concede this time as one's feet are the most important body part in hiking, as I have continually preached to you.'

After a prolonged stay I was happy to be on the road again. Twenty minutes into the journey a car pulled up in front of us and the driver beckoned us forward with a wave of the hand. Colin said to me, 'I wasn't looking for a lift as it's not far to go. Still, what do you think?'

'I will go along with what you decide as I had my way earlier.'

Colin laughed at the remark. 'OK, we'll go for it then!'

Colin opened the door of the car and driver shouted, 'I'm going to Pitlochry, if that helps.'

'That's fine!' said Colin.

'Put your rucksacks on the back seat and tell your friend to get in along with them. Oh, you're the bulkiest so you had better come in the front.'

Colin laughed as his massive frame created problems in confined spaces. 'No problem,' said Colin.

The Hillman Minx was a popular car of this era, a sturdy, reliable family car, and this one was well kept. I was surprised the gent offered us a lift as I knew my dad would not have even contemplated such an idea. Let strangers into his pride and joy with dirty boots and a lot of bulky baggage on his clean seats? I don't think so!

Before driving away the driver introduced himself. 'I'm Tony, by the way, and I work as a mechanic at the local garage. I was down in Perth this morning picking up spare parts for an engine, and I'm just on my way back to the garage. I enjoy getting out and about now and again as it breaks the monotony.'

'Pleased to meet you,' said Colin. 'I'm Colin and this is my pal Jamie in the back.'

'Pleased to meet you both,' said Tony.

'It will only take us twenty minutes,' said Tony. 'How long do think it would have taken you?'

'At least two hours, depending on Jamie's feet,' said Colin.

Tony then asked, 'Have you got sore feet, Jamie?'

'Only when Colin treads on them,' I said.

'Oh, is that the way it is with you two – a little Scottish banter to keep you both on your toes, if you'll pardon the pun!'

'We don't fall out,' said Colin, 'but we like our say.'

'Are you lads studying for your highers?' asked Tony.

'I've sat mine in April and now await my fate,' said Colin.

'What about you, Jamie?'

'Mostly O levels with the exception of music and art.'

'I'm sure you'll have passed,' said Tony. 'Speaking of music, I'm in the local band. I'm playing tonight in a hall at the edge of town next to one of the big hotels. Here, I have a couple of spare tickets as my sister and husband can't make it.'

'That's very kind of you,' said Colin, 'we would be delighted to accept them.'

'That's brilliant!' I said.

'Yes,' said Colin, raising his hand in the air but forgetting the height of the car roof, then giving a howl of pain at his stupidity.

Tony laughed. 'I am glad I didn't do that. I'm on guitar tonight. You will hear a bit of everything tonight as we try to mix our routine for all ages.'

He dropped us off in the small town centre which was bustling with tourists. 'See you tonight lads.' Then he was off.

Chapter Fourteen

We decided to have a look at the shops as we had more time on our hands due to the unexpected lift. What I did notice was the number of kilts on display. Rarely had I seen so many men actually wearing it as normal dress. If it was to impress the tourists then they had a winner.

Most of the serving staff were adorned in a fitting way to match their particular job of work. Two lovely girls in mini-kilts were the immediate attraction to Colin.

'Did you see them?'

'I sure did,' I said, 'but we haven't time to pursue them as my stomach is beginning to ache. I haven't had a fish tea for a while,' I exclaimed. 'Let's break out with some of the money we've made.'

'OK,' said Colin, 'this once.'

It's not easy going into a cafe or restaurant with rucksacks. The only way to do it is to remove them from your shoulders before entering. Well, so I thought!

On my blind side was a table near to the door; too close for comfort for one as clumsy as me. No sooner had I entered than I caught a plate of scones and sent them spinning across the floor. Oh no, I thought, here we go again! My blushes were spared by a young, slim girl who apologised for the lack of space in the premises. It seems they had had to fit two more tables in the room to accommodate the summer influx of tourists.

'I'll put your rucksack in a small closet till you have finished your meal. Well, you'll need to put them in!' she said, laughing. 'I don't think I could lift them. You must be very strong to carry such a load and still be able to walk!'

'No problem!' said Colin, whose biceps she could hardly fail to notice.

'You have arrived at a convenient time as we have three tables about to be vacated.'

Waiting till she cleared a table I began to feel impatient, as my stomach was beginning to rumble even more. The wafting aroma of fresh fried food from the kitchen added to the urgency.

'Well, what is your order, boys?'

'Two fish teas with lots of bread please,' said Colin.

Within a minute our table had a large pot of tea and a plateful of bread and rolls laid on the table. We could not wait for the main course and set about devouring the brown bread and rolls. The young waitress came across and stared at Colin, saying, 'You must really be hungry. I'll bring you another plate of bread and rolls with your meal. It will be ready in five minutes.'

She was as good as her word; another full plate of rolls and brown bread was promptly displayed on our table.

Again she came across to Colin. 'Have you enough tea? Or do you need another pot?'

'Another pot, please,' said Colin, as he stared into her eyes.

She wore a lovely white fitted blouse with emblems and shapes emblazoned on it and also a brooch in the shape of a thistle. Completing the attire was a long straight tartan skirt in deep green and black. I have to admit she was as pretty as a picture.

Not a scrap was left on the table and although we knew this would be expensive the extra pound was well worth it.

Having the tray placed before us, Colin beckoned the lovely waitress and without warning he asked her straight out: 'Are you doing anything tonight?'

'Me?' she asked.

'Yes, you!' said Colin. 'Will you come to a dance with me?'

'I don't finish till six-thirty,' she said.

'The dance doesn't start till eight o'clock,' said Colin, producing two tickets from his pocket.

'Oh yes, I'd love to then! I think The Leaves are a great group.'

'Where shall I meet you?' asked Colin.

'If you'll be there for eight o'clock I will meet you there.'

'That's great,' said Colin. 'By the way, I'm Colin McLean,' he said, offering his hand.

'I'm Fiona McKenzie. Pleased to meet you, Colin.'

'Very pleased to meet you, Fiona McKenzie,' said Colin.

After all the pleasantries we retrieved our rucksacks and bade farewell.

'How are three of us going to get in to the dance with two tickets?' I enquired. 'That was a little presumptuous of you, taking the two tickets without asking me.'

'You worry too much. We will cross that bridge when we come to it,' he replied.

We made our way to the campsite and had our tent pitched in double quick time. The art of keeping things in order was now getting through to my thick skull. Having everything in the right place simplifies a task, such as putting up the frame of a tent.

After the wedding in Lochearnhead we had been given two kilts by our thankful friends. Although they were a weighty burden we wore them part of the time while walking.

We made for the site washrooms, but before reaching them I spotted the camper van from Yorkshire. With all the other things occupying my mind I had completely forgotten that Thelma and her mum and dad had planned to stay in Pitlochry.

I pointed the van out to Colin, but his mind was elsewhere at this point. 'Give me my ticket, Colin! If you're taking Fiona then I will take Thelma!'

He replied, 'Well, OK then, perhaps I've been a little selfish. I was kinda hoping you would find something to do tonight.'

'I still can't believe you were going to take both of those tickets for yourself, Colin.'

'Sorry Jamie, I was totally out of order. My only thoughts were to ask Fiona out. I forgot all about you. Never mind, I've said I'm sorry.'

'Well, what are we going to do about it then?' I asked.

'Let's see if there is a phone number on the ticket,' said Colin, 'maybe there are few still available.'

'They are one pound fifty each!' I said.

'Yes, but we only have to buy one each,' said Colin.

'Oh, I never thought of that. That's OK then.'

'You go and see Thelma while I have a wash.'

'OK!'

'She might not want to go with you anyway,' said Colin.

I left the camp with Colin still laughing; he did like to tease.

I am such a shallow person, I thought; here am I going to ask Thelma out after all my deliberations the last few evenings about the lovely Bonnie. Oh, how I wish I hadn't a conscience. Maybe I should say to Thelma, it's just a night out with a friend. Oh bother, I'll just go along with what comes along. She might not want to go out, as Colin has already said.

Knock, knock, knock.

'Who is it?'

'It's Jamie Cameron!'

George opened the door and grabbed my hand, shaking it wildly. 'Great to see you Jamie! What a surprise. Never thought that I would, though! You'll be going down the pub later, I suspect.'

Before I could reply I was pulled into the van and there stood facing me was Thelma. She's as pretty as a picture, I thought to myself.

'What are you doing here?' she asked.

Again before I could speak I was being hugged and kissed by this over-affectionate Yorkshire lass.

'I saw your van before we pitched our tent and I thought I'd pay you a visit. We arrived here earlier than I expected as we got a lift today from a chap who sings in a band. Oh, he has given us two tickets for the dance tonight and I wondered if you would be interested in going with me? Come for a walk and I'll explain everything!' I said.

She stepped out of the van with me and I told her that I would need to buy another ticket if she chose to go with me. It didn't appear to matter what I was saying – it seemed to be going over her head as all she seemed to want to do was hug me.

Once she had taken what she felt was satisfactory she snuggled under my right arm so that we could walk as one. With my right arm now over her shoulder she grasped my right hand with her left giving her full control.

'What was that you were saying? Again?'

I repeated everything with even more clarity now that she had came to terms with my sudden appearance.

'I'll ask my mum and dad if they wish to come along – they were looking for something to do. Oh, you don't mind, do you?'

'Of course I don't! Your parents are good company.'

We returned to the van and Thelma told her mum and dad what we were planning to do that evening.

'You don't mind if we tag along then?' said George.

'Colin and I would be delighted if you and Marg came with us.'

'Don't forget me!' said Thelma.

'Not forgetting Thelma,' I said, which brought on a beautiful smile from her.

'Let's give this number a ring from the shop,' said George. 'Come on you two, you're coming with me.'

George called the number and on receiving an answer, began bellowing down the phone in his deep Yorkshire accent. 'Four tickets please for tonight!' he said.

'What method of payment, sir, and when will you collect them?' was the message from the hotel receptionist. George handed the phone to me and I told the girl that I was a friend of Tony's in the band and that he would vouch for me.

'That's all right then. You can pick them up at the door – and, by the way, these are the last tickets available, it's now officially a sell-out!'

With everyone delighted including myself I quickly headed to tell Colin of our good fortune.

Colin was already spruced up by the time I returned. I was sure he would be the main attraction of the evening for the unattached, and most possibly all the attached as well. If he could look that good I could surely be more positive and raise my esteem to a higher level. With the confidence seed firmly planted, I could now look good and feel good. The female population were in for a treat.

White shirts and kilts were the attire for the evening. Our woollen socks were not quite dry yet, but if you can imagine what a wringer does then you should try to visualise what Colin was doing to them with his bare hands.

At seven we rapped the camper van door. The door opened and there stood Thelma in a short mini-kilt. I edged Colin aside as he was transfixed by her legs. 'Move over!' I said, so that I was the one prominent in her view.

He turned and whispered in my ear, 'Aye, Jamie, what about Bonnie now?'

He was right of course and I had no answer for him. Thelma held her hand out for me to enter.

Marg then called us. 'C'mon in lads!' she said. 'We are not quite ready yet. I'm sure you can eat a piece of apple pie and have a cuppa while you are waiting.'

I couldn't take my eyes off Thelma and thought, is it possible to have three girls and love them all?

I had a vision of all three together and quickly erased it as the consequences of such a meeting could be fatal. Live for the day and the moment was Colin's philosophy. Well, so he said, but I doubted it very much as he had not been the same man since leaving Lochearnhead.

'My, you are dashing in your kilts! Are you true Scotsmen?' said Marg.

'Nothing worn below our kilts, everything in good working order,' Colin replied, laughing.

They were all actually ready to go but you don't do anything before putting the kettle on for a brew, especially if you are from Yorkshire.

'Let's go then!' said George.

As we set out Thelma had positioned herself in such a way that I had to put my arm over her shoulder, leaning and snuggling so I felt as if I were carrying her. I was relieved it was only a twenty-minute walk. Any further than that and I would have had to give her a piggyback. Or maybe vice versa.

The attendant at the door was very helpful when we told him that we had booked four tickets earlier by phone. Thank goodness our tickets were at the door. We would never have been allowed in otherwise. No problem, the chap said, pay the girl at the desk when you enter. Although we received the tickets they were clearly marked 'TO PAY' on the reverse side.

The place was bursting at the seams but the one good thing was that the young ones stood around a makeshift bar. I didn't go near it though, as it was an over-eighteen dance. The fact we were with family helped and no questions were asked of Thelma or me. We both would have passed easily for over eighteen, especially Thelma, who had adorned herself with all the fashionable make-up of the day.

We managed to find a table and I looked for another two seats for Colin. Thelma, with her mini-kilt, had managed to secure them from some male admirers, to my horror.

We had left Colin at the door, where he was impatiently waiting for Fiona. It's a woman's prerogative to keep a man waiting; why, I'll never know or understand. She didn't have him standing too long, for they entered the hall about five minutes after us. He was beaming with delight, and no wonder. Fiona wore a short black dress which enhanced all her curves and displayed her long, slender legs.

After all the introductions the band struck up and, boy, what a noise. We were treated to the best rock music of the era and the floor was bouncing. When Tony had said 'a bit of everything' he had sure meant it.

Marg was interested in how Fiona and Colin had met and went about finding out in the way women do. Fiona was an assured person and therefore had no qualms about telling where she worked and how Colin had asked her out. 'How romantic,' said Marg.

After the break the band announced Ceilidh time. 'Strip the Willow' was the shout. Everyone in groups of eight – most of the regulars knew the routine so at least two of them were in each group. We seemed to go round and round and round again. I could feel my head spinning and Thelma was trying hard to throw me about but with little success. This was a dance for big women and strong men in kilts swirling to the tune.

Big George was giving it his all. He was sweating profusely from the holiday ale he had consumed over the week. He let go of Margaret a little early and Colin was lucky to catch her.

'I'll get him back for that!' said Marg, 'I'll wait my chance.'

Sure enough her opportunity came round. When he was least expecting it she let him go and, oh boy, he went crashing into our table, taking all the drinks with him. We had to take our group of eight to clear up the mess in case someone slipped.

George was still in fits of laughter as he tried in vain to apologise for his stumble to the waiting staff. After gaining his composure he said to the waitress, 'I'll pay for the glasses, lass, and here's a pound to yourself.'

After the commotion George caught the attention of Marg. 'You got me back good and proper there, luv!'

'What makes you say that, darling?' was Marg's reply.

Before anything else could be said, Tony called Colin on to the stage for a song. I can't remember the song, but it was one of those where the girl clings to the guy and the dance becomes a motion of one. Colin was staring at Fiona as he sang and I could see from the side of my left eye that she obviously wanted a close dance.

There was little room to move on the floor so Thelma made the most of this by pushing herself full against me. She was trim and easy to hold – so much so that I really began enjoying it. These moments should last for ever. Were these the words of a song, I wondered? I didn't know and didn't care!

It's always good when the band finishes with a last two or three slow numbers and this is what they did. Fiona made the most of the final number with both arms stretched over Colin's shoulder.

Before 'Auld Lang Syne' we went up to the stage to thank Tony for his generosity and congratulated him on his fine playing.

'I'm sure you'll go far,' I said.

'Thank you!' Tony said. 'We enjoy what we are doing and we know it's appreciated out there. They say if you are happy within, then it shines on your face. Well, I'm happy, Jamie!'

This guy had it all. He exuded charisma. I was sure he would make the big time.

We bade him farewell and it was time for the road; luckily it was dry and fresh, perfect conditions for a walk. We all declared it had been a wonderful evening with fun and laughter galore. It had also been fraught with danger when George and Marg were let loose on the dance floor.

'What a night!' said George.

'I'll second that!' said Marg.

We said farewell to Fiona, who had proved to be a good sport and talented dancer. Colin decided to see Fiona home, which happened to be only a short distance away. We all offered to wait till he returned but he declined our offer, preferring to make his own way back to camp.

Thelma had found her favourite position below my right shoulder, locking me once more by holding my right hand with her left hand. I had thought her demure at our first meeting, but she certainly had come out of her shell when she was clear in mind what she wanted. I didn't object as she was soft and cuddly and most probably vulnerable.

She suddenly stopped and pulled me down to her, saying, 'Am I just one of your frivolous holiday romances, Jamie Cameron?'

The question caught me unawares and off guard, as I did not expect to be quizzed directly by her. I was totally flummoxed by it and unable to reply. I felt such a heel: I do love Bonnie, and here I am holding another girl in my arms.

Seeing my plight, she said, 'I'm just teasing.'

Thank goodness for that. But it still left me feeling a little low. I was really enjoying her company and I told her so.

'I have had a fabulous time with you and your folks, especially with you. I never wish to offend you in any way as you are such a genuine, beautiful person.'

'So you think I'm beautiful, then, Jamie?'

'Of course I do! And the hall full of young lads will back me up on that.'

George and Marg had made their way back to the van, leaving us together in the moonlight.

'Perfect moon,' I said.

'You are a right charmer, Jamie Cameron.'

'Och, I can't help it.'

'Never change. You have a kind way with you and it shows. You are probably in love with love at this moment in time.'

'Thanks, Thelma. I've been so fortunate to have you as part of my life.'

'The girl who gets you, Jamie, will never let you go. It might be me when you mature. I'm in no hurry. I'm sure you will choose the right one eventually.'

With that I pulled her close and our lips met with a long lingering kiss.

'Goodnight Jamie!' – and she ran away from me to the van.

As she left me I was motionless, and gazed longingly at her slender figure and perfect legs which were exposed by that tantalising mini-kilt. One thing for certain was there would be no shortage of suitors if she was of a mind. The reaction of the guys at the dance had proved that beyond doubt.

I had mixed feelings about that night, with the affection I felt for Thelma. She had it in a nutshell when she hinted that I was immature. I could even see it for myself in my indecision. My inability to take responsibility was only part of the problem. I had to find out for myself what love really meant.

There were obviously different kinds of love. One was intimate, which meant total commitment to another, involving sex of course. I had no idea of what to do about it, and as far as I could see Colin was more mixed up than me, so there was no point in asking him.

I felt love for Thelma and didn't want her to be cut out of my life, but I knew that she would never settle for being just friends. I thought of Bonnie once more and there was no way I wanted to be without her either. Oh, what a mess love can get you into! I thought. I realise now why Colin was in a mood after we left Lochearnhead. Bother, I hope I grow up soon!

I strolled back to the tent looking to the heavens for guidance; with the stars sparkling all around me I regained peace of mind once more. Colin had not returned so I turned in. No doubt he would be unwilling to leave Fiona.

Chapter Fifteen

About nine o'clock I was awoken by a voice outside the tent. 'Are you lazy things not up yet? Mum has sausage, bacon and eggs ready for you!'

Colin and I both popped our heads out of the tent simultaneously to the amusement of Thelma. 'We will only be a minute,' said Colin.

'It'll get cold if you don't come quick,' said Thelma.

I looked at Colin. 'When did you get back last night?'

He pointed to his nose and didn't answer, so I guess that was that.

Hurriedly we arrived at the van and Marg greeted us saying, 'Come away in lads, your plates are on the table.'

'Thank you again,' I said.

'Don't thank me this time, thank Thelma. She insisted we have you for breakfast. I think she wants to eat you,' said Marg. This brought a burst of laughter from everyone. Even Thelma saw the funny side. 'I'd want him well done!' said Thelma.

'We are off to Inverness today in a couple of hours' time – if you lads want a lift?' asked George.

After some deliberation Colin asked if he would drop us off at Killiecrankie, a few miles up the road.

'It is our intention to spend a few hours in Killiecrankie, then walk to Inverness with a night or two in the tent on the way.'

'No problem, lads, if that's what you want,' said George.

We broke camp as quickly as possible after breakfast, then washed before taking our luggage to the van.

George had loaded up by the time we arrived so he told us just to keep our sacks on our laps as it was only a short drive away.

About twenty minutes later George said, 'That's us!' pulling in at a lay-by.

George shook our hands and wished us well. 'Now remember to come and pay us a visit. You will like Otley, it's nice and quiet.'

Marg gave us a big hug and left Thelma to wish us farewell. Colin kissed her hand then her cheek, which made her laugh.

It was difficult to say goodbye to someone whom you were fond of and when you had hit it off so well together. Nevertheless it was time to go, so I hugged her... but she wanted a kiss.

Oh God, now she was crying. I had no alternative but to kiss her. I had promised myself earlier just to say farewell with a hug; now I was in full embrace and she wasn't for letting go.

'Goodbye!' I said.

She didn't say goodbye, only, 'You have my address and telephone number!'

Thelma closed the van door, leaving Colin and I staring at the departing vehicle.

'Time for new adventures,' said Colin.

'I wonder if we will ever see them again,' I said to Colin.

'Who knows, Jamie. We have to move on. That's what life's all about.'

Killiecrankie – a name that stands out. It has a certain ring to it. I always puzzle how places are given names, especially one like the Braes of Killiecrankie.

I had read about the Jacobites in my history class and had heard of the Soldiers' Leap from Colin. It was a case of leap for your life across a deep gorge with the river thundering below. If it were the case that they did jump, then the soldiers must have been facing death from a fierce enemy. Mind you they were at a disadvantage, being on lower ground.

We used the footpath trail down to the river. It must have been raining further up north as I could hear a deafening noise of the River Garry with each step that we took forward.

We found the perfect vantage point of the gorge. 'This will be close enough,' said Colin, pointing to a nice large rock that we could sit on, with an uninhibited view.

'Wow!' I said.

Roaring above the din, Colin shouted, 'If you have any poetry in you then it should be unveiled now! Let your thoughts drift to all that has happened in the past few weeks. All the excitement, the love, the pain the sorrow! Then be still and then write!'

I nodded, not wishing to strain my vocal cords. I found it

awkward to concentrate, as my thoughts were so taken with the scenery below. I will write my poem afterwards, I decided, when I feel the mood.

The River

Who could have thought from falling rain and
    mountain dew,
That this mighty river was born just like you.
It derives its source from high on a hill,
To give it strength and have its fill.
Other waters have crossed her path and she at once
    has shown her wrath.
Gathering force throughout the night,
Leaping and bounding with all her might.
Through the gorge with power and thrust,
Like the echoing sound of a cannon burst.
To surge for the coast she must abide and let not wait
    the calling tide.
The dawn awakes to set her free and rest her heart in
    the open sea.

Jamie Cameron

I wouldn't have liked to be fighting down here with wild Scotsmen. I could only imagine how the redcoats felt with little option but facing death by the sword or drowning in the torrent below. The fact that they tried to leap at all only goes to show the fear they had of the enemy, and the consequences they faced in not attempting to escape across the chasm.

After buying a snack I felt I should let Colin peruse my poem.

He took the paper from me and scrutinised it, taking in the depth of what I had put to paper. 'Mmm, yes, not bad!' he said. I was a little dismayed with his lack of enthusiasm. However, I knew he was the best in his class with composition essays and analysis of literature. Therefore his opinion was very much valued by me and I knew it would be unbiased and fair.

'You have a start and you will improve as your experiences

grow. It takes knowledge to attain the higher level. As Churchill once said, "Youth is wasted on the young." We have youth on our side but only time will make us wise! Unless you're a child prodigy.' Colin laughed out uproariously.

At least he thought my poem was passable, which gave my ego a boost.

'I wouldn't have fancied fighting down here,' said Colin. 'One trip or false step and you're dead.'

'I had much the same thoughts,' I replied.

'Right, time to go. We are heading for the great wilderness now, Jamie lad.'

I couldn't help but wonder why we hadn't gone in the van when it was offered. It was the sense of achievement of looking for new adventures that inspired him. A new challenge was required; the offer of the lift obviously took away that. It would have been too easy for him and he might miss a new opportunity.

We reached Blair Atholl where the splendid green scenery takes the eye. Yet only a few miles ahead the rugged Grampian Mountains waited for us.

After we had walked for just over an hour a grey Morris van stopped and the driver called to us.

'Inverness any good to you?'

'Yes,' yelled Colin. 'You can drop us off at Aviemore, it's on the way.'

A lad opened the van door and told us to put our rucksacks in. 'Close the door and come up front. We'll manage you in somehow,' he said.

We placed our luggage in and closed the van door, and without warning the big gangly lad sprinted to the front passenger door and jumped in, closing it behind him. The van then sped off, leaving us bewildered and stranded in the middle of the road.

Colin looked at me stunned at what had just taken place. We were truly speechless, rooted to the spot. Neither of us used profane language, even though it would have been appropriate at this particular instance.

'What do we do now?' I said.

'Maybe they were just having a laugh and will return shortly,' said Colin.

Before I could reply the van was returning, heading back to Blair Atholl. It slowed down as if to stop and two clowns inside started waving. Was this a ploy to distract us? I thought. Yes it was! The vehicle began to accelerate as it passed us.

'Registration! Colin!' I shouted, 'get the registration. Can you see the plate number?'

'R... 6'

'What did you get Jamie?'

'R, Y... 6! Well, it's a Morris 1960 grey van with this plate or your plate number. There won't be too many of them running around here!' I said.

'How do you know it's a 1960 van?' asked Colin.

'Dad has a 1961 Hillman Minx and it has an S reg.'

'That would seem about right then,' said Colin. Nothing else for it, Jamie, we'll have to head back to Blair Atholl.'

The mere fact we had to go back annoyed Colin. His pet hate was going back the way he came.

It would normally have taken about a half an hour to cover the distance back to Blair Atholl. We had only our kilts, shorts, socks, plus underwear and shoes left in our possession. You could say we were now travelling light.

We reached the hotel on the main road, which was pretty busy with tourists. Colin made his way to the receptionist and took charge of our predicament. The girl pointed to a pay phone on the wall in the corner and I could see Colin gesture in acknowledgement of information.

Colin phoned the nearest police station at Pitlochry and relayed the story. 'I'll have a car pick you up in half an hour,' the desk sergeant told him.

While we were waiting, Colin lamented on the stupidity of what we had just done. 'How could we have been so lax as to lock our gear into a small van and not notice there was not room for passengers in the front seats? They must think we are a right pair of twits.'

'Never mind,' I said. 'It's not the end of the world. We still have all our money in our shoes.'

A police car picked us up outside the hotel and took us back to Pitlochry. We explained to the constable what had happened and how we had been duped. 'I'll keep an eye out for any Morris van with an R-reg plate,' he said.

After a grilling by the sergeant at the station we were given stern warning from a senior officer about taking lifts from strangers. 'This is what can happen when you put trust in the wrong hands. I hope that will be a lesson to you both!'

It certainly had made us very wary.

We gave our home addresses and phone numbers to the desk constable in case the rucksacks were found. 'If our investigation proves fruitful you will have to return for possible identification of the culprits,' said the officer. 'Have you enough funds to return home?' he asked.

'Yes,' I said, 'we carry our money separately.'

'That's lucky then,' he said.

It's not luck, I thought to myself, it was the genius of my uncle and his hidden wallet innovation. 'Yes, we are lucky!' I said, not letting the cat out of the bag.

'Well, I hope it all works out for you and I suggest you take a train home.'

'What do we do now Colin?' I asked, knowing full well he would not pay for a ticket willingly.

'Let me think for a moment. I'm sure I'll think of something. I know!' said Colin. 'Let's go to the garage and see Tony. He may be able to help us.'

'What a good idea, Colin!' I said. I wished I had thought of that.

Tony was working when we arrived and was slightly startled when he saw us. 'My goodness, what are you doing here? I thought you'd be in the middle of the mountains by now!'

'It's a long story,' said Colin.

'Well, if you can wait outside I'll catch you up during my break in twenty minutes. You can fill me in then,' said Tony.

As we sat on the wall outside waiting for Tony to appear, our mood was anything but pleasant.

'All right, what are all the long faces for? Nothing can be that bad, can it?'

After explaining the loss of our rucksacks and tent to Tony, we told him we had decided to return home.

144

'We have little alternative,' said Colin. 'Without our gear there is no point.'

'I'm headed for Crianlarich tomorrow morning to collect a spare part for a car if that's any help to you,' said Tony.

'That would be great,' said Colin. 'We will find it a lot easier to get a lift from there. If not, the train fare will be a lot cheaper to get home.'

'What shall we do about a bed for tonight though?' I asked.

'You can crash on my living room floor tonight. My mum and dad won't mind under the circumstances.'

'We are off to the restaurant for a bite to eat,' said Colin.

'Aye! And that's not the only reason, I bet!' said Tony, 'I'm sure Fiona will come into that equation somewhere.'

For the first time I noticed that Colin was really flustered by the remark as his cheeks had gone slightly red. So he's human after all, I thought.

I entered the restaurant behind Colin; he made sure of it by leaving me in his wake as he made for the door. Fiona was serving a table when we came in and hadn't seen us. Imagine her surprise when she turned to see Colin standing before her. Her face immediately lit up and she came running towards him. She then took his hand and led him to a table next to the kitchen. As Colin sat down he held on to her hand in a way that allowed no one in the room to see what was taking place.

'I'll bring some bread and rolls for you, gentlemen,' she said, keeping her decorum lest someone might suspect something.

The meals in this establishment were first class, along with the service, although you might say we were biased through having the special attention of Fiona. Colin called Fiona over to pay the bill and asked, 'What time do you finish?'

'Around six-thirty, depending of course on people finishing their meal. We just can't throw them out, you know,' she said, laughing.

'That'll be in about an hour then,' said Colin. 'I'll collect you then if that's OK?'

'Wonderful!' she said. 'I'll look forward to it.'

'Bye now, and thanks once more for the generous helping,' said Colin.

'Sh, sh, shh!' said Fiona. She turned away quickly as the restaurant was still very busy.

'Did you manage to tell Fiona what happened?' I asked Colin.

'Not a lot! I told her I would fill her in on all the details later this evening. I am sure she was just happy to see me whatever the circumstances. It's your favourite saying again and I'm becoming familiar with it: "Something good out of evil!" '

We both laughed.

'I'm glad we kept our kilts on this morning,' I said.

'That was a blessing in disguise,' said Colin.

'I'm not going to play gooseberry so I'm going back to the garage to see what Tony's up to tonight. He should be about finished for the day.

We arrived in the nick of time as he was about to drive off. 'You back again!' he said.

We told him we had had our meal and asked what the prospects for the evening were.

'Jump in! You can wash and brush up, but only after me. I'm in need of a scrub much more than you. I've been up to my eyeballs in grease and oil all day. I love it, though; there is nothing else I would rather do. What do you think of this car?'

'She's a beauty!' I said.

It was an Austin Cambridge 1600, ink blue, and it was shining like a shilling, with leather interior, walnut dash and chrome fittings. It was easy to see that this was his pride and joy as it was in immaculate condition.

'If you take care of a car like this it will be on the road for many a year,' said Tony.

On arrival at his home he explained the situation to his mum who, upon hearing what had happened, welcomed us with open arms.

Tony showered first and I nipped in before Colin, much to his annoyance. It was good to have a shower; oh how good did that feel. I must have been in there about ten minutes when Colin knocked on the door.

'How about it – are you going to take all night? I've only forty-five minutes before I meet Fiona!'

'Be out in a minute!' I said, laughing.

'You took your time,' said Colin.

Both Colin and I had newly bought underwear as we had nothing to change into because of our plight. I had rinsed my old ones along with my socks, but how was I to dry them I wondered? I asked Tony when I got downstairs.

'Mum, I'll put the boys' underwear and socks in the wash, is that OK?'

'That's all right son, I'll have them ready in the morning.'

Although I had eaten about an hour ago the smell of baking pie in the oven was tantalising and driving my taste buds wild. My appetite had improved immeasurably in recent weeks with good fresh air in my lungs.

'I've made you some cheese toasties, I'm sure you will manage them.'

By this time Colin was already in the living room having completed the fastest wash ever recorded.

'Oh, you're so kind,' said Colin, 'how will we ever repay you?'

Colin finished his meal and departed, informing me he would be back for eleven o'clock. 'See you then!'

'Jamie, I'm going down town to meet the boys,' said Tony. 'We sometimes play in one of the hotel lounges, depending on how busy they are during the summer season. Do you want to string along?'

'Brilliant!' I said.

'They have a piano in the lounge if you should want to play. I'll lend you a pair of slacks and a shirt for the hotel.'

'That's great! I kind of wondered what I'd wear.'

Tony introduced me to the rest of the lads in the band. 'He's a pianist and singer boys.'

'We'll he'll get his chance tonight. The hotel manager has told me there are two bus parties staying over. They're from the English Midlands and they like a good time.'

'Do you play any of the old-time stuff?' asked Tony.

'I do them all,' I replied. ' "Mother Kelly's Doorstep", "Run Rabbit", "Silvery Moon", etc.'

'We'll get paid for this one, lads, and we might get a few tips on top. Well, maybe! If anyone offers you a drink tell them to leave it with the bartender and you can collect at the end of the night. That way you only drink one or two pints and share the proceeds.'

He went on to tell me of an uncle of his who played the accordion. 'Aye. Johnny just kept taking drink from punters till he fell on the floor drunk. That put an end to his career as an accordionist.'

'Is he from around here?' I enquired.

'No, he lives way up north.'

The group played a few Elvis numbers then they turned to me for the old-time music hall. I played and sang for over an hour with all the singalong music. Then I sang a Scottish medley: 'Down in the Glen'... 'Song of the Clyde'... I had everyone join in so much so I could hardly hear myself above the din.

We had a break, which I was glad of as my fingers were feeling the strain. 'Well done lad!' was the united chorus from the group.

'Maybe they will want to dance for the last hour,' said Tony.

'Hope so,' I said.

With a mixture of waltzes, quicksteps and country dances the night turned out great, with rapturous applause.

Tony called me to finish with the songs 'We'll Meet Again' and 'The White Cliffs of Dover' instead of 'Auld Lang Syne'. They loved it! I could almost feel the roof rising.

Unknown to me, Colin had slipped in just after the break. Fiona and he were snuggled in the far corner. It was Tony who had noticed, pointing them out. He told me he had seen them slow dancing earlier. I made for their table instantly.

'I didn't see you come in,' I said.

'You were a bit busy,' Colin said. 'We had a great time and its good to be discreet now and again, Jamie.'

'I'm glad you enjoyed it,' I said.

'Did you have fun playing?' asked Colin.

'Loved it!' I said.

Fiona spoke softly and said she had had a splendid time. I kissed her cheek and said goodbye again. 'This is becoming a habit!' I said. She smiled with a tinge of sadness but said nothing.

'See you later Colin!' With that I joined Tony and the company for a five-minute time call.

'Jamie, you've got two pounds from the hotel and two pounds ten shillings from behind the bar!'

'Oh, that's good news,' I said. 'I'll get a shirt and slacks for that.'

We made our way home by foot, as Tony had taken two pints of beer.

'I don't care to drink and drive,' he said. 'I have no time for anyone that does. Anyway, my livelihood depends on my ability to drive.'

I couldn't help but wonder how poor Fiona felt at Colin turning up suddenly and unexpected. It would indeed be heartbreaking to let him go again so soon once more. No farewell kiss for Colin tonight! She had indeed shown her emotions the night he left and I'm sure she desperately wanted him close, but he would have to give some sort of commitment that he would return to see her.

'That was a heartbreaking goodbye for both of us, Jamie,' said Colin. 'I just cannot commit myself at the moment, wish I could! If ever I want to date her later on then I would have to do the pursuing. Fiona has made that abundantly clear.'

Chapter Sixteen

I t was up early the next morning as Tony was leaving around eight fifteen. With everyone wanting a shower and breakfast it would be a tight schedule. Tony's mum and dad were now in the equation as they started early. Women's work is never done! Our smalls and socks were washed and ready. Four packed lunches ready. Boiled eggs, toast and tea set on the table. Perfection! Where do we get mums from?

I had taken all this for granted before, with little appreciation. I thought, I know I will have to show my gratitude to my mum when I get back home. I'll say 'You are so good to me, Mum!' She'll say, 'Say your prayers and eat up.'

I thanked Tony's mum with a hug and told her how kind she was to put up two relative strangers.

'You were no trouble! If I can't help someone in need then I'm not much of a mum.'

What an angel, I thought.

We managed to scramble into the car on time, waving farewell to them both.

'Travelling light again!' I said to Colin.

'Only a packed lunch and spare underwear,' said Colin.

'It should only take us an hour and a half to get to Crianlarich,' said Tony, 'around ten I think. I hope that will be all right for you.'

'Do fine!' said Colin.

Tony put on his radio and sang along most of the way. 'Well, that's us nearly there. Are you planning on taking the train or are you going to try for a lift?' asked Tony.

'I will check the train times. If we have to wait for a couple of hours then I think we may try for a lift. What do you think, Jamie?' asked Colin.

'That's fine by me,' I said. I agreed as I didn't fancy sitting in a station for a couple of hours.

'Goodbye again, lads. I hope everything goes well with you. Stick in at the music Jamie, you never know – I could see you in the charts some day.'

'Not before you!' I hastened to say.

'Good luck! Good luck!'

We shook hands and Tony drove off to collect his spare parts.

'It certainly was lucky meeting Tony,' I said.

'What a stroke of luck that he was heading down to Crianlarich,' said Colin.

'Aye, and an angel for a mum,' I said.

'I heartily agree with you there. We have a packed lunch into the bargain,' said Colin. 'Now let's head for the station.'

It was easy scrambling up the stairs to the station without our rucksacks. Wouldn't it be great if someone took our equipment ahead and we just did the walking, I thought.

On checking the timetable we discovered the next train south would be three hours away.

'That's made up my mind,' said Colin, 'I'm not hanging around here for another three hours.'

I had to agree. 'Might as well start walking now,' I said.

'We should eat first,' said Colin.

I bought a bottle of coke and Colin purchased a bottle of clear lemonade as he didn't like colouring in his drink. We tucked into our packed lunch on the outskirts of the village.

'What a feast! No wonder Tony is in no hurry to get married. He is in love with both his car and music,' I said.

'Not forgetting his mum,' said Colin.

There was a lot of mist on the Ben as we set out for Ardlui, which is the nearest village south, where we had had fun with the girls from Balloch hostel, which of course included my Bonnie.

I had a heavy heart as I didn't relish going back home with five weeks or more still left of the holidays. It was difficult. I should be going north, not south, I said to myself. Have to try to be positive and rid myself of negative thoughts.

'How are you feeling this morning, Jamie me lad?' said Colin, poking fun. 'You look a little down in the mouth to me! Look on the bright side – we have plenty of money to spend and you are going up to Inverness in two or three weeks' time to be with Bonnie. So spare a thought for me.'

'Where will you go?' I asked. 'Will it be Lochearnhead or Pitlochry for your last week?'

'That's a really difficult choice,' Colin said. 'I honestly haven't made up my mind. I love Jean and Fiona both so much,' Colin lamented. 'Fiona made it crystal clear she wasn't going to have her heart broken by someone coming in and out of her life no matter what her feelings were for them. I didn't even get a farewell kiss, only a peck on the cheek.'

'Well, I told Kate and Thelma that I had Bonnie, though I could see it hurt them both. I wish I could date all three!'

'Not possible!' said Colin.

'Yes, I know! I tried to visualise all three of them together. What a mistake! Total mayhem. Squabbles, fights and pulling each other's hair out. It just doesn't bear thinking about.'

'Just think if we hadn't met any of them our life would be all the poorer for it,' said Colin.

'I tried to paint a picture of life in my head without Bonnie. I stopped immediately as it was unthinkable.'

'No, I don't want to think like that!' said Colin. 'If I tried anything as stupid, I would end up with a sore head.'

Interrupting my final few words on the subject, Colin said, 'Look, there's a car in the lay-by down yonder and it looks as if it's stopped in a hurry – the two front wheels are nearly in the ditch! Hold my sandwiches and small bag of clothing and I'll run to see if I can assist.'

Colin's knowledge of first aid had proved to be an asset when we were boating on Loch Tay; I would need to take a course when I returned. Everyone should have basic training, as I had found out. I would have been useless without him.

When I got closer I could see him talking with someone in the passenger side of the car as I approached. He beckoned me with a wave as if to say 'move yourself'. I hastened to the car as swiftly as possible. He gave me a quick rundown of what had happened and what his plan was.

Following his instructions I helped lift the elderly gentleman into the back seat. It was a big car; a Vauxhall Cresta, two toned in shades of blue. We were able to put him almost full length on the seat due to the breadth of the car.

Colin asked the lady, 'Can you drive?'

'I only drive in and around the city. I'm not comfortable on roads with hills and bends.'

'That's OK,' said Colin. 'Jamie will drive as he has a provisional license and you can sit beside him. I'll go in the back with your husband and put a pillow on my lap and he can rest on it.'

'That's very kind of you,' said the lady, introducing herself as Helen Ballantine.

John had a high temperature, so Colin gave him a couple of aspirin and some water and the old gentleman nodded off to sleep.

'It's best we take him to hospital,' Colin explained to Mrs Ballantine. 'Do you know where the nearest hospital is?'

'The Royal Alexandra in Dumbarton is probably the nearest general hospital to here. Is that all right with you lads? It's only about an hour and a half away if we don't get held up in traffic,' said Helen.

Loch Lomond road is busy with day trippers and tour buses this time of year, as we had experienced, and the road is exceptionally narrow at some points. I was slightly nervous to say the least driving on such a road, but circumstances had dictated that I did so.

Helen told us that they had been staying with friends in Fort William for the week but John had not been feeling too well the previous day. So he had decided he just wanted to go home early. He had been up the Ben – well, halfway up – on Sunday and had got caught in the rain. 'Silly old man,' she said 'Sixty-two and climbing hills. Anyway, that's how he got his fever. He didn't feel too bad when we started out earlier but began to shiver later on the journey.'

I got the impression from Helen that she wasn't entirely happy at having her holiday spoiled by returning home early.

'I told him he's far too old to be climbing hills at his age but he's a determined one and made the attempt anyway,' said Helen.

'He was trying, maybe, to show you that he was still fit and capable,' I said.

'I told him to get a fishing rod. That's what he's fit for now.'

Oh-oh. I'll just leave it at that, I thought.

What a machine this big Cresta was, what a cracker! It was easy to handle. The only thing wrong was I felt it taking up half the width of the road. If I were buying a car this would be the one; or should I say if I could afford one. It had big tail fins at the rear – nothing like the American versions, more sedate, yet noticeable all the same. The suspension was superb; it was like being on a boat when you hit a bump, not like most other cars.

There were some tight corners on the way along the loch which I found exhilarating. What a thrill! I was sorry in a way to part with the Cresta as I left it parked in the hospital grounds.

We stayed in the waiting area with Helen while John was being examined by the doctors. Helen decided to call her son, David, in the interim, to let him know what had happened.

'He will drop you lads off at St Enoch's Station after his visit,' said Helen.

'That would be great,' said Colin, 'as we are not sure how to get to the city from here.'

The doctor returned after approximately one hour. 'He's got pneumonia,' he said. 'We'll have to keep him in for a few days. It's nothing to worry about at the moment as you brought him in before it became serious.'

'Thank you, doctor,' said Helen. Helen then turned to Colin and me. 'I don't know what I would have done without your help. It was so good of you!'

Colin shrugged it off. 'We needed the lift anyway,' he said.

Just at that moment David arrived and Helen updated him with his father's condition. David asked if he could see John, but the doctor told him he was sound asleep and preferred that he remained undisturbed.

Helen introduced us to David and told him all that happened to us in the past few days. 'Imagine stealing all they had!' she said. 'Poor lads are having to go home early.'

'Wait a minute,' David said, 'do you think you could see yourselves in a cabin for a few days by a loch?'

Colin and I stared at one another in bewilderment. After the initial surprise Colin responded by enquiring, 'What cabin might that be?'

'I have a cabin in Lochgoilhead overlooking the loch,' said David. 'It's yours for the week if you wish.'

'Yes please!' we both said in unison.

'That's settled! It's yours,' said David, 'I'll take you there after I have taken care of some urgent business. Mum – will you manage the car over to Bearsden?'

'That won't be a problem, son, I'm used to driving in the city limits. It's those narrow winding roads that I don't like.'

He kissed his mum and said, 'I have to take care of the lads now but I'll pick you up and we can visit Dad tonight.'

'Bye, son! I'll see you later then.'

'Right, lads, give me a minute. I have a couple of urgent calls to make. Wait outside in the car park for me.' Five minutes later David reappeared. 'I'll take care of you lads now.'

Turning to Colin he said, 'We will have to find one of those outdoor activity shops for you and see if we can't get you kitted out once more.'

We headed to the car park and, don't you know it, he owned a Mark 2 Jaguar. It was a silvery grey colour with the chrome gleaming in the sunlight in absolutely mint condition.

'Like it?' asked David, with a smile that lit up his face.

'Oh yes!' I said. How fickle I'd become now. I liked this car better than the Cresta.

This guy had everything. He was tall and lean with dark hair cut to perfection. He was well groomed; his suit was obviously made to measure. His dark brown shoes were mirrors of polished excellence. He wore a white satin shirt with a deep blue tie. His jewellery included gold rings on his wedding finger and a watch with cufflinks to match. This indeed was a man of considerable wealth, I thought to myself.

The interior of the car was of black leather, which softened under my weight. I was a little uncomfortable though at never having been in such an expensive vehicle. To tell the truth I was afraid that some crumbs or pieces of heather would fall off my kilt and mess up the car.

David glanced over his shoulder towards me and asked, 'Are you comfortable, Jamie?'

'Yes, I'm fine!' Mmm… I wonder if he noticed that I was a little tentative?

'Now, I'm sure there is an outdoor shop in the town centre.'

After a five-minute drive Colin spotted one. 'Look, David, over there is one at the corner of the street!'

'You will only need one rucksack, lads. I have a spare one in the cabin you can use,' said David.

Given the quantity of items required we were both worrying about the cost as I tried to tally up the amount. David, sensing our fears, said, 'Look, lads, this is on me, the complete bill. It's my way of thanking you for what you have done for my mum and dad. Pick up two of everything you need, including thick socks and shirts.'

David led the way to the serving till and said to the girl, 'I'll pay for this equipment.'

Colin and I were so grateful for this and expressed it by thanking him and shaking his hand. We would never know the exact amount that David paid for the goods simply because he might have been offended if we had asked. I don't think he would divulge it anyway!

'Let's find a grocer's store now and we'll get you stocked up for the week,' said David.

Colin had now planned ahead for the next few weeks with the help of our newfound wealth. 'What a difference a day can make in your life!' he said.

He handed me a note with the following:

- Seven nights in Lochgoilhead climbing and walking;
- Seven nights between Fort William and Fort Augustus;
- We will split up near Invermoriston and I'll head for Gairloch and Ullapool;
- You will then go to Inverness to meet Bonnie.

After reading the itinerary Colin asked, 'Is that OK by you, Jamie?'

'Absolutely!' I said, relishing the thought of a cosy bed for a week.

As we loaded up the boot with our provisions my thoughts strayed back to John and Helen; I thanked God that we gave a little help, for indeed we had been paid back a hundredfold for a small charitable act.

Colin found it difficult to conceal the fresh smile on his face at the outcome of events. 'Are you as happy as I am, Jamie?'

'Ecstatic!' was all I could say.

'I can't wait to see this cabin,' said Colin.

'Neither can I! I find it hard to believe that someone has bought everything we need.'

'Well, the man insisted, so we have to go along with his wishes.'

'Right boys, close the boot and we will be off,' said David.

I must admit I like to daydream, and boy was I enjoying this one on our way to Lochgoilhead.

It was a cloudy day as we returned up Loch Lomond with the sun bursting through every so often. This time I was able to enjoy the scenery as I lay back in my chauffeur-driven Jaguar.

Going into Arrochar I had a splendid view of Loch Long and the Argyll forest which stretches all the way to Lochgoil and then to Holy Loch at Dunoon. I had a perfect view of the Ben Arthur, affectionately known as the Cobbler, which dominates the sky above.

We followed the A83 trunk road to Inverary and Campbeltown. Up the very steep incline called 'The Rest and Be Thankful', which is difficult for heavy vehicles. I had heard of cars being stuck on it in winter before it was upgraded; now I knew why.

David held back to let a few slow cars get a run at the hill. He then masterfully accelerated at the precise point to give him a chance to reach the top without changing into lower gears. I'm sure he wanted to show off a little.

On reaching the top we stopped to take in the view at the summit. It was breathtaking and I felt as if I were on the top of a mountain.

After our short break we took the narrow single-track road towards Lochgoil, with its passing places set out strategically for oncoming vehicles to pass, or vice versa. I'm not positive but I thought I heard David say, 'We go down hill for about seven miles from here.' Anyway, it's some slope!

We reached a small junction where at last a sign pointed us in the direction of Lochgoilhead. Half a mile further on, we came on a sign for the village and to the right one for Carrick Castle.

'I'll let you see the village first,' said David, going over a small bridge straddling the stream. The village had few buildings; nonetheless it was furnished with the essentials, including church, hotel, public bar, post office and shops.

'You will find everything you need in the main shop,' said David, 'including fresh milk and bread.' He parked in the main car park which is only feet away from the edge of the loch.

'This will be one of those panoramic views that Colin has told me about,' said David, laughing. Colin had obviously been referring to a statement I make when I'm overwhelmed or in awe of the scenery. He would pick on me if I overindulged on a particular expression. 'I'll have a word in your ear later, big ape!' I said to Colin.

David pointed to the cabin which was about a mile away on the edge of the loch, exactly as he had stated earlier. 'You have an uninterrupted view of the loch at night which is a bonus if you wish to stay up late, boys. Let's get over there and get you settled in.'

It only took a few minutes back over the bridge along the stream and by the loch.

'This looks fabulous!' said Colin.

I'll need to remember that word and shove it back at him if he uses it again, I thought. The cabin was just off the road. Oh yes, I said to myself, a week here for free – who would believe it?

David gave us a quick run round the cabin pointing out all accessories and utensils. 'There is a list of instructions on the door and these must be adhered to rigidly. I don't want any parties, either, so if you behave then I won't have to chastise you.'

'You needn't worry on that score,' I said. 'We are only too grateful for what you have done for us.'

'Likewise!' said David.

He pulled a rucksack from a cupboard and handed it to Colin. 'This should be all right for you.'

So I'm to have the new one, I thought. I wonder what Colin will have to say about that later? Maybe David thought that I was more deserving, having driven a tricky road with only a learner's licence. Who knows?

'Come outside, lads!' Walking up the small garden he then showed us two kayaks. 'You are welcome to use these whenever you want. The paddles are underneath and can only be freed by releasing the outer chain.'

Handing Colin the key, he said, 'Keep this in the cabin at all times and always put it back when you have released the chain. That way it will stop you from losing it, especially in the water.'

'We will obey all the rules,' said Colin. 'We are also good swimmers and I have a life-saving certificate.'

'I can believe that!' said David. 'Now, I have to rush; I have a few things to catch up on when I get back. Enjoy the cabin and have a wonderful time. I will let you know how my father is when I return.'

'Bye, David. Thanks again for your generosity,' said both Colin and I.

'Oh, I almost forgot. Hand the key of the cabin in next door if I don't turn up before you leave. Bye, then,' said David.

Chapter Seventeen

We took a look around the cabin and chose our separate rooms. Well, I say chose, but we tossed the coin for the front room which had a view of the loch and I won the toss. Being fair and not being greedy I chose to take the last four nights in the front room and offered Colin the first three nights, which he accepted.

'Thank goodness we didn't call home. They would have expected us home tonight if we had told them what happened,' said Colin.

We had promised our parents that we would call home every four days so that they would not worry about what we were up to.

'I'll give mine a call tonight from the hotel in the village,' I said to Colin. 'To let them know I'm OK and they will pass on the message to your folks.'

'That's fine,' said Colin. 'Saves us two calls!'

I lay down for an hour as I felt exhausted after such a busy day.

It was mid-evening by the time we had made the meal and cleaned up the mess.

'Miss your mum for this?' Colin asked.

'Aye! I honestly never washed pans and dried dishes before.'

'We don't know we're born. Truly spoiled when you think about it,' said Colin.

I still felt really tired. The fresh air here made me feel so sleepy. After another short nap we decided to go into the village for a beer. Well, Colin decided.

I remembered what David had told us before he left. 'Put on your skip bonnets you bought today. It'll keep the midges away from your face.' A place as beautiful as this had to have some sort of drawback.

The little blighters seemed to enjoy Colin's skin more than mine. Perhaps he was a little liberal with his deodorant.

'I'm itching to death,' he cried.

'I told you to wear your slacks, not your shorts here, but you wouldn't listen.'

'I'll have to go back,' said Colin.

I told him I would wait beside the water until he returned.

This was a tidal loch which was fed by the Atlantic via the Clyde estuary. It was good to have half an hour of private time after the problems of the past few days. A cabin to ourselves for seven nights: amazing.

My mum and dad and the whole family could only afford a caravan holiday and that had been only in the past few years. Wealth has its benefits and its drawbacks. David had bought the cabin primarily for his own use. He had told us it was easy climbing – or hillwalking as it was called round here. It took pressure off him and gave him power and motivation once more, relieving him of worry, a common complaint.

'Feel better now?' I said to Colin on his return.

'Yes, I should have listened. It would have saved a lot of trouble. It's just that I like the fresh air on my legs.'

'I'm kind of thirsty now, Colin, so let's step up the pace. It's about a twenty-minute walk to the hotel and we have to follow the road as the river flows into the loch adding an extra half mile.'

'Great to relax over a pint!' Colin sighed.

'It was a tough day but, boy, look how it's worked out for us!' I said.

It was dark when we strolled back to the cabin. The trees began to close in on us and we could only hear the flow of the river. It was really eerie, then all went pitch black.

'Where are you, Colin?' I shouted.

'Over here!'

'Where's that?' I cried.

Next thing I knew I was in the bushes. 'Help, get me out of here, Colin, I am being jagged to bits!'

'Make some sort of noise continually so I can locate your whereabouts, Jamie. One of the tunes you're rubbish at will do!' Colin howled in the darkness.

I hummed my tune then finally I felt Colin's hand on my shoulder. Believe it or not he was on all fours as he wasn't sure of his own whereabouts either.

'Let's get you out of here!' Colin laughed, tugging my arm. 'Take my hand and we'll back track to the crown of the road.'

That's sensible, I thought.

'OK, let's go,' said Colin.

If someone comes round this corner, I thought, with a torch or even worse car headlights; what will they think when they see two grown adults holding hands in the middle of the road? Fortunately nothing like that transpired and we were both relieved to see the flicker of light coming from the loch.

I just remembered what David had said at that point. 'He told us to take a torch if we were going to be out late!' I reminded Colin.

'Oh, so he did. Well, one of us should take responsibility for that – you, Jamie!'

That was me told! 'OK!'

What luxury we had, and freedom with it. This was going to be a wonderful few days. So far the weather had been exceptionally kind to us. In fact it had been a great summer from the start of our holiday.

We awoke to see a little mist rising from the loch. The view would be an artist's dream when the sun breaks through, I thought to myself.

'Full English!' Colin said while turning the eggs. He was more than able to look after himself when required.

'Yes please,' I said.

'Be ready in five minutes. You take a quick shower and breakfast will be served up pronto.'

After the meal and tidy-up Colin decided that we should spend the day on the loch with the kayaks. 'I fancy a bit of canoeing today.'

'That's fine by me,' I said excitedly.

After completion of chores Colin decided it was time to go. 'Ready, Jamie?'

'Yip.'

We unlocked the padlock, releasing the chain from the trailer. Then we pulled out the kayaks one by one.

'They are quite light!' I said.

'Aye, they'll be no bother,' Colin replied.

We were only yards from the road and beach. We decided it would be easier lifting one kayak at a time on to the beach as there was a five-foot drop at least to the beach from the grass verge. Having completed the task we found a spot where we could board the kayak without wetting our feet, as we were wearing plimsolls.

We were only about five-hundred yards out when Colin turned too quickly. I think he was about to say something but the words were never released as the boat capsized, taking him head first into the water.

He managed to right the boat in a matter of seconds. As he surfaced his face was a picture and I couldn't help myself as I burst into fits of laughter; almost in tears!

'Were you testing the self-righting technique?' I howled.

'Only renewing my skills!' he replied with a grin, all the while trying to regain some dignity. Of course, he knew full well that he would be teased at every available opportunity in the pub by me.

'I'll have to go back and change,' Colin said. 'I don't want to catch a cold with four or more weeks' holiday left to enjoy.'

We made our way back to the small beach. Colin was dripping wet as he alighted from the kayak. 'Be back as quick as I can!' he informed me.

'Take your time,' I replied. 'I'll dry your boat out as best I can.'

I was left by myself for a short period which I did not mind at all; the one thing I had learnt, even as young as I was, was to enjoy one's own company. Be happy with yourself and you will spread your happiness wherever you go. I suppose my church background came to the fore every so often. Christ's teaching is to 'love one another as I have loved you'. So if you are happy only then can you give love.

It always pains me to see people taking advantage of soft and shy-natured beings. Have they had the misfortune of being brought up without love, and are only content through dominance, I wonder? I have also found out that these individuals can easily detect weakness and exert their will on the unfortunates, as they know very few will stand up against them.

Which brings to mind the thieves who stole our gear. Were they deprived when they were small and had to fight for every crumb of bread? One thing is certain: they took advantage of our trust. To my mind the gravest sin!

Colin returned wearing his new swimming shorts. They were dual purpose as they could be used for both swimming and walking. They were one of the purchases made in Dumbarton.

He was better prepared this time with all his change of clothing in poly bags, one inside the other, making things watertight should a second incident occur.

'What were you going to say before you fell in?' I asked him with a snigger.

'Oh yes! The barman told me if we wanted to fish we could get some bait and tackle at Carrick Castle. Apparently mackerel come in with the tide to feed and are simple to catch.'

'I thought you were trying a new method of fishing! Ha! Ha!'

'Very amusing, Jamie, and very childish I might add.'

I let it go as I had one up on him now. I could see his pride was hurt.

I was not surprised at all that Colin had overturned and fallen in. The physique of the man filled the recess on the kayak leaving him little room for manoeuvre. Colin had an idea that we could fish from the boat with his line. Frankly I couldn't see it, so I asked how we would be able to land our catch, if any.

He always came up with an answer. 'By towing the fish to the nearest beach!' he replied.

Well, that's certainly unique, I thought.

We paddled for about twenty minutes, keeping to the middle of the loch with the shadows of pines and fir trees reflecting on the bright water. The Argyll forest was all round the loch, reaching up the steep hillsides on either side of us.

I thought of the planting of such trees and wondered how they managed to plant them in such precarious places. I suppose machinery plays a good part, with diggers, etc. However, this did not explain what I wanted to know. I would have to research the methods of planting forestry when I returned home and find out who or what determined where the planting took place.

We reached Carrick Castle about half an hour later, after a leisurely paddle. There was a small jetty for crafts of various sizes to tie up for a short period allowing people to embark or board. A white cabin cruiser was leaving the pier as we approached. Aren't they lucky, I thought. I would have been more envious of the people on the sleek vessel had it not been for the fact that I was staying in luxury accommodation myself.

As the craft passed us, two bikini-clad, beautiful young females began waving to Colin, who was twenty yards ahead of me. Oh-oh. For a second I thought the worst – he was going to capsize! He managed fine. Perhaps it was pride that kept him upright, as he wanted to show off his skills to them as he turned and waved back.

We made our way past the jetty to a small, lush, green bank where we could beach the boats. 'When we get ashore you stay with the kayaks. We don't want anyone pinching them,' Colin said.

'OK, but don't be too long.' I knew full well if the shop was fully stocked he would check out just about everything. Just as I thought, he was away over an hour – and the shop was within my sight. So it obviously was to his liking.

I closed my eyes and lay facing the sun. I might as well enhance my tan. David had provided us with suntan lotion along with everything else. There wasn't much got past this man, I thought. I hope his dad has recovered. I'll give him a phone call this evening to ask for his health and his mum also.

I had drifted into serious unconsciousness when I was abruptly awoken with a boot on my backside. 'Waken up, you lazy turd!'

'What kept you?' I asked. 'I'll bet it was the pretty assistant!'

'Nonsense! In a tackle shop?' laughed Colin. 'I had a blether with the proprietor and he has told me we can hire a motorboat for fishing. It's reasonably priced so I have booked a charter for four hours tomorrow. If that's all right by you?'

I wasn't bothered either way but I felt he could have at least asked me first. I'll take a book with me, borrow one of David's from the cabin, I thought.

'Yes that's fine,' I said. 'I want to look at the castle for five minutes, so just you sit with the kayaks!'

'OK,' said Colin.

I was disappointed to find that the castle was just a ruin and not open to the public. Probably unsafe, I thought. Never mind, I would check on its history when I returned home.

I always like to have a little knowledge of the history of an area. My dad said it shows you were attentive to your surroundings of the time. It is also good for storytelling, at which he surpassed any of my teachers with the depth and intensity of the subject he was engaged in.

'So take note, listen, learn and read and you will carry knowledge with you always,' he would say.

When I returned to the bank Colin brought me back down to earth with a bump. 'What cloud were you on there, Jamie boy? No, don't answer that! Anyway, that white cruiser came back up the loch again and those two babes were whistling and waving at me!'

So much for his abstinence from women for the next few weeks, I pondered.

'I wish I'd booked the motorboat for today now,' he said. 'You had better remove your top and shoes. We don't want you getting wet. Anyway I can't afford you getting the sniffles!'

Better do as he says, I thought.

'I'm told the tide will be going out in about an hour's time. That should be about the same time you wasted looking at an old ruin.

At this I bit my tongue, not wanting to get angry. It was all right for him to spend over an hour in a fishing tackle shop.

'OK! I'll help you in, we don't want you losing all your bait at the water's edge!' I said. 'You ease yourself in. I'll hold the back of the kayak steady then hand you your line and bait.'

'Good thinking, Jamie,' said Colin.

He was a big lad so it was sensible to follow the correct procedure. He manoeuvred gingerly and finally made it. He sailed away from the bank with everything intact, including his dignity as a few holidaymakers had now ventured on to the pier.

As I joined Colin alongside I was sure our audience had gathered to laugh at the sight of two rookies in the hope we fell in. 'Let's give them a laugh,' said Colin. With one push he had overturned and was facing into deep, murky water. Easing himself out of the craft he swam beneath my kayak and quickly jolted the stern. With his weight there could only be one outcome. Yes! And over I toppled, into the water.

He must have known what would happen if I went in the water as I dive regularly and am a good swimmer beneath the surface. This had to be pre-planned, as why else did he tell me to remove my clothing and put it in a bag? The main thing I had learnt about Colin was to expect the unexpected. When I surfaced he was there before me grinning like a Cheshire cat.

'Caught you out there, Jamie!' At this he started howling with laughter. 'I thought I would give our spectators a little entertainment! Do you honestly think I could fish off of this thing?'

'Possible for you, maybe!' I said.

'I admire the faith you have in me, but it would have been difficult to bring in any catch without joining them in the water! Anyway, I've booked a boat for four hours tomorrow.'

'We'll have to dry off now,' I said.

'I'll ask the shop if we can change into our other clothes,' said Colin.

The gentleman offered us a small cupboard-type room to change in, for which we were very grateful.

Having dried out we returned to our boats which had dried in the sun.

'Fancy a race?' Colin asked.

'OK then, I'm up for that! But I want a two-minute start.'

'All right, Jamie, you've got it.'

I should have said five minutes as I had little chance of beating him over the distance. I paddled as fast as I could to try to gain as much advantage as possible. I knew I had little hope as I had found it difficult to keep up with him earlier. He hadn't a watch on so we both counted, one, two, three…

I turned to see if he had started but he was still motionless. I counted another twenty and turned once more to see if he had started. Again he was motionless. I gave him the thumbs up and he raised his oars instantaneously.

I didn't look round for ten minutes. I finally took a glimpse to see how close he was as I could not hear him behind me. OK – oh no, he was in the middle of the loch and heading for Lochgoil.

'See you in Lochgoilhead and first round is on you tonight,' he roared from the distance.

By the time I reached the beach he wasn't to be seen. I carried my kayak back to the cabin. Looking towards the village I could see the distinct colour of the kayak. He must have gone shopping, I thought.

Keeping an eye from the window I saw him return from the village. I went to the beach to give him a hand as I didn't want him toppling into the water with his purchase. He handed me a bag, saying, 'Fancied a bit of sirloin tonight so I decided to go into the village. I thought I still could have beaten you even with the detour.'

'That's great,' I replied. 'Are you cooking?'

'Who else!' Colin retorted.

'You must be fed up about me talking about my appetite but there has to be something in the air, as I am always ravenous.'

A full plate of potatoes and veg and large well-done steaks. Delicious.

Colin's was what I call underdone but that's a matter of taste. Who's complaining? I washed up. After all, he cooked the bl— dinner.

We rested on the veranda and snoozed for a couple of hours, after which we strolled into the village hotel for refreshment, not forgetting to take our torch.

The air made me very sleepy. I can't ever remember sleeping so soundly in my life before.

Chapter Eighteen

'Well,' Colin said, 'how about getting fit again with a jog to Carrick Castle?'

'Fine by me!' I said.

'OK. If we leave at ten-thirty that gives us two and a half hours before collecting our charter boat. It's only about six miles – a doddle for you, Jamie boy.'

'All right then, but we will have to make up lunch and dig some bait before leaving.'

'So we'll carry a small bag each. That won't handicap us, will it?'

'No, not at all,' I replied.

After one hour on the road I was beginning to feel the pace. Thank goodness it was only another half mile up the road.

'We managed to make the castle with plenty of time to spare. I told you it was a doddle,' said Colin.

I grinned and agreed wholeheartedly. 'You were right, it was easy,' I said. What a fib that was! The last thing I wanted was for him to see that I was struggling, as he was clearly in his element.

The thing is, he is a long-distance runner, which takes stamina and determination. I know for a fact that he will achieve much more than myself in life, simply by his sheer stubbornness and will to win; also his zest for life. On the other hand I'm a sprinter. I like to make quick decisions. My pet hate is people who talk in circles without providing answers. I say you either know or you don't know when faced with a problem.

We had plenty of time to spare before our booked boat so we made for the green bank and sunbathed on the grass while we were waiting.

'If ever we want peace and quiet in our lives we should return here,' said Colin. 'I'll stroll over and have a look at the tackle available. You watch our bags.'

'Aye-aye, captain,' I said.

He left laughing. I'm sure he was happy with the tag.

About thirty minutes later he arrived at the jetty, all smiles, with his new toy. 'Not bad, eh! What do you think, Jamie?' asked Colin.

'Should do the job OK,' I said, not wishing to show over enthusiasm.

It was a small row boat really, with an outboard engine; nevertheless it was substantial enough for fishing purposes. The craft was about nine foot long and painted all in white. The outboard motor was fitted with a steering rod. It also had a set of oars in case of emergency.

'Let's see if we can have a fish supper tonight then, Jamie,' said Colin.

We sailed down the west shore past Carrick Castle and into the middle of the loch. The water was much darker and therefore deeper so Colin decided we would cast our lines out there.

Colin became increasingly frustrated after trying six or more locations without success.

'Why don't we try the entrance of Lochgoil next to Loch Long?' I said.

'OK we'll try that. There is nothing doing here, anyway,' said Colin.

It took about ten minutes to find a spot that Colin was comfortable with.

'By my reckoning this is where the fish will have entered the loch for feeding when the tide came in. It is due to go out shortly so we'll have to be patient,' said Colin.

'Then we have just wasted an hour!' I said.

'Not at all,' said Colin, 'they are feeding at the moment. Unfortunately we didn't pick the correct spots.'

'We have less than an hour left to catch our supper then, and it's a little choppy out here,' I said.

'It won't capsize, if that's what you're thinking!' said Colin.

He joined up his two-piece rod which he had borrowed from the cabin and added his coloured bait which would hopefully attract the fish. I had a hand line which Colin had purchased at the shop. 'See if you can catch anything with that!' said Colin, laughing, as he handed it to me with lures attached.

After about five minutes I felt a tug on my line. I reeled it in slowly – well, that's the only way you can do it with a hand line. 'Yes, you beauty!' I said. It was mackerel, about a foot long.

Colin took it off the hook and did the necessary; I'm afraid I couldn't deal with that. 'A few more of his friends will do nicely!' said Colin.

I thought perhaps he might have been a little miffed at me bringing in the first catch. I have to say the opposite was the case.

'Is that the tide going out now, Colin? The reason I ask is I feel the boat starting to drift.'

'Yes,' said Colin. 'You will have to take charge of the oars, and forget about putting your line back in the water.'

'Fine,' I said. 'I'm happy with my catch!'

I put the oars gently into the water and moved them only slowly with as little disturbance as possible. Colin now could concentrate on his line; he had changed his bait and replaced it with the same type he had put on my hand line. 'This should do the trick!' said Colin. I could see that he was pensive and intent as he reeled in his line then released it, obviously trying to attract his quarry.

All of a sudden the line went taut, and I mean taut, as the rod dipped sharply into the water. 'I have at least two on!' said Colin, reeling in slowly. Not two but three mackerel were on the line. 'Whoopee!' shouted Colin as he dealt with them individually.

'Are we trying for more?' I asked.

'You bet!' said Colin. 'We have twenty minutes' time left.' He lowered in his rod once more and in a matter of seconds his rod was tilting to the water and being pulled downward by the ensnared fish. 'Another three!' he cried. I felt sure they could hear him at Carrick Castle with the din he was making.

'Is that us, then?' I enquired.

'One more cast!' shouted Colin.

'OK,' I said, 'but we'll never eat any more than this lot in two days as it is!'

'I'm still going to try for more!' said Colin.

He cast the rod into the water for the last time. A few minutes passed and nothing. 'I told you we had enough, but you wouldn't listen. The shoal will probably be back out to sea by now,' I said.

'We'll give it a couple of minutes yet,' said Colin. 'There may be some stragglers.'

I wish I'd kept my mouth shut. A minute later the line became taut once more. With the extra tension the rod dipped towards the water.

'Told you so!' said Colin, reeling in another three mackerel. 'Now I'm satisfied. We can head back in once we bring in the oars and restart the engine.'

With all the fish in a bag and the rod dismantled I brought the oars on board while Colin put his bait carefully in a small tin for safety. 'That's us now, Jamie! I'll start up the engine and make for the anchorage.'

As Colin was about to pull the cord a white private cruiser passed only a few feet away then turned to come alongside.

'I wonder what they want.' I said.

'We'll know in a minute. They are about to stop,' said Colin.

The boat eased along side and two bikini-clad girls leaned over the side to speak with us. 'Are you in distress?' said one of them, giggling all the while.

'No, we are fishing!' said Colin.

A male voice from the cabin called the girls, interrupting their fun. 'All right, Dad, I'll ask them!' said one of the young ladies. 'Dad wants to know if you have caught anything,' said the young lady. It was apparent to me the launch had deliberately stopped for this reason and not to see if we were in distress as the girls had made out.

'Yes, we have,' said Colin.

One of the girls then left to inform her dad, who was presumably at the wheel. On returning she said, 'Dad wishes to know if you want to come aboard for tea and hopes you will share your catch.'

Colin looked at me. 'What do you think, Jamie?'

'I have no problem with that. It will save us cooking!'

The girls went inside to confirm our acceptance. On returning, they gave the following instructions, 'Dad wants to give you a tow, so we'll move ahead of you then throw you a line.'

'Great!' said Colin.

Colin caught the rope and secured it to the boat; he then

pulled the rope so that we were alongside the stern, which had a small aluminium ladder to the deck. Once he was on board I threw him our bags, then our catch of fish; finally I clambered up the steps and on to the deck.

Colin went up to the wheelhouse to converse with the skipper – or Dad, as the girls called him. I was taken literally by the hand to the main lounge by the girls, who had by now introduced themselves as Evelyn and Carol. They pulled me in to meet Mum and a large black dog which was sprawled over the floor.

Colin came down to the lounge and I introduced him to Mavis, Evelyn and Carol. He always oozes charm and took each hand and kissed it as it was held out. Oh, get me a hankie! He knew that women like to be made a fuss of and boy could he show it.

Colin began to explain the situation about the boat. 'We have to return the boat by 5 p.m. to the owners at Carrick Castle anchorage, which is only ten minutes away. So we'll have to leave right away. Bobbie knows what is happening and he will pick us up at the pier after we anchor the boat.'

I got on board our motorboat first, which I have to say was not easy; my main concern was Colin. The size of the man on this small boat was difficult enough without having to have him reboard in the middle of a loch. I held it as steady as I could, pulling the rope tightly so that we were against the cruiser. The only thing left for him to deal with was the slight swell.

'Right! Now put one foot on!' I shouted, as the motorboat rose up in the water. His timing was perfect. I needn't have worried; I just didn't fancy trying to pull him aboard from the loch. In my mind, I could see the boat turning over in the middle of the channel and us having to try to right it. I quickly disposed of such thoughts as it would have been virtually impossible for two of us to get back on.

When he was settled he asked, 'Why didn't you stay on board?'

I told him, 'The girls insisted that I should meet their mum! Anyway, I wanted to see the vessel for myself. I didn't want to hear his rants about the cuisine.'

'Oh, that's all right then!' said Colin.

Colin had arranged for Bobbie to follow behind us.

We delivered the boat to a small jetty and tied up. Colin then dealt with the usual deposit and paperwork. The cruiser could be seen from our vantage point as we walked back towards the castle. 'The craft's about to berth at the pier!' I said.

'Well, let's make a dash for it then!' said Colin.

The girls started waving as they saw us approaching. 'Fallen on our feet again, Jamie boy!'

Evelyn held her hand out to Colin and Carol did the same for me as we climbed the short steps. 'Welcome aboard, landlubbers!' they said in unison. We were led to the lounge once more where a place had been set for us both. Evelyn was beside Colin and Carol had reserved her place alongside me.

'Mother has already gutted the fish and is making a fish pie, which I'm sure you will enjoy, lads,' said Evelyn.

'Sounds great,' said Colin.

'She didn't take long!' I said.

'Most of the preparation had already been done and we were heading down towards the Clyde to pick up some essentials when we spotted you fishing.'

'That was convenient,' said Colin.

'Yes, it certainly was,' said Evelyn.

Bobbie came in and introduced himself to me and asked the girls to release the mooring ropes so that we could move to a sheltered spot for lunch. It was about ten minutes before the sound of the engines faded; I then heard a loud splash which I assumed was that of the anchor being released. Bobbie then joined us at the table with some good English banter, football being one of the subjects close to his heart. Mavis and the girls were attending to us as if we were paying guests.

What a meal that was! I'd never tasted anything like it. I didn't ask the recipe, I just ate. Colin was in total agreement and voiced it: 'That was really exceptional. I don't recall ever tasting a meal as delicious before!'

'Have a glass of wine, lads. It's only table wine and has very little alcohol content,' said Bobbie.

He went on to tell us that he was originally from Rothesay and he had chartered the boat through a friend from a marina on the Clyde. 'You know how it is with these boats. I'm quite sure a lot of them are purchased for tax purposes and they lie in their moorings for most of the time.' He went on to say, 'This is our second week here and we have had marvellous weather. It's the girls' first time. I'd promised them for some time I would let them see where I belong. They have been running around in swimming costumes all week as if they were in Spain.'

Colin and I hadn't failed to notice the costumes, which were barely holding their almost perfect figures.

'My sister lives in Rothesay. She loves it so much and doesn't understand anyone wanting to leave. She has enjoyed our company, not having seen us for such a long time.'

'Why did you leave?' I asked.

'Simply for work! If I hadn't moved I would not be able to afford the lifestyle I have now,' said Bobbie.

'I intend to move abroad in a few years' time to make my fortune,' said Colin.

'What about you, Jamie?'

'Oh, I'm a bit of a home bird. I would like to go abroad but not permanently,' I said.

The subject changed quickly and one of the girls said, 'We are heading back down to Rothesay tonight, boys, there is a dance on. Do you want to come with us?'

'Jamie, come out on to the deck! I want to hear your thoughts on it without any pressure,' said Colin. He knew I would probably have said yes right away under the circumstances. The girls wanted company and were keen on the idea of having escorts. 'Well, Jamie, do you or don't you want to go with them? Straight answer please!'

'It's the fact I'm going to meet Bonnie that bothers me, nothing else. I'll make it plain it's just for fun, then.'

'OK. Do you want to tell them that or will I?' asked Colin.

'You tell them we will be coming along with them, please.'

'That's settled then!' said Colin.

Colin returned to the lounge and told them the outcome of our little discussion. 'We have decided to go to the ball with you!'

This message of intent was greeted with howls of laughter from Carol and Evelyn and not forgetting Mavis. 'It's a fancy dress party! What are you going to dress up as?' asked Evelyn. The devils had sprung one on us.

Colin pondered for a moment. 'We shall go as two High-landers!' he said. 'We have our kilts in the cabin.'

'Oh boy!' said Mavis, 'I'll look forward to that!'

'Mum! It's for us to say that, not you!' said Evelyn.

'Why not? I like to see a man in a kilt! Don't you?'

Evelyn was left speechless by the quick retort from her mum and was clearly embarrassed. Colin came in quickly to spare any blushes. 'We have nowhere to sleep and cannot afford accommodation in Rothesay.'

'Dad, can they sleep here on the lounge floor? We can provide them with sleeping bags,' said one of the girls.

'It's fine by me. But I think it's mainly up to the lads, as they are the ones who will have to endure the cramped conditions. Oh, and your mother uses the lounge the most as she is up early. If all parties are happy, then so am I,' said Bobbie.

'I don't mind!' said Mavis.

After another parley, Colin told them, 'We have no problem sleeping on the floor as we have experienced much harsher conditions camping.'

'Right, I'll start up the engines and we can be on our way,' said Bobbie.

We were two thirds up the loch so it was only a ten-minute trip to the cabin. Bobbie took the craft in as close as he dared. He turned to face the exit of the loch then dropped anchor. The stern was now facing the cabin, which would allow us to put the dinghy into the water and paddle directly to the shore.

I wasn't taking any chances. I let Colin go on the dinghy first in case of any calamity. He was such a big lad that there was only room for two of us on a four-seater dinghy. Tentatively he put one foot at a time on to the craft while holding on to the rope being held by Bobbie and me. But he slipped at the last second and fell backward straight into the boat. Fortunately he managed to cling on to a holding rope which stopped him from falling into the water.

Once he had gained his composure he started laughing and said, 'Well, that must be a unique way of boarding!'

The girls were, by this time, trying desperately not to laugh at his misfortune. There was a sigh of relief when Colin made light of it; they could take their hands away from their mouths and finally release their mirth.

I managed on the small boat easily to the delight of everyone. Bobbie loosened the rope and Colin started to row for the shore.

'I thought I was for an early bath there!' said Colin.

'It was really funny from where we were,' I said. 'The girls were in fits.'

'I know, that's why I made light of it. The only thing I was afraid of was that I might strike my head on something sharp.'

We pulled the dinghy on to the beach and Colin said, 'I think we should carry this up to the cabin. I don't want to take a chance with someone else's equipment.'

'I have to agree,' I said. 'It's not heavy. I think you could lift it yourself, Colin.' He just laughed as we both lifted it on to the road from the beach, which was only five yards away.

It was a quick dash for the shower, but Colin blocked my way and there was no way that I could get past. I had to wait patiently for ten minutes before I could wash. As a result I had only a three-minute shower as I had to put on my shirt and kilt.

The big oaf was ready and parading himself in front of the mirror when I exited the toilet. 'You not ready yet, Jamie boy?' enquired Colin.

I ignored him completely and hurriedly got dressed.

Chapter Nineteen

It would be around a half an hour later when we made our way back to the cruiser. Bobbie appeared when we were only a few yards away. 'Throw me the rope!' he cried.

I aimed carefully and he caught it first time.

'Well done, Jamie!' he said. 'I couldn't have done any better myself. I'll pull you in alongside if you place the paddles in their appropriate position.'

I took the paddles out and put them in the recess. 'OK, that's us, Bobbie,' I said.

I made sure that I got off first as I didn't fancy a dip with my kilt on. Carol took my hand and I was pulled by the other by Evelyn. Here we go again, I thought, I hope Colin doesn't fall in; he is so awkward in confined areas. As he made his way forward the dinghy began to tilt dangerously; seeing this he decided to jump and made a leap to the cruiser. Bobbie and I grabbed an arm each and held him till he found his feet and was able to scramble aboard.

'All aboard, we can now head for Rothesay,' said Bobbie. 'I'll let you steer if you like, Colin!'

'That would be something new,' said Colin.

'As we go out of Lochgoil, steer to the middle of Loch Long,' said Bobbie. 'It's pretty deep water all the way down. You have to keep an eye out for yachts and Navy boats as well. We should reach Rothesay in just over an hour all going well.'

Indeed there were numerous yachts out taking advantage of the stiff early evening breeze. Therefore Bobbie was forced to take charge in the latter stages. He finally berthed after waiting for the ferry to leave the pier.

'I'll take Butch over to my sister's. You go with the lads and the girls, Mavis. Keep a seat for me at the hotel,' said Bobbie.

'All right, dear,' said Mavis.

'Are you not changing into fancy dress, girls?' asked Colin.

Fits of laughter ensued. 'I think they have put one over on us, Jamie,' said Colin.

'Looks like it,' I said.

'When you said you were going to put on your kilts we hadn't the heart to tell you we were only teasing. Anyway, we all wanted to see you in your kilts,' said Evelyn.

'We'll forgive you this time,' said Colin.

The girls took our arms when we disembarked. We walked in a fivesome with Colin and me on the outside and the girls in the middle. Mavis preferred to be called one of the girls.

The place was mobbed; a newly formed pop group from Glasgow had been booked and the young ones were taking advantage. Teenagers were dressed as adults with all their make-up – eyeshadow and lipstick were the dress code. They also wore tight slacks or short skirts – all the latest fashion accessories.

'We are going to sweat tonight,' I said to Colin.

'Especially with these kilts on,' Colin replied.

'We won't be doing any jogging tomorrow,' I lamented, and he nodded in agreement.

In no time at all Evelyn and Carol had grabbed us for twists and rock. My kilt seemed to be everywhere. The girls hardly broke sweat, wearing only flimsy costumes. When Colin and I were finally allowed to sit down we were dripping with perspiration.

'That'll keep you fit, lads!' said Bobbie, who had made his way down to the table after having a quick pint at the bar. Mavis wanted a dance and informed us as much, since Bobbie was more intent on a pint of Tartan Special, which is an exceptionally good ale in Rothesay.

Mavis was bobbing like a young thing at a rock and roll number with the girls in hysterics at her antics. She was a big girl and, as I had said earlier, when they throw you about then down you go – which I did on at least two occasions. I was pleased when she retired through exhaustion.

'She takes a bit of keeping up with, my girl,' said Bobbie, soaking his thirst with yet another pint of Tartan ale.

'Last dance!' was the cry from the band.

'Already! Can't be!' said Evelyn.

'Thank goodness!' Colin said to me.

Evelyn grabbed me for the last two numbers and Carol nabbed Colin simultaneously. It was really a first chance to have a talk with her. She told me she and Carol both had boyfriends in Stockport where they lived. Their dad was an accountant in Manchester and it was a big change for them to be in such a quiet rural area. They liked having the boat, without which they would have had little to do, plus they had met us, which was a bonus.

'It's been fun to meet you both without any ties. We are all thoroughly enjoying your company!' said Evelyn.

'We'll see you over the next two days, won't we?' I said.

'Of course you will. Mum and Dad will see to that.'

She just snuggled in for the final dance so I didn't bother to tell her about Bonnie and Kate.

It was great to be back in the fresh air after the heat and noise of the past few hours. 'I need a cuppa,' said Mavis as we strolled towards the cruiser. 'Make sure he doesn't fall in,' said Mavis to Colin, 'I think he's had one over the eight.'

We were quickly settled with a tea and cookie and then off to bed. Well, I say bed – it was two sleeping bags on the floor on top of lilos. I had slept in far worse conditions; the tent for starters.

If anyone has sleeping problems I can recommend this type of holiday. You'll sleep like a baby. In the morning it was after ten o'clock before anyone stirred. That included me.

'Will someone volunteer to go and get the morning rolls? Oh, bacon, eggs and the morning papers also!' asked Mavis.

I volunteered immediately as I wanted to take in the sights. Evelyn decided to go along when she heard I was going. It was a pleasure to walk with a pretty girl and I enjoyed the fact that other guys were giving her the eye when they passed by. For the first time I had a chance to tell her about Bonnie and how we had met in Balloch.

'I'm pleased for you! I have Charlie, who is a gentleman, and I know I'll marry him in a few years' time.'

This is fun, I thought, that we are both open to each other's ideas and we know there is no fear of broken relationships. Just good friends having a chat and confiding in one another.

'I only wish you and Colin were my brothers. I'll miss you

both awfully much when we leave. You must promise that you'll both keep in touch in the future. I want you both at my wedding, even though it will be three years away at least.'

'I promise! Cross my heart,' I said.

'I'll hold you to that, Jamie Cameron!' said Evelyn.

Everyone was up and raring to go when we arrived back with fresh supplies, including Bobbie.

'I'll head out now, darling,' said Bobbie. 'We will have breakfast in a nice quiet spot away from here. There is a small beach not too far away if I remember correctly. I saw it on the way down.'

'I'll prepare as much as I can while we're on the move,' said Mavis.

'Oh, I hope he means he'll be stopping shortly as I'm beginning to feel rather peckish,' I whispered to Colin.

My fears were allayed when we anchored in a small cove. 'I was right, dear, it wasn't far,' said Bobbie.

Five minutes later we were all round the table once more with the girls serving. Mavis excelled herself with another perfect meal. 'That was just what I needed, dear!' said Bobbie.

Colin was chatting away to Carol and they were laughing loudly at something mischievous by the sound of it. I told Evelyn the full story of what had happened to us in the past week as I had only managed to fill her in with some scraps owing to the intensity of the past twenty-four hours. She listened intently to what I had to say and, when I had finished, said of the thieves, 'They are just poor unfortunates who need help,' said Evelyn. I thought that was very charitable of her. 'Look at how the problems brought by them actually changed your lives. You would never have been able to help that old couple, for one. In turn, their son would not have been able to return his gratitude by being generous to you. Good from evil, if you do not harbour vengeance, is my motto.'

'You should be a philosopher,' I said.

Evelyn smiled and said, 'If only.'

The sun had filtered through and the girls began to feel a little frisky. They went below deck and returned wearing their tiny, flimsy bikinis. They had brought out half a dozen hula hoops with a few plastic balls. Both Colin and I were wearing our shorts, which were dual purpose for walking and swimming.

Carol now gave us instructions of the game. 'We start off with one hoop which is thrown in the water; we then throw a ball into the middle of the hoop and the person who has dived must come back up through the middle of the hoop and throw the ball back on board,' she explained. 'I'll start,' she said.

The first hoop was thrown in by Carol and when she had dived through, Evelyn threw the ball into the middle of the hoop. Carol resurfaced under the ball, chipped it, and threw it back on board.

'That's easy!' Colin said, and he proved it by doing it in quick time.

'Well,' Carol said, 'you want to play hardball? Right, then, we are up for that!'

With another demonstration two hoops were put in the water and balls placed inside. 'This time you must surface dive, come up, and retrieve the ball over the hoop. Surface dive then come up under the second hoop and bring two balls back to the boat.' The girls made it look so easy as they slid over the hoops and brought the ball back.

Bobbie and Mavis and Butch the dog were all enjoying the fun and I could see their eyes light up eagerly waiting to see the antics of us. We both managed easily with the help and cheers of the onlookers.

'Right then!' Carol said. 'It's up to three balls this time. You can use your underarms or between your legs!'

This should be fun, I thought to myself.

Carol went first. One ball, then two. She caught the ball under her armpit for the third and back to the boat.

'Easy, lads!' she taunted.

Excitement was bubbling over. I couldn't let girls beat me, so I gave it my all. Alas, when I surfaced I lost the third ball from my armpit.

'Hard luck!' was the cry resounding in my ears. I don't think I've ever found anyone with such competitiveness. The girls were really up for it.

'All rests with you now, Colin!' I said.

'Surely they can't do four balls,' Colin said.

'Want a bet?'

Carol was first. One, two, three, then slowly on to the fourth hoop clutching it with her underarm. She took all four under, came back up and threw them on to the deck. 'Beat that!' she shouted, gazing at Colin.

'Come on, my man!' I said.

'I'll give it my best shot,' he retorted.

One, two, three, with difficulty this time. Surfacing slowly and intently. We all kept still as he eased towards the fourth hoop, still clutching it under his arm. He disappeared below the water and returned to the boat where mass hysteria reigned.

Evelyn's turn, which she managed with relative ease.

'They have had plenty of practice at this!' said Colin to me.

Carol then gave out further instructions. 'The third ball has to be caught and shown between your legs when you surface.'

'That's impossible!' said Colin.

'We'll see!' said Carol.

In she went. One, two, then she surface dived below the third hoop and up come a set of legs and pulled the ball away.

'So that's how it's done! But it must have taken a lot of practice to do that. You're up against it here!' I said to Colin.

Evelyn went next. One, two, then the same steps, gripping the ball with her thighs. Unfortunately her bikini bottoms had been lost when descending. Her dignity was still intact as no one had seen her misfortune. When she resurfaced she frantically pointed to her top and then her bottoms. I got the message instantly and dived into the water, heading straight for the third hoop where she had plucked the first ball. Fortunately they had clung to the hoop and I was able to hand them to Carol, who was in the water by this time. She surface dived and helped Evelyn guide her legs in to the bikini bottoms. A much-relieved Evelyn began smiling once more.

After the slight commotion, Carol shouted, 'Evelyn is disqualified for discarding excess clothing in order to gain extra advantage.'

This was greeted with howls of laughter and even Evelyn found it difficult not to join in.

'Just you and me left, Colin!' said Carol. 'Do you think you can beat me?'

'Yes,' he replied.

Colin started; he surface dived and a moment or two later two huge legs came up through the hoop, gripped the ball between his thighs, and pulled the ball below the water.

'He's done it!' cried Evelyn.

We all cheered. It was a draw.

It might as well have been a victory for Colin, who took centre stage with a hug and kiss from Mavis, then Evelyn. Carol waited, but nothing came her way, so she was forced to give Colin a kiss. Eventually Colin said, 'Wasn't a draw a fair result?'

Cheers greeted his words.

Butch, who had been straining his leash all the while, was now free and Bobbie threw his ball into the water. 'It's time for Butch's swim now,' he cried. The dog went straight over the side without hesitation and retrieved the ball for Bobbie, who was waiting on the low side of the stern. Full of enthusiasm it barked for more.

'Colin, you, Jamie and the girls all swim to the beach. Keep throwing the ball for Butch and he will go along with you. Mavis and I will follow you shortly and bring the picnic hamper in the dinghy.'

After a good splash about we reached the shore with Butch still wanting more. Bobbie found a perfect spot out of the sun and set up his small encampment.

'Please take Butch for a walk, someone,' said Mavis.

Evelyn volunteered herself and included me, which of course I didn't mind one bit. She was great company and very intelligent into the bargain. We had fun throwing the ball for Butch who continually returned it with speed. 'He's making the most of this,' said Evelyn, 'after being tied up for a full day.'

We proceeded along a small track just off the beach and found a perfect spot where a small stream ran into the sea. 'Let's have a seat on that old fallen tree beside the water,' said Evelyn. By this time big Butch was exhausted and went into the stream for a drink. 'You'd better watch out, Evelyn, he's about to shake himself!'

Oh-oh! I was too late. She got the full brunt of it as her back was turned. Butch then jumped up on her and her clothes were now completely soaked. I couldn't help myself as I burst into fits of laughter.

'So you think that was funny, Jamie Cameron! Well, see if you think this funny!'

I forgot I was standing on the bank of the river. Evelyn lunged at me and there was only one way we were headed. Yes! Straight into the water!

I emerged first, coughing and spluttering after having swallowed half the river. As she surfaced I was waiting, and as soon as she had regained her breath I pushed her head under. When she came up the second time it was behind me and before I could do anything I was once more immersed in water. I came up heaving for breath and Evelyn was waiting. 'Had enough?'

'Truce!' I said.

All the while Butch was in the water making mischief.

'I'm glad I have my bikini on under my skirt and blouse,' said Evelyn, in the process of removing her wet clothing.

'I'll have to take my shorts off and let them dry, leaving me in my underwear. I hope you don't mind, Evelyn.'

'I won't look. We'll just lie on the bank till your shorts dry,' she replied.

The sun was now warm and we dried out quickly; Butch fell asleep following his daft half hour.

'Jamie, can I ask you something?' asked Evelyn.

'Go ahead!' I said.

'It's a little personal and I can't talk to my parents about it. My boyfriend is putting me under pressure to have sex with him as we have been going out for around nine months. He says all his pals and their girlfriends are sleeping with one another. What do you think I should do?'

'It's a sign of the times,' I said. 'Two of my friends had to get married last year and they were only sixteen. It can work out if you really love someone, but in a lot of cases it was just the want for sex and it ended up a disaster as the boys felt trapped.

'It's up to you to make your own mind up, and he shouldn't

be forcing you if he loves you. There is so much at stake for someone as young and lovely as you.'

'I could kiss you, Jamie! Oh, come here!' And she gave me a long kiss and a hug. 'I won't ever tell Bonnie you kissed me!' And she started laughing.

'There is a lot of hilarity back at camp,' I said.

'Dad will be telling some of his stupid jokes and Mum always finds them funny. He hears them down the club on a Friday night,' said Evelyn.

Bobbie had a small stove and hamburgers in the pan. 'Where have you been, you pair? Any longer and Colin and I would have had your share,' he said.

A quick snack and we returned to the cruiser. 'All aboard!' said Bobbie. Colin and I helped the girls from the water and Bobbie managed to bring Butch on, receiving a cold shower for his trouble. 'Let's head for Lochgoil, and we can have supper at the hotel on me,' said Bobbie.

No sooner had we boarded than the wind got up. 'I think we are in for a squall!' said Bobbie. 'I forgot to check the shipping weather this morning. With all the sunshine we've been having it plain slipped my mind.'

He made a call and told us to check for anything loose. 'Batten everything down – seems a squall got up in the Irish Sea and it's heading this way,' said Bobbie.

I said to Colin, 'I didn't think it could get rough in these parts.'

Colin and I were off the Holy Isle halfway to Arran last year fishing when we were hit by a stormy sea. The skipper of the boat came running out saying, 'Get your lines in double quick and put your tackle in your bags. I mean right now!' By the time we got our lines in, a wave came right over the bow and washed my weights and floats away.

That didn't half give us all a fright. Before the next wave struck all fifteen of us were below deck or in the wheelhouse. 'We'll have to head straight for Arran!' the skipper screamed. 'If I try to head for port there's a fair chance she'll capsize.'

'That's the longest thirty-five minutes I've ever experienced in my life,' I remember Colin saying. We were pounded the whole time. Swirling up, one huge wave would smash into the second, with its violent spray crashing on the wheelhouse and deck. Twenty minutes of this, then we were hit by a fierce one engulfing us and taking down the radar mast. I thought, This is it – drowned at sea in my youth.

Finally we reached the sheltered waters off Arran. What a relief! We made a full sweep turn keeping as close to the shore as possible then headed for port. 'Don't know what to expect when we lose our shelter!' shouted the skipper. We reached the main channel and were pounded on the starboard side for five minutes. Then the skipper nestled us between the waves.

I would never have believed had I not seen it for myself. He held the craft at the same speed as the waves and nestled between them. Only twice did we go over one, which meant we hardly felt as if it was stormy at all. 'Glad I'm heading for port!' said the skipper. 'Hope the lads further out have made shelter in time. The lifeboat is already out in the channel checking.'

Fortunately we were far enough up the Clyde estuary so we were only treated to a six-foot swell. The girls were enjoying the spray, until Bobbie told them to get inside. They weren't pleased, but obeyed his command.

It was rough for around half an hour till we reached the relative calm of Loch Long and then on to Carrick Castle and finally Lochgoilhead. It was a little choppy so the dinghy was out of the question, but we managed to tie up at a private jetty. It was at least a half-hour walk back to the cabin, so we would have to hasten our step if we wanted a bar meal.

'Bye-bye! See you folks at the hotel around eight o'clock.'

'OK, lads!' said Bobbie and Mavis.

The girls were off to doll up before we could say cheerio.

'Typical,' said Colin. 'Women! Appearance comes before anything.'

'You'll have to get used to it,' I said.

'It's almost six-thirty just now,' said Colin. 'We have still a forty-minute walk back to the cabin then another thirty minutes' walk back to the hotel. They have only a ten-minute walk each way!'

'Stop moaning!' I said. 'Let's put the foot down and sing while we walk.'

I always find it amazing what happens when you take your mind off the task you are trying to accomplish, which in our case was to walk faster. It seems less of a chore that way. A quick shower and into our slacks and shirts provided by the generous David Ballantine.

'Are you ready yet, Jamie?' asked Colin, who had beaten me to the washroom once again. He was one to talk of women and their appearance. As I looked in, he was ego-boosting at the mirror, probably saying to himself, 'How can any girl resist me?' I'm sure if he were made of chocolate he would eat himself.

'In a minute,' I said. Seven-twenty should give us time to spare for our table at eight o'clock prompt, I thought.

We had spent nothing of the money that we had come with so we could afford a night out once in a while. So I would tell Bobbie we would pay our own way.

'What kept you?' cried the girls as we entered the dining lounge.

'Typical!' said Colin. 'You were already washing and dressing up while we were on our way back to the cabin.'

They enjoyed winding us up and continued the ploy. 'You might have dried yourself,' said Carol to Colin. Colin was dripping with sweat after the robust walk from the cabin and the air was balmy; plus he was in his new slacks, which he hardly ever wore.

Once we had settled a selection was made from the à la carte menu, with Bobbie ordering a bottle of wine. After the meal the discussion about activities for tomorrow began. Colin had planned to go hill walking and suggested that we all go. Mavis declined immediately. 'I'll be lucky to get up 200 feet without an oxygen mask,' she laughed out.

Bobbie was up for it though. 'I must get some photos to go back with, especially one of us all up at the waterfall.'

The girls were not going to be left behind and declared their interest immediately. 'What shall we wear?' asked Carol.

'Boots, shorts and a sweater,' said Colin.

'And your underwear!' said Bobbie.

'DAD!'

The girls proved to have the same attitude as Colin: doesn't matter what you're doing, you've got to look good.

Mavis volunteered to make up our picnic on the one condition that all of us returned fit for the barn dance in the evening.

'We forgot all about that!' said Evelyn.

'Are you both going, lads?' Bobbie asked.

'Of course they are. I've bought them their tickets and I want to see those kilts twirling!' said Mavis.

That's that, I thought, the decision has been taken out of our hands completely.

After we finished our coffee we decided to head for the cabin as it was already ten o'clock. 'I hope you don't mind,' said Colin, 'we have a full day ahead of us tomorrow so an early night won't go amiss, and it is a good walk back.'

'We'll not be far behind you, lads,' said Bobbie.

'See you in the morning, folks,' said Colin. 'You will have to walk to us!' he added, laughing. 'Bye-bye… night, girls.'

We had our torch with us this time. What a difference it made when we reached the point where the trees overhung and met across the road, blocking the sky completely.

'Pretty frightening here,' I lamented to Colin. 'Would think twice of walking on my own down this road.'

'Big pussycat,' said Colin. 'Scared of the dark, are you?'

'I was always glad to come out of the thicket,' I said.

The most marvellous part is seeing the stars after coming out of the pitch black. I never knew the heavens were as busy. In fact I will tell anyone who likes to stargaze to come up here. It has to be unique, hills all around with stars and planets lighting up the loch.

A quick wash and off to bed. I was so grateful to God for looking after us in such a way that sleep came easily.

Chapter Twenty

C olin was as bright as a button in the morning, much to my disgust. I preferred to awaken from my slumber gently and take my time washing and dressing. Colin had been into the village and bought the rolls and a paper. It was a mile walk and he had completed it before I was even up.

'Come on, lazybones! You not up yet? We have a journey ahead of us today. I've met Mavis and the girls already at the grocery store and picked what we're having for lunch in the hills.'

'I'm getting there,' I said.

We ate breakfast and put our walking boots on. David had put out some pairs of gaiters for us to wear. They fitted over our stockings, protecting the shin and calf – similar to a footballer's shin guard. At the bottom, they had a loop of elastic which fitted under the boot. They were also clipped to the boot on one side, to hold them firmly in place. They provided both waterproofing and added protection should you encounter an adder in the grass on the hills.

There was only one set so he had left out two poly bags with the bottom cut out. 'You slip them over your boot then use tape to keep the bag in position,' he had explained. 'This will afford the same protection as the gaiters if you follow my instructions.'

'I thought it would be difficult,' said Colin. 'Instructions can be confusing and hard to follow when you have no one there at the time to show you. It was a doddle, though.' I was pleased he gave me the gaiters as the sound of rustling bags would start to annoy me after a short time.

The girls and Bobbie arrived at the cabin. 'Nice place!' said Bobbie.

'This is great!' said one of the girls. 'You should book one of these for us another time, Dad!'

The girls had short-cut jeans on and I can only guess how they managed to get into them. They had half a shirt on baring their midriffs and both carried a sweater. They wore small chunky boots and tiny socks.

Bobbie had on a Hawaiian shirt and khaki shorts and a pair of light tan shoes. 'I'll be sticking to the Forestry Commission path mainly,' he said.

The girls started on Colin, who of course enjoyed any attention lavished on him from the opposite sex.

'Why are you wearing poly bags? Have you got holes in your socks?' sniggered Carol.

'They are for keeping my catch of fish from the stream coming from the falls,' explained Colin.

That flummoxed them, I thought, looking at the bewilderment on their faces.

'Had you going then for a moment!' Colin mocked, bursting into fits of laughter. He went on to explain to them what they were for and how they offered dual protection from rain and snakes. 'If you are going into long grass you should put these on at the falls.'

'Oh, we will,' said one of the girls, 'can't stand snakes or creepies.'

'It's only a precaution we were told to take. There is no record of anyone being bitten as far as we know,' said Colin.

The road up to the falls is quite steep and I wondered if Bobbie would make it. He was getting a good tug from Butch the dog, who seemed desperate to be free of his shackles. It took us an hour and a half to reach our destination and Bobbie was relieved. 'That'll do me!' he exhaled. 'I'll have my lunch, take some photos and play with Butch.'

'We'll press on then,' said Colin. 'It will be two-and-a-half hours before we return. If you wish to go back by all means do so,' he said.

Carol decided that she wished to climb to the summit as she wanted photos of her feat.

Evelyn said, 'I'll stay with Dad and Butch,' and divided the lunch pack up equally.

'Have fun and be careful,' Bobbie said, concerned.

'You too,' said Colin and I.

'Oh, we will,' said Bobbie.

Colin insisted that Carol put on the poly bags for protection, much to her dismay. But she knew in her heart that it made sense. It was a steep climb and some parts were pretty soggy and I'm sure we all were glad of the damp protection.

After an hour and a half we finally made it. 'Get your camera out now,' said Colin. 'Look at the views of the water and hills from every angle.'

'I want one of me in all the views!' demanded Carol, who had found it tough going. She really had been struggling the last 200 feet.

After our photo shoot it was time for lunch and as usual Mavis did not disappoint with a variety of sandwiches. Carol had also brought a flask of tea, which was most welcome. Checking our map Colin pointed to various landmarks and wrote down for her the direction of every picture taken.

'I can't wait to get home and show that big lug of mine what I have done,' Carol mused. 'He wouldn't believe me if I didn't produce the evidence.'

'Well, that's all the evidence you'll need,' said Colin cheerily.

We sat for a while just admiring the scenery. 'Peace,' I said, 'perfect peace. We are lucky to have such a country.'

Starting down we angled our descent so that the incline was not too steep. This made injury unlikely if we took a tumble. We reached the falls in well under an hour; it's always quicker on the way down, which is relief to all.

Evelyn was waiting for us on her own. 'Where's Bobbie?' I enquired.

'I'll tell you on the way down,' she said. With that, she took my arm and snuggled into me. 'I've been sitting here on my own for over an hour and I was a little scared.'

'Why didn't you go with your dad, then?' I asked.

'I honestly thought you would have been here earlier,' said Evelyn.

'We were taking photos and enjoying the view. Then we lay down for a short rest,' I said.

'Wish I had come up with you now! I'm sure the views are stunning.'

'You should have,' I said, 'I missed your company.'

'That's nice! I felt I had to wait and keep Dad company. Carol needed to prove to herself she could do it, for herself and also to show off to her boyfriend.'

'Carol has taken lots of photos. I'm sure she will share them with you.'

'I'll have to settle for that, then,' said Evelyn.

'You were saying earlier why your dad had to go back down.'

'Oh yes. We had let Butch off the lead and started playing with the ball. We decided to have a little fun with him and threw the ball into the pool below the falls. Butch didn't like the noise coming from the water and wouldn't fetch the ball. Dad tried to retrieve it by stretching out, but overdid it. In he went, head first. As he came out he toppled into the mud. You should have seen the state of him, he was absolutely filthy.

'I was afraid to go near him so he took off his shirt and washed himself as best he could and that's when he decided to go back down. I heard him laughing as he was going down, but I'm sure he wouldn't have wanted you to see him like that. So you could say he was sparing his blushes.'

'Can I tease him?'

'Oh, he'll tell you all about it before that, I'm sure,' said Evelyn. 'May I steal a kiss? I'm still a little shaky.'

'Oh, OK then, I'll not tell your boyfriend!' I said.

Pulling my arm, Evelyn asked what my plans were for the next few weeks. 'Where are you going next?' she asked.

'We are heading for Crianlarich then on to Glencoe next week. Plans don't always work out as we have found out recently. So we will take things as they come.'

She began tickling under my armpit and said, 'You're only trying to sidetrack me!'

'OK, OK, I give in. I'm afraid I'll give you a black eye with a stray blow from my elbow.'

'You'd better not. Whatever would I tell big Charlie?' said Evelyn.

'After Crianlarich we will camp on Rannoch Moor then spend a night or two in the hostel at Glencoe.'

'Sounds scary staying on the moors for the night,' said Evelyn.

'Colin has been there before. He has camped all over so I'm in safe hands.'

'I suppose it's better to have company. I know how lonely I felt on my own half an hour ago,' said Evelyn.

'Bonnie's brother is picking us up at Ballachulish. His youth club are camping around the Oban area at the moment. They are making their way to Fort William and intend climbing Ben Nevis along with some other pursuits.'

'Sounds like a lads' week, then,' said Evelyn.

'Yes, it is. Bonnie wanted to go with them but big brother Angus would have none of it.'

'Oh, the beautiful Bonnie! Are you crazy about her?'

'Well, you could say that,' I said.

'So would I stand a chance if I was interested? Just teasing!' said Evelyn.

'You are a devil!' I said.

'I know,' said Evelyn. 'Where are you meeting Bonnie? And where are you taking her?'

'That's a lot of questions,' I said.

'I'll start tickling you again if I don't get answers.'

'OK, OK! Anything for a quiet life! Colin will be heading up to the Kyle of Lochalsh then Gairloch and Ullapool. We will go our separate ways near Invermoriston and I will then head straight for Inverness to meet up with Bonnie and stay with her aunt for a couple of days.'

'Then where are you taking her?'

'Come on, Evelyn!' I said.

'Do you want me to start tickling again? We girls like details, and that means all!'

'Well, we will take the train down to the Kyle of Lochalsh then sail to Skye, where we will stay with another aunt on her uncle's side.'

'Wish we were going with you, with the exception of next week,' said Evelyn.

'It's your turn to spill the beans,' I said. I couldn't say I would tickle her in case my hands went on to the wrong place.

'I may tell you later!'

Typical! I thought. You tell a girl everything, then they tell you nothing.

'Isn't that your dad there, Evelyn, at the bottom of the hill? He is about to go on to the main road,' I said.

'Oh no! What an embarrassment, he hasn't put his shirt back on. I hoped he'd be back on the boat by now. He's hardly covered any ground at all!' said Evelyn.

'He should try to lose some weight. I'm sure carrying all that excess isn't good for him.'

'Perhaps you should take him with you,' said Evelyn. 'Oh look, he's jumping up and down now and swatting something!'

'It's the midges, it has to be! They are after his sweat. We had better get to him quick and give him Colin's sweater or he'll be eaten alive,' I said. We managed to reach him in time before he became too irate.

Evelyn said to me, 'Close your ears as he'll let out a few oaths, Jamie.'

While he was pulling on Colin's sweater which I had given him I did indeed hear him utter a few profane adjectives.

'You can wash and tidy up at the cabin,' I said. 'It's only twenty minutes away.'

'That's fine, Jamie.'

All the while silent oaths were pursed on his lips. He saw the funny side after a cup of tea and a wash that seemed to have settled his nerves.

'I can't believe I fell head first into that river! Where are you? You stupid dog! It's all your fault!'

'Leave him alone,' said Evelyn.

'Just kidding, darling.'

'Are you fit to walk back to the boat now?' enquired Colin.

'Yes, I'll manage. I hope Mavis has my dinner ready. I quite fancy it early as I don't want to be dancing on a full stomach.'

When we arrived back at the boat Mavis had everything ship-shape and, oooh... the aroma of cooked food. Delicious.

'Get yourselves to the table. Everything is ready,' said Mavis. Music to all of our ears after the challenge of the day.

'I'm ready, dear,' said Bobbie.

'Well, get yourself in there, then,' said Mavis.

At the table the events of the day were discussed. The most hilarious ones were obviously the renderings of Bobbie, who illustrated the story with wit and gestures and a few silent adjectives under his breath. Mavis was in fits of laughter at his antics. 'Wish I'd been there!' she said.

'I would have beaten you to the top, dear,' said Bobbie, 'leaving you exposed and a spectacle of overweight halfway up, plus a meal for the midges!'

'I don't think so, luv. You've obviously had too much sun,' said Mavis.

The whole table was in hysterics.

'I'm quite sure you would have lost,' said Colin.

'You might be right,' said Bobbie.

'We'll have to go now,' said Colin. 'It's almost eight o'clock already.'

We disembarked and waved to the girls from the shore.

'See you both at ten o'clock. Don't be late!' said Colin.

There wasn't a breeze as we hurriedly made for the cabin.

'I would gladly rid myself of this shirt,' said Colin, 'but the midges would enjoy it even more than I. How would you rid us of the midges round here, genius?' asked Colin.

'Simple!' I said. 'Do you see those horses over there?' I asked.

'Yes,' said Colin.

'Look at the swarm of midges above them. They are obviously attracted by scent.'

'I'm with you,' said Colin.

'Well, all you need is a large Hoover, suction machine. It would be shaped like a mini-tanker which supplies garages with petrol. The grille would be small enough to suck up only the midges and it would be battery operated like a milk float on wheels, making it manoeuvrable and efficient. You would add whatever scent was required next to the grille. Then you drive it along the road, stop at each tree, and draw off your quarry. I'm sure there would be very few midges left after only a week.'

'Why don't you get one made?' said Colin.

'You need to fund it, which is out of the question,' I replied. 'It's not always the inventor who gets the credit for his findings. That's the reason Japan is on the up. They find quicker methods of doing things. They are not well known for inventions.'

We finally arrived at the cabin unscathed.

'I'm going to put my head down for an hour,' sighed Colin. 'It's going to be a long night, and the women will be demanding.'

'You can say that again!' I exclaimed.

After our short nap we hurriedly washed and freshened up. It was time to try on my new shirt, with the kilt of course. 'What do you think?' I asked Colin.

'They'll be fighting over us, Jamie me boy!' he said, twirling his kilt and showing off his tanned legs.

'I think it's you they'll be fighting over,' I replied. 'Thank goodness we don't have to do the walking back to the cruiser after that hike.'

'It's great having the dance fifty yards up the road,' said Colin.

'I wonder if Bobbie will be fit enough to come at all. He was all in earlier,' I said.

'Did you not hear him tell us that his sister and husband are coming from Rothesay, and they are spending a night on the cruiser?' said Colin. 'And the girls are spending the night on the floor as we did the other night. Oh, the other thing is they are being taxied by the brother-in-law in his Land Rover to save a walk.' There was a knock knock at the door. 'That will be the English clan,' said Colin. 'Let them in.'

Indeed it was the girls; they were dressed in mini-kilts and light white blouses, leaving little to the imagination.

'Are you ready, lads?' said Bobbie. 'I'm dying of thirst,' he shouted from the jeep.

'Yes!' I said.

'We'll be off then! See you there!'

The girls decided to walk with us the short distance. Evelyn took my hand as we exited the cabin and Carol was already enfolded under Colin's huge shoulders.

'Evelyn,' I said, 'I don't stand a chance of a dance with you this evening dressed like that!'

'Dressed like what?' came the reply.

'I mean every boy or man will demand your company because you and Carol will pass for models. I'm complimenting you, not taking you down.'

'Oh! Thanks, Jamie, I thought you thought we were a bit over the top.'

'No, I think you are beautiful.'

'Now, my big Charlie might not like that.'

'But do you?' I asked.

'Oh yes!' She smiled at that and clasped my hand tight as we made our way to the dance.

It was about 10.30 p.m. when we arrived at the barn. The band had only just started as many people were still queuing to get in, which included us. 'They come from all over to one of these ceilidhs!' a voice was heard to say from the gathering.

Handing over our tickets, Bobbie and his brother-in-law Tommy instinctively headed for the bar, which was made up of half a dozen tables joined together at the top of the barn. As you can imagine, everyone else was of the same intent, so another large queue faced them.

'We'll get the drinks,' said Bobbie. I was quickly summoned to assist while Colin took care of the ladies. As usual!

The hay was unevenly spaced and also at different heights, giving a theatre-type atmosphere. Just as I had predicted, the girls were the choice of the young male stags of the area. They had only turned to sit down when another pursuer would charm them for a dance. It was an hour before I finally managed to have a dance with Evelyn.

'Thank goodness it's a waltz!' said Evelyn, 'I won't last until two o'clock at this pace.'

'There is a break at eleven forty-five in ten minutes, then it starts again at twelve-thirty which will give us time to re-energise,' I said.

'Oh, that's good!' said Evelyn.

Colin by this time had danced with, I reckon, nearly every eligible female in the room. Even Mavis and Joan were enjoying the evening. Bobbie had even been up for the 'Strip the Willow' along with Tommy. The both of them were now sweating profusely in the heat of the barn.

'I'll need some more ale to keep me cool tonight, lads,' said Bobbie. 'Poor Tommy will be on lemonades as he is driving.'

After the buffet it now went into full swing. The fiddles appeared to go faster and Bobbie and Mavis were leading the charge with Colin, me and the girls in hot pursuit. Mavis was becoming even more boisterous as the vodka took effect while Joan and Tommy were lapping up the fun. Being a little older they had decided to take in slow dances only latterly.

On the floor, one of the big lads in his full regalia let Mavis go a little early; she only just managed to keep her feet. I could see the twinkle in her eye and read her mind: So you want to have a little fun, luv? I'll show you fun.

Every time she was twisted she let her partner go earlier and earlier until one went crashing down on the floor with his kilt over his head and small G-string-type trunks sparing his blushes. You would have to have been there to imagine the expression on his face as he tried to regain his composure. It will be a while before he attempts that again, I thought to myself.

It was a huge dance floor so a nice young man approached our group and gestured with his hands to calm it. We all laughed and nodded to him. With the little frolic over we continued in a more dignified manner.

The night finally came to a close and the whole eight of us were dancing with the partner we came with. With hugs and kisses at 'Auld Lang Syne' I could see the girls were a little sad as they were heading home the next day, which was actually today at noon.

Evelyn took my hand as we left and began crying.

'I'm so glad I've met you! I can't believe that I'm in love with two boys,' she said.

'Oh, you'll get over me quickly!' I said.

'I don't want to!' she said. 'I want you to promise to come down to Stockport to see me next summer. I won't be getting married for at least three years, anyway. I'm only eighteen and I have my degree to get and career to pursue.'

'I promise,' I said, reassuringly. 'Anyway, I thought you told me it was five years.' I got a jab from her elbow for my remark, which had bought a smile to her face once more. The desired effect achieved, Jamie boy. I am learning, I thought.

Carol was kissing Colin goodbye and Evelyn, seeing this, quickly pulled me to her, kissing and hugging me as if for dear life. She let me go and joined Carol, hastening their step as they left us, waving goodbye and running to the Land Rover.

Bobbie and Mavis wished us all the best for the future and were grateful for our company, which had made it such a memorable holiday for them.

'If you want, next year I'll book a big boat for a couple of weeks on the Norfolk Broads, lads. There will be room for us all!' said Bobbie.

'We'll keep that in mind!' said Colin.

'I would love that,' I said. 'Even if Colin can't make it, I will.'

'Well, the offer is open,' said Bobbie; with a handshake, he left.

Mavis hugged and kissed us both. 'Now, keep in touch,' were her parting words. She then followed Bobbie.

The car left with everyone waving and all the women in tears.

'Well, that's another chapter in our lives over,' said Colin. 'Oh, I've really enjoyed it.'

'Me too!' I said. 'Evelyn is great to be with, she's a cracker.'

'Aye, they both are. Never mind, it's off to bed for us and see what tomorrow brings,' said Colin.

Chapter Twenty-one

We awoke to the sound of a klaxon from the loch. Looking out of the window we saw the cruiser had came as close to the shore as possible. Hurriedly we put on our shorts and shoes and ran to the water's edge.

The girls were waving frantically; it was obvious they didn't wish to leave without seeing us once more. They were now dressed with shorts and blouses for going away. There was a small conversation between them, then they bent down and picked up their bikini tops and started waving them.

'What a pair of devils they are!' said Colin.

'Aye, they are all that. I really will miss them.'

'Bye!' I yelled.

'Bye!' cried Colin.

A couple of blasts from the horn from Bobbie and they sailed down the loch and into the distance.

'Well, what's the itinerary for today?' I asked Colin.

'Take it as it comes, Jamie boy,' he replied. 'I'm starving. Let's get dressed and head for the store. We are badly in need of fresh supplies.'

'I agree. What time is it, anyway?'

'Believe it or not it's nine-thirty. We must have had a sound sleep,' said Colin.

We quickly washed and changed and Colin asked, 'Fancy a jog into the village? It will do us the world of good.'

'I'm up for that,' I said.

Ten minutes was all it took. 'Pretty good, Jamie! That wasn't bad, considering the night we had last night.'

'The staff look kind of weary this morning. I wonder if they were out late at the dance.'

'Don't ask, Jamie. It's not the thing to do. Women tend to volunteer the answer to that kind of question themselves.'

We were a little longer jogging back with the extra purchases. I ate four rolls – two egg ones and two bacon ones – plus a few biscuits and some fresh juice.

'Feeling better now, Jamie?' asked Colin.

'Sure am!' I said.

The weather had changed to a light drizzle as we returned to the cabin. 'Never mind,' said Colin. 'I'm not going to complain. We have had sunshine for most of the holiday.' We finished washing and drying the dishes then we did a bit of tidying up. 'Right, let's go over the events of the last few days,' said Colin.

Suddenly, before I could respond, there was a knock at the door.

'Wonder who that can be, Colin?' I said.

'I'll get it,' said Colin.

Colin opened the door wide and there stood David Ballantine. 'How nice to see you!' said Colin. 'What can we do for you today?'

'It's what I can do for you!' he replied. 'Have you any plans for today?'

'Nothing planned at all,' said Colin.

'In that case, if you wish, you can come along with me today. 'Is that OK with you, Jamie?'

'Great,' I said, 'you don't need to ask me twice!'

'You won't need much with you. The forecast is good for the afternoon,' said David. 'I'm going to mass. I have to leave now to catch the service in the Episcopal Church in Inverary.

'Just give us a minute,' said Colin. 'You start the car and we'll do a check before we leave.'

I didn't mind going with David at all. After all, he had one of my favourite cars. It was the one weakness that Colin ribbed me about, calling me a shallow person.

As we made our way out of Lochgoilhead, David took the left fork towards Dunoon, 'It's only a matter of choice which way we turn. However, I find there's less traffic on this route, plus it gives you a change of scenery,' said David.

The road was no less steep as we twisted our way round sharp bends. Hope we don't meet anything coming down, I thought to myself.

'There's a good view of Loch Fyne when we reach the main trunk road,' said David.

'That will be one of Jamie's "panoramic" views then,' said Colin.

Big oaf! I meant to pick out one of his favourite words and throw it back at him. I'll bide my time.

David laughed at Colin's remark but made no comment.

He went on to tell us that the Catholic Church had an arrangement with the Episcopal Church to allow mass to be said on Sundays. 'I think the nearest church from here is back in Dumbarton or further on to Oban district. I remember you telling me, Jamie, that you are a Catholic. That is one of the reasons for offering you a trip today.'

'I have only managed mass once since coming up north. I'm sincerely grateful to you for the opportunity of going.'

'How about you, Colin?' asked David.

'I keep my faith very much to myself, but if you are both going then I'll tag along.'

We reached the main road after about fifteen minutes and indeed we had a splendid view of Loch Fyne as David had said. The road carried round to the start of the loch at its source, as most roads do in Scotland. Who was complaining though, going at speed in a classic Jaguar? Certainly not me!

'I'm pretty sure this road was built for this type of car,' said David. 'The only problem we have is in autumn. On the far side of the loch the trees surround the road and shed their leaves making it very dangerous, so I wouldn't be going at this pace.'

I dreamt of having a car like this with Bonnie beside me; maybe one day.

As we came closer to Inverary the road opened up and we could see the town clearly, with the castle and grounds to the right. 'The castle is worth a visit if you wish to stay here for the day, or you can come to Lochgilphead with me if you wish. The choice is yours,' said David.

'I'd prefer to visit the castle, Jamie. What do you want to do?' asked Colin.

'I'll go along with that – I'm interested in the Campbell clan history.'

The town was much smaller than I had imagined. It had only one main street which was crowded with visitors. The harbour and frontage of the loch faced us as we arrived. All in all it was very scenic.

'It might be difficult to find a car space today, going by the throngs of people about. I'll go back to the big car park below the main arches and look for a spot,' said David. We managed to find a space after a few minutes. There were two or three places available, 'Thank goodness!' said David. 'That's a find, as we haven't got much time to spare.'

'Is the church far away?' I asked.

'No, only five minutes away,' said David.

We arrived at the church. It looks like standing room only, I thought to myself.

'Oh it seems very busy – more than I realised,' said David. 'The problem round here is there is only one mass and it looks as if everyone has checked the time of it. Never mind, we will accept it as our penance for today.'

The church was set in the trees, partially hidden with a small lawn to the right. It would probably have been built shortly after the Reformation. It was constructed of soft cream sandstone with a small bell tower, and would have used the masons' skills of the time to achieve the impressive finish. It felt nice and homely with little to distinguish it from the Catholic church; the similarity was extraordinary.

I had often wondered what would have happened if Henry the Eighth had stayed faithful to his wife. Perhaps there would be no Church of England. Maybe one day they will find a way of unifying the church once more. I hope so.

We waited in line for five minutes to let the front of the queue find their seats. Having finally got in we were huddled into the back recess against the wall without a seat. The church would have seats for just over 100, but there seemed to be twice as many in the congregation today.

Colin and I were asked by the pass keeper to collect the gift offering, which we took as a compliment. We gladly accepted the task. The service lasted over fifty minutes, which was normal for a mass. I was relieved, though, when it finished, as I was not used to standing in the one place for so long. The sermon I will always remember well; the main theme was 'With faith you can achieve everything!'

The heat had built up inside and I inhaled the wonderful fresh air to my relief as I exited the building.

'Right, time for lunch! And it's on me, boys,' said David.

'No, we can't accept any more from you,' said Colin.

'Nonsense!' said David. 'I have to tell you that my dad had not only chill or flu-like symptoms as first thought. Other health issues were diagnosed during his stay at the hospital. Tests revealed that he had a blood disorder, and failure to have it treated would eventually cause him to have a stroke. So I thank you again once more for your help towards a stranger.'

'How is he, then?' asked Colin.

'He has nearly recovered and is hoping to get home next week,' said David.

'That is good news,' I said. 'Your mother will be pleased.'

'Yes, she will. But not as half as pleased as Dad,' said David, with a grin. 'Now for lunch, and no arguments. I'll see to it Dad pays.'

We had to accede to his way; he would not have it any other way. I was sure that was why he was a successful businessman; positive in nature and a will to have his way, while taking into consideration the views of others.

It was indeed a treat for us at the restaurant, with sirloin steaks all round. After we had our fill, David had to leave for Lochgilphead and excused himself. 'I'll collect you in three hours from now. If you make your way to the car park, where the car is at the moment, I'll pick you up there.'

'We'll be there!' said Colin.

'Have a nice day, lads. I will pay the bill on the way out.'

'Thanks again,' said Colin.

'I am finished. I think we should head for the castle and make the most of the day.'

'OK, let's go then!' said Colin.

We bought a brochure on the history of the castle while we were waiting on our guide to show us around. The information to hand would give the historical background of the castle and the Campbell clan. The castle itself is a unique piece of architecture incorporating Baroque, Palladian and Gothic, featuring four imposing French-influenced conical spires. This castle was the first of its size and type built in Scotland.

The construction of the castle began in 1720 with a sketch prepared by Sir John Vanbrugh, the architect of Blenheim Palace and Castle Howard for the Duke of Argyll.

After the death of Sir John Vanbrugh the design was developed by Roger Morris, who saw the start of construction in 1746 and worked with William Adam, then the most distinguished architect in Scotland. Both Morris and Adam died in 1748 after completion of the designs and it was Adam's sons John and Robert who saw the project to completion for the 5th Duke of Argyll in 1789.

The 10th Earl was granted the dukedom in 1701, as thanks for the regiment he raised for the crown known as Earl of Argyle's Regiment of Foot. This was the unit given the task of carrying out the notorious massacre of Glencoe, an episode inaccurately classed as a clan vengeance by the Campbells. I recommend that everyone should read the history of Scotland to form their own unbiased opinion, as there were many factions fighting.

Our guide took us round the building showing us all the state rooms and paintings, a tour that was well worth the visit as David had said.

We sat in the gardens and discussed what the castle had to offer, not least the artefacts.

'Right, Jamie, we better get a move on. The day has flown and David will be back to collect us in half an hour.'

'Most enjoyable. I feel like a historian now.'

This put Colin into one of his fits of laughter. 'You have a long way to go and a lot to learn before you can say that.'

Chapter Twenty-two

The walk is picturesque along the side of the loch with a clear view of the town. 'We'll have to hurry, it's taken us longer than I realised,' said Colin.

We were a few hundred yards from the main arch when I saw David's car drive beneath it into the car park. 'That's David now, Colin!' I said.

'You're the sprinter, Jamie. If you want to make a dash for it I certainly won't hold you back.'

'You wait here then and I will let David know where you are.'

'That suits me. On you go, then,' said Colin.

I left Colin and ran on and met up with David who was scratching his head when I arrived.

'I thought for a minute that you might have forgotten where we had arranged to meet,' said David.

'No, we lost track of time, that's all,' I said. 'Colin is on the outskirts of town waiting to be picked up.'

'Let's do it then,' said David.

It took only a couple of minutes to reach Colin.

'Too much for you Colin, the jog that is?' asked David.

'I sent my sprinter ahead of me,' said Colin, grinning at me.

'Well, lads, did you enjoy your day?' enquired David.

'Fantastic! Brilliant!' Colin and I replied in unison.

'Let's be off, then.'

We headed out of town towards Lochgoilhead, only to find a traffic jam a mile onward. A lorry was unable to drive over the humpback bridge with its heavy load. Its width had blocked oncoming traffic coming from the south.

This is going to be fun! I thought. I wondered what or who would come up with the solution.

I didn't need to wait long. A lorry driver without a load emerged from behind us and stopped beside the stricken vehicle. There was a gesture between the drivers – obviously a discussion about tactics. I could see them nodding, which meant they were of the same opinion as to the remedy.

The driver nearest to the stricken vehicle was then spoken to, whereupon he alighted from his car and made his way towards us to the back of the queue. Watching out of the back window I noticed the last car reversing about 100 yards distance up the road, then the next, and so on until it came to our turn.

The chap explained to David that the truck would need to back up at least 100 yards to have a run at the bridge, hence the reason for the movement. David hurriedly obliged and the cars in front began to follow suit until the chap who had spoken to us put his into reverse, completing the chain.

'Jamie! Colin! Take a walk up to the bridge,' said David. 'You can fill me in with all the details later.'

'Will do!' we said.

'I wonder where they have come from and where they are delivering the load to,' I said to Colin as we approached the bridge.

'I don't know, but I don't fancy following him to Glasgow. It's not a dual carriageway and it has some steep inclines before going down the 'Rest and be Thankful' to Arrochar,' said Colin.

'Then you have the road along Loch Lomond. It's a nightmare!' I sighed.

'You can say that again,' said Colin. 'I think the problem here is he is unable to get enough speed at the bridge in order to get over the humps.'

The lorry backed up as far as it could, then the second lorry attached a metal tow bar to give it extra power. All ready, they started up their engines. I thought to myself, this should be a doddle with double pulling power. I was proved wrong, however, as the two lorries came to a standstill three quarters of the way up the short steep incline, with diesel fumes spewing from both their exhausts. Slowly they trundled backwards to their starting positions.

'What now?' I asked Colin.

'Looks like they need more pace,' Colin replied.

'Oh look, there's a chap walking towards us coming out of that lorry heading for Inverary,' I informed Colin.

'Good-oh! I wish I had a camera.'

After a consultation with the other two drivers the chap returned to his lorry and unhitched his trailer. He re-emerged with the front cab only and attached it to the other two. 'It's all or nothing this time!' said Colin. All three engines burst into life and they were off. It was easy to see they had gathered more momentum as they approached the hill.

The lorries were in low gear and noise was deafening as all three vehicles met the incline. The air was awash with the stench from the exhausts as they powered forward and over the top, to the cheers of the onlookers.

'Did you see the amount of snaps people were taking?' I asked Colin. 'That should give them something different to show their relatives when they return home!'

'Not quite the usual holiday snaps,' said Colin.

The traffic build-up was finally eased when one of the car drivers took the initiative and waved twenty cars in turn in each direction alternately, thus relieving the congestion.

David collected us on the south side of the bridge. 'Well, fill me in! I couldn't see much from back there,' said David.

Colin gladly related the moments of failure and success with relish.

'Oh, by the way, I have decided to stay at the cabin tonight and have a night with you at the hotel in Lochgoil,' said David. 'I phoned my wife for permission from Lochgilphead,' he added, laughing heartily.

'That's great!' said Colin, 'I'll take you on at darts.'

David was cool for his years. I used to think someone at thirty-five was an old man, but I changed my mind completely after meeting him.

We stopped at the cabin for only a minute or two, mainly to park the car for the night. 'Let's make the most of my free night, lads!' he said. As we walked to the hotel, he told us of his aspirations in his younger days of becoming a top badminton player. However, he had found his lack of agility a great dis-advantage as an inability to stretch causes energy loss in a gruelling tie. 'I play for fun now. I also play tennis in the summer, mixed doubles with my wife and friends. By the way, that's where

I met her. I couldn't take my eyes off her legs! Best set I've ever seen, and still are!'

'Well that's a good start!' said Colin.

Colin had a pint along with David and I just stuck to my usual cola. David ordered three pies along with the drinks which we demolished in minutes. 'I should have ordered six,' he joked. 'I'll get another three with the next order.'

Some of the locals challenged us to a game of darts. This was right up Colin's street, as he was a formidable opponent for everyone back home. It wasn't long before he got into his stride. David and I took turns at being his doubles partner and although we faltered at each turn, he more than made up for the handicap we posed.

The evening seemed to fly as last orders were called. We bade farewell to our newfound friends and promised to return at a future date.

Walking back to the cabin David enquired of our plans for the coming weeks, as an eventful week was about to close. Colin explained the problems posed by not having our tent and how he proposed to get round them.

'Wait a minute,' said David. 'I have an old two-man tent. It will keep you dry, and that's the main thing, isn't it?'

'Yes,' said Colin.

'Well, I'll dig it out for you when we get back,' said David. He spoke of his love for the area. 'The view of the heavens I promised was correct, was it not?'

'Fantastic!' I said.

'I've never seen anything like it,' said Colin.

'I can see further development in the future,' said David, 'as tourists discover its beauty.'

'As long as they don't spoil it,' said Colin. 'Oh, Jamie has an idea how to combat the midge population. Maybe you can help him find a backer for his project.'

'If it's good enough it will always come through, that's my philosophy,' said David.

Arriving at the cabin, David fetched the tent out of the cupboard. 'Looks as if it will stand up to a few camps yet, boys!' he laughed.

'That's fine,' said Colin; 'should do the trick.'

We hit the hay and were sound asleep in no time.

David woke us early as he was going straight into work. Eight o'clock and we were all loaded into the car, along with rucksacks and tent.

'Well you've had a wonderful time here and I'm sure you'll be back one day. I find it best to leave a place without saying anything at all. Just leave it to your memories and it will be with you all your life,' said David.

It was a wrench to leave the cosy and comfortable cabin. I would spend the whole summer there if it belonged to me. If I ever had any misgivings about going to Lochgoilhead then they were clearly gone.

I had to master the art of looking after myself – and of course Colin (just kidding) – with danger, thrills and being at the mercy of the weather once more. 'Living on your wits gives a sense of self-reliance that can only be gained from experience,' said Colin.

David provided us with a full breakfast – enough to satisfy our hunger pangs for a good part of the day.

'I'll drop you off at Tarbet, then,' said David.

Colin had decided that we should stick to the main trunk road rather than take the route used by many hikers on the east side of the loch. As we had to meet Angus, Allan and Duncan with their youth group at Ballachulish in a few days, we might need a lift should we be delayed by some unforeseen problem. I had phoned Bonnie from the hotel the previous night and she relayed the details of where the coach would pick us up. The intention of the group was to spend a few days in the Fort William area. This would of course include a climb of Ben Nevis. At 4,406 feet it is the highest peak in Britain. Colin wanted desperately to add this conquest to his feats.

My heart had almost melted hearing Bonnie's voice once more. 'I hope you are behaving yourself!' she said. 'How many other girls have you charmed?' she asked inquisitively.

'None but you!' I replied.

'I detect a little flutter in your voice and the hesitancy of a guilty man. So I'll want all the details of your time without me! I'm looking forward to meeting you in Inverness in two weeks' time. Love you!'

Oh-oh. I hope she will forgive all my little flirtations, I thought to myself. 'I can hardly wait! Bye now, baby.'

David pulled in at the Tarbet Hotel to drop us off. 'Well, lads, it's been a pleasure and I'm only pleased to have returned a favour.'

'You have been more than generous,' Colin said in gratitude. 'We won't forget this week and what you have done and are very happy that your dad is now making a full recovery.' Colin shook his hand and I followed his lead. His hand was firm and strong, emitting genuine warmth.

Before exiting the car he gave us both his card and told us to contact him when our studies were finished. 'Bye, lads, nice to have met you!' With that, the big Jaguar sped off into the distance. With a wave he was gone and so another chapter in our short life disappeared.

'Some experience, eh, Jamie?'

'It certainly was. It's good to know there are guys like him around,' I said.

'Let's get the rucksacks on and head back up to Crianlarich,' said Colin.

'How far is it?' I asked.

'I'll just check my map.'

'No need – there's a sign for Crianlarich, Fort William and Oban,' I said. 'It says eighteen miles.'

'That's a doddle. We'll manage it in six hours with a couple of rests along the way,' Colin mused.

'I hope you remembered to Vaseline your feet this morning, Jamie. Too much of the good life last week!'

I stopped him before he uttered another word. 'Hey, I had to waken you the last two mornings after your indulgence in the local ale house.' There was not a word from him at this. Perhaps he had taken the huff.

It was a quiet time as we picked our way between traffic. The road became very busy over the next stretch owing to the sharp turns. Coaches passed one another with inches to spare. Some even had to pull their mirrors in towards them to pass.

'It'll take us longer than I thought,' Colin said.

'Maybe we should have taken the other route instead,' I said.

'You're possibly right, but we'll just have to make the most of it now.'

We walked on the beach wherever we could to get away from the fumes of the traffic and the incessant noise. It was a relief to reach Ardlui after such a taxing walk. Colin had a couple of pies and a pint and I had two bacon rolls and cola, which went down a treat. The conversation revolved around Crianlarich and how events had taken us south instead of north.

'You could say it's a case of déjà vu,' said Colin. 'We've been here before and here we are again.'

Colin set out his plan for the rest of the day. 'It will take us at least another two or three hours to reach Crianlarich so we'll be in time to have a bar meal around six o'clock, then we'll head up to Tyndrum.' As he spoke he pointed to the map. 'There's a stream just south of there where we will be able to camp for the night. We won't need a fire as it will be late by the time we arrive.'

'That seems fine,' I said to him.

I enjoyed the break as I found the last mile or so hard going and a bit of a slog.

Leaving possibly the most awkward and tedious part of road behind us, I felt invigorated seeing the road stretch out before us, with Ben More to the north-east of us in the distance. It was a steady uphill walk to Crianlarich and it had taken fully eight hours, including stops, to reach the village.

We were fortunate indeed to have money to pay for our meals. We managed to find a small restaurant with suitable meals and reasonably priced at that. We duly tucked in and left not a scrap on our plates.

'I hope you're fit to walk for another hour or so,' laughed Colin.

'No bother!' I replied. 'I've replenished my tank and I'm re-energised.'

'You can't beat a cup of tea to boost the reserves,' said Colin.

'Aye, and a good glass of Scottish water!' I affirmed.

'According to the map, it's three miles to the stream,' said Colin.

'That'll be an hour and twenty minutes away, then. We should be there by nine forty-five, well before dark,' I said.

The weather changed after a bright start to the day. 'Scottish mist coming down,' Colin sighed. 'It's the high mountains draw it down around these parts.'

'I hope we can see where we're going,' I said.

'If it gets any worse we'll make camp not too far from the main road, make sure we don't lose our bearings,' said Colin.

The mist continued to thicken but we made our destination in time. There was a steep bank up towards the stream and what looked like a tent on the opposite bank. Colin spotted it almost at the same time as I and said, 'Someone has decided to camp here for the night, I can see a light coming from inside the tent. Wonder if it's male or female?'

Typical! I thought. My first musings were, I wonder where they have come from, and are they foreign?

As we approached, a well-proportioned female came out of the tent. 'Oh, you don't half give a girl a start!' she said in a half-scared voice.

'Hell… sorry, I'm Colin Mclean and this is my young friend, Jamie Cameron.'

'Pleased to meet you. I'm Maureen, and Liz my young sister is in the tent.' At the mention of her name a young, slender girl appeared from the tent. I reckon she was my age at least. She offered her hand positively, not shyly, and said, 'Pleased to meet you.'

'Do you mind if we pitch our tent just a few yards over from you? I prefer to be on higher ground should the stream rise over night,' I asked.

'No problem, pet!'

I liked the Geordie accent. It was right down to earth.

'Let's find a flat area then, as best we can, Jamie, under the circumstances.'

This was out first attempt at putting up our new tent; well, this old second-hand one. After ten minutes we seemed to be getting nowhere. I think we're in for some ridicule, I thought inwardly. Sure enough it came seconds later.

'I can see you lads have had plenty of experience at camping!' giggled Liz, with a grin a Cheshire cat would have been proud to own.

'We have just acquired this one,' said Colin politely, but not pleased.

'What second-hand store did you purchase it from then?' said Maureen.

We were still painstakingly trying to set the framework out when we were met with even more backchat.

'It's a two-tone shade, or is it faded, do you think, Maureen?' said Liz.

Colin was becoming irate and frustrated as he always maintained the upper hand as far as the ladies were concerned. I finally solved the riddle. The crosspiece was bent and that was what had thrown us off. I said to Colin, 'Look, hold these two pieces apart and I'll join them up one at a time.'

'Yes, that's it! Thank you, Jamie,' said Colin.

We then placed the base inside the framework before attaching the canvas itself. Having completed the tasks in hand we again were tormented by the Geordie lassies.

'Is it supposed to sag in the middle?' enquired Liz.

'Yes,' said Colin, 'it's an innovation for this type of model!'

'Maybe it can droop further to give you separate compartments,' said Maureen, much to Colin's disgust.

Having teased us to the point of someone being strangled, they now offered us refreshment. 'We have some spare soup if you want?' asked Liz.

'That would be great,' said Colin. 'You have a handy cooking implement there.'

'It's only a light gas portable stove, very handy for heating tea and quick meals, but it only lasts a few days until we need a refill.'

'As long as it does for the purpose. I'm ready for that soup now,' Colin said, scenting the aroma.

'Have you been long on the road?' asked Liz.

'Since ten o'clock this morning,' Colin informed her, 'although we left Lochgoil around seven-thirty.'

'How about yourselves?' I enquired.

'We left the Stirling area this morning, walked for three hours, had lunch then managed to get a lift to Crianlarich. We thought we might make Tyndrum but it got misty so we just decided to camp here for the night.'

After our bit of banter the communication became a little less strained, thanks to the sharing of their soup.

'Are you on holiday for a week or two?' I asked.

'Two weeks in all,' said Liz. 'We intend to spend a few nights in Oban at the youth hostel and then on to Fort William, plus the rest of the holiday in Skye. Then it's back to Whitley Bay.'

'Whitley Bay!' I exclaimed.

'Yes, why, do you know it?' asked Maureen, entering the conversation.

'I'll never forget it!'

'Why? It's not that bad a place!' said Liz.

'It's the lighthouse which stands out the most in my mind,' I said. My mum and dad took me to the top and I had to be carried down screaming my head off. I have never recovered. I'm still terrified of heights and probably always will be!'

'It's the tallest in Britain,' said Liz.

'I know. When I got to the top I felt as if it was leaning to the one side.'

'Leaning Tower of Pisa!' said Colin.

'Well, it felt like that! You know of course that it's cut off from the mainland when the tide turns?' I said.

'Yes, we both have been to the top. Don't know what your problem was,' said Maureen.

'Well, I was barely ten at the time. Surely that has to come into consideration!'

I was beginning to feel like a wimp when Liz came to my rescue. 'You'll get over it probably, because you were forced up. You have kept the memory alive in your head too long. Best thing is to do heights gradually. I do hope you get over it, for life includes all manner of doing things at high levels.'

'I have good memories of Whitley Bay as well.'

'What are they?' asked Liz, with whom I had struck up a rapport.

'Well, the rail station is the first thing that springs to mind. Upon leaving we met with a group of young lads with what we call a "guidy". It's a cart, basically, with four old pram wheels and a wood plank and a box at the rear, where one can sit or put belongings – in our case, luggage.

'The lads asked us where we were lodging for the holiday. We gave them the address and they then placed our suitcases and luggage on the cart, saving my mum and dad the carry, and of course the taxi fare.'

I didn't need to explain to the girls – they knew of the practice.

'For a few pence it was worth it. Having five children and little money wasn't easy in those days. A taxi didn't even figure in the equation. It was good to see youngsters using their initiative to profit from their labours. These boys would be about fourteen and still at school, so any extra pocket money was most welcome.

'I feel things are going wrong at the moment as friends seem to have more money and less to do, resulting in a few of them being sent to borstal,' I said.

'Lads do like their drink back home, I must confess, but in the main they're not bad,' said Liz. 'They love their football more than anything.'

'Oh, we all love football,' I said.

'Do you remember the street you stayed in?' asked Liz.

'No, I can't remember,' I said.

'Pity!' said the girls.

'Why?' I asked.

'Well, our older brother Terry did that very job,' said Liz.

'Small world!'

'It is indeed,' said Maureen.

'I do remember one thing though – or maybe make that two,' I said. 'Yes, the landlady cooked all the meals but my mother had to provide all the food. It seemed strange at the time to me, but I can only surmise that food was expensive and that it made sense to buy what we could eat and what my parents could afford.'

'What else?' enquired Liz.

'Well, the pack pudding we had was chocolate. It was one of those seven-day packs. Not one of us could eat it. Including Mum and Dad. The landlady came through to see how we were getting along.

' "What's the matter with the pudding?" asked the lady.

' "I always have to throw the chocolate one away as no one will eat it," explained Mum.

' "Oh, you should have told me! Do you all want ice cream, boys and girls?"

' "Yes please!" we smiled with our reply. Without more ado the plates were removed and ice cream was served. "That make you all happy?" she asked then. "Oh yes!" we shouted.'

'That's a nice happy memory,' said Liz, 'I'm glad it was from Whitley Bay.'

'It was a good holiday,' I said. 'Before we left, the old gentleman showed us his handiwork. He built warships. I loved them as they were so realistic. I'm sure he made them of matchsticks but it's the one thing in my memory that I can't be exact about. I don't know whether or not he had been in the Navy as I was too young to be included in any discussions of that nature.'

'Anything else?' asked Liz, who seemed to be amused by my memories of the place.

'Oh yes, the Spanish City show ground!'

'Yes, you're right!' said Liz.

'It was the first time I'd been on the ghost train, and it gave me the creeps.'

'Is that it?' asked Liz.

'The only other things that come to mind are the high cliffs and big waves on the beach.'

'I would say you passed your exam on Whitley Bay with flying colours for a ten year old, Jamie. We have lost most of the holidaymakers as everyone is heading for the sun now when they can afford it.'

'I don't know anyone yet among my friends, with the exception of my aunt and uncle who are in business, that go abroad,' I said. 'I'd love to see Australia! One of my friends has gone there to live. He was advised to leave this country for health reasons. I got a card from him. It looks fantastic. Surfing and sunshine and the girls. I couldn't stay, though, I'm a homebird and probably always will be,' I said.

'I like listening to you, Jamie! Will you tell me more about your life tomorrow?' asked Liz.

'Yes, of course I will.'

'I'm glad someone likes his conversation, he bores me to death,' said Colin.

'Ha ha,' I said.

Chapter Twenty-three

I t was time for hitting the hay as darkness was falling.
'Don't be trying to creep into our tent tonight,' said
Maureen. 'I've a pan at the ready for any intruders on funny
business.'

Liz began giggling at the antics of her big, protective sister and
I guess the speech was being addressed to me.

Though the conditions were cramped owing to the size of
Colin it was snug and warm as a chill had came down latterly
turning the air fresh.

I awoke with a start as I was staring at the sky and feeling just a
little shivery. 'What the BLAZES?'

I got up quickly and saw that our tent was packed, frame and
all, on top of our rucksacks with the exception of the groundsheet
which we were lying on. I stood up and saw the girls were bathing
their feet in the stream.

I gave Colin a quick nudge. He arose from his slumbers,
cursing below his breath.

'What the…!'

As he awakened fully I explained to him what had happened.

'So they want to play games!' said Colin. 'I think they need an
early morning bath, don't you? Quick, they haven't seen us. Let's
creep over behind them through the long grass.'

'I'm all for that,' I said.

We got within a yard of them with Colin's prowess and skill.
Colin sprung out of the undergrowth first, taking Maureen by the
waist. His momentum carried them both into the deep water
pool. Maureen had hardly any time to scream and only a small
startled shriek filled the air. On the other hand Liz more than
made up for her with screams of excitement as I tried to grab her
and pull her into the water. She turned so quickly, giving me a
glancing blow. In despair, I caught the only thing I could as I was
plunging into the water. Unfortunately it was her shorts that I

gripped, and they ended up round her ankles leaving her in her scanty briefs. That was the last thing I glimpsed before being engulfed by the flowing water.

I must have swallowed half the pond before surfacing, as I had fallen awkwardly. Resurfacing I was met with a four-letter word and a smack on my face from big sister Maureen. She had misinterpreted my intentions and was administering the punishment without trial.

Liz by this time had managed to restore her dignity and approached Maureen, shouting 'Stop! It was an accident. I'm sure Jamie came off worst, first with me giving him a glancing blow, then tripping him, and now you follow up by slapping him. Sorry, Jamie! I hope you'll forgive me!' said Liz.

At this she gave me a big hug. Maureen then came forward and gave me a hug also and said that she was sorry. 'I just got it wrong! I reacted on the spur of the moment. Sorry, Jamie, I mean it.'

We broke camp and packed up quickly, eager to start the new day. The girls, I felt, were overloaded for camping and hiking, but that was what you would expect. Colin commented to me, 'They are obviously relying on lifts mainly, as it is not possible to carry that lot.'

'It's not as if we are able to help them, as we have the tent now,' I said.

It was about an hour before reaching Tyndrum and the girls were exhausted. We used the facilities to wash and change before our meal.

Colin and I finished at the same time while the girls were only halfway through. Liz offered me half a plate of fries which were left on her side plate.

'I'll not finish them so you might as well have them. I can see you are very hungry.

'My mum would say "I'd rather have your photograph on the sideboard as you are too expensive to feed." '

Maureen had a ferocious appetite but hadn't finished her plateful. Her meal seemed to me to be a little overgenerous. Colin asked if he could finish the scraps. 'Do you mind if I clear the plate for you?'

I think she was a little surprised at the request and somewhat reluctantly agreed, as Liz had already offered me her leftovers.

'OK then, if you're that hungry, lad,' said Maureen.

'So you're off to Oban then?' I said. 'It's a pity I don't know where big Angus and his group are camped.'

'Who is Angus?' asked Liz.

'Jamie's girlfriend's brother,' said Colin. 'He and his brother Duncan are going to pick us up with his bus at Ballachulish in four days from now at the ferry.'

'You will be travelling to Fort William at that exact time,' I said.

'More's the pity then,' said Maureen.

'Not only that, they will be climbing the Ben with their party and Colin and I will join them. The bus must have a few empty seats when they have offered us a lift. The other thing is they have travelled up from the Borders; that can't be far from you down in Newcastle, is it?' I asked.

'Oh, that makes me want to meet Angus all the more! Is he single?' asked Maureen.

'Yes, all six foot eight of him!' I said.

'Wow!' said Maureen. 'Tell me more!'

'I can only go by what Bonnie has told me, but she says he's a mild-mannered bloke, a real gentle giant of a man, but he's not to be crossed either. He prefers honest people with no uppity or snobbery.'

'Oh, that's me!' said Maureen.

'Stop getting carried away,' said Liz. 'What's Duncan like?'

'Both he and Angus play rugby. Nothing grand, though, only with a local side.'

This answer did not suffice. 'But what's he like as a person?' enquired Liz.

'Oh, he's a little shorter at six foot four.'

'I think I like Duncan! Tell me more,' said Liz.

'He has fair hair with blue eyes and is very quiet,' I said.

'Mmm! I like a challenge, and he is a big challenge. Oh, I like the sound of Duncan,' said Liz.

'Well, we will just have to make sure we arrive at Glen Nevis in three days,' said Maureen.

'We weren't sure about this type of holiday but it was all we could afford,' said Liz.

'Is it becoming more to your liking now?' I asked.

'You bet!' said Liz. 'I'm holding you to your word that you will introduce me to Duncan.'

'You have it,' I said.

'Don't forget me,' said Maureen, 'Angus is mine.'

We paid our bill then loaded our rucksacks on each other's back. The girls walked the short distance with us to the main junction: Oban to the left and Fort William to the right, displayed on the signpost.

I got a great big hug from Maureen. 'Now remember me to Angus.'

'I will. See you in a few days then!' I replied.

Liz then grabbed me. 'Tell Duncan that a lassie from Whitley Bay is looking for him.'

She had mischief in her eyes. I wondered if Duncan would stand a chance!

They both nabbed Colin simultaneously, landing kisses all over him, right left and centre. 'Pity you are taken, gorgeous,' Liz and Maureen said. I don't know why she said that. Perhaps Colin was still showing emotion for Fiona. Women have built-in instincts for this sort of thing. I'll never know.

'Bye-bye! See you in three days, girls.'

'Byeeee…'

'I don't think they will walk far, Jamie. It took them an hour to walk less than a mile.'

'Just as well they are girls, then,' I said.

'Hey, I don't fancy your future in-laws' chances if they ever meet. They will have them down the aisle quicker than they can blink,' said Colin.

'What will be will be! I intend doing nothing to influence the situation.'

The girls had only just left us, but in a matter of minutes were picked up by a heavy goods lorry.

'I told you, Colin, they would get a lift, but I didn't reckon on one as quick as that.'

'Good luck to them! It's always easier for the girls to get a lift,' said Colin.

'I don't begrudge them it, they were really nice and we had a bit of fun.'

'How's your jaw by the way?' Colin asked with a hint of laughter.

'Fine!' I replied. 'How far to Glencoe?' – trying to change the subject.

'It's about thirty-odd miles if we keep to the road. I prefer the road as I feel we will get there quicker. I'm willing to take the walkers' path if you feel it's safer, though.'

'The road doesn't seem too busy, so I'll go along with that,' I replied.

'We can pick up a spot of lunch at the Bridge of Orchy then,' said Colin.

'That will do nicely,' I said.

It was a steady incline towards this area and I was beginning to feel the pace.

'This is what we came for!' said Colin, striding out. 'This separates the men from the boys!'

He had donned his Lochgoilhead bonnet to protect his head from the sun. The sweat was dripping from his forehead, as from mine. The scenery gave a real sense of total isolation with rare views in all directions. Bridge of Orchy was a welcome sight, a small haven in the mountains.

After we had replenished our water supplies and eaten lunch, Colin began studying his map. 'As it's hot I think we will try to save about two miles by taking the walkers' path on the west side of Loch Tala and Black Mount. We will make camp on Rannoch Moor just before the track meets the main B2 road to Glencoe. What do you think?' asked Colin.

I was just a little tentative, but when I thought about being in a real wilderness with only the stars I knew I had to experience it for myself. This is what Colin preferred: camping alone and feeling the breeze of the night air as he gazed at the wonderment of the heavens.

'That's OK! I like the idea of being out alone,' I lied. I only said these words to try to instil some confidence into my mind, for I knew Colin told me the more self-reliant I became the more powerful a person I would become.

The walk in the past hour had excelled everything so far. Perhaps it was the sense of being totally alone with only the sound of the wind and the shriek of a bird of prey.

I felt safe with Colin. Although I was strong I knew I lacked the prowess and skill of the man. We rarely spoke, taking in all the features of the loch and surrounding hills. The path was more prominent than I had imagined, which I expect was partly due to the volume of walkers and the dry spell were having at present.

We nodded to a few walkers who were heading in the opposite direction from us. I wondered if they were from Fort William or whether they had decided to do the return journey. Colin had taught me that it's not always good to know all the facts. This leaves room for imagination and surprise. Maybe they're on the run, maybe they are on a sort of sponsored walk. This is what keeps one alive he would say. The spice of life indeed.

I hadn't given it much thought before but I knew then that Colin and I would go in different directions, simply because he had imagination and drive. Would it be Canada, America, New Zealand, Australia? Who was to know? But he was the sort of man that a small country like Scotland could not hold, I feared. I could envisage him living in any one of those places.

I was unable to describe or put to words the feelings I had at that time. But I was determined to enjoy the moment and take what life threw at me. I knew I would travel but I also knew I would never leave Scotland.

We pitched the tent as the sun was slowly setting on the moor. I decided to miss out on the 'panoramic' and 'spectacular' in case Colin poked fun at me. 'Isn't that something else?' I said. 'What an array of colour! Open Rannoch Moor from east to west and Etive Mor to the north, with the mountain range to the south.'

'What a place!' said Colin. 'That's the main road to Glencoe over there.' He pointed to the mountain range north-west of us.

Although the scene was desolate to me, Colin's eyes sparkled as he looked out on the moor. He had a gift which I know I could never have; there was uniqueness in the man which I would never be able to emulate.

'We might as well hit the hay early,' said Colin.

'You go to bed if you wish. I want to look at the stars for a half hour,' I said.

I awoke next morning to the sound of rain on the tent.

'Wakey! Wakey! Jamie, I hope you have your bonnet and weatherproof jacket handy.'

Oh no! Oh well, it had to break some time, I thought.

'Here's what's left of the grub,' said Colin, handing me a sandwich and a packet of crisps. 'Might as well eat them here.'

'Thanks,' I said.

'The sky is looking heavy so we should get underway as soon as possible.'

Pulling the tent down and stacking it in its holder took much longer than I anticipated. It was wringing wet and more difficult to fit. Colin insisted on us doing all this in our underwear so that we could put dry clothes on for walking. This would have been one of those 'capture moments' as Bonnie called it, in other words, a photo shoot. We managed to shelter and help each other dress as we were now completely naked. I now know what a naturist feels like: cold!

With our kit on we headed for Glencoe, which was just under three hours' walk away. The pack felt much heavier. Indeed it was! We were carrying the excess water soaked up by the tent. There was no possible way of expelling the water; only fresh air could do that.

We had walked for one hour or so and were close to the mountain range surrounding Glencoe, which stands at just over 3,000 feet. Words actually fail me this time as to how to describe their beauty.

'I feel fatigued,' I lamented to Colin.

Colin admitted it was a hard slog going up the steady incline against the wind and rain.

'Look,' I said, 'it's starting to clear from the west!'

'We will rest in about ten minutes then,' said Colin. 'With a little luck it will be off by then.'

Sure enough it had dried out when we reached the falls in Glencoe. The water was pouring a fair distance over the rocks owing to the overnight deluge. Close to the falls, the noise was almost deafening as the cascade plunged into the pool below. With the sky now clear blue this was a magical experience.

We took off our wet tops and shirts as the sun was beginning to heat up the early afternoon air. 'A little sun won't do us any harm,' said Colin, now bare to the waist, as he opened the tent up and spread it on to the rock. I followed his example and spread the inner sheet on the ground and we lay down on the soft grass and snoozed for a while till everything was dry.

My thoughts returned to my visit to Inverary Castle and the lament which the piper had played in remembrance of the Glencoe massacre. I read a copy of the book, *White Shadow over Glencoe*, according to which the murders took place in the snow. I felt saddened with the outcome but enjoyed the book.

With the extra money we had made earlier and the particular savings on the tent we were still well in pocket. I myself had more money than I had started with.

'Now I am feeling extremely peckish,' I said to Colin, 'are you hungry?'

'I really am very hungry myself now,' he replied. 'Well, let's find a hotel or a restaurant!'

'That's what I wanted to hear. I don't think I could have gone to the hostel and then gone for food to return and cook it.' My energy level drained at the thought of this!

'I'm starved myself. Let's get a move on. The nearest hotel is only forty minutes' walk away and the village is the same, as I remember,' Colin lamented.

We arrived around one fifteen in the afternoon, only just in time for lunch. Home-made steak pie with trimmings was the chef's special of the day.

'We'll have two of your special,' Colin said, all the while making eyes at the pretty, smart little waitress.

'Sorry sir,' she said, 'I've only enough left for one portion. The only other main course is a ham salad.'

Colin without hesitation instructed the waitress to bring one of each, and to make them large portions along with a side plate of chips.

'Yes, sir, I'll see what I can do.'

Colin turned to me and told me not to worry – that he would halve the pie with me.

'That's fine, then!' I said curtly.

'Don't go into the huff, Jamie, you know I always share.'

I can honestly say that lack of food is my Achilles heel and is the only thing that makes me grumpy. The meal arrived very quickly to our gratification.

'That's smart,' said Colin. 'Look at the size of the pie, it's huge.'

'It was probably not sufficient enough for two portions,' I said to him.

'I'll halve it and put it on your side plate of chips,' said Colin.

'That will do nicely,' I said.

We tucked in and the plates were empty in no time at all.

'You lads must be very hungry!' said the young waitress, setting her eyes on the empty plates. 'We have half a dozen buttered rolls left from this morning's breakfast. You are both most welcome to them if you wish,' she told us.

'Will you charge us for two bags of crisps each, so that we can have crisp rolls later, which is one of my favourites?' said Colin.

'Which flavour of crisps do you prefer?' asked the young girl.

'One bacon, two cheese and onion and one plain, please,' Colin said.

We finished our cup of tea and the waitress returned with our order.

'Thank you very much for your hospitality and excellent service!' smiled Colin. 'I can recommend this establishment to my friends.'

The girl laughed and smiled broadly and said goodbye and disappeared. I let my imagination run wild. *Again!* No wonder she is laughing. The only friends out here we could have are the birds and the sheep, I thought.

We loaded up again and began our short journey to the youth hostel. Walking along the road near the hotel I saw a cycle go into a ditch a good distance from us. It was about five minutes before we eventually reached the spot. By then two girls had emerged, one holding a chain from her bicycle. She started pushing the now encumbering machine. The other walked her cycle as if in sympathy.

They had only walked a few yards away from the scene when Colin shouted, 'Can we help you?'

'No, you can't!' said the fiery redhead. 'We will manage fine by ourselves, thank you very much.'

Colin was lost for words. I'd never seen him so horrified before. We let them walk on and I spotted tyre marks in soft earth at the side of road. 'She must have lost control and gone into the ditch here, Colin!'

'You are probably right, Jamie!'

'If she is holding the chain I will bet the coupling and spring will be here. I'm quite sure neither of them would know what to look for,' I said.

'I don't know what to look for either!' said Colin.

'It just looks like the chain itself, only it's a very small part,' I said. 'You look for something made of metal and that will be fine.'

'OK, that sounds reasonable,' said Colin.

About five minutes later he produced the coupling. 'Is this what we're looking for?' he asked.

'Yes!' I said. 'Where did you find it? We need the spring to join it up to the chain.'

Colin showed me the spot and I found the missing part in a matter of seconds. 'Got it!' I said. 'I think I will play little mind games with them if they are staying at the hostel tonight. They obviously have had bad experiences with guys. Are you sure you haven't met them before somewhere, Colin?'

'That was a little below the belt even from you, Jamie boy' said Colin.

'Just kidding!' I said.

Although the girls were pushing their cycles they were still able to outpace us.

'That's them at the hostel now,' said Colin. 'Yes, they have stopped! I was right. I still find it strange, the attitude they adopted when we were only offering a hand.'

'Let that be your challenge for the week then, Colin,' I said.

'What challenge is that, Jamie lad?'

'Why they hate guys?'

'OK, you're on. If I get the answers then you buy me a couple of pints!'

'You're on!' I said, as I was sure he was going to fail.

'The hostel is only a short distance along the road from where we are. Further on it leads to Loch Leven and Glencoe village,' said Colin.

'I'm still in awe of the road through Glencoe and mountains towering above us – splendour yet with an eerie sense of foreboding. You can sense something sinister happened here, Colin,' I said.

'I have to agree. I'm sorry to use one of your adjectives, but it is a dramatic scene.'

I can't ever remember having felt small as I had done in the past few days with the vast openness of Rannoch Moor the previous day and the close proximity of the mountains above this day.

'Colin,' I said, 'the first thing I have to do this evening is to phone Bonnie and find out the exact time and place where Angus and Duncan will pick us up.'

'That's one lift we don't need to look for,' said Colin.

It will be a bonus just to hear her voice, I thought to myself.

'Does it feel good that you are set on Bonnie?' asked Colin.

'It does! I'm really smitten by her, even though I have other distractions.'

'I have had clear insight to those distractions, and very pretty they were too,' said Colin, tormenting me again.

Not to be outsmarted I challenged him, 'Where does your heart lie, Colin, Pitlochry or Lochearnhead?'

He was caught unawares by the swiftness of my reply and stammered an answer.

'I have to say that I love them both equally, which probably means I don't love either of them enough. On the other hand, it may be that I don't wish to commit to myself as you have done with so much at stake in the future.'

'Will you go back down to Pitlochry or Lochearnhead?' I enquired persistently.

'I haven't made up my mind yet.'

I wasn't about to let him off the hook that easily. 'Haven't made up your mind or won't tell?' I said.

'I am going back down to Pitlochry to see Fiona. I have phoned her three times since leaving her.'

'Three times, you sly so-and-so, and you never let on. No wonder you are good at cards, no one's ever going to guess your hand.'

We were now close to the hostel so I let the subject drop as I felt as though I had found his Achilles heel. When we arrived at the hostel I saw the cycle with chain missing and I made an excuse to Colin that I wished to wash my hands in the stream. 'You go on in and book us in. Remember, I want a bottom bunk!'

I took off my pack and made for the bicycle; the chain was lying on the ground beside it. That's a stroke of luck, I thought to myself.

Without more ado I set about fitting the missing coupling to the chain. I then took my Swiss knife from my pocket and proceeded to press the coupling on the connecting spring. This is the most difficult part and a strong hand is required and, dare I say it, it's a man's job. Having completed the task I then placed the chain on the cogs and worked it into position. Five minutes and the job was done. I retreated quickly into the hostel so that no one would be any wiser to what I had done.

Colin had found us a perfect bunk where we could look out on to the trees. 'I have chosen two top bunks for us,' said Colin. 'There is no one below us at present, which is a bonus, and the bunks are solid wood.'

'Oh, this is marvellous! I wish every hostel was like this one,' I said,

'We are lucky – it's midweek, and that is why it's quiet. The warden says there are only a few beds available at the weekend for walkers,' said Colin.

We went into the main lounge and had a cup of tea and generally relaxed. I felt myself nodding off with the walk and heat in the building, when suddenly I was prodded from behind. Startled, I rose to my feet.

'Did you interfere with my cycle outside?' came a loud demanding, voice at me. Interfere? That is not what I did. Gee whizz! What's with this girl?

By the time I was ready to answer her friend had appeared and Colin was nowhere to be seen. I'll have to choose my words carefully here, I thought.

'The thing is,' I said, 'my friend and I found the coupling for your chain just off the road and on seeing your cycle I thought I might as well fit the part in case you should need to go somewhere.'

Both the girls stood staring at me, then turned to one another before one spoke.

'Our behaviour was totally inappropriate towards you and I hope you will forgive us, as we really appreciate you fixing the bicycle.'

'No problem!' I said. 'Glad to be of service. Oh, I would get the chain tightened at the garage before you set off from the hostel. It's only a minor adjustment and it should only take two minutes. Perhaps if you smile at the mechanic he won't charge you.'

This remark brought an instant smile from them and they thanked me once more.

'Maybe if we see you in one of the bars we will buy you a drink.'

'That would suit me fine!'

'Bye for now then!'

On the road to the hotel, I told Colin all that had happened. 'Maybe they will tell you what their problem is with guys, seeing I have broken the ice.'

'Perhaps!' said Colin.

The trees seemed to close in on us as we headed for the village pub. 'I have a big thirst tonight,' said Colin. 'I fancy a few pints.'

A few pints he had, and he wasn't kidding. It was the happiest I'd seen him since he left Balloch, which seemed a lifetime ago. He confided in me that he knew Fiona really wanted to see him again, but he still had feelings for Jean. So he had decided to go back to Lochearnhead at the end of holiday and see whom he preferred. It was the only way he could think of to try to end his dilemma.

We left the public bar early as I was afraid Colin would not be allowed into the hostel. We walked for over an hour and I gave him a few mints to suck in case anyone smelled his breath. Luckily no one came near him as he made straight for the dormitory, and he went out like a light as soon as his head hit the pillow.

I slept well myself. This is the best hostel bed I have slept in – it must have been built with climbers in mind, I thought.

Chapter Twenty-four

'Wakey wakey, Colin me boy.'

'Oh, my head!'

'Serves you right spending all your money on the local brew,' I said. 'Come on. Get up and we'll get some good fresh air.'

He wasn't long in gaining his stamina once more after a hearty breakfast. On finishing our chore Colin decided that a walk to Kinlochleven would be the best cure for him. Half an hour into the walk he sighed, 'Ah, this is good, I feel so much better now. I hope you forgive me, Jamie, for being a pain in the butt.'

'No problem. As long as you don't make a habit of it.'

'This is a lovely walk, Jamie. The hills seem right on top of us and the loch is shimmering below us.'

'How far is it to Kinlochleven, Colin?'

'About five miles from here.'

'It's good to be able to stride out without the rucksacks; I feel I'm walking on air.'

'I felt like that last night, Jamie!'

I went into fits of laughter.

'Hey, isn't that those two girls' bikes in the ditch, Jamie?'

'Yes it is! That pair seems to like ditches,' I said.

As we got closer we heard a scream for help. 'Looks like one of them is in trouble!' said Colin.

'It's coming from over that ridge,' I said.

'Looks like we are in for a spot of climbing,' said Colin.

The big man scrambled up on all fours to the top of the ridge before I could even think about what to do. I followed cautiously behind as I had my previous encounter with danger still on my mind. Colin had disappeared by the time I got to the top but one of the girls greeted me and told me what had happened.

'Colin has told me to go down to the road and stop a car if possible and tell them to get the mountain rescue and ambulance for Nancy.'

'I'll come with you. What's your name?'

'Oh, it's Barbara.'

'Right, Barbara, we'll go sideways to get down and I'll go first.' It was a little slippy but we made it to the road without incident. 'This is where you come in,' I said. 'Blokes will stop for a woman in distress quicker than for a man.'

'Well, if you're sure,' said Barbara.

The first car that came along stopped as I said it would. We asked the occupant to phone the emergency services from the village and tell them to be as quick as possible.

While we were waiting, Barbara filled me in on what had happened and why they were so frosty towards us earlier. Apparently Nancy had wanted a photo from the top of the ridge, which she thought would show the full expanse of the loch. 'She lost her footing while taking the picture. I tried to reach her but I couldn't. That's when I started screaming. I was so relieved when your friend came so quickly.'

'Don't fret; Colin is well trained in first aid. I'm sure he will be able to console her till help arrives,' I said.

The mountain rescue team arrived in a matter of minutes, followed by the ambulance. In quick time a stretcher was at the ready, taken up and lowered to where Colin was. Two men preceded the stretcher to give a hand to raise Nancy on to it. It was a delicate operation, but Nancy, being only seven stone, was easily lifted on to it. I'm sure Colin could have managed it himself if need be.

The team above lowered a rope to the stretcher, which was attached by the team below. Once they were all in position they pulled up the stretcher slowly guided by Colin and his new mates. It took about five minutes to raise her as it had to be done very slowly. Once this was achieved she was lowered back down to the road and the waiting ambulance.

Although in a lot of pain Nancy thanked us for our assistance before going off to hospital. Barbara gave us a hug as she had been advised to go along to check if she was suffering from shock.

'Will you take the cycles back to the hostel for us? Oh, you are welcome to use them for the rest of the day if you wish,' said Barbara.

'Oh, that would be great, it will get us to Kinlochleven much earlier, allowing us to explore the area, not to mention the saving of energy and time on the way back,' said Colin.

The rescue team thanked us for our assistance, but Colin said, 'No, we thank you! I don't know what people would do if there was no mountain rescue.'

We waved them farewell and picked up our newfound transport.

'Do you fancy a cycle trip round the loch to Kinlochleven?' said Colin, laughing.

We arrived in the sleepy town and lay beside the loch, discussing the events of the day.

'Well, Jamie, tell me why they hate men!'

'That's easy,' I said. 'Nancy was to be married this week but her boyfriend got cold feet and disappeared two weeks ago. Apparently he hasn't been seen since.'

'That certainly explains it,' said Colin. 'She is obviously still suffering and so is her bridesmaid.'

'I forgive them! Do you?'

'Oh yes! The poor thing has a broken ankle into the bargain, along with her broken heart. I hope she meets someone nice soon, else the male population round her is in for a troublesome time. Right, Jamie, time for food.'

We were told by the warden in the morning that Nancy indeed had a fracture and she and Barbara wished they could say thanks to us personally. The warden let us off without a chore that morning owing to our excellent behaviour towards others.

'It's good to feel good about oneself, Jamie.'

'Yes it is, Colin.' I had to admit he had excelled himself in front of others and I was proud of him, but I never gave him too many compliments. I felt he didn't need his ego boosting.

Fort William now beckoned, which I was looking forward to. Bonnie had confirmed that her brothers Angus and Duncan would pick us up at the road adjacent to the Ballachulish ferry. We could have taken the ferry ourselves across the loch and waited for the bus on the other side of Loch Leven. However, this might have caused confusion and it also meant we would have to wait an extra half an hour for the bus to go around the loch via

Kinlochleven. To save hanging around we decided to wait for the bus on the south side of the loch, where we were at present.

'I'll let them know that,' said Bonnie on the phone. 'I miss you so terribly much. I wanted to come up to Fort William but Angus was totally against the idea. "Don't want you throwing yourself at this chap!" he said.'

'He is only protecting his little sister and you can't blame him for that, can you?' I said.

'I suppose not. I'll just have to wait till I see you in Inverness.' She sighed. 'Bye! Love you, can't wait till I see you.'

We set out on a dull, damp morning for Ballachulish. There was no hurry and it was only ten o'clock so we had two hours to enjoy the view along the loch towards the ferry. Again the weather changed, as it so often does up there. The sun broke through the clouds exposing the mountains to the full rays of the sun.

'That's the pap of Glencoe now visible through the mist,' said Colin, pointing to a strange-shaped peak. 'I'll let you work it out for yourself why they call it that!'

The trees were now basking in the sunshine, lit up and sparkling with light from droplets, giving an array of colour to the valley beyond.

'I like this place,' said Colin.

'You like everywhere you've been! You're the same with women. There is always something to match or better than the last.'

'Are you saying I'm shallow, Jamie?'

'No – whatever makes you think that?' I laughed out my reply.

We arrived at the ferry with about twenty minutes to spare. Feeling peckish we had a bag of crisps and a cola beside the loch. As the ferry crossed back and forth I noticed something familiar in the shape of a Morris van.

'Hey, Colin does that van have any resemblance to the one that stole our gear near Blair Atholl?'

'Let's take a closer look,' Colin replied.

'Not too close!' I said. 'In case they spot us.'

'No sweat!' said Colin. 'Look, they are both out of the van

now. One is having a smoke and the other is drinking a bottle of juice.'

The ferry had taken most of the original queue away, although the queue still remained the same length with the continual build up of traffic to make the short crossing.

'That's definitely them!' said Colin. 'I'd remember that gaunt chap anywhere. I didn't get a good look at the other one although I could see he had a chubby face with a sort of reddish fair hair much like yours, Jamie.'

'Look, I said it has an R-reg plate! It must be them!' I said excitedly.

Before we could say another word we could see a bus approaching. 'This must be Angus and Duncan coming,' I informed Colin.

The bus pulled alongside us and out jumped what could only be described as a man mountain.

'Hello! I'm Angus, Bonnie's big brother. Are you Jamie Cameron?'

He stood at six foot eight with the build of a Sherman tank.

'Pleased to meet you,' I said tentatively. 'I'm Jamie.'

'So you're the one that's captivated my wee sister's heart!'

I had no answer to that. Verdict... guilty.

Colin offered his hand and introduced himself to Angus.

'Please to meet you,' said Angus. 'Put your gear in the front two seats. We have no one in them. It will save us opening the boot. It's pretty full anyway.'

'Before we leave, there is something I should tell you, Angus.'

'What is it?' growled Angus. Obviously my choice of words was taken in the wrong context. I went on to explain: 'Did Bonnie tell you that we had our two rucksacks and tent stolen?'

'Indeed she did,' said Angus. 'If I get my hands on them...'

'Well, the thing is we are sure the two culprits are about to board the ferry the next time round.'

'Are they, by Jove!' growled Angus. 'Duncan! Duncan! Get your arse out here!'

Out stepped man mountain number two, an absolute giant of a man, maybe an inch or two shorter than Angus, with the exact frame of Colin. Colin whispered to me, 'I wouldn't like to fall out with your intended relatives!' Angus filled Duncan in on the developing situation. All I could hear was, 'Oh aye! Aye!'

Angus went into the bus and told the driver to collect us on the other side of the loch as we were all about to board the ferry. The bus drove off with everyone peering out of the rear window. I couldn't count the number of heads staring at us. They were obviously expecting some sort of action. This is where you put yourself in their shoes and let your imagination run riot. The boys will be betting on a punch-up or fight of some sort, I thought.

'Right!' said Angus, immediately taking charge. 'We won't all go together in case they take fright!'

Angus then walked with me down to the approaching ferry. After the ferry had been unloaded we boarded as foot passengers. Duncan and Colin waited for the last vehicle to go down the slipway before joining us. 'That's handy,' said Colin, 'the van is right at the back of the craft.'

As the ferry moved off Angus walked nonchalantly towards the van. Both occupants were at the back of the ferry and had no idea of the approaching Angus and what was taking place at the front of the van. We had all joined up by this time. Angus checked the van. 'That's a stroke of luck!' said Angus. 'The keys are still in the ignition.'

Angus growled his instructions to Duncan. 'Go down to the rear with Jamie one at a time, with a minute apart. I'll saunter down first and pass the time of day with them. Colin, you follow me.'

Angus manoeuvred into position then informed us that he was about to go down towards them, telling us to remember to space out the time. We could hear Angus strike up a conversation ever so gently.

'Right, Colin,' I said. 'You go now!'

As Colin joined them they obviously hadn't recognised him as laughter filled the air. 'They seem to be hitting it off well,' I said to Duncan.

'Right, go now Duncan,' I said. He walked slowly and began to lean over the railing before joining in any dialogue. It was now my turn. I moved forward. Duncan by this time was positioned at the rear of the passenger side. With no one able to see us we now moved in for the confrontation.

Angus, with a deep and complete change of attitude, glowering, said, 'Do you know these two lads?'

'No never seen them before! Why, what's the problem?'

'Problem is you stole their possessions up near Blair Atholl!'

'Not us!' said the burly one.

'How is it you're wearing Jamie's cap, then?' said Angus.

Their faces began to show the strain of the predicament they found themselves in. 'Well, maybe. It was just for a laugh,' said the slim one.

'The game's up!' said Angus. Seizing the burly one, he lifted him straight up with ease, while Colin grabbed his feet.

By now the ferry was fully halfway across the loch, which could be better described as a river when the tide is out. The loch was flowing very fast, so before ejecting him from the ferry, Angus enquired of him, 'Are you a good swimmer, lad?'

'Aye, why? You're not going to chuck me in, are you?'

'I sure am, boy!' said Angus.

With one heave he was in the water!

By this time Duncan had the thin one up in the air by himself. I was merely a bystander as he tossed him in the water without any assistance from me. With all the noise and commotion there came shouts of 'man overboard!' One of the deckhands came running to the stern and asked Duncan if they had fallen in.

'No,' Duncan replied, 'they quite fancied a dip as it was getting a bit hot for them.'

'It's against the law to dive off ferries,' the man said angrily.

'Ach, aye, they're only having a swim. You can overlook it this time, surely?' Angus asked.

'Well, just this time, but I'll give them a good talking to when they come over.'

'You do that!' said Angus.

'Oh, by the way, they left the keys in the van so that we can drive it off for them. They want to walk as well so they will collect it at the nearest lay-by. They want to get fit again. Trying to impress the ladies, I guess.'

'I'll tell the skipper what has happened, then. When he gets cross they'll feel the wrath of his tongue. You just don't mess with him.'

'That's OK,' said Angus. 'I'm sure they'll take it on the chin.'

The ferry docked and we all boarded the van, Angus and Duncan in the front and Colin and me in the rear. Angus waved to the staff as he as he drove off and they returned the compliment.

Angus parked the van just off the main Fort William road so that we could view the confrontation with the swimmers and the captain of the ferry. As they reached the shore they were met by a furious man gesticulating menacingly at them while they stood dripping wet.

'Serves them right,' said Angus. 'I'll move the van 100 yards or so and then let you lot off. The bus should only be a minute or two away by now. Tell the driver to pick me up at the next lay-by. I'll park it there for our friends.

'Oh, before you go there is a wallet with fifty pounds under the seat. How much was your gear worth?'

Colin replied, 'Well it wasn't new. We could pick up most of the equipment including the tent for thirty pounds.'

'Thirty pounds it is then,' said Angus, handing Colin the said sum. 'I'll be off, then!' He then replaced the wallet below the seat.

The bus arrived in a couple of minutes as Angus had said. We loaded our gear on the front seats and settled down. Angus, meantime, had parked the van and was waving towards the bus a few hundred yards forward. As he entered the coach there was an almighty cheer. Obviously word had spread quickly of his dastardly deed.

He bowed to the applause and then turned to face me before taking his seat. 'Oh, with all the excitement I quite forgot about a letter I'm carrying for you. Yes, it's from my wee sister Bonnie. I see that pleases you!' The very mention of her name made my heart leap. On receiving the letter I thanked him.

'No problem! I love Bonnie and I don't want her hurt,' said Angus.

'So do I, and I would never hurt her.'

'That's OK then. We understand each other.'

I wondered what Bonnie had to say in her letter! I only managed to resist the temptation of opening it because Colin was sitting beside me and would have seen the contents.

It's a scenic journey from Ballachulish; the main trunk road follows the shores of Lynnie all the way to Fort William. Colin commented on the views ahead. 'That's Ben Nevis now, just to the right of us, overshadowing the town.'

'It's a strange shape – not what I envisaged,' I replied.

'Ah, you have to go over to Corpach for the best views. If you have seen any calendar pictures then most likely they would have been taken from there.'

Finally we turned towards Glen Nevis and my frustration was now beginning to get the better of me. Then Colin said, 'You can read your letter shortly, Jamie boy. I'm sure you are desperate to find out what she has to say.'

He was correct and I felt I had to respond. 'Yes, I can hardly contain myself, only I want to read it in privacy.'

'No problem. That's us now. You stay on the bus and I'll tend to all gear and lend a hand should Angus require it.'

I nodded and he left me.

I ripped the envelope apart and quickly unfolded the letter. It read:

From your naughty Baby,

I tried so desperately to be with you this week; but my older sibling Angus, being overprotective, would have none of it. Even pleading with my parents failed to bring any joy. He went as far as to say that he didn't want his young sister throwing herself at the first boyfriend she has gone out with, whom she knows virtually nothing about. I said that's not fair!

However, he continued to find excuses and insisted there were no other women or females in the company. I told him I have my own tent. He persisted by saying, 'You are still not going, and that's the end of it.'

I wish I could still come but it's out of the question now so I'll have to wait patiently till next Saturday.

Till I see you in Inverness
All my love
Bonnie
xxxxxxxxxxxxxxxxxx

Chapter Twenty-five

The eager young lads were not long in emptying the bus of its contents. Sprightly at fourteen and fifteen, they were enjoying the freedom of the fresh air and were bursting with energy. They performed every task with enthusiasm and virtual ease. While one lot were setting up the tents the others were making the charcoal fire for cooking under the supervision of the teacher.

A large bag of pre-peeled potatoes were put into three large pots, plus two large tins of mince, onion and peas, which are used for catering purposes. The meal was ready for all in under an hour which was a credit to all concerned.

'Everything has to work like clockwork when you have twenty-five hungry lads to feed,' said Angus.

'How do you afford the coach hire?' I enquired.

'Oh, we get it on the cheap! The company is owned by uncle,' said Angus. 'The lads save up two shillings a week throughout the year to pay for all the other overheads.'

'I'll bet they look forward to the break,' I said.

'It's good for lads to get into the hills and experience the wildlife first hand. It helps build up character,' said Angus.

'I can see they don't seem to mind the chores,' said Colin.

'It's for their own benefit,' said Angus. 'The sooner camp's set up the quicker we eat. Appetite is a big thing. I'm sure you both will relate to that.' We nodded in agreement.

The boys all had their own plastic cup, plate, fork, knife and spoon and had the charge of keeping them clean. Even small things like washing and cleaning add up to their responsibility. My impression of Colin's washing and cleaning was non-existent, as he used his charm on women to his advantage.

After supper, which was at nine o'clock in the evening, we all gathered round the campfire. Angus produced a guitar from the tent but before he could start playing the coach driver gave him a time when he would return to pick them up.

Big Angus and Colin burst into song and the boys sang up even if it was only to mock and make fun. After a while I rendered a few songs and most of the lads joined in.

'Right lads,' Calum shouted, 'ten fifteen. I want you lot up bright and early. We are taking a stroll over to Corpach first thing tomorrow morning.'

There were two large tents with just enough room for twenty-five boys with sleeping bags, and a bell-type tent for the four leaders – Angus, Duncan, Allan and Mike. Colin and I pitched our tent in close proximity to the bell tent.

When all the other leaders had retired, Angus decided to call it a night. 'Right, lads, we have an early start tomorrow, time to hit the hay.'

It was a quick wash at eight-thirty in the morning. Another sunny day beckoned. Colin and I took a rucksack between us as we wished to be free to explore the area by ourselves, free from company. We found a nice spot where were could enjoy the views.

Later that day after our walk we returned to camp and dinner was prepared. Angus asked if we wanted to join them. 'It'll only cost you a shilling each for a full meal.'

'Fine,' said Colin, and I nodded in agreement.

After dinner the lads hadn't burned up enough energy and suggested a tug of war. 'Give us half an hour to let our dinner go down and the six of us will take on the lot of you,' said Angus. The lads waited patiently until big Angus signalled he was ready. 'Right, Jamie, Colin, Allan, Duncan, Mike. We can take them,' laughed Angus.

The rope was produced from the tent by Duncan. 'Let's make a mark here!' With a stick he made a deep incision on the ground.

'Right,' Angus said, 'twelve of you against the six of us.'

The boys became animated and stood in line facing Duncan.

Angus was our anchor man. The boys had their heaviest youngster in a similar position.

'OK! When I say pull we all take the strain. Then we heave when ready.' The rope became taut at the call from Angus. 'Heave!' shouted Angus, and we caught them off guard. As we pulled them over the line there were cheers from the leaders.

'Right,' Angus said, 'sixteen of you. Let's see if you can take us.' This time the boys held firm and it was only after a matter of minutes, when their stamina gave in, that they were forced over the line.

'Give us time to get our breath back and we'll take on the lot of you,' said Angus. There were two dozen in all.

'We'll never do it,' Colin sighed to me. 'We might as well save the effort.'

Angus had other ideas, though – he was going to cheat. 'Right, go and fill the water buckets for supper,' he said. When they were out of sight, Angus said, 'Now go and fetch the water container beside the tent, Colin.'

Cunningly, when the lads were out of sight, Angus poured water on the area on the opposition side but only at the middle where it might not be too obvious. By the time the lads returned to their position the water had been soaked up by the dry earth, hiding the evidence.

'Right! Are you ready?' shouted Angus.

'Aye!' the cry was.

The rope went taut; I could see by the expressions on the lads' faces that they were determined to beat us. I felt a slight movement towards the line from our side. We're beaten this time, I thought.

'Come on!' Angus bellowed. 'Let's have one last tug.'

With this the lads started to slip. The power and momentum, along with the slippery conditions, brought them slithering over the line.

'Victory to the leaders,' said Angus.

A spokesman for the boys complained that they felt that they could not win because the surface had become slippy.

'Aye, well, seeing that there was as many of you the weight would bring the dampness to the surface,' said Angus, turning and winking to us all the while.

'We want a second chance,' said one of the boys.

'OK, tomorrow or the next day,' Angus said.

Satisfied, the boy returned to the group.

I asked Angus and Duncan how they came to be involved with the youth group – as my dad says it's wrong that MBE and OBE nominations are given to people who are just doing their job. As a youth leader himself he said he would give money to clubs in poor areas where government has failed. 'You are a perfect example of what my dad spoke about. You are helping youth by encouragement and example along with adventure. Yet you get recognition from no one.'

'We don't do it for silly medals. We do this because we are still boys at heart,' explained Angus. 'We like to pass on our skills as well and hope the lads will follow in our footsteps.'

'My dad says that one day governments will see the error they are making and will be forced to pay for good youth leaders.'

Before retiring we saw two girls approaching the fire. 'Look, Jamie,' said Colin, 'it's Maureen and Liz – the girls we met camping near Tyndrum before we went to Glencoe.'

'So it is!' I said.

'Well, you've made it,' Colin said to the girls. I introduced them to Angus and the rest of the company. I could see that Maureen was fascinated by Angus and was not shy in her manners. Likewise with Liz towards Duncan, making it quite plain she would take him as a challenge. Had we found a match for the two big men, I wondered.

'We are climbing the Ben tomorrow, girls,' said Angus, 'and you're welcome to join us if you wish.'

'We'll try, but I'm not sure if we will be able to reach the summit,' said Maureen.

Wait till I tell Bonnie that two girls have joined the group to climb Ben Nevis tomorrow at the invitation of big brother Angus, I thought. Boy will she give him dog's abuse when he returns home. So much for it being a men-only outing! I'm sure he will be eating his words.

Colin and I left the leaders with Liz and Maureen, who were in fits of laughter at the stories being told by Angus.

'Now there's a match if ever I saw one! Or is it two?' said Colin.

I was glad Colin had opted for an early night. I had never climbed any higher than a few hundred feet, but I had a fair idea that climbing a Ben would sap a lot of energy on nearing the summit with the thin oxygen level.

After breakfast the next morning a guide joined us in camp. His name was Archie and he was a native of Fort William. He took part in the yearly race up the mountain. He was a well-mannered chap, but also very strict. 'I don't stand for any tomfoolery on this climb. You will obey my rules to the letter,' he said. 'The important thing to remember is to follow the track and don't deviate from it. If you cannot go on, tell someone and remain where you are and we'll collect you on the way down.'

He went on to tell us that he entered the race every year and there were many entrants, mature as well as female.

'Races up!' I said to Colin.

'They actually do run up it,' said Colin. 'A good few years back they even drove a car to the top.'

Aye, and the band played, I thought to myself.

The bus took us to the starting point, which was a bonus. Having retrieved our rucksacks from the boot we set off with Archie leading. I shared my rucksack with Colin. I made sure I took it for the first half of the climb, for two reasons: one, I wanted make sure there would be something to eat when we stopped for a break; two, I felt it would be easier to scale the final ascent without any encumbrance.

It was game for Liz and Maureen to attempt the climb, but I'm sure they had ulterior motives. After an hour of continual walking we stopped for a well-earned break.

'Tough, isn't it, Colin?' I said.

'It's certainly steeper than I imagined,' said Colin.

The girls all the while were sticking close to Angus and Duncan while the teachers took charge of the boys, who were bouncing about as if it were a Sunday afternoon stroll. I thought I was pretty fit but they made a mockery of that.

'The girls are faring well, Colin, maybe they have done something similar in the past.'

'It's possible. Remember, they are Geordie lassies,' said Colin.

We set off once more and had a few more stops before reaching the final incline. To the delight of the youngsters there was snow on the final approach.

Without warning a missile hit me on the back of the neck and all hell let loose as another followed. This continued for about five minutes with both Colin and me the prime targets. Did we retaliate? Yes, of course we did!

It was brought to an abrupt halt when Angus and Archie spotted the mêlée.

'We're for it when reach the summit,' said Colin.

'Aye, it'll be another earbashing lecture from big Angus,' I said.

The girls were really in trouble now they had hit snow. Angus had given his rucksack to one of the youngsters and had taken Maureen by piggyback on the final stretch. Liz, not to be outdone, had fallen at the feet of Duncan and was now being transported in similar vein.

'I think they will really be enjoying themselves now,' said Colin, laughing.

'You could be right,' I said.

On reaching the top, Angus gathered us all round for a group photo.

'He won't be able to hide the evidence from Bonnie now!' I said to Colin.

The girls all took separate pictures and promised to send us all copies. The view from the top was superb and I asked Liz to take photos of Loch Lynnie and the surrounding mountains.

It was time to return and I felt we could get down a lot quicker, but Archie insisted that he should take the lead as more accidents tend to happen on the way down. I could understand that, but there were moans from the younger party.

There were a few stories to tell round the campfire with all having their own versions of events. Angus and Duncan by this time had been persuaded by the girls to have an evening at the pub. Colin and I duly obliged to stay with the lads and have a few fun games.

The boys were in their tents by the time that the foursome returned, leaving Colin, me and the teacher to the quiet of the evening.

'They will be tired now,' said Duncan, 'after the climb.'

'I'm starting to feel it myself,' I said.

'I'll second that,' said Colin.

We retired after a short chinwag with the girls and not

forgetting Angus and Duncan. The girls had had such a wonderful time – so much so they told Angus and Duncan they wished to remain with the group for the duration of their stay, which the leaders readily agreed to. Not only that, Angus promised to take them back to the Borders on the coach and then drop them off home in his car.

'What do think, Jamie boy, are they heading for the altar?'

'I don't know about that, but one thing for sure is they are in for some strong words from Bonnie. I can hear it now, "You can take strange women on holiday but not your sister!" It is odd how things twist and turn though.'

'Night all! See you in the morning!'

We awoke to a fresh morning.

'This is a good day for walking,' said Colin.

'Yes, it is,' I said. I could tell he was getting itchy feet. He wasn't a boy who liked organised sports or group activity. Although he had a main plan of direction it was never set in stone. Spontaneity suited him, changing direction on a whim at the time he dictated.

'Whenever breakfast is finished we will set out for Fort Augustus,' said Colin.

'That suits me fine,' I said.

The boys had the meal ready for us when we got up. 'Well done lads! You will make some girls very happy,' said Colin laughingly.

The girls and the crew gathered to say goodbye. 'We have enjoyed your hospitality over the past few days!' I said.

'I'm pleased to have met you,' said Angus. 'My wee sister has made a good choice after all. You have a good holiday with her and tell all my relations I'm asking for them and I hope to visit them shortly.'

Big Duncan shook my hand and wished me well. 'I'm glad we were able to assist you down at the ferry the other day.'

I had quite forgotten that, with all the other excitement going on. Thanks again for that!' I said.

'No problem!' said the big, quiet man.

By this time, the girls were hugging Colin, as usual. I gave them both a hug and wished them well for the future. They knew what I meant and both went into fits of laughter.

'Bye-bye!' – from us both, and we were on the road once more.

Colin set off at a brisk pace with his plans set in his mind. 'It's around twenty-five miles to Fort Augustus. We will have our first stop at Spean Bridge, which is roughly ten miles away,' he said.

I had read an article about Spean Bridge telling how the commandos trained for combat during the war. This was thought to be an ideal place, through its isolation, for honing their skills in the art of sabotage. According to the findings, it proved to be a valuable asset and a memorial has been set up to commemorate those brave men who fought and died for their country.

I had to tell Colin to slow down a little as I felt he was over-doing it. The confinement to camp had obviously not agreed with him. I'm quite sure that if I hadn't wanted to stay with the group he would have climbed the Ben and moved on.

'Hey, Colin, are we jogging to Spean Bridge?' I asked.

'I feel really fit this morning and I am enjoying the fresh breeze.'

'Spare a thought for me, then. You have long legs, therefore I have to make three strides for your two.'

I remember having our photos taken by Colin's friend who, after having them developed, referred to me as 'your big pal'. Colin found this amusing as I was four inches shorter than him.

I have a long back and short legs, so when I sit down I look as if I'm taller than Colin. The friend had never seen me standing up and looking at the prints you would not condemn him for the confusion.

Chapter Twenty-six

We arrived in Spean Bridge in two-and-a-half hours, which was our best time ever with the tent.

'How are you feeling now, Jamie boy?' asked Colin.

'Not bad, considering,' I replied.

'We have made good time!' said Colin.

The girls had prepared some sandwiches for us before we had left camp. Boy, were they welcome!

The signpost ahead of us said Fort Augustus straight on, Roy Bridge and Newtonmore to the right. We were about to set off on the road once more when a car pulled alongside us.

'I'm going to Fort Augustus, if that is any help to you?'

'It certainly is!' said Colin. 'That's where we are headed for the next two nights.'

I was surprised that a young woman on her own had stopped for us, especially an attractive one. Colin was in his element and was not long in requesting the reason for her visit to Fort Augustus. 'Have you relations in the area?' enquired Colin.

'Not as such,' she replied. 'I am staying with a friend I met when on holiday.'

'Oh, that is nice,' said Colin, commanding all the conversation.

'I was travelling in Europe doing much the same as you when we met up three years ago. We have remained friends ever since.'

I now realised why she picked us up; being a hiker herself she had obviously taken lifts from many strangers herself.

I wouldn't like Bonnie taking lifts from anyone, I thought. Maybe I'm overcautious! I feel a woman is very vulnerable on her own and even with a partner. Still, it's their choice.

My ears were still ringing from the lecture we got from the police officer in Pitlochry about taking lifts which could jeopardise our well-being and also give them extra work.

Not wanting to be left out of the conversation I asked where she came from; although she spoke perfect English I felt that she was not from Britain.

'Are you English?' I asked.

'I should take that as a compliment! But the answer is no. I'm from Sweden.'

Colin now entered once more into the conversation. 'I should have known that.'

'Why? What makes you say that?' said Inger.

'Your lovely silk blonde hair for a start, and your name of course,' said Colin.

'I suppose that is a giveaway,' she replied.

'How long are you staying in Fort Augustus?' I asked.

'For one week only,' she replied. 'I'm actually living and working in England at the moment.'

'Whereabouts?' asked Colin.

'What you call the Midlands,' she said.

'May I ask what your profession is?' said Colin inquisitively.

'Oh, I am on a three-year study working for British heavy industry, looking into work-related back pain and injuries. It's quite complex as you have all manners of different shapes and sizes working in industry. The number of days lost through back pain and injuries is absolutely staggering and that is why a special team has been called in.'

'You will be looking into how people lift and stretch, I imagine,' I said.

'Yes, that is one essential part of the study,' she replied.

'You are a back specialist then,' said Colin.

'I am indeed. I have a degree in the orthopaedic study of the body.'

'Have you an opinion on the matter yourself?' I asked.

'Yes, but it's only a personal one, I have to emphasise. Most men at forty start to develop tummies and are not what you would call fit. They may still have strength but they lack the suppleness of youth. Strangely we have young men prone to backache for no apparent reason, hence the study. It's hoped that our findings will help to find the main causes and then a solution towards resolving it.

'Before you tell me about yourselves will you take a look at the car behind? It has followed me all the way from Kinlochleven!'

My first thought was of *The Thirty-nine Steps*: murder and intrigue. Had she been mistaken for a spy? Was the car we were in bugged, and were we about to be taken hostage? Get real, Jamie! Check the number plate first.

'Slow down a little so that we can take a note of the registration,' said Colin.

For once he was ahead of me in thought.

'I missed it,' I said, 'but it's a Vauxhall, which helps.'

'You say it has followed you all the way from the Kinlochleven. Are you positive?' I asked.

'Well, come to think of it I may have seen it as I left Glasgow, but I didn't pay it much attention as the road was pretty busy. It caught up with me on a slow part of the road which wasn't a busy stretch and then it started flashing its lights behind me. It then tried to force me off the road when overtaking me. My car has a more powerful engine and I managed to outrun him by anticipating his intentions.'

'He is definitely after something,' said Colin.

'Put on your radio!' I said.

'Why?' asked Inger.

'There may have been something on the radio which can connect to your car to the pursuer.'

'It's on the hour,' said Colin, 'so the main news will be on now.'

'HERE IS THE SCOTTISH NEWS. THERE WAS A JEWEL ROBBERY IN GLASGOW AROUND TEN O'CLOCK THIS MORNING. THE ROBBERS ESCAPED WITH TWO BOXES OF EXPENSIVE RINGS AND A RARE NECKLACE, WHICH WERE PLACED IN A LARGE BROWN ENVELOPE AT THEIR INSISTENCE. IT HAS BEEN REPORTED THAT ONE MAN, THOUGHT TO BE ONE OF THE THIEVES, WAS ARRESTED HALF A MILE FROM THE SCENE OF THE CRIME. ON QUESTIONING THE SUBJECT SAID THAT HE WAS RUNNING FOR A BUS AND KNEW NOTHING OF A ROBBERY. HE HAS NOW BEEN RELEASED WITHOUT CHARGE AS NO EVIDENCE OF IDENTIFICATION CAN LINK HIM TO THE INCIDENT. A BLUE VAUXHALL CAR IS BEING SOUGHT AS IT WAS SEEN SPEEDING AWAY FROM THE AREA.'

'Well, that's a blue Vauxhall that's behind us,' I said.

'That doesn't explain why it's following you then, Inger, unless your car may be carrying the stolen goods,' said Colin.

'Where could they have put them?' asked Inger.

'Was your boot locked?' I asked.

'Yes, I think so,' said Inger.

'Well, we are certainly not stopping to find out!' I said.

'I'll second that!' said Colin.

'What do we do?' said Inger.

'We drive straight to the first police station in Fort Augustus,' I said.

'I still can't fathom how they put it in the car if your boot was locked. Were you parked near to the jeweller's mentioned, Inger?'

'I was parked in a piece of land which was cleared for development. There were twenty or more cars parked and mine was right at the rear,' said Inger.

'That would explain why they would select your car, as it was out of view to the public eye,' I replied.

'I wish we could see in the boot,' said Colin. 'We will look pretty foolish if there is nothing there.'

'Wait a minute!' I said. 'Was your little pilot window open when you left the car?'

'Yes, it was!' exclaimed Inger.

'The newscaster said that the two boxes containing the rings were put in a brown envelope. If they pushed it through the window then it would have gone under the driver's seat.'

'You may be right!' said Colin. 'I'll try to make room so that I can check below Inger's seat. First of all I'll have to put the rucksacks on the passenger side.'

Colin is somewhat cumbersome in confined spaces. I wouldn't like to be as bulky as that. It must be really awkward at times for him. I have a perfect frame and size – well, maybe unlucky to be a couple of inches lacking in height. It took Colin minutes to rearrange the rucksacks and then it was still going to be a struggle for him to look under the seat. After a few attempts he gave up, saying, 'I just can't get down to see!'

I was beginning to get a little frustrated with him at this point. 'Well, use your initiative!' I blurted out.

'What are you saying, Jamie! I am thick? Is that what you are suggesting?'

'No! What you should do is lean over and feel under the seat with your hands. You will have to stretch over the top ridge under the seat, though.'

'OK, got you,' he said.

Fumbling around for a minute or two, with the added vocals of a few moans, he finally shouted, 'I have something. It's definitely an envelope!'

'Well, bring it out then!' I said excitedly.

'I would if I could, you impatient little brat!' he shouted.

'Now boys, behave!' said Inger coolly. 'I'm sure Colin is doing his best.'

Huh! The women always take his side, I thought bemoaningly to myself.

'I've got it!' Colin suddenly exclaimed jubilantly. Colin produced a large brown envelope and quickly opened it without tearing it. He emptied the contents on to the seat and sure enough it produced two boxes.

'Do you wish to open them?' said Colin to me.

'No! You go ahead,' I said.

'Boy oh boy!' said Colin. 'No wonder they are chasing you. This lot will be worth a fortune. There are forty rings in each box. Not only that, the diamonds are huge!'

'They obviously chose the biggest diamonds so that they can be broken up,' I said.

'Is the car still following us?' asked Inger.

'Yes! It's even closer now. They must be becoming very impatient,' I replied.

'I only hope they don't get desperate before we reach a police station,' sighed Colin.

The words were no sooner out of his mouth when the blue Vauxhall tried to overtake us on a straight stretch of road. 'Put your foot down, Inger!' I shouted. 'We don't want them ahead of us as that would surely be to their advantage.'

They obviously felt compelled now to make their move before we hit the next town. Inger could handle the car well. I have never been in Sweden but I can imagine there will be many treacherous roads through the mountains, not to mention the snow and icy conditions.

'I can see you are no slouch when it comes to driving!' I said.

'What is slouch?' she asked.

'Never mind,' I said.

'I have been driving since I was eighteen. The roads, especially in the countryside, can be tricky! Is that how you would say it?' She laughed.

'Yes,' I smiled, 'that is how we would say it.'

'Where I live it is important that I drive. It enabled me to be free to drive to university and of course other chores. Both my brothers and sister drive. My dad taught us round the yard so we would pass first time.'

The big Ford car leapt forward as she put the accelerator to the floor and we were flung over the seat with the ferocity of the surge.

'That caught them out!' said Colin.

'I suggest you go as hard as you can,' I said. 'Decelerate before the bends and put the foot down when you're on the curve. This will stop them from passing. Both cars are similar in engine capacity so it will depend on you, Inger, to outdrive them.'

We were only a mile short of Fort Augustus when the worst possible thing that could transpire did occur: a puncture!

'OH NO!' shouted Colin. 'The tyre's blown, I don't believe it!'

'OK, don't panic,' I said to Colin.

I told him to replace the boxed diamonds inside the envelope and put it back under the seat. 'Let's play dumb. I'll do the talking,' I explained.

'OK, Jamie.'

Colin followed my instructions to the letter. Moments later, we pulled into a convenient lay-by. Before we could exit the car two masked men approached, one brandishing a gun.

'Get out of the car!' We readily obliged. 'Keep your hands down. We don't want to draw any unwanted attention, do we? Now open your boot and start replacing your wheel with the spare.'

The other robber searched the car and shouted, 'It's below the seat!'

'OK, let's go. Why didn't you stop earlier?' asked the gunman.

Inger answered, 'I panicked because I was by myself in the car!'

They both gave a sort of grunt which I took as their being satisfied with the explanation.

They made off and the first thing I checked was the number plate. 'Clever lot,' I said, 'they have obscured the number plate with dirt, making it illegible.'

'They had planned the robbery carefully but things never work to plan!' said Colin.

'They had clever masks on – quite funny as they looked like the Lone Ranger twins but for the moustaches!'

'Do you think they were real?' asked Inger.

'No,' I replied. 'I have never seen a moustache as thick as that before.'

It was a clever idea and worked in practice. When we were forced out of the car no one would notice their disguise from behind, not like a hood with holes. Anyone passing by would have spotted a hood and alerted the police.

'Right, let's get the spare on and get out of here,' said Colin.

We had the spare fitted in quick time and were now underway.

'Right, what do we do now?' I asked.

Before Colin could reply to the question he let out an oath.

'What is it?' we asked.

'One of the rings is on the floor. It must have fallen out when I was closing the box.'

'I hope they don't check the contents or we are in for big trouble!' I said.

'You spoke too soon, Jamie! Look, they have stopped their car on the verge just up the road.'

'Oh they must have checked the contents,' shouted Inger in a panicky voice.

'That's for sure!' said Colin.

'Put the foot down, Inger,' I said in a slightly raised voice.

'He is moving out!' shouted Inger.

'Give it all you've got. We have the advantage at the moment being up in speed,' I said.

We were level with the robbers now and they turned the vehicle in an attempt to hit us broadside. In a quick manoeuvre, Inger's skill at the wheel came to the fore. Guessing what they were up to, she braked quickly, catching their rear bumper a glancing blow. The blue Vauxhall then went out of control and hurtled through the hedge on the driver's side. If it hadn't been so serious, it would have been funny.

'Do we stop?' shouted Inger.

'Not on your life!' yelled Colin. 'Let's head for the nearest police station.'

'I hope they are all right,' said Inger.

'Who cares!' replied Colin.

'Do you think they were concerned about our plight when they were trying to run us off the road and into a ditch?' I asked.

'No, I suppose not,' replied Inger.

Chapter Twenty-seven

Twenty minutes later we found a small police station in Fort Augustus, much to our relief. Colin took command of the situation by relating all the facts to the desk sergeant. He also handed over the ring which was a stolen item in the robbery.

'I'll contact Inverness and Glasgow right away,' said the officer on duty. 'I'll have to ask you to stay here till I find out what action will be taken, in case you have to be questioned further by CID.'

'No problem,' said Colin, 'only glad to be of service.'

I wasn't too sure about this. What if we had to wait till someone came up from Glasgow?

According to the message from Glasgow, it was in the best interests of all concerned that we should be kept in a cell overnight, while Inger was taken home. The car was to be kept at the station and assistance would be sent from Inverness.

'It's six o'clock now,' said the sergeant. 'I'll have a couple of CID officers with you before ten o'clock – well, that's what I have been told – so you make yourselves comfortable in the cell and I'll send out for a meal for you.'

Inger kissed us goodbye and said, 'Sorry for giving you so much trouble.'

'Don't fuss,' said Colin, being his usual gallant self. 'We have enjoyed the thrill!'

We put our rucksacks in the cell, feeling slightly downhearted.

'A fine mess this is,' I said to Colin. 'You should have been more careful when you closed the box.'

'Sorry, Jamie! I just didn't see the ring fall on the floor,' he replied.

'It's OK. I just don't fancy spending a night in here.'

'Neither do I, but what can be done?' asked Colin.

'Not much I suppose. We'll have to grin and bear it,' I said.

We were given a fish and chip tea which was excellent under the circumstances. I lay down on the bed as I felt quite exhausted by the morning's walk and subsequent events. What will my mum and dad say when they find out I have spent a night in a police cell? I thought inwardly.

'Wake up, Jamie,' said Colin. 'Two detectives have arrived and want us to tell them all the events of the day.'

The two policemen were in plain clothes and were well spoken.

'I want you to tell me everything from the beginning, lads. Jamie and Colin, is that correct?

'Yes, it is, sir,' I replied.

'Your friend Colin will tell us his version to my sergeant and then we will check whether your stories match up and see if there is anything left out.'

After I had given my account of events he left me to join his sergeant, who had completed his task with Colin. About half an hour lapsed and they returned to the cell where Colin and I were placed.

'OK, lads, your versions match perfectly so I assume nothing has been overlooked.' He went on to tell us about the robbery itself and that this gang was dangerous.

'Look, lads, I can't hold you but I recommend you stay in the cell until tomorrow at least till we try to establish the whereabouts of these individuals. There was no sign of them at the place you spoke about. However, a large hole in the hedge was discovered which would back up your story.'

It was late now so we reluctantly accepted B&B in the station.

We were awoken early with a shout from a young constable not much older than ourselves.

'Wakey wakey! Here is your breakfast, lads. Sleep well, did you?' he enquired.

'Not bad, considering,' said Colin.

'Well, it's double eggs and sausage with bacon rolls. Is that acceptable to you both?'

'Brilliant!' I replied.

'Well at least we won't set the forest on fire this morning trying to cook breakfast – and last night's dinner for nothing!' said Colin, whispering in my ear.

One thing Colin had in his favour was his quick change to

happiness from an extreme low point. I envied that as I tended to hold on to the menace that had caused me concern. Colin's philosophy was to get it out of the system as quick as possible and focus on the opportunities that lay ahead. He had immediately pointed out the benefits of our night in voluntary custody such as savings on food.

About ten o'clock the two CID officers came to see us. 'Well, lads, you can go if you wish. Circumstances have overtaken the events of yesterday.'

What did he mean?

'There has been another robbery, this time at a post office twenty miles from here, which is quite unique in this part of the world. I can only put it down to the gang that were chasing you. Probably they were short of cash and picked their target at random.

'Well that's it, lads, leave your contact telephone numbers with the desk officer and you're free to go. Thanks for your help! Bye.'

We picked up our rucksacks and gave our home telephone numbers plus Bonnie's aunt's at Inverness.

'Have a nice holiday lads,' said the officer.

We stepped into the fresh air quite relieved at being free to move on once more.

'Colin,' I said, 'I'm not convinced that the post office robbery was down to our pursuers.'

'They were short of cash, that's what the detective said.'

'I know that, Colin, but he didn't say it was an armed hold-up.'

'Let's forget it, Jamie, and enjoy our holiday,' Colin replied.

We had only gone 100 yards up the road when a car pulled up beside us. It was Inger. 'Are you all right?' she asked. 'I haven't slept a wink thinking about the two of you.'

'We're fine,' replied Colin. 'Jamie is just a little traumatised.' Without warning Inger gave me a motherly hug and kissed me on both cheeks.

'I'm sure he'll feel much better now!' Inger said.

'Oh, by the way, did I say I was feeling a little below par myself?' Colin moaned.

'Oh, come here!'

She gave him a hug as best she could – usually it's him that does the hugging – then she kissed him.

'Is that better?' she asked him.

'Much!' replied Colin.

By this time her friend Karin had joined us and Inger introduced her to us. 'This is Karin and she is my travelling companion I was telling you about.'

Colin took her hand and kissed it. He's at it again, I thought. The charm this man can turn on! Her face was filled with excitement by his advance towards her. She was much younger than Inger. She looked about sixteen, but was probably in the region of twenty-two.

What gave this away was the fact that she was in her final year at university. Inger had told us earlier that Karin had a year gap from her studies to explore the world.

Karin then shook my hand and said, 'I wondered if you would wish to stay at our place for a couple of nights and we will show you around the area. I'm afraid there is no spare room at the house but we thought you could pitch the tent in our back garden. It's spacious and secluded for you. You will be able to use our toilet and washroom facilities. What do you think?'

'Absolutely perfect!' said Colin.

'Yes!' I said instantly.

'That's fine. We'll take you home to get a wash and freshen up. I'm sure you will want to change after spending the night in there.'

'Are you saying we stink?' Colin asked with a grin on his face.

Karin was more than a match for him and responded by saying, 'The only thing fresh about you is your tongue, my boy!'

I could see this relationship would have some good old ding-dongs ahead of it.

Karin took us home where we had a bath and change of clothing. Both Inger and Karin suggested that we set up our tent in the garden right away and they would lend a hand. Boy, were they hopeless! Every piece they attempted to join up was the wrong one. I'm quite sure they were doing it to create a little mischief.

'No one could be as handless as that,' Colin said to me quietly.

'Correct,' I replied.

After a few moments' thinking, Colin suggested they go inside and hold up the tent to enable us to put the parts together. In other words the girls became the two main pillars. They fell for it and went inside. They were now effectively supporting the cover themselves while Colin and I sat laughing on the grass.

'Where are you?' shouted Karin. 'You must have the frame put together by now.'

Inger then cried, 'I can't hold it up any longer, and her side went down in a heap followed by a screaming Karin, who yelled 'Wait till I get my hands on the pair of you!'

'That will teach you not to take the mickey out of us,' Colin said, lifting up the tent cover while I gave them my hand and pulled them both out to their instant relief.

'I was suffocating in there!' said a not-so-pleasant Karin.

Inger said to me quietly, 'She will get you back for that little stunt. Of that I am sure.'

Karin then started laughing. 'You put one over on us there.'

We put the tent together in a matter of minutes and Karin offered to show us the area in her car, as Inger's car was still being held as evidence. 'I'll take you to the abbey first. Then we will go down to the loch later for a swim,' Karin said, 'and maybe I can help you with a little history of my town.'

There was a serene sense of peace in the area. Whether it was to do with the monastery I do not know, but I certainly liked the tranquillity.

'I like Fort Augustus, Karin!'

It's a lovely place to stay,' she acknowledged. 'I hope to get a post in Inverness as a librarian when I complete my studies at university, which will allow me to return home at the weekends.'

'You love it that much,' I said.

'Oh yes! I'll show you my favourite place tomorrow. Inger and I will make up a picnic lunch and we will make a day of it. I do hope the weather keeps up though.'

We stopped well short of the abbey and took in the splendour of the building and surrounding countryside. Suddenly through the trees in a small cutting a gentleman appeared in front of us. 'Good day,' he said. 'Are you enjoying your walk?'

'Yes indeed,' said Colin, 'we are admiring the abbey also.'

'Ah yes! Would you like to come and visit the chapel? The pupils are all on summer vacation as I imagine you are yourselves.'

'We would love to,' I said. All nodded in agreement. 'It's very kind of you to take us round,' I said.

'Not at all. I enjoy telling the story to all who are interested, especially as you are of the faith and your ancestors once lived not far from here.'

The organ was huge and extremely well kept. 'It would grace any cathedral, an organ such as this,' said our guide. He explained the complex details of how it had to be kept and cleaned. I was amazed at the length of the pipes. They seemed to reach the ceiling. They would give it the low pitch, I presumed.

After we had seen the stained-glass windows in the church, and following our visit to the chapel, the priest was kind enough to tell us the history of Fort Augustus.

'The Fort was constructed between 1729 and 1742 to a design by General Wade, and taken by the Jacobite army in 1745. The 14th Lord Lovat purchased the buildings from the government in 1867 and used part of them as a hunting lodge. In 1870 the buildings were leased to the monastic order of the Benedictines. The monks converted the Georgian fort to a Gothic abbey and extended the existing buildings to provide an independent school and monastery. Further buildings were added which included the construction of a church. The barrack square was replaced by Gothic cloisters and a lawn.

'History has lent the abbey many interesting features, in particular the refectory with its panelled walls and stained-glass windows, and the original guardroom with its vaulted ceiling, recently used as a chapel.'

As we were leaving, on a lighter note I broached the subject of the Loch Ness monster.

'Do you think it's a gimmick to bring in the tourists?' asked Colin.

'Ah now! I can see the loch from my window and, yes, I do believe there is something in the water as I have seen strange movements first hand,' said the man in black. 'People will believe what they want. Most want to see it for themselves, though!'

I'm not sure if our guide was a priest or a monk teaching in the abbey but he certainly knew his way about. 'It's the summer recess and that is why it's so quiet and I'm able to show you around,' the man told us. We thanked him for the tour and the history talk. He said that it wasn't a problem and that he had enjoyed showing us the Abbey. He wished us a happy remainder of our holiday. We waved farewell and headed back to the car.

The girls had prepared a lunch basket and suggested we find a quiet spot on the loch. Karin knew exactly where to go, having been brought up in the area.

'This is perfect,' said Colin.

I agreed wholeheartedly. 'Spot on!' I said.

Girls are good at making up a packed lunch and our two companions didn't let their sex down. We lay on the shore relaxing and also discussing the trauma of yesterday. 'I'll be happy to have my car returned,' said Inger. 'I hope they finish what they have to do soon.'

'Never mind that,' I said. 'Let's have a swim!'

'We have no costumes,' said the girls.

'Neither have we!' retorted Colin. 'Underwear is fine, we won't look.'

Colin and I had our shorts and our tops off in a jiffy and were in the water before the girls had decided what to do. The water was freezing. 'I can't see them coming in, Colin!' I had only just uttered these words when the girls came plunging into the water from behind us. Karin had a white bra and panties covering her modesty, while Inger wore black, which did look like a bikini.

Inger had obviously swum in cold water before and started splashing a spray at us. She was a girl who liked fun. Colin was of the same nature and the noise from the pair of them must have gone right up the loch.

Karin looked cold and was shivering so I made for her and started splashing, which really annoyed her. I thought I was going to get an earful but instead she dived in and grabbed my legs, pulling me under.

'So you want to play then?' I said to her.

Free now, I surface dived, caught her legs and pulled her

under, then lifted her out of the water then dropped her and dunked her. She was squealing every time she surfaced.

I finally let her up and she splashed and splashed till she felt she was satisfied with her retribution.

'We are going out first!' said Inger.

'OK,' we replied.

They went behind a tree, removing their scanties and drying themselves as best they could with a napkin. 'You can come out now!' said Karin, wearing her shorts and blouse without her underwear.

Colin and I dried ourselves with our T-shirts and put on our shorts.

'Give me your underwear, lads, and I'll put them altogether in on bag,' said Karin. Turning to Inger, she then said, 'I hope no one sees us in our street, especially without my knickers. Does it show?'

'Not much,' said Inger.

Well, it was noticeable to us because we couldn't help but stare at their bottoms, but we said nothing.

'Let's be off then,' said Karin.

She stopped in her street and checked there was no one about. 'We'll make a dash for it when the coast is clear. I don't want that nosy parker Irene seeing me without a top and no knickers below,' Karin moaned. She certainly wasn't hiding much as the darkness of her skin reflected through her blouse and what was there was quite apparent. 'Come now, Inger, we'll run in the back door!'

Their cause was futile, however, as the neighbour from hell came from the rear of the house and met them head on. Irene had been chatting to Karin's mum about the tent we had erected in the garden. We found this out later.

'My, you must be feeling it hot! Your clothes are sticking to you and you're showing the boys all your assets. Oh, it must be good to be young,' said Irene.

Karin and Inger smiled and said, 'If that's what it takes!' and continued running.

Both Colin and I waited till the girls had gone in before exiting the car. We put on fresh underwear in the tent and then went to the house.

Karin's mum and dad shook our hands and asked us to come in for tea. Hannah and Calum were exceptionally nice people and were only too happy for us to pitch the tent in their garden after hearing of our problems.

'Would you care to go to the hotel with us for a drink?' asked Karin and Inger.

'Thought you'd never ask!' said Colin.

The girls had a quick change (again!) and collected us from the tent.

We had a wonderful evening with them. Although they were older, they did not treat us like a pair of adolescents. Karin had already told us she hoped to be a librarian but was looking for someone to love. I have to say, she was a lovely looking girl, but she showed she liked being in charge of any situation that arose, which is sometimes a turn-off for guys.

'I'll take you to my favourite spot tomorrow,' said Karin.

'We'll look forward to that then,' we replied in unison.

We walked back in a group, not as partners, with Colin cracking jokes, some of which were at my expense. I didn't really mind as it always ended in a laugh.

'Goodnight, boys!' said Karin as she leaned over and kissed me full on the lips.

'I needed that!' she said. 'I haven't had a kiss for a while. Hope you don't mind an older woman taking advantage.'

I didn't let go and I pulled her forward and kissed her in return. 'I certainly don't mind!' I replied.

She ran into the house and left me standing there. Colin meanwhile only got a handshake from Inger, who retreated quickly after Karin.

'You are a little devil, Jamie! You are attracting more girls than I am now!'

I laughed and we turned in for the night.

Chapter Twenty-eight

T he girls let us have a lie-in. It was almost mid-morning before we surfaced to face another day.

'We thought you might be exhausted,' Inger said, 'so we didn't disturb you.'

'Thank you,' I replied, 'it was very kind of you.'

'We have your breakfast ready if you come now,' she informed us.

'Right away!' said Colin. As far as food was concerned no second invitation was required.

Karin laid our plates on the table but did not join us. Perhaps she regretted the advances she had made towards me, I thought, and maybe she is feeling vulnerable in the cold light of day. She might also have been caught unawares by my reaction. I would have to find out, anyway.

After breakfast, in an effort to break the silence, I offered to help wash and dry the dishes along with her. 'How are you this morning?' I enquired.

She did not answer the question but rather deliberated for a moment before saying, 'About last night – I'm sorry if I've given you the wrong impression!'

'Not at all!' I said. 'Why can't a lovely girl get a kiss now and again without feeling trapped? I enjoyed it and I wouldn't mind doing it again, but I have a girl that I love so I only treat a kiss as a kiss with a dear friend, who is beautiful by the way.'

'You are a charmer, Jamie Cameron! You have learnt a lot from your friend in the past few weeks I bet.'

'Well, you may be right, but I like to be around girls and especially ones like you.'

'So you think of me as a girl then, even at twenty-two?'

'Why ever not? You only look as if you're in your teens and I like you a lot, so if you want to kiss me again then do so and we will both enjoy it.'

She put her arms around me and said, 'Hold me, Jamie, I've been badly hurt and let down. I desperately need to find someone to love and love me back.'

She kissed me and began to cry.

'Stop it!' I said. 'Whoever he is, he is not worth it. He is blind, anyway, to throw away someone as affectionate and loving as you.'

'But I loved him so much. I can't see me feeling the same way ever again.'

'Look, Karin, I'm only sixteen, yet I have an old head on my shoulders. I know what is right and what is wrong. This guy is wrong for you and it's better that you have found out now rather than later.'

'Oh, I forgot your age, and here am I laying all my troubles before you. I'm sorry.'

I gave her a kiss and held her without saying a word. She tried to speak, but I hushed her. 'I promise you will find someone much more loving and suitable even if I have to search for him myself.'

'You would do that for me, Jamie?'

'You bet I would. Now, come on, give me a smile.'

She began laughing. Maybe it was because I had started to tickle her.

'Tell Colin to stop flirting with Inger. I need her to give a hand with the picnic.'

'Right away, boss!' I said.

I had to duck a flying arm from Karin as she mused over my remark.

We loaded up the car and Karin insisted that I sit in the front passenger seat beside her. She had put on a miniskirt instead of her usual shorts which I can honestly say was driving me to distraction. Her skirt was half the size it was after she sat down in the driving seat. Her legs were perfectly formed and her skin was lightly tanned. I found myself looking at her legs more than the road ahead. I can't imagine how someone could give up girl like this.

'Something wrong?' she enquired.

'Yes,' I said, 'your legs are driving me bananas.'

'Why, what's wrong with them?'

'Nothing! They are perfect and I can't take my eyes off them.'

'Jamie Cameron, you naughty boy.'

'Well, if I have to find a boyfriend for you I can honestly tell him you have a smashing pair of legs that match my girl, Bonnie's.'

Karin smiled and said, 'Keep your eyes on the road or I'll belt you when we stop.'

'I certainly will not – the view's worth a belt.'

She gave in and went on to say, 'This is my favourite spot in the whole world that I told you about yesterday, and what a perfect day to see it. We have been fortunate indeed this year with the weather.'

'It's the best summer I can remember,' said Colin.

'You haven't seen as many as me!' said Inger.

'You poor old things,' said Colin.

'That's it! You're both for it now. We have had enough of your nonsense!' said Karin.

At least Karin was back to her old self once more. I had been a bit worried about her that morning. I do hate to see someone cry.

'We'll park here,' said Karin. 'You and Colin can carry the hamper as part of your punishment.'

'Only part! There is more?' I asked.

She pointed to her legs. 'Much!'

'I think I will just about manage it,' said Colin, lifting it with two hands and then resting it on one arm, maintaining the balance with the other.

'Show off!' said Inger.

We walked past the locks and out to the loch. 'Right, this is where we spend the day. Inger, put the blanket down on the grass verge here at the end of the path,' said Karin. Inger didn't need to be told twice and followed the instructions to Karin's satisfaction.

'What a view! Picturesque is the only way to describe such a setting as this,' I said.

'This is the part of the Caledonian Canal, which joins up with Loch Ness. It runs all the way from Fort William on the west coast to Inverness in the east,' said Karin.

The Caledonian Canal runs through the Great Glen, a natural

fault line from Fort William to Inverness. The canal is one of the great waterways of the world. It is sixty miles long and is made up of twenty miles of natural lochs. Even by today's standards, it is an amazing piece of engineering. It first opened in 1822, constructed to help commercial shipping avoid the treacherous journey round the Pentland Firth and west coast. The canal, purpose built for sailing boats, was overtaken by the invention of steam and therefore never paid for itself.

The mountain scenery on the route gave it a new breath of life, with ships and cabin cruisers coming from all over the world. With walking and climbing readily available, not to mention the wildlife, is it any wonder success has now rightfully come its way? Spending a day watching the boats navigate the locks is very entertaining.

'It must have cost a fortune in those days to build this, Colin.'

'Aye, it would be the taxpayer who footed the bill as usual, I imagine,' said Colin in a sarcastic tone.

'It is some place though,' I said.

'I have to agree with you,' said Colin.

The place Karin had chosen was the entrance to Loch Ness from Loch Lochy, or the exit from Loch Ness into the Caledonian Canal down towards Loch Lochy, depending on which way you are headed. I could have sat there all day watching the small craft going to and fro.

We all went for a walk on the beach, throwing stones into the water like kids. And why not, I thought.

Karin decided after our little stroll that we should put our hamper back in the car and spend the last hour watching the locks open and close. 'Right, let's lift this lot, you pair of lazybones,' she said.

We couldn't say anything – after all, the girls had prepared the food. 'If we are to be treated like lackeys then so be it, we will act like them,' said Colin thoughtfully. 'You prepared it, so we are at your command.'

'That's good to know,' said Inger.

'They are planning mischief again,' I said to Colin.

'I know!' he replied.

As we headed for the car I said to Colin that I hadn't realised the work involved, nor was I aware of the procedure in the filling up of the locks. 'I can only say I don't fancy falling in.'

'I'm sure if you were with someone experienced then you would soon get the hang of it, but it's certainly not for novices,' said Colin.

Colin gave me a nudge. 'Is that our friends back there on the third lock?'

'I'm not sure,' I replied.

'I'm positive it is them, even without their masks. There can't be two tatty shirts like the one that chubby one is wearing.'

'You may be right. But what can we do if it is them?' I asked.

'We'll play it by ear,' Colin replied.

I hope he is not going to do something foolish, I thought. This lot are dangerous.

As a large ship, which resembled a sea cruiser of some sort, reached the last lock, Colin told the girls to return to the car. We watched while the lock filled up, and when it was almost level with the loch, Colin moved forward to the boat and shouted, 'Excuse me a minute' – grabbing the unsuspecting chap by surprise – 'you are one of the culprits who tried to put us off the road two days ago!'

'I don't know what you're talking about!' he exclaimed. Before Colin and I could engage him in any further conversation we found ourselves in the water. Someone had crept up silently behind us and pushed us in.

Oh no! I thought to myself. Why did Colin not just go and fetch the police. Too late now though!

As I surfaced, an outstretched hand was offered to me from the boat which I gladly accepted. I was pulled on board to my relief, which proved only to be short-lived as I was struck from behind by something heavy and I blacked out immediately.

I was barely semi-conscious, but I felt myself being raised and bundled on to some sort of craft. I could hear what sounded like an engine, but I blacked out again before I could honestly say that for definite. I can only assume the same thing had happened to Colin, for when I awoke he was lying beside me, groaning in pain on the shores of the loch.

Obviously we had been brought ashore by the small boat and

dumped at this spot. They had probably thought it would be some time before we recovered and they would be out of reach before any alarm could be raised.

'That's a fine mess you got us into there,' I said to Colin. 'Oooh! My head is throbbing.'

'Mine is bleeding!' said Colin.

'Have you any idea what happened?' I asked.

'One of the robbers pushed you in first. While I was grappling with him someone hit me on the head from behind. The next thing I knew I was in the water struggling for dear life. I managed to surface and someone held out a hand from the boat in the lock. When I was pulled on board I was struck again. That's the last thing I remember,' said Colin.

'If they were intending to murder us then that was an ideal time to get rid of us.'

'You're right, Jamie! I think they carry the gun just to put fear into their victims,' said Colin. 'Also, if they killed someone, it would make life extremely difficult for them. I'm sure they enjoy stealing and want to continue in a life of burglary.'

'It would be too high a profile for them if they had murdered us, then, Colin!'

'Yes, I'm positive of that, Jamie!'

By the time we had gathered ourselves together we heard the girls calling us.

'Are you all right, Jamie?'

I blacked out once more before I could reply…

I awoke to find Karin leaning over me. My head was on her lap and she was cradling me like a baby. I might as well milk this moment, I said to myself. This feels really good to me, held in the arms of a beautiful woman!

'Are you OK, my baby?' said Karin, stroking my face and head gently.

'I'll be fine in few minutes if I can rest here for a little just to recover.'

'Take as long as you need, I'll just cuddle you.'

'What more could a guy ask for!'

'Is this where it hurts, Jamie?' asked Karin, as she leaned over and kissed the lump on my head.

'Oh yes!'

'We'll have to take you to the doctor when we get back then. Why did you go near those ruffians anyway? You are just foolish boys!' said Karin.

Meanwhile Colin was receiving the same attention from Inger. He looks happier now, I thought, probably overdoing it as usual, but who am I to begrudge him a little pampering? I am one to talk, soaking up all the attention like a sponge.

I had one more good cuddle and I said, 'I'll try to get back on my feet now, Karin.'

Karin put my arm over her shoulder and I pressed my cheek to hers, making the most of my injury. 'I think you are making the most of this!' said Karin. She then gave me a big kiss. 'Does that make it better?'

'Nearly,' I said.

'One more then.'

Oh, what a kiss! I really did feel better as she helped me back on my feet. We walked slowly back to the car.

Inger found it impossible to do this so she took Colin's arm and followed us. When we got in the car I asked, 'How did you know where to find us?'

'We happened to turn round at the moment you were both struck on the head and decided to follow the boat up the loch by road, all the way to Inverness if need be,' said Inger.

'We were afraid they would dump you in the loch and you might never have been seen again,' said Karin.

The local doctor saw us as an emergency and declared we had only been badly bruised. He recommended that we rest for a few days, however. With a few compresses and painkillers we would make a complete recovery.

We then returned to the police station to make a statement and informed the police that the boat was heading in the direction of Inverness. 'Problem is, officer, we were three quarters of the way up the loch, so by the time we arrived back at Fort Augustus the boat could be at sea.'

'Never mind,' said the constable, 'I'm sure we'll find it. Someone must have seen it go through the locks. Leave your contact telephone number in Inverness if you intend going there tomorrow.'

Inger and Karin took us to a small restaurant for our farewell meal. They treated us well and Inger apologised for all the havoc she had brought on us.

'We enjoyed the excitement,' said Colin. 'The headache is the worst part of it all.'

I nodded in agreement.

Inger had received her car back from the police and was now at liberty to drive once more. Both the girls had arranged to go to Fort William the next day and Inger preferred to drive.

'We will miss you both terribly,' said Inger.

'Likewise,' I replied.

Inger went on to say that she was dating an engineer down in the Midlands and that she liked him very much.

'I'm not surprised you have a boyfriend, a beautiful girl like you,' I said to her.

'Karin and I are agreed that we had never been paid as many compliments as we have had in the last few days,' said Inger.

As we walked home, Karin took my hand and said, 'I'm sorry for my aggressive behaviour towards you and then more or less demanding a kiss. It was unforgivable. You must think me an awful old hen.'

I couldn't help laughing – it was so funny the way she said it. Having contained myself I said, 'I loved every minute of it. I confess I made the most of the cuddle you gave me on the beach, plus the bonus of seeing your legs close up.'

'Oh yes, I owe you a belting for teasing me about my legs, but I can't because you're hurt.' She laughed and nudged me on the side. 'Oh you… I wish I could give you another bump!'

'I will find you a nice guy, I promise,' I said to her. 'I'm sure there will be someone up in Inverness looking for a beautiful, intelligent girl like yourself. Bonnie's bound to have some big cousins.'

'So you're off to meet your Bonnie tomorrow then?

'Oh yes! I can't wait,' I said.

We were now at the tent and Inger said, 'We have camped when we were younger, but are accustomed to the good life now. Isn't that right Karin?'

'Yes,' Karin replied. 'I like hot and cold running water, preferably in a nice bathroom.'

Karin took me to the side and once more said, 'Will you find me someone to love, Jamie? I am so lonely!'

'I promise,' I said to her sincerely.

With that she asked me for a parting kiss. I duly agreed and put up no defence. I asked her not to tell Bonnie of this close union. With this we retired for the night.

After a breakfast we didn't waste much time and said our goodbyes quickly so as not to incur too many tears. We made a pact to keep in touch and that I would fulfil my promise to Karin. And we were on our way.

We were fully loaded and on the road again. Colin was at his brightest when walking, despite the bumps on his head from the assailant. The lump on his head was clearly visible and did not suit him at all. 'How am I to explain this to the female population over the next few days?' he said.

'I'm sure you will come up with something that will fascinate them,' I said.

'You were clearly whacked with the same force as me, yet you only have a small lump. I always said you were hard-headed, Jamie boy.'

'Are you saying you are soft in the head, Colin?'

'You are getting smart, Jamie! That's one up to you,' replied Colin.

'You have forgotten that you were hit twice on the head, though, Colin.'

'Oh, that is why my lump is so big!'

'Look, that's the sign for Invermoriston now, Colin.'

'Yes, Jamie, and where we part.'

I hadn't given it any thought, with the goings on and the delight of the thought of seeing Bonnie today. It had completely slipped my mind that we would go our separate ways after being together all these weeks.

'I completely forgot all about it, honestly, Colin.'

'I'm not surprised. With all that has happened to us it's a blessing we are still here at all. I'm sure you learnt plenty with all the experiences we have had – some for the good others best forgotten.'

'I wouldn't have missed it for the world and I'm thrilled I

came with you, for no one else could have enlightened me on the ways of life and made it so worthwhile.'

'Thanks, Jamie! I have Bonnie's aunt's number so I'll give her a call and hope to have a chat with you there. Three is a crowd, so you have a good time with your girl. She is a lovely girl and I won't tell her of your clan of female followers that you amassed since seeing her last. You have been pretty faithful under the circumstances with all the lovely West Highland lassies throwing themselves at you... Bye, Jamie.'

'Bye Colin!'

He loaded the tent on to his rucksack and walked into the distance. It took a man of his stature to carry it. I was now free of half my load, which delighted me. I waited by the roadside junction and watched him as he sang merrily on his way.

Believe it or not, two minutes after he left me a Land Rover pulled up alongside him and offered him a lift. Before he entered the car he looked back and waved furiously and gave me the thumbs up sign. I could visualise the grin from here; he had been positive he would get a lift as he had said someone would feel sorry for him carrying that amount of equipment. Yes, he was right again!

Chapter Twenty-nine

Before we had parted I had asked Colin, 'Where are you heading, anyway?'

'First stop will be the Kyle of Lochalsh, maybe over to Skye, and then on to Ullapool. I will head down Aviemore later. I might pick up a job beating the heather in early August which will tide me over.'

'I can't imagine you beating the heather. You're far too big and likely to get your head blown off.'

'Thanks a bunch!' said Colin.

I knew he would do it anyway just to say he had done it. 'Oh, have fun then, it will be free board and accommodation for a few days. I have some extra money if you need a few pounds.'

'Thanks just the same, Jamie, but you will need all your pennies to keep that gorgeous girl of yours happy.'

'I'll phone home for the both of us from Bonnie's aunts, Colin. You know how my parents worry. I tell my mum to keep your folks up to date as long as you tell me what you're up to.'

'That's fine, Jamie. Don't worry, I'll keep you informed.'

It was strange being on my own but I liked the lighter load; I was able to stride out and slow down whenever I wished. Colin was a hard taskmaster and accused me of having LPG – I didn't know what that meant until he woke me one morning after oversleeping. 'You have definitely got the 'Lazy Pig Gene', boy. Get up, you lazy good-for-nothing.'

I had learnt a lot over the weeks about myself and what I could and couldn't do. Colin was right: this is the most important time in your life for character building, also to experience trials and hardship, and the manner in which you deal with them brings a sense of well-being. To experience the problems of others and offer assistance whenever possible is the real meaning of charity.

I felt pleased with myself and was truly thankful to have a friend so kind and motivated as Colin. The most important assignment I now had in life was to pass on what I had learnt and teach others the skills I now possessed.

It was a winding way along the loch. Ah, this spot looks familiar – yes it's where Karin rescued me yesterday, I remembered.

I had plenty of time to reflect on what had happened, how those bandits had thumped us both on the head and got away with the goods. One thing I hoped to find out was that the culprits were all behind bars by the time I reached Inverness.

Passing Drumnadrochit I saw Urquhart Castle sitting out on a piece of headland. It was set on a rocky peninsula commanding views of the complete length of the loch. The castle had a chequered history. It was blown up in 1692 to prevent it falling into Jacobite hands. It was strategically placed where one could control the loch. It had been purchased by a Mr Chewitt in 1930 for his family but never used.

I took a stroll through the ruin and viewed the loch. It was very peaceful and I sat for a short time just relaxing. I worked out that I had only about twelve miles to walk to Inverness which would take me roughly three hours. Not long till I see Bonnie again, I thought.

I had walked only about a half a mile when I felt a burning sensation on my heel. Oh no, I had forgotten to buy some Vaseline jelly for my feet! This was going to prove a painful twelve miles. I took my boot off on road verge to have a look at the heel. It was inflamed but there was no blister yet, which was a blessing. I poured some cold water on it. I then put on two socks instead of one making my boot tighter, thereby easing some of the friction.

I had gone only a few yards when I placed my foot on a loose stone and over I tumbled into the ditch. 'You stupid oaf,' I said to myself. Fortunately I did not twist my ankle or bruise myself in any way; luckily I had fallen on spongy moss. The only thing that was hurting was my pride. Gathering myself together, I wondered why it had got dark all of a sudden. I turned round to find a huge tanker had pulled up beside me. The cab door flew open and a voice from within yelled, 'You OK?'

'Yes!' I bawled back. 'I only tripped and tumbled over.'

'I'm headed for Ullapool, but I can drop you off near Inverness if you wish.'

'Near Inverness is great!' I said.

'Climb aboard as quick as you can, my boy, I have little time to waste.'

'Yes, sir!' I said, throwing my rucksack in first and then jumping up after it.

'Comfy now?'

'Yes!' I replied.

'Hello, I'm Alec!' said the driver. 'I'm not supposed to pick up anyone on the road but I noticed you falling over and I thought you might be hurt. I'll put it down as an emergency stop should anyone report me or put in a complaint.'

'It's good of you to stop and compromise yourself in such a way. I will defend you if the worst should happen. Speaking of emergencies, do you have a plaster by any chance?' I asked.

'We have to carry a full medical kit on board. Go to the back seat and you will find all you need.'

'Thank you again!'

I cleaned my foot and put Vaseline on the area which was inflamed. I then put on a bandage which would stop any more rubbing. 'Oh, that feels good now, Alec, what a relief.' I left my boot off for the rest of the journey which in fact was only half an hour. 'It would have taken me over three hours to get to Inverness and goodness knows what condition my heel would have been in had you not stopped,' I said.

'Only glad to help, son.'

'My, what a view you have from the cab!' I said.

'It helps a lot on winding roads. I'm able to see well ahead, which is much more than the motorist can.'

'It must be a lot of responsibility on your shoulders being in charge of such a vehicle.'

'Yes, it is. The secret is never to become complacent and always be aware of the danger this could impose if I lose control. I put many things that go wrong in life down to downright carelessness and casual manners of rogue companies who bend the rules to suit themselves. You will experience what I have said later on in life and that's for sure.'

'I will take note of what you say,' I said.

'That's my turn-off now, Jamie. I'll take the turning and stop at the nearest lay-by. You will have at least a mile to walk but I think you will manage that now. Have a good holiday with your girl.'

He stopped as he said he would. It was a mile and a half back, but I was pleased that my heel no longer ached. I threw my rucksack on to the verge and clambered out.

'Bye, Alec, I hope I can repay you some day.'

He laughed and drove off, leaving me with a hoot from his horn.

The weather had been misty most of the way along Loch Ness, which was unfortunate as I was so much looking forward to its scenery. I'm told it's deeper than the height of the mountains that surround it. Still, it was Inverness at last. I had had problems along the way but they were only memories now.

I strode out to the station where I was to meet Bonnie. The Edinburgh train was arriving at four o'clock and I had timed it to perfection. Well, my good fortune had saved me.

It was three-thirty as I crossed the span bridge across the River Ness. I looked down at the clear, pure water. No rubbish, was my immediate thought. How fortunate they are in this part of the world I thought, as I compared it with the rivers back home.

The sun had broken through by the time I reached the station. With only fifteen minutes to wait until the arrival of the train I paid for a platform ticket and sat on a bench thinking about what Bonnie would say. My daydream was disturbed by the sound of a bell in the station. I'm sure this is what they called the distant signal bell relayed by the signal box further down the track. I had been told this by my mum, who was one of the few signal box woman in Scotland during the war. Having taken ill with a blood disorder at Ardeer she needed to take blood injections all her life. After recovering she was sent to train as a signal woman; everyone had to have a job so she was allotted a signal box after six months' training.

Railways were busy then and she passed the Royal Train and Winston Churchill while on duty – moments she was keen to talk about all her life. No recognition of any kind came her way; again, an unsung hero of her time, like millions of others.

I jumped up as I heard the sound of wheels on the track. Looking into the distance I could see the train approaching. Having sensitive hearing I placed my hands over my ears as the train came thundering into the station. It had over a dozen carriages so I followed the first one until the train came to a halt.

Sometimes it's difficult to see clearly into a carriage, with light reflection playing its part. This was one of those occasions, I have to say. I couldn't make out anyone clearly. I moved along to the second and third carriage, and then from behind came a call. 'Jamie! Jamie!'

I turned round and there was the most beautiful girl you could ever imagine standing before me. A sheer vision of loveliness. She was even sweeter than I remembered and a sense of guilt washed over me. All because of my straying in the last few weeks.

Before I knew she was in my arms. Having placed hers round my neck she swung herself in a way that left me no alternative but to catch her.

'How I've missed this! I go to sleep every night with the thought of you holding me. This is my favourite position. I hope you have missed me too!'

'I have Bonnie! Like you'll never know.'

She pulled me down with her arms to enable me to kiss her.

A porter who had been helping passengers with their luggage clapped his hands on Bonnie as he was passing. 'Let him come up for air, darling girl, he's turning a funny colour!'

At this Bonnie laughed and replied, 'You're only jealous.'

'I am indeed! I hope he appreciates you. You are one of the bonniest wee lassies I have ever seen.'

Bonnie had no answer for flattery and was bemused by his remark.

'He is right, you know. You are beautiful and I am the luckiest guy in the world.'

'Would you listen to yourself! It's I who is the lucky one to find someone so young and caring who's about to turn seventeen in a week's time.' She pulled me towards her once more and kissed me. 'Oh how I longed do that all the way from Edinburgh.'

I put her down gently and lifted her rucksack. It was much daintier than mine but it was packed to capacity.

'I'll put my rucksack on if you help me. I want you to hold my hand while we walk.'

As we exited the station Bonnie turned to the right towards the river.

'Does your aunt stay on the north side of the river?' I asked.

'Yes, but it's not too far,' said Bonnie.

It was heaven to be with her again; to feel her hand clinging to me tightly was all I had dreamt of.

As we crossed the bridge over the River Ness I remarked on the clarity of the water. 'Look how clean and clear the water is here. No industrial pollution. Where I come from there are only small parts of the river which we are able to fish; only upstream remains uncontaminated.'

'Our rivers are pretty clean down in the Borders. My dad and uncle both fish in the Tweed.'

'Oh, that reminds me, Colin goes down to fish there,' I said.

'I completely forgot about Colin. How is he?' asked Bonnie.

'He was fine when I left him and he sends his regards. I hope your aunt won't mind as I gave him her telephone number so we can keep in touch.'

'Oh, I'm sure she will enjoy the excitement of having a young man calling every now and again.'

It was about half an hour after we left the station when we finally arrived at the cottage. 'This looks really nice,' I said. 'They must be quite well off.'

'My aunt is a little house-proud, so take off your boots when we go in.'

'I will do that, Bonnie. I'm dying to take them off anyway.'

Bonnie knocked on the door and a tall, attractive woman appeared before us. I put her in the age group of late forties, much the same age as my mum. She had a winning smile, which was similar to Bonnie's.

'I can see the resemblance right away, that you are related to Bonnie,' I said, taking the initiative.

'Oh, this must be the well-mannered young man you met in Balloch! I'm Mary, by the way. Bonnie's dad is my brother. Come away in and meet Stephen, my husband.'

Stephen was a big man just as I suspected. Every relation of Bonnie's was on the large side.

'Get yourself settled in first, then we can have a chat,' said Stephen, taking my hand and giving it a good strong shake.

I laugh every time I recall Colin's first comments when he first met Angus and Duncan: 'Wouldn't like to get on the wrong side of your intended relations!'

I was shown a small room at the rear of the cottage. It had a single bed and a small wardrobe which was adequate for my needs. It was a palace compared with the tent I'd been living in over the past few days.

'This suit you all right?' asked Mary.

'This is absolutely perfect, with a view of the garden thrown in – what more would I want?'

'I have left you out a bath towel. The hot water is ready if you wish to use it now,' said Mary.

'I hope you can wait till Jamie is finished, Bonnie, we girls like to spend a little longer than the boys in the water.'

'I can wait,' said Bonnie, 'but not too long,' – tickling me while replying.

'Thanks, Mary, I'll take a bath right away if that's OK with Bonnie?'

'Even better if you're taking it now, it will give me plenty of time to soak after that tedious journey,' said Bonnie.

I had completely forgotten how far Bonnie had travelled to get there. 'Are you sure you don't want to go in first – after all you have been travelling all day?' I asked.

'No, honest. You go first, Jamie.'

Oh, my poor heel. It was still raw under the bandage. I am sure though, that had I not got a lift when I did it would have been badly blistered.

A bath… nothing quite like it for relaxing. I am sure if Bonnie hadn't knocked on the door I would have nodded off.

'Have you gone to sleep in there?' she enquired.

'Just about! I'll be out in a minute.'

I lay down for a snooze while Bonnie washed. I must have fallen over, for the next thing I remember was someone blowing on my face.

'That was a lovely way to waken someone, Bonnie,' I said.

'Mum always does that with dad so as not to have him jump up with a start,' said Bonnie.

'May I try it with you?' I asked.

'Yes, but do it gently though!' she said.

I then blew gently in her ear. 'That tickles,' said Bonnie.

I then blew an almighty blast into her ear. You're going to regret this, I said to myself. I jumped up immediately and Bonnie came after me, chasing me round the room.

'Wait till I get my hands on you, Jamie!'

I tripped up and landed on the bed; the next thing I knew I was being tickled under my arms, which she knew I could not bear.

'I give in! Help! I give in!' I cried.

'What's all that commotion up there?' It was Bonnie's aunt – thank goodness for that, I had thought I was going to die laughing.

'Jamie tripped. But he is all right for now,' cried Bonnie.

Meaning what? That she wasn't completely satisfied yet with her retribution, I thought.

Bonnie took my hand and led me downstairs. 'That should teach you not to mess with me,' said Bonnie, giving me a kiss.

'Never again!' I said.

Mary had prepared a lovely casserole for us. 'I'm sure you both must be very hungry after your journey,' said Mary.

'You can say that again,' I said.

Stephen repeated what Mary had said, and we all burst into laughter.

'About tomorrow – you have nothing planned, I hope?' enquired Stephen.

'No,' both Bonnie and I responded.

'That's good! I'm told it's your birthday the day after tomorrow, Jamie. Is that correct?' asked Stephen.

'Yes it is. Who told you?'

'Bonnie of course – her birthday is the same day,' said Mary.

Stephen went on to say, 'I have booked a chalet for the four of us down at the new Aviemore Centre as my present to you both. It's not officially open as yet but I'm sure there will be plenty of activity for you both.'

Bonnie began jumping up and down. 'Thank you! Thank you!' she cried.

I was flabbergasted. 'I don't know what to say – I'm speechless.'

'Just be happy we love Bonnie very much. I don't have a wee girl of my own to pamper so I like spoiling my brother's pride and joy,' said Stephen.

'I like to see young ones happy and I like fun. Not much around these days though.' He went on to say 'My son Charles is a lecturer in English literature at the college. He has his own flat in town. He takes on pupils for extra tuition at their homes. So we don't see a lot of him as you can imagine.'

'What do you do for a living, Stephen?' I asked.

'Oh, I'm a figures man myself.' Looking at Mary, he said, 'Fell for that one right away!' laughing heartily.

'Shush!' said Mary.

'Still in good shape yet, Jamie!'

'Oh be quiet, you!' said Mary.

'I'm the same myself, Stephen. I can't take my eyes off Bonnie's legs.'

'Wait till I see you later!' said Bonnie.

The ladies departed for the kitchen with few 'hmphs'.

'Look at the verbal abuse we're getting, Jamie – and we are only paying them compliments, after all,' said Stephen. 'I'm a banker,' he continued. 'Started off as junior then a teller and then finally bank manager. I have more difficulty remembering a name than a number.'

'I have the same problem! I remember a telephone number easier than someone's name.'

'Then your path is carved out for you,' said Stephen. 'You can be a bookkeeper, an auditor or an engineer.'

'Funny you should mention engineering, as I like taking engines apart and putting them together again. My older brother is an auditor with the civil service, which falls into line with what you are saying.'

I went on to tell him of my love of art and music and that I paid for music lessons from performing and doing odd jobs.

'You have another year at school yet, Jamie, so my best advice to you is to study hard now as it gets more difficult as you get older and time is more precious.'

I went on to tell him of the problems we had faced over the past few weeks.

'My, you have had an eventful time,' said Stephen. 'Can't wait to hear big Angus's version of events of the ferry incident. I'm glad you told me about the robbery, though! I know what to expect if the police arrive at the door.'

Time had flown and before I knew it was ten o'clock.

'I think you children should have an early night seeing as we are leaving early tomorrow for Aviemore,' said Mary.

'That's a good idea,' I said.

Bonnie agreed and asked if I would walk her to her room. With that wonderful warm smile of hers, how could anyone refuse?

We bade goodnight to everyone.

Bonnie took my hand as I walked to her room. 'Carry me, Jamie, I love being in your arms, it's all I dream about every night!'

'My pleasure.' I lifted her up, then she put her arms around me and kissed me, long and tender. Without warning she pushed her hands under my armpits and I went into fits of giggling. As a consequence we both landed on the floor with Bonnie on top of me, still doing her tickling act.

'Did you think I had forgotten, Jamie?'

'Oh no, I give in!' I howled uncontrollably. I was so afraid I might lash out and cause her an injury.

Aunt Mary came to the rescue once more. 'What is the trouble?' cried Mary from along the corridor.

'It's Jamie, he has fallen again!' replied Bonnie.

'That boy has trouble keeping his feet Stephen, don't you think?' we heard her say.

'Mary, the boy is head over heels in love with Bonnie and she knows it and is loving it. If she wanted she could have him eating out of her hands just the way you were with me. Remember, dear?' said Stephen.

Mary said nothing. She must have given him a hug as everything went quiet.

'I think we should have an early night, and don't forget you have to do the driving.'

'Yes, dear!

'You heard your aunt, Bonnie! Now, off to bed with you too.'

'One more kiss then!'

I lay awake for a little while having spent time reflecting on the wealth of the people I had met over the summer. I thought: in comparison to what I'm used to they are in a different league totally. I live with my mum and dad and three siblings with my elder brother returning at weekends. You could say the place is somewhat cramped at times. Then we bring in our friends who are not averse to sleeping on the floor at weekends. But it's a home and mum always manages to squeeze in an extra plate of food if necessary. I wouldn't wish my life to have changed in any way. You could say our house was a real home.

Chapter Thirty

Would you believe, it was eight-thirty in the morning already. A voice called, 'Are you up, Jamie? The toilet is free and everyone is having breakfast.'

I had meant to get up at eight but I guess I was a little tired and they let me have a lie in. It was a delight to my heart to hear that gentle voice at my door. 'I'm just getting up!' I replied.

'If you don't hurry up I'll come in and challenge you to a tickling match,' said Bonnie.

'I'm up! I'm up!' I replied quickly, as I couldn't bear to be tickled first thing in the morning.

I washed quickly and hurried to the dining table where a full Scottish breakfast was ready and waiting. I devoured it in minutes to the delight of Mary.

'My, you have a healthy appetite, Jamie!' Mary said.

'Just a growing lad,' Stephen said to his wife.

A quick tidy up and we were off on our schedule for the day. Bonnie had put on a pair of three-quarter-length trousers at breakfast, perhaps because I'd mentioned her lovely legs the evening before. However, when she came to the car with her small bag she had changed into a short minidress.

'We all ready then?' asked Stephen.

'OK,' was the reply from us all.

'Let's be off then.'

Bonnie leaned towards me and lay on my shoulder as we drove off. After we were on the road for ten minutes she whispered in my ear, 'Do you like my skirt?'

'What's to like, there is little of it?' I said with a wry smile. 'How can I look at the countryside when you are driving me mad with that perfect pair of pins on you? I'll miss all the scenery!'

'Just getting my own back, Jamie. Anyway, you say you love all of me.'

'Oh, never mind,' I said. Boy was she really enjoying teasing me. After five minutes she put her top over her legs. She had won and she knew it.

It didn't take long for us to reach Aviemore, though we had stopped at Carrbridge for lunch to give Stephen a break from the driving.

'After you hit the fifty mark, twenty-five miles driving at a time is enough for anyone. Well, myself anyway,' Stephen said.

During lunch he took time to tell me of the history of Aviemore and all about the new centre. Three years previously the first chairlift had been completed on the Cairngorm.

'It was around about fifteen years ago that skiers and climbers first began to converge in numbers to the area,' said Stephen. 'Next came the Aviemore Centre. Where you have people you need conveniences so developers chose Aviemore as a prime location on the main rail and road links to the North and the South. The Fraser family built the Aviemore Centre at great expense and it proved a boon to the area, giving much-needed employment to the locals. It was officially opened in 1966 although building work had started in the early part of the sixties. Wait till you see what it boasts in terms of the amenities.'

'I have no doubt it will have its critics,' I said to Stephen.

'I'm sure the job creation won the day!' Stephen laughed. 'Actually I'm looking forward to seeing what it looks like now that it is almost complete. I have only seen photos of the plans in the paper myself, so it will be a new experience for us all.'

As we reached the village I could see the River Spey on my left and the forest beyond, then further still the dark mountains of Cairngorm. I felt happy – I had taken an instant liking to the place for some unknown reason.

The chalet apartment consisted of a toilet and two sets of bunk beds. It was spacious, but it was for a family.

Stephen, seeing the expression on my face, smiled. 'Did you think I'd booked us all into this one! No, no, we men need a bit of space. We will live upstairs.'

'Oh, I did wonder how we would cope with the women about when changing and using the facilities.'

Stephen was in fits of laughter. He had just remembered booking a sleeper on a night train. A case had been open on the bottom bunk containing women's clothing. 'I thought I was sharing with someone in drag. To my astonishment a young lady came in and quickly ran out again. I don't know who got the biggest surprise or shock. The expression on her face was similar to the one you had earlier when you thought we men were sharing with the women. Anyway, the attendant sorted it out eventually to the satisfaction of all,' said Stephen.

Just moments later, Bonnie knocked on our door and entered. She quickly pointed to the new Swedish duvet. 'These are really good. They are so light and warm, there is no need for old blankets. I'm going to ask my mum to get one when I return home,' she whispered in my ear, saying, 'I wish we were all in here, it would have been fun.'

'I would have to run around with my eyes closed – and what about your aunt?' I replied.

She smiled and said, 'She would cope.'

'Naughty!' I smiled in return and the girls left.

'A shower – how wonderful, how wonderful!' I said out loud.

'You thinking what I'm thinking, Jamie? Well I'm in first if you don't mind,' Stephen said.

Now changed and ready we knocked on the ladies' apartment. 'Ready girls?' cried Stephen. 'If not, we're off without you.'

The centre was really busy, with everyone wanting to view the new facilities and to test them out. I loved skating and swimming. However, both were very busy so we decided to try later.

'What about lunch?' Stephen asked.

'Yes, let's,' we replied.

The self-service was perfect and the available selection was excellent. I overheard one of the staff say they had served around 1,500 meals already that day.

After our quick tour Stephen wanted to explore the area and suggested a trip up to the ski slopes. It's a half-hour road trip up to the chairlifts and the lift itself takes an hour after that. Beyond Loch Morlich the road had not been fully tarred and there were bumps and potholes all the way. I'm not too keen on heights as I've already mentioned, and the last two miles of steep incline are quite hair-raising for someone with this phobia. Stephen didn't seem to bother as he throttled his big Rover up the hillside. I shut my eyes as we approached the first bend as I could see the whole of the valley below me, with Loch Morlich looking like a big puddle.

Bonnie was thrilled with the view. 'Isn't it marvellous?'

'The view is superb, Bonnie, but there is no barrier to prevent us going over the edge.'

'Oh, Uncle Stephen's a good and careful driver. You scaredy cat, Jamie Cameron.'

The car park was huge and full to capacity even though it was only midsummer. I walked with Bonnie back to the bend to admire the view. 'Is that much better, my love?' Bonnie asked me.

'Oh yes. I am not too keen on going back down as we will be right on the brink.'

'Oh come here!' – and she kissed me. 'I'll sit on the passenger side going back down and you can look at my legs.'

'Deal!' I replied with a smile.

We waited half an hour to get on the chairlift but it was well worth it. There was no sensation of height with the towers only thirty feet from the ground, all the way to the summit, which I was relieved about.

Stephen had his binoculars with him and I'm quite sure he was lucky to have them to himself for a minute, as Mary and Bonnie continually prodded him for them.

'Glad I brought the binoculars for you, girls, I'm sure you would be lost without them,' Stephen laughed.

About an hour passed and a cool breeze got up so we made our way down.

'This is great going down, you see everything,' said Stephen. 'I wonder what it's like in the winter.'

'A bit chilly for me,' Mary replied.

Bonnie was as good as her word; she sat on the passenger side to spare me from looking over the ridge.

'All right now, Jamie?' she asked pointing to her legs.

'Perfect!'

Stephen had noticed a small lounge which sold all the Scottish malt whiskies and after parking the car asked if Bonnie and I wished to go along. Bonnie was now eighteen years of age so was eligible to have a drink, and expressed her wish to go along. She had a glass of wine while I had a shandy. Stephen and Mary were still intent on the malts and couldn't make up their minds, so varied was the choice. We spent a couple of hours there and Stephen was in fine fettle with jokes of all description.

Bonnie decided she wanted to see the new cinema, so it was a quick wash and change for us, leaving Stephen and Mary to sample maybe one or two more malts. The cinema was set out like a theatre with perfect vision of the screen from all areas. 'I wish we had cinemas like this near to us,' said Bonnie. 'Not much chance though as we have only a small population.'

The movie was rubbish but I had Bonnie sitting next to me so I lay on her shoulder and snuggled in close.

It was a little milder when we came out so we walked into the village to look for a snack and ended up with fish and chips. As we were returning to the centre we saw two girls jumping up and down on a trampoline. 'Look at them, they must have been drinking, their skirts are almost over their heads,' said Bonnie. She had hardly finished her words when one of the girls failed to come back up from the trampoline. Then there was a horrible scream, and a call for help from her friend filled the air. I raced to the scene with Bonnie behind me. When I got there I found that the young girl had caught the top of her groin on one of the springs as she had fallen into the gap.

I quickly decided what to do and told Bonnie and the other girls to take the trapped girl's arm. Luckily a middle-aged gent came along and was able to assist. I told them I had the strength and power to pull the spring apart and all they had to do was lift the girl when I said the word. The girl was clearly embarrassed, but the pain she was in put all this to one side.

I put one hand under her thigh, grabbed the spring, and pulled with all my might till she was free. 'Now!' I shouted, and all three lifted her clear.

Although still in shock and in severe pain she thanked me. The gentleman and the girl's friend then took her to the first aid centre.

'Well done, Jamie! My, what strength you have. You couldn't have failed to notice the lump she had on her thigh after the spring was removed,' said Bonnie.

'I don't think she will ever try that again. What foolish things young ones of our age do. They take too much alcohol and their judgement is impaired.'

'I want a carry!' said Bonne. She jumped into my arms! Oh how I had missed this over the past few weeks.

'I wish I was in the same chalet as you.'

'Well, you're not. So that's that,' I replied.

Next day after breakfast Stephen had planned that we take a trip and see where the ospreys nest. We drove into the forest and followed a footpath along to the hide. Special binoculars, more like a telescope, were present, allowing us to watch the nest where the chicks are fed. The system has the benefit of protecting the nest from egg collectors who care nothing about the ospreys but are rather intent on having a collector's item.

The trail also led to the red squirrel habitat. If you remain still and quiet and sit beside a tree, and if you are patient, the squirrels will run around you as if you are not there, which I thought was a wonderful experience.

Stephen was a hungry man, much the same as me as far as food was concerned. 'Right folks, time for lunch,' Stephen said sharply. After about ten minutes he found a nice hotel at Nethy Bridge. 'This will do nicely,' said Stephen.

Four lemonade shandies was the order, with the emphasis on lemonade. 'That's nice,' said Bonnie, 'and it's ice cold.'

'Let me taste it, Bonnie,' I asked while I was waiting for my drink to be presented. I took a big gulp and handed the glass back.

Her eyes flashed, and she retorted, 'Why, you greedy thing. I will be having some of yours!'

The young barman laughed, took her glass and handed her the one intended for me. 'I think you will enjoy this one better, miss,' he said, winking at her to my disgust.

'Why, thank you, sir. At least there are still some gentlemen about.'

Stephen ordered lunch and pointed for the girls to sit at the far table.

'Mind if I say something, Jamie?' Stephen said. 'Never take advantage of a woman's generosity, especially when it involves drink.'

'I was only having fun. I think she knows that and she is good at games.'

'She is a little older in the head, Jamie.'

'Point taken, sir.'

'You'll learn!' Stephen laughed.

Just at that a fisherman entered the bar and asked to see the manager or chef. After a brief conversation the fisherman left, and a minute later returned carrying a huge fish. 'Looks like lunch has arrived,' Stephen laughed heartily. The chef then appeared from behind the bar with a set of scales. Everyone's attention had now been drawn to the situation and complete silence reigned.

'It's a big one!'

'Aye,' said the chef, 'It's a pity it's of no use to us. It may be used for pets' feeding if you wish. I'll take it off your hands anyway,' he concluded.

The fisherman went on to explain that he had fought for twenty minutes to land the fish. As everyone was now intent on what he had to say, he turned to face us, saying, 'I thought I'd caught a salmon. It looked like one as I was trying to haul it in. Unfortunately it was a large pike, which is usually found at the merging point of streams where they prey on small fish. He looks as if he's had the pick of streams by the size of him. Maybe I'll catch some more trout now.'

He smiled and waved goodbye. Probably to go and catch more fish, I thought.

After lunch Bonnie started tickling me in the back of the car. 'Got you in the bar,' she said. 'Were you worried?'

'Just a little! I'd hate us to fall out.'

As she kissed me she explained that girls like to be the ones to play games. Stephen had already told me this, so I would learn in future. I smiled and nodded and gave her a cuddle. 'You are beautiful, Bonnie.'

'Shush!' she replied.

Stephen took us sightseeing: Grantown-on-Spey, Boat of Garten, Loch Morlich. Afterwards we returned to Aviemore.

It was about supper time when we got back and I fancied a swim. Bonnie and Mary declined, saying they wanted to look at the shops. Stephen and I made for the pool after gathering a few odds and ends from the chalet. The pool was perfect and not too busy at this time.

Stephen decided on a race. Stephen was a bigger man than I, which was a distinct advantage in the water. He was taking three strokes to my four. I thought, surely he can't keep that going for four lengths. My instinct was confirmed at the fourth and final length. He started to labour and I managed to ease to the finish with a few yards to spare.

'Well done, Jamie!' Stephen said, struggling to find his breath.

We hadn't noticed, but the girls had come to spectate. I say girls, because Stephen always viewed Mary, his wife, as just a girl inside, which I think is really nice after about thirty years of marriage. Bonnie had been cheering me on though I hadn't noticed, and Mary had been egging Stephen on.

We got dressed quickly. The girls had decided they wanted to go skating. 'This will be fun!' I said. We were all handed skates to fit our requirements. I couldn't help but wonder if Bonnie or Mary or even Stephen skated in their spare time. I thought that Stephen was a bit of a dark horse. I would have been willing to bet that he could skate.

We met at the barrier, with no one anxious to take to the ice first. Finally Bonnie put her skates on the ice and had to grab the barrier quickly to break her fall. Was she kidding, I wondered?

Mary next took to the ice and, oh yes, she could skate. Then the dark horse himself. I knew it; away he went like a professional.

I went on to the ice and joined Bonnie. 'Do you skate, Jamie?' she asked.

'Yes,' I replied.

'Well, let's go then!' With this she was off.

'Why, you little devil!' I shouted, but she didn't hear me.

Bonnie turned to look at me and mouth back, 'Naughty baby, that's me.' She was enjoying this; she had the same nature as Stephen, caring, but with a mischievous streak.

For our final birthday treat Mary and Stephen arranged a meal for us, then an evening at a small folk club. Without a doubt this was the best birthday party I had ever had. After everyone singing 'Happy Birthday' to us, the final song was 'Wild Rover' which everyone knows. I swear they must have heard the din in Inverness.

We thanked Stephen and Mary for all they had given us. I gave Mary a kiss and shook Stephen's hand. 'I'm so glad I've met you both,' I said.

'Feeling's mutual,' Stephen replied. 'I hope you will love Bonnie the way I love Mary. If you do, you will be happy all your life, I promise.'

I hadn't much to spend on Bonnie but I managed to buy her a bracelet for a few pounds. 'Just a little memento for your birthday, baby.'

'Oh Jamie, it's beautiful. Thank you! Thank you! I'll treasure it always.'

She then kissed me until I ran out of breath.

Bonnie asked her aunt and uncle to stop and let us off at Culloden on the way back from Aviemore. It felt sad as I stood beside the gravestone where the Cameron men fell. Wars... What waste they are! Yet if my grandparents hadn't fought Germany, where would we be today? God help us. I'm sure half of us just wouldn't be here.

I'm quite sure if dictators were analysed they would all be institutionalised or given treatment for their delusions. What I can't understand is that history always points to their downfall. Do they think that life and justice will never catch up with them? I wondered.

I bought a book on the Jacobite cause so that I could learn much more of my ancestors' plight. The visit was worthwhile but eerie.

Chapter Thirty-one

Before our last full day in Inverness I was hoping for a good night's sleep. Unfortunately it rained heavily and I awoke at two in the morning with the noise of the wind and rain on my window. I think it must have been around five o'clock before I finally fell asleep again, as it appeared to be getting quite light.

Bonnie was as bright as a button at the breakfast table. 'Did you sleep well, Jamie?'

'No, not really. Did you not hear the rain last night?' I asked.

'No,' she replied, 'was it heavy?'

'I'll say it was! It hammered my window all night.'

'Oh, I'm at the back of the building. Probably that's why I couldn't have heard it,' she said.

'I wish I'd been in the back last night.'

'You could have joined me then... only teasing!' laughed Bonnie.

'What are the plans for today?' I asked.

'Nothing wild, just a stroll along the river will do me,' Bonnie said, smiling.

'That'll do nicely. I was hoping for something more active but I'm not up to it today. Maybe we could take a walk to the canal later, though.'

'That will do me. Oh, I want to buy one or two items for next week if that's OK,' said Bonnie.

'Settled then!'

You don't spend five minutes shopping with women. Every shop has to be checked out to make sure they get the best bargain, and also the first to the last garment, whatever it may be. It didn't matter what she tried on, she was gorgeous in all the items.

'What do you think of this one?' she asked.

'Perfect!' I replied.

'But you said that about them all, Jamie! Don't you have a preference?'

'I just think you're beautiful whatever you're wearing.'

I could see she was becoming frustrated with this so I opted for the previous top and shorts. 'I think the light blue or turquoise set you had on before and the red shorts with pink blouse were my favourite.'

'So you did take notice after all,' she smirked. 'I'll take the blue set and I'll try the navy skirt and blouse on again.' After a few minutes, which seemed like an eternity, she emerged decked out in these items. 'What do you think?'

'Yes, I was right, a perfect match for your colouring.' Thank goodness! Now I can get some fresh air, I said to myself.

'Right, you next!' said Bonnie.

Oh no, I had completely forgotten my shopping needs. We strolled towards the gents' area. I wasted no time and found what I was looking for in a matter of minutes.

'Good taste, Jamie! You weren't long,' Bonnie said.

I had had a good idea what I was looking for and luckily for me they had all the tops in my size. The purchases were lightweight so we didn't need to return to her aunt's to drop off our bargains.

The first stop after this was the baker's for our picnic food and a walk along the river. It was fantastic to be out in the open air again. Bonnie said that she enjoyed walking along the riverbank.

'I could see that shopping didn't agree with you, Jamie. I peeked through the curtain when I was in the changing room and saw the frown on your face.'

'Oh no, it's just that the choice for women is so extensive and it must be difficult to chose such arrangements. I can only say I'm glad that I am not a woman.'

She kissed me on the cheek and said, 'You're an angel.'

When we reached the river I was amazed at the height and speed of the flow. 'Look at the speed of the water!' I said. 'I wouldn't like to fall in there.'

'You were right, Jamie. It must have been a heavy downpour through the night.' The water was nearly on the road and I wondered if it ever flooded here.

We found a quiet spot. I took off my shirt and sat on it, then Bonnie lay on my lap. I told her at length what had taken place over the past few days.

'You were bumped on the head! Whereabouts?' she asked. I pointed to the spot at the back of my head. She got up immediately and touched the bump with her hands. 'Oh, my poor baby! Have you seen a doctor?'

I explained that the doctor had said the lump would go down in a few days.

'Here, I'll kiss it better. You have certainly been up to some mischief. Do you have anything else to tell me?' Bonnie enquired.

'Lots,' I said, 'but let's enjoy the day for now.' I didn't want to tell her about all the girls I'd met but I wanted to tell her about that pair of brothers of hers. I'll wait until she broaches the subject, I thought. She will be furious with them when she finds out women were on the bus on the way home. Oh, I'd almost forgotten Karin. 'Oh, by the way, have you any cousins up here?' I asked.

'Yes. Just Charles, my aunt and uncle's son. You haven't met him yet. He has his own flat in town. He is a clever boy, twenty-six years, same age as big brother Angus.'

'What does he do?' I asked.

'Why do you want to know? Why all the questions?'

'I am asking the questions,' I said.

I like the way she reacted when I was purposeful in my questions of her. Her expressions were remarkable and if I could catch them on canvas they would indeed be priceless.

We had a tickling match which Bonnie by all accounts won and I had to tell her the story about what had happened during the previous weeks. I went on to tell her all the parts that I had omitted – Inger, who given us a lift, and about her friend Karin, plus everything else that had gone on later. I had to tread carefully so as not to give the wrong impression.

I told her about Karin's long-term boyfriend and how he two-timed her and got engaged to a friend. Bonnie interrupted my story with a cry of, 'Some friend!'

'She is a beautiful girl – well, actually a woman.'

'Yes!' she said, laughing. All I could think about was that I was grateful that she was laughing. 'Well I haven't seen her, but more the fool he is to dump a girl as nice and pretty as her. So you fell for her!' said Bonnie.

'No! Of course not! You're making up your own story,' I said.

'I'm sorry,' said Bonnie. 'Go on.'

'The thing is she is desperately looking for someone to love, and I told her when I got to Inverness I would find out if you had any relatives or friends that might fit the bill. She is studying to be a librarian and hopes to work in Inverness when she has completed her studies at university.'

'Ah!' said Bonnie. 'I think I have the very man for her. He is tall, though.'

'That goes without saying,' I said, 'having seen the size of your brothers.' She started tickling me again. 'OK, OK! I'll shut up.'

'You had better or you'll get more of the same!' she said.

'As I was saying, he is tall, handsome and quite like Duncan. He has a master's degree and teaches English at college.'

'I must say he sounds perfect for her,' I said. 'She is very vulnerable and needs someone stable and strong.'

'He has all those qualities,' said Bonnie.

'Why is he not married or going out with anyone?' I asked.

'You will have to ask him that, but my guess is that it is mainly down to his workload and all the special tuition after working hours that he does.'

'How do we get them together, is the question?' I asked.

'Let me think for a moment and see what we can come up with. I'll need to find a man for this girl or else I might have big competition on my hands!' At this Bonnie smiled and took my hand.

'She has no chance!' I said, and kissed her.

'Wait, I have it!' Bonnie said excitedly. 'I'll make an appointment for a lesson on the weakest of her subjects. I'm sure she will make use of the knowledge even if our efforts to unite them fail.'

'That's a great idea!' I said. 'I'll phone her tonight after you arrange a date and time.'

'Do we tell him what we're up to?' asked Bonnie.

'Not a chance!' I replied. 'He's better being in the dark about it. Any blind dates my friends have been on have proved to be a disaster.'

'Are you going to tell Karin?' asked Bonnie.

'No. Only that it is in her best interest that if she wishes to fulfil her ambition as a librarian then this appointment has to be kept.'

'That should do the trick,' said Bonnie.

We had just finished our rolls and scones and felt quite pleased with our proposed plan for our unsuspecting friends. As we started to put our bits and bobs together a blind man walked past with his dog.

'What wonderful animals dogs are, and how clever to lead someone who is blind,' Bonnie commented.

'They are well trained and must not be of nervous disposition,' I said. 'Their owners love them to bits and rely totally on them when out walking, especially in town where there is heavy traffic. I have a friend who is blind, and his dog is both pet and leader. They are quite inseparable.'

The pair had only walked about 100 yards when the blind man slipped on the wet grass and started sliding towards the river. Instinctively the dog grabbed his jacket with its teeth and tugged him until he was at a standstill on the embankment. I was amazed at its quick response and the action it took.

By this time Bonnie and I had dashed to the scene, but we were unable to avert the crisis that was about to unfold. The dog lost its footing and slipped backwards into the river. Its paws were filled with soft mud and it was therefore unable to grip on the slippery surface. I couldn't believe the dilemma I was about to be faced with, but instinctively I decided I had to save the animal if possible. I have heard of hundreds of cases where owners have drowned trying to save their dogs, only for the animal to be rescued by someone else. I shouted to Bonnie, 'Take care of the gentleman – he should be safe on the flat piece of banking.'

'No, Jamie! No, Jamie! No!' were the last words I heard from Bonnie as I dived into the swift waters of the River Ness. The water was absolutely freezing, much colder than the Tay and colder than any loch I had swum in. As I surfaced I saw the dog ten yards ahead of me. I couldn't believe the speed of the river. I felt as if I was doing about fifty miles per hour. Though this might be an exaggeration, anyone who has a small car will tell you that the lower you are to the ground the greater speed feels. This was one of those situations.

I had no problem catching up with the dog; a dozen or so strokes and I caught his lead and drew him to me. There was no panic from the animal, only a bark when it closed in on me. I felt it knew that I was helping.

Oh no! I saw the town centre bridge ahead. Some people had spotted me by this time. I passed under it very quickly though.

A crowd had gathered on both sides. I could imagine what they were saying: 'There's a poor blind man, and there goes his dog with him.'

I wasn't afraid of the water; my only problem was getting out as I didn't know which side would have the best exit point. I decided to go with the left bank, which would be north, as I knew the canal would run into the estuary on that side. Sure enough I then spotted a slot and made for it immediately. I knew I had to react quickly, which I did. I was fortunate indeed as two bold fishermen had spotted me as I neared the side. Without hesitation a rod was held out for me to grasp, with both men holding firm.

I grabbed at it and entwined the dog's lead round it, giving me extra grip. With the lead now over the rod I was able to get both hands on the dog's harness and leave my fate to the fishermen. It was enough! They managed to ease the dog and me into the side.

One of the men then left his rod on the bank and ran forward a few yards. He reached out his hand, gripping the reins, and pulled the dog to safety while I held its harness. I was still hanging on as the water was pressing me forward. Thankfully the other fisherman now came to my rescue, leading the dog forward up the bank. He grabbed my shirt, then my arm, and eased me on to the embankment. What a relief – I had thought I was a goner there!

'Are you blind?' asked Sammy (I later learnt his name).

'No,' I said. 'The dog needed a little exercise and I thought I might catch a fish for tea at the same time.' I laughed.

Sammy and Fred burst out laughing. 'Thanks again!' I smiled as I pulled myself together. 'I'll have to rush back with the dog to its owner – and my girlfriend will be distraught.'

I hadn't realised the distance that I and the dog had travelled until I started to walk back. When I finally arrived at the town centre bridge I was greeted by massive applause from a huge crowd who seemed intent on asking if I was all right. 'WET! I'm only wet,' I shouted. The dog had shaken itself dry but we humans need to be dried. Finally I managed to weave myself through the crowd to where Bonnie and the blind man were standing.

The relief on her face was immense. She couldn't leave the gentleman but she waved frantically for me to hasten to her.

After I reunited the dog with its owner, Bonnie grabbed me and hugged me. 'I thought I had lost you! You fool, why do you do such foolhardy things?' she asked me.

'I couldn't let the poor dog drown. It needed me,' I said.

'Let's get back so that you can get changed and have a warm drink.'

'I don't need a wash, just a hug,' I said.

At this she thumped me and then hugged me and told me never to be such a hero again.

The gentleman thanked me kindly for saving his beloved dog and said he could never repay me. I wished him well. 'You and Barnie take care now, and stay away from the water.'

As we walked back to Bonnie's aunt's I noticed one or two flashes, which I presumed were freelance photographers taking my photo for the daily newspaper.

At tea Bonnie explained to Mary what had happened and how I had dived into the swollen river to rescue the blind man's dog. 'That was brave of you, Jamie. You will be glad you bought a change of clothing today then,' said Mary.

'I certainly am,' I replied.

'I will have all your clothes washed and dried ready for your journey in the morning.'

'Is it all right to use your phone, Mary, as I wish to phone home? I hope you didn't mind me giving Colin your number, also. I had to give a contact number to the police.'

'No trouble at all,' said Mary. 'I'll send you the bill.' And she walked away laughing.

I phoned my mum and told her I was fine as I didn't want her to worry. I phoned Karin next and told her that I had arranged an appointment with an English lecturer.

'That's good of you. I can ask all the little niggly questions that some teachers seem to shy away from,' she said.

'Bye now,' I said.

'She didn't suspect anything, Bonnie. What about your cousin – does he suspect anything?'

'No, he only said to me that he was happy to take on our young lady friend from Fort Augustus for a special lesson when I called earlier. At a discount, of course,' Bonnie smiled.

I took Bonnie into town and we sat with a glass of wine and a cola. I told her about the ship which had dumped us on the shores of Loch Ness and that I believed it had headed this way. I wanted to go to the canal but she was having none of it.

'Not on your life. You have had enough problems and heroics for today and the rest of the past week without any more trouble. Everywhere you go something happens. It's a matter for the police and you have done more than your fair share, so let it rest.' She was right of course; I knew this. We strolled hand in hand and enjoyed the rest of the day.

It was time to leave once more. Mary and Stephen had been wonderful to me and I had to promise that I would come up and see them often.

'Now I don't want any excuses from you both. You know we have plenty of accommodation so I want to see you soon,' said Mary. 'Give my regards to my sister. Tell her I'll be over to see her in September. I'll give her a call to finalise a date.'

She hugged me, which seemed to last for ever. Obviously she had taken to me and wasn't afraid to show it. While she was hugging Bonnie, Stephen gave me a firm handshake and told me to stick in with my studies.

There was a knock at the door just as we were about to leave. Stephen opened the door and a plain-clothed policeman stood before him, producing his credentials. 'Is Jamie Cameron here?' he enquired.

'Yes,' said Stephen, 'but he is about to leave for the Kyle of Lochalsh in a few minutes' time.'

'Don't worry, I won't hold him back,' he said.

The officer took me to the side and said, 'We have searched the boat you and your friend described. It was on its way to the North Sea. Unfortunately we found no trace of the diamonds or the two robbers on board. We had nothing to go on so we reluctantly had to let the boat sail. It means of course our friends are still at large. If you do hear or see anything, contact us and we will deal with them. We don't want you getting involved again.'

'Yes, sir.'

'OK, have a nice holiday and I'll get your holiday number from your friends,' said the officer.

Mary handed him the telephone number of her sister in Skye saying, 'This is the contact number should you need it, sir.'

'I'm obliged, madam.' He then took me aside and said, 'I promise to keep you informed, Jamie, of any new developments should they arise; again, have a good time.'

I filled Stephen and Mary in on what he had told me before leaving.

'Bye, my loves!' said Mary.

'Take care and look after one another,' said Stephen.

Chapter Thirty-two

Bonnie and I decided to walk to the station so that it would not be a weepy send-off. 'They are lovely people,' said Bonnie, 'but they make me want to cry every time I say goodbye when I leave.'

'You leaving him already?' a voice from behind was heard to say.

It was that cocky young good-looking porter who I think fancied Bonnie. He was the one who had told her to let me up for air.

'No, for your information we are going on holiday together,' said Bonnie.

'Oh, that's me told then! What train are you catching?' he asked.

'The one to the Kyle of Lochalsh,' I said.

'That's it sitting over there,' the young man said. 'You can board now. It leaves in fifteen minutes.'

'Thank you,' said Bonnie.

'Anything for a beautiful girl,' he replied.

'He has to have a crush on you. Are you sure you haven't met before?'

'He may have seen me once or twice at the station,' said Bonnie.

The train left bang on time and I was looking forward to the journey across country, another Scottish gem. We hardly spoke the whole way, merely pointing to each new splendid view as it passed by. Mary had prepared a packed lunch for us which was mmm... wonderful. Bonnie had to hold me back at times. 'Slow down, Jamie, you have to chew your food. It's not good for you swallowing whole.'

The views along Loch Carron were worth the trip in themselves. I recommend the excursion to everyone.

After the stunning journey we finally arrived at the Kyle of Lochalsh. We walked only a short distance into the small town.

'That's Skye over there,' said Bonnie.

'Is it?' I replied.

'You're not looking!' she shouted.

'I'm sorry. I was daydreaming.' The truth was I couldn't stop looking at her; she was so cute in her outfit of shorts and tiny boots.

'If you can take your eyes off me for just a minute I'll point out where we are going.'

'Well, if it's just for a minute then,' I said.

She smiled, then kissed me. 'Now behave.'

'Only if I get another kiss,' I said with a grin.

'OK, one only,' she replied.

I couldn't hold her as we were both wearing our rucksacks so I just held her hand, and continued to do so all the way to the ferry.

It's only about fifteen minutes across to Kyleakin on the ferry. Bonnie pointed to the one just arriving. I had to show that I was truly listening to her by asking questions, which I really didn't want to do, but the last thing I wanted was to make her cross. I asked all the usual questions – how long they stayed on the island, etc.

'I'll tell you all about them in the next few days,' she said.

At that moment I wasn't bothered about that at all.

We boarded the ferry which was pretty full of foot passengers. 'It's a nice view of the mainland from here,' she said, looking back to the Kyle. I couldn't help myself! 'It's not as good a view as I'm seeing in front of me!' She smiled that gorgeous smile at me and I desperately wanted to kiss her at that very moment. I was handicapped as I had her rucksack between my legs, plus my own on my shoulders. Seeing how restricted I was, Bonnie took the initiative, leaned towards me, gave me a hug and kissed me.

'May I sing to you?' I asked.

'You better not!' she said with an embarrassed look.

That didn't deter me. Without warning I was being kissed again.

When we parted, I said, 'Well, if that's how easy it is for me to get a kiss I'll sing to you all the way to your aunt's cottage.'

After disembarking from the ferry we took the main trunk road to Portree. 'My cousin Gordon will pick us up at the junction of the Armadale road around four o'clock. It's only two o'clock now so we have plenty of time,' said Bonnie.

Unfortunately we were caught in a heavy shower which

drenched us both. 'The clouds hit the Cuillins to the west and the rain tends to fall round this way!' said Bonnie.

No sooner than it had materialised than it disappeared in the same fashion. The air was mild so we dried in no time at all.

'Are you all right,' I asked Bonnie, 'as I felt a slight shiver?'

'Just my hands,' she said. 'It's a little cold.'

I pulled her to me. 'Give me your hands and we'll sit on this rock.' I took her rucksack off and clasped both her hands in mine; I then hugged her. 'If I didn't have this rucksack I could carry you all the way to the cottage, Bonnie,' I said.

'I know you would,' she answered.

I put my arms round her and held her tight. I kept one hand round her and took both her dainty little hands and held them in my right hand.

It was almost four o'clock, and Cousin Gordon turned up in his open truck spot on time.

'Hi, I'm Gordon. You must be Jamie,' he said in a clear voice. He stuck out his hand and gave a very strong handshake. 'Sorry, only room for one in the cab! You'll have to jump into the back, Jamie.'

I placed both our bags in the rear then boarded the vehicle. Bonnie was for none of it, and after a word with Gordon she held both her hands out for me to pull her up into the truck. I did so with ease and took her close to my chest. 'I like this!' she said, 'in fact I like it a lot!'

'Well, I'll have to acquire a truck of my own, then,' I replied.

She huddled into me all the way to the cottage. I honestly saw nothing of the scenery. I've been so lucky, I thought to myself, however did I manage to get a girl like this?

After about forty minutes we arrived at the small bed and breakfast which was about a mile or two off the main road. The road was so narrow that it was left to the conscience of the individual driver to put to one side and make way for oncoming traffic. I was surprised that everyone was so courteous.

I jumped out of the truck and Bonnie stretched out her arms for me to lift her. I ignored her for a second – and I mean a second – to look at the rucksacks. I turned back and her face had changed to that of a child with a slapped backside, or a child who had just lost its toy.

I quickly put my hands on her waist and lifted her from the truck. She clasped my neck with her hands and stared at me and, rubbing nose to nose, said, 'Are you teasing me?'

'Just a little,' I replied,' remember Ardlui?'

'How can I forget!' With that she kissed me.

By this time her aunt had appeared. She was a small, sturdy lady with hair the colour of salt and pepper. 'Give the boy a chance to breathe, girl!' she said. 'I'm Agnes, by the way, and I take it you're Jamie, the one I've heard a lot about.'

'I am,' I replied. 'Very pleased to meet you.'

'Bring in your bags and I'll show you your rooms. I've put you downstairs, Bonnie, in accordance with your mother's instruction. My sister says I've to take good care of you. As if I wouldn't. I think she forgot you were here with the girls last month, but never mind! Tell Jamie to take his boots off and leave them in the hall. There are plenty of spare slippers if he wants to use them.' She seemed to say all that without taking a breath. Amazing.

My first impression of the small farm was how close it came to a little place called the Lamb, in a small village on the Somerset/Devon border. It had hens and a donkey and also a goat. I'm not sure if it had a milking cow. My dad had made an overnight stay there on our way to Torquay. I vaguely remember being told that Dick Turpin had slept there. My dad said there was room for his horse in the bed.

This was so similar and if I had been the age I was then I wouldn't have known if I was in Skye or Devon. The kitchen had a large table with room for a dozen seated around it. I told Agnes about the similarity to my lodgings in Devon.

'Not to worry! I'll match the food you got there, no problem.'

I had made no mention of food, but bring it on, I thought, as I was rather hungry.

'This is your room, Jamie. You have a great view of the loch. It is good if you can't sleep. You have a small cupboard toilet. The basin is over in the corner with the mirror above.

'Oh, the shower is in the main hall, only one cubicle. We allow you five minutes and that's plenty of time to wash for anybody, including girls.' Again, all this in one breath.

After giving us the tour of the house, Bonnie's aunt left us to get organised. She informed us that tea would be served at six-thirty and that this should give us plenty of time.

After an hour's nap I awoke to find Bonnie leaning over me, stroking my hair. 'How are you, sleepy head?'

'What are you doing in here?' I asked her.

'Shush! Don't let Aunt hear, I'm banned from coming upstairs. I only want some hugs and kisses and to be beside you.'

'Two minutes!' I said, 'I mean it!'

I lifted her up like a rag doll and ran her out of the room.

'Oh, I can take plenty of this!' she said, giggling.

'I know, but right now get down the stairs before your aunt hears us.'

Refreshed after the shower I headed for the kitchen. I had forgotten it was a bed and breakfast establishment and when I entered the dining room the place was filled to capacity. 'Evening, evening!' came a chorus of voices.

There were the usual questions and requests for information that people like to gather in these sorts of places. It so happened that there was an elderly couple from Ayrshire and this prompted even more questions.

The aroma from the kitchen was driving me mad, as yet again my appetite was insatiable. A large terrine was brought in by a young lady who was Gordon's girlfriend. They were due to be married in September. The information was relayed by Bonnie. Bonnie called her over and introduced us.

'I'm told you have a healthy appetite,' said the young girl.

'Well, I do get rather hungry,' I said, all the while trying to play it down.

'Don't worry, I'll make sure you get the biggest portion of pie.'

She was as good as her word. My plate was heaped up twice or three times the size of Bonnie's. Steak pie with potatoes, carrots, peas, onion and cabbage, and that was after the starter, home-made potato, leek and veg soup. Hot apple pie and custard to finish, 'Oh boy!' I said to Bonnie. 'Yes, she's matched Devon, all right.

'Do you want to go for a walk down to the river?' I asked Bonnie after dinner.

'No, I've some chores to do for Aunt Agnes.'

I took a look outside around the property to see if there was something or other needing repair. I immediately noticed that a gate that held the chickens was held together with a rope. I wondered if I could fix it for Bonnie's aunt.

Agnes appeared and I asked her if she would like me to repair the gate.

'Oh, that would be a godsend as none of us can find the time to repair it. Donald is too busy, and the same goes for Gordon. There is plenty of wood in the shed with all the tools along with it,' said Agnes.

After checking what wood was in the shed I came back and told her that I could fix it with a little help from Bonnie.

It didn't take long to saw the planks and put them together with crosspieces. 'I don't believe it!' said Bonnie. 'It's taken shape before my eyes.'

After removing the old gate from the brackets I now fixed my masterpiece to them and added a new bolt. Bonnie had run to get Agnes a moment or two before I had finished. When she saw what I had done she was amazed.

'My! Jamie, I thought you were pulling my leg. Well, Bonnie, you won't have to do any more chores this week. Jamie has done enough for you both,' said Agnes.

When we had finished supper Bonnie asked, 'Do you mind coming with me to Portree and then on to see the Cuillins tomorrow?'

'Not at all, that's what I'm here for, to be with you.'

'My cousin Gordon is a plumber and he has to visit both areas. He says he'll be in both places for about two hours at a time.'

'That sounds great. You can't come to Skye and not see the Black Cuillins,' I said.

'I will go and tell Gordon – he's just finishing his tea.'

Bonnie returned full of excitement, saying, 'We leave at eight-thirty. Gordon has to be in Portree by ten o'clock.'

'That's fine,' I said, 'as long as you don't keep me awake with your snoring.'

'Why, Jamie Cameron… I'll—!'

I had to run for cover after this remark, and I mean run!

Agnes had our breakfast prepared for us and her other guests at seven-thirty; nothing to her, though, as visitors liked to be out early. Gordon had checked the weather forecast for that day and it sounded promising, which was a bonus. I didn't fancy getting a drenching in the back of his truck, as I had already tasted how the weather can turn on you.

I lifted Bonnie on to the van without asking, as I knew she would rather be in the back with me. It was good that Bonnie had been here as a regular visitor and was able to point out the various landmarks as we headed towards Portree.

Gordon stopped on the outskirts of town and told us he would take us to see the Old Man of Storr, a landmark along Glen Varragill. You have to see it and the Cuillins to say you have visited Skye. It was an hour extra on to Gordon's day. It was really kind of him to go out of his way for us.

'That's worth a picture, Bonnie,' I said, 'and the visit.'

She quickly snapped the view with a head shot of me in the frame.

'I can now tell my friends that you are the old man of Storr.'

I couldn't help but laugh and said, 'I'll autograph it for you, then!'

We arrived in Portree early enough for a morning tea, which I never refuse. Gordon left us at the cafe and promised to meet us back there in two hours unless there were any unforeseen hitches.

Bonnie wanted to have a browse round the shops so I had to agree. Having found what she was looking for we decided to go down to the harbour and watch the fishing boats make ready for sea. There was an abundance of small craft including pleasure boats in the sheltered anchorage. As we sat hand in hand admiring the view I took the opportunity to tell Bonnie of my time in Fort William with her two brothers, Angus and Duncan.

'I have to tell you there were two girls along with them on the climb up the Ben.'

'Who were the girls?' Bonnie asked.

'They met them at the campsite and got really friendly with them. They come from Whitley Bay, just north of Newcastle.'

'So are they going to meet up with them again, Jamie?'

'Well, as far as I know they are taking them back to the Borders on the coach, then Angus offered to drive them back home. I hope you are not angry with them?'

'No, I'm not. I always hoped they would meet someone. They are pretty shy with girls after all. I will have a go at them, though, for not letting me come with them and then having the audacity to allow two strangers on the bus. Boy will I have fun with them. I'll make sure Mum and Dad hear my ranting.'

'You are a little devil!'

Time flew and we headed back to meet Gordon, who appeared from a baker's shop as we arrived.

'Perfect timing!' said Gordon. 'Right, I have to shift. I need to be in the Dunvegan area in under an hour.'

We boarded our transport once more. One good thing about being in the back of a small truck is the uninhibited view of the landscape.

'Breezy, but an excellent way of seeing the island, Bonnie,' I said.

'I have never been in the back before so this is a new experience for me,' said Bonnie.

'What about your friends?' I asked.

'If you recall they had their own transport.'

'Of course they did. I completely forgot.'

The colours changed with the light, which added to the splendour of the area. Gordon dropped us off at the castle and promised to return in an hour and a half at the latest.

'An hour and a half should be plenty of time for you to see the castle,' said Gordon. 'I'll take you back through Glen Drynoch on the way home.'

Dunvegan Castle is about twenty-two miles from Portree on the western side of the island. Though I was sure the castle would have some very notable artefacts and historic records we decided not to tour there as it had turned warm and we had little enough time to spare. Instead we opted to buy a brochure and read it in the gardens, and not to forget all the photo shoots.

The castle had a picturesque wooded garden where we found a perfect spot to read up on its history. Parts of the castle are thought to date from the ninth century, but building work has been carried out in almost every century since the 1200s when the MacLeods moved in. It is said to be the oldest inhabited castle in Scotland today. Inside there are family portraits galore with antique furniture, books, trophies and weapons.

Showcases containing all sorts of medals and relics display such intriguing items as a lock of Bonnie Prince Charlie's hair and a pincushion embroidered by Flora MacDonald. Also on display is the famous Fairy Flag, of which precious little now remains. Legend has it that this sacred banner, believed to date from the seventh century, will bring success to the chief or his clan if unfurled in an emergency. However, the charm will only work on three occasions and it has already been used twice to secure MacLeod victories in battle.

Time was up and we had to run, else Gordon would be kept waiting. We made a promise, though, to visit the castle at a later date.

Although I had heard Skye was unfriendly at times to visitors, I found the exact opposite. Maybe it was because I had Bonnie's relations there.

We didn't have to wait long at our meeting point as Gordon was punctual. 'We'll go back by Glen Drynoch as promised,' said Gordon.

'You do keep good timing Gordon, every bit as well as Jamie,' said Bonnie.

'Better!' said Gordon.

'That would be good of you,' I said, 'I would like to see the Cuillins if you don't mind.'

Gordon's knowledge of the area proved to be beneficial. He told us that there were around 1,500 residents in that part of the island alone. 'You can imagine how the place could have flourished if everyone had stayed. Think of the population – it may have been a large town by now,' said Gordon. 'Sadly, little remains to show us the presence of that time.'

As we drove up the glen the Cuillins become clear to our eyes and then red hills appeared just before the tiny village of Luib. Glamaig is the best known of the red hills.

'I'll leave you for an hour beside the loch. You can take some pictures and take in the wildlife around you,' said Gordon.

Bonnie took various snaps and then was content to lie down and take in the views as Gordon had suggested.

'I was here with Lisa and Heather about six weeks ago,' said Bonnie.

'Oh, I completely forgot about that!' I said.

'Do you want to know what happened here?'

'Why? Are you going to tell stories like Colin?' I asked.

'Maybe not as well. But I'll try. Well, the three of us were walking along here and we decided on a swim, or should I say Heather decided. We had no change of clothing, as usual, so, as there was no one about, I was in the altogether.'

'You were starkers, Bonnie?'

'Afraid so, Jamie! Well, a car stopped near to ours on the roadside. As far as we could make out the owner was changing a wheel, so we didn't bother. When we were about to get out of the water Heather spotted two young lads wandering towards us. They came to the water's edge, lifted some stones and started throwing them near to us. Unfortunately they were a little too close for comfort and Heather could stand it no longer.

'I think they got a shock of their life when they saw a naked woman running out of the water at them. They weren't long in shifting and we managed to get into our clothes without any further mishaps.'

'I wish I'd been there!'

'Why, Jamie Cameron!'

'Sorry, Bonnie, I didn't mean it like that.'

'I'll forgive you this time!' said Bonnie.

'Shall I tell you about the gardens down in Armadale, Jamie? It's what I've been told by Heather and Lisa as I haven't been myself.'

'That's OK. I'll look forward to it if it's as good as the last story!'

I had to stop, she began to tickle me. 'No more nonsense, I promise, Bonnie, as long as there are no more naked girls included!'

I got up and ran but I tripped and she made the most of it. I was screaming!

'I give in. I can't stand being tickled.'

'OK, that's enough nonsense from you, my boy, for today.'

'I give in. I promise! May I say something afterwards, please?'

'Yes, you may, Jamie! I'll continue now.

'The castle is part of the Clan Donald history from around

1750 and has vast gardens. I don't know whether we can visit on the way down to Mallaig.'

'I think we will have to give it a miss this time, Bonnie. Anyway, it will give us another place to visit when we return.'

'I was supposed to go with Heather and Lisa, but my aunt needed me to do some chores. So I really can't give you a first-hand report on the gardens and castle,' said Bonnie. 'Now, what were you saying, Jamie, about hiding on Skye?'

'Well, looking at this place I find it difficult to see anywhere you could hide if you were a fugitive, unless it was high in the mountains or in some cave or ravine. I was thinking of Bonnie Prince Charlie and how terrified he must have been with no army left to defend him.'

'It certainly can be inhospitable at times, Jamie.'

'I only hope the people who sheltered him were never caught. They were certainly brave to hide him. Who knows what the consequences were for harbouring a man whom they saw as a pretender? Going by what I have read about the torture of Wallace, I can only hope they were not as barbaric at that period in history.'

'I think you know more about history than you let on, Jamie.'

I laughed and said nothing. I was about to kiss her but she interrupted me by saying, 'It's time for us to go again, Jamie. Gordon will be here shortly.'

'OK, baby.'

'You forgot something Jamie… my kiss.'

'Just testing…' I had to run again. What I did notice from this was that when she wanted a kiss it had to be there and then. Her Uncle Stephen's words rang in my ears, about how to treat a woman… carefully!

Gordon arrived pretty much on time. 'Have a good day, you pair?' he enquired.

'Lovely, thanks,' I said.

'I'll bet she didn't give you much peace, Jamie.'

'I'm not going to answer that, Gordon; I'm already treading a fine line.'

'Enough said, Jamie,' said Gordon. 'All aboard then. Oh, I'll stop and let you see the Northern slopes of the Cuillin from Sgurr nan Gillean to Bruach na Frithe.'

Bonnie had her camera out once more with a picture of me and the Cuillins in the background.

'Thanks again, Gordon, for the tour.'

'You won't thank me when you see my bill,' said Gordon, before setting off.

I hadn't yet met Bonnie's uncle as he kept irregular hours looking after his sheep. After breakfast the next morning Agnes asked if we could take a haversack to Sandy, who was on the hills. She pointed on the map where he could be found.

'Silly man is away without anything. He'll be starving. If you don't find him, take Bess with you, she'll find him all right.'

The weather had been bad overnight but had abated early in the morning. It was dry with a stiff, mild breeze when we set out to find a man I'd never met.

'With one thing and another he seems always to be busy. My aunt hardly ever sees him,' said Bonnie.

'Is he on the hills by himself?' I asked her.

'He has Spot and Patch with him. They go everywhere he goes. Bess likes it round the cottage and my aunt likes to have her here too.'

'Here, lass!' Bess licked my hand and tugged at my feet.

'She likes men,' Bonnie said.

'Don't you?' I replied as she tried to tickle me, but she wasn't quick enough. 'Let's go then, baby!'

'Yes, my dearest,' said Bonnie, laughing. 'Oh, my aunt has given us these two staffs. She says they are good for going uphill with.'

We climbed a few hundred feet and I had to admit the staff was very handy. Two small streams blocked our path which we were forced to jump as they were swollen with overnight rain. I made the jump first on each occasion. Bonnie followed and always insisted that I catch her. She made the most of every opportunity available. I obliged by playing her little game for my own selfish reasons.

We had been out for over an hour and still no sign of Sandy. Surely we should have sighted him by now; there were plenty of sheep on the hills but no evidence of any other life form. I scanned the horizon, but still nothing.

We approached a deep gully with a waterfall cascading into a deep pool, not as dangerous as the one at Inverbeg but still frightening.

'Stay back!' I said to Bonnie but she insisted on coming forward.

'Stay back!' I repeated. 'We'll have to go back and cross this further down.' She didn't listen and came forward to have a look. 'Go back, Bonnie!' I said once again. 'I've told you, we'll have to cross further down. God, she slipped, and I was helpless to stop her from sliding into the chasm. Visions of Inverbeg came flooding back. This can't be happening again! I thought.

I had no Colin to help me now so the decision of what to do rested solely on my shoulders. I crawled to the edge of the bank and looked over. There she was, holding on with her fingertips, panic stricken and clinging on for dear life. Bess howled as if she knew of the dilemma.

There was nothing else for it. I had only one plan and that was to go to her and try to save her. I tried to show her what I was going to do by holding up my arms in the hope she would respond directly to the gesture. It was now or never, she could not hold on much longer anyway. I took a deep breath and I slipped over the edge and for the second time in my life I was utterly terrified. My instincts told me to slide on my bottom as the ground was slippy, not jagged.

Over I went, positioned perfectly to catch her; hopefully she had interpreted my strategy and was willing to trust me. If she didn't trust me my attempt could be in vain. She had had plenty of practice at clinging to me when she wanted lifting. It was her favourite passion to be held like a baby.

As we met she let her hands go and pushed with her feet on the bank so that she could clasp my neck. Perfection indeed! I then pushed the edge of the bank, holding her tight, and headed into the bubbling pool below. We hit the water with a mighty splash and went under.

I couldn't see a thing for froth from the falls splashing all around the pool. I didn't let Bonnie slip from me. I had one hand round her waist. You would have to have cut my arm off to release me from her. Finally we surfaced and were being washed down by the current.

Bonnie was clinging to me like a leech and I could see the terror in her eyes. Fortunately the stream widened out and although it was raging we found ourselves in only two feet of water. We went over a small fall with height equivalent to a weir which I might have enjoyed in an altogether different circumstance.

I finally managed to get on to my feet, still carrying Bonnie. Although the current was powerful I scrambled for safety. Having reached the opposite bank, still a bit out of breath, I reassured her everything was fine, as she was crying. She said nothing but just stroked my cheeks.

After a few minutes she spoke. 'What would I do if I didn't have you?'

She then kissed me for what seemed like for ever.

Playing everything down, I said, 'I dived off of bridges higher than that into deeper water. I knew perfectly well I had tried and tested all other jumps and dives before any attempt was made.'

'You are only saying that because you really want to scold me for being a naughty person and not doing what I was told.'

By this time Bess had come down from the cliff and swum across to meet us. The dog was so excited it kept licking me as if it knew what I'd done.

'You have another girl eating out the palm of your hands,' said Bonnie.

I look off my shirt and socks to let them dry in the mild air.

'Take off your underwear as well,' said Bonnie. 'I'll turn my back. They'll dry in a short time.'

I did what I was told. After a half hour I had everything back on.

'Turn your back so that I can take my underwear off now,' said Bonnie. I did this reluctantly but I am a gentleman and always will be. She was left wearing only a cotton blouse and her shorts. I tried not to look at her cleavage but it was extremely difficult.

'I know you want to look!' said Bonnie. 'In any other circumstances I would say no, but you can if you want.'

'I do want to, but I won't. I love you too much so I will wait.'

With that she pulled me to her and kissed me once more. 'I love you, Jamie boy!'

'Me too!' I said.

With that we both burst out laughing.

Bess was beginning to grow weary of not getting any attention, and let it be known by letting out a few barks of discontentment.

We sat on a large rock for a few minutes gathering ourselves together after the ordeal. Bess began prodding at me again.

'Hello lass! What's the matter?' I said, stroking her head all the while. 'You want some love and attention too, don't you.'

Bess lay down wanting her tummy rubbed, and I duly obliged while Bonnie stroked her head.

'She'll take that kind of attention all day,' said Bonnie.

'Much the same as yourself then,' I said.

Bonnie laughed. 'Yes, we girls can take all the care and attention that's going.'

We had forgotten our purpose of being in the hills after the near disaster on the cliff.

After a brief rest Bonnie decided to put her underwear back on. It had dried quickly in the stiff breeze.

'I'll go behind the big rock over there,' said Bonnie. 'I don't want to be exposed naked to the whole world.'

'Why not?' I said, laughing.

'Behave, Jamie!'

Five minutes later she appeared from her shelter smiling once more. 'That's much better. I felt like one of those girls who decided to give up their bras,' said Bonnie with her beautiful brimming smile.

'Let's go and find your uncle now,' I said. 'Come on, Bess, find Sandy! Find him, Bess!'

Bess ran off into the distance sensing what I was telling her. 'Do you think she understands?' I asked Bonnie.

'With my experience of her I'm sure she understands,' said Bonnie.

Fifteen minutes later we heard the sound of barking. 'That has to be Uncle Sandy's two collie dogs,' said Bonnie.

'Look, Bonnie! Look there! It's two collies. They are coming down the hillside, they have seen us and are very excited.'

They reached us in a matter of minutes and greeted us with

moans and howls. 'They are trying to tell us to follow them, Jamie, I can tell.' Bess also sensed the urgency.

'Here, Bess, lass, what's the matter?' She whimpered then jumped up on me and tugged my shorts. 'You're right, Bonnie,' I said. 'Go, lass, go!'

'I told you they are clever dogs, Jamie.'

'Come on, Bonnie, there must be something wrong. We'll have to hurry. I'm afraid something might have happened to your uncle.'

The collies were running up the hillside with us in pursuit. 'This will be a real test of stamina for Bonnie,' I thought. To my surprise she was quicker going uphill than I.

When we reached the peak we rested for a minute before continuing.

'Look, Jamie, down to your left. All three dogs are standing by someone. It must be Uncle Sandy! Oh, I do hope he's not too badly hurt.'

'Be careful on the way down. I can't afford to carry you if Sandy needs to be carried.'

'Are you scolding me, Jamie?'

'No, baby, I just don't want you hurt!' I leaned over and kissed her.

'I forgive you then,' said Bonnie.

We found Sandy in a ditch. He had gone over on his ankle and was in pain. I lifted him easily as he would only be about ten stone, a tall, slight-made man with dark hair growing grey at the sides.

Bonnie gave him a cup of tea from the flask and a couple of sandwiches.

'You must be Jamie, then,' said Sandy.

'That's me!' I replied.

'Heard a lot about you, son.'

'It's not true!' I replied.

'Well, it seems to be all good what I heard,' said Sandy.

'It is!' said Bonnie, quick to agree. 'He's fixed the gate for you, Uncle.'

'Well, that's good news. It'll save me another earbashing from your Aunt Agnes.'

'How are you now, Sandy?' I asked. 'Think you can walk leaning on my shoulder?'

'I'll give it a try. Can't sit here all day and night.'

I eased him up to his feet. 'How's that?' I asked.

'It's a little easier now. I don't think it's broken. Just a little swollen,' said Sandy.

'It's about six miles back to the village,' said Bonnie.

'It's only three miles to the road,' said Sandy.

'Oh, that's good,' I replied. 'I can carry you for the last mile if I need to.'

After an hour and a half we were making little progress so I said, 'There is nothing else for it, Sandy, I'll have to carry you the last mile to the road.'

I gave him a piggyback and the dogs were delighted, jumping and running all around us.

'Go on you silly beggars!' Sandy shouted, noticing they were taking full advantage of the predicament he was in. You could hardly fail to notice that they loved their master.

'That's the road now, and with a little luck we might find Gordon on his way home if it's around six,' Sandy said.

We had hardly reached the road when Bonnie spotted the truck in the distance. 'There's Gordon!' Bonnie said excitedly.

'That's a godsend. We couldn't have planned it better than this,' I sighed.

He pulled up beside us. 'What's the matter, Dad?' Gordon shouted from the truck.

'Over on my ankle, son!' Sandy informed him.

'I'll take you to the doctor, then,' Gordon replied.

'No, I want to go home! I'll see the doctor in the morning, son,' Sandy said wearily.

I helped Sandy into the truck with the help of Gordon.

'You don't mind the back of the truck, Jamie?' Sandy asked.

'No, Bonnie doesn't mind either!' Gordon said, winking at me.

I lifted the dogs in. They were enjoying it and had obviously experienced the ride in the truck before. Jumping up myself I then offered Bonnie my hands to pull her up. This time, however, she insisted that I lean over so that she could cling to my neck with her hands. This made it impossible for me to refuse to kiss her as she was totally in control.

'I love this!' she said with a smile.

'So do I!' I replied.

Gordon shouted out of his cab window, asking us, 'Are we all settled in?' knowing full well what Bonnie was up to.

Agnes put on a cold compress and gave Sandy two painkillers to alleviate the pain. Within an hour he felt much better.

After dinner Sandy told us that they were having a celebration for Gordon and his fiancée in the church hall down at the village. 'Nothing fancy,' Sandy told us. 'You and Bonnie will be leaving the following day. Is that right, Jamie?'

'Yes, it is, Sandy. We hope to catch the early morning ferry from Armadale to Mallaig.' I related all the details of the impending trip.

'Seems you had a very busy day, Jamie, carrying me with a swollen ankle – and I've just been told you saved my niece from the river.'

'All in a day's work!' I said. 'I just happened to be there at the appropriate time. I was forced into decisions which were for-midable to say the least. The outcome was satisfactory, though, as I got the girl.'

Bonnie stretched out her hand at that.

'You're just a wee pair of love birds!' said Agnes. 'I'll tell your mum you're in safe hands, Bonnie!'

We all had an early night. I was truly exhausted after the events of the day. I kissed Bonnie goodnight and told her to go to bed as well. 'You're bound to be tired after all that excitement,' I said.

'OK, Jamie, just one more cuddle,' she replied.

Next day I overslept and no one bothered to waken me. Agnes had told Bonnie to let me rest. Although I was being modest about the events of the day it was bound to have taken its toll.

Chapter Thirty-three

I looked at the clock and it was ten-thirty. It was nearly lunch time. By the time I had washed and changed it was eleven o'clock when I entered the kitchen.

'Ah, there you are!' Agnes exclaimed. 'You'll be in need of a big breakfast.'

'Yes, Agnes, I am hungry!' I replied.

'Just sit yourself down and I'll make it.'

'Where's Bonnie?' I asked.

'She's off to Portree with Gordon. She wants to get an engagement present for them.'

'Of course, it's the party tonight!'

'Yes, it is,' said Agnes. 'I've been baking since I got up.'

'I could smell it from the top of the stairs. That's what brought me down.'

In a matter of minutes Agnes produced a full breakfast, which was delicious, and she added a few freshly baked scones.

'You take Bonnie down to the loch today and just relax. She will be back shortly,' said Agnes.

'That sounds good,' I said.

'It'll be a tonic for the both of you.'

Bonnie arrived while I was sitting on the porch. 'Is this what you do when I'm away?' she asked.

'Sunbathing and reading a good book, it's great for the nerves,' I said to her.

'You lazy thing. I'm up early for groceries and a present and you were still in bed when I left at nine o'clock. When did you rouse from your slumber?' she asked.

'Around eleven,' I replied.

She was now beside me. 'You deserve it, after what you did for me yesterday.'

'Well, where is my present then?' I said.

'I have only one present for you!' With that she kissed me and put her arms round me and sat on my knee. 'Is this not the best of presents?' she said.

'Yes, it certainly is.' I reciprocated with an affectionate kiss on her forehead.

'I'll show you the present I have bought Gordon and Isobel,' she said. She opened a box and produced an iron. I was surprised at the choice of gift but Bonnie enlightened me to the facts.

'It's not what I would have chosen, but Isobel asked me to buy something practical. I obliged by bowing to her request. I could see the puzzled expression on your face. Are you content now?' she asked.

'Yes. That's perfectly reasonable and very practical.

'Your aunt says that we should take a walk down to the loch, and has offered to make us up tea and sandwiches for our picnic,' I said.

The air was fresh as one would expect in this part of the country. There was a slight breeze on our backs as we left. This made the walk relatively easy. We had only a light haversack borrowed from Agnes, which I carried, allowing Bonnie to get up to all sorts of mischief being free of any encumbrance.

At one point I was forced to take the sack off. I grabbed her after a short chase and lifted her into my arms.

'How is my naughty baby today?' I asked her.

'She is in heaven or on the next best thing,' Bonnie replied.

I put her down and clasped her hand and retrieved the picnic bag. In just over an hour we found a sheltered spot on the shores of the loch.

'I have been here before!' Bonnie exclaimed. 'It seems so much nicer with you here, though!'

'You know, I feel the same way about you,' I replied. 'I have experienced this phenomenon on a few occasions. When Colin comes into the room you can almost feel the atmosphere change. He has an inward air which he exudes and I'm sure everyone knows it.'

'Do you think he'll ever settle down?' asked Bonnie.

'If he finds someone like you I'm sure that he will,' I replied.

'That's very kind of you,' said Bonnie.

'It's true!' I said.

We lay in the sunshine for a little while. 'Look, Bonnie, fish are jumping to catch flies now that the breeze has dropped.'

'It's a gorgeous day now,' said Bonnie. 'Oh, look over there, it's a young hind taking a drink from the stream flowing into the loch.'

'It looks unsteady on its feet. It can't be very old,' I said.

'Oh no, it's stuck in the mud! Look, it can't move its right leg. Can't we help?' asked Bonnie.

'We can't do a thing!' I said, 'it would only panic and it might break its leg if we go near.'

'Wait a minute, Jamie! Isn't that its mum coming down the stream?'

'Yes it is, Bonnie. I'm sure she will help it.'

Sure enough the doe came alongside and leaned on the fawn till it was freed. 'Isn't nature wonderful, Jamie?'

'Yes it is! I remember reading that elephants are most protective of their young, and not only their own. If a calf gets into difficulty all the females gather round to help. The herd instinct, I guess.

'I'm sorry, Bonnie! I don't want to leave but it's time to go back. We have to change for the party as it's at eight o'clock, so we will need to get a move on to be home for six o'clock.'

We were almost at the cottage as I could now see it clearly from the small hill where we were standing.

'That's the view my Aunt Agnes has from her window every day. Isn't she lucky?'

'It's fantastic and she knows it!' I said.

With only one stile to get over Bonnie insisted on me lifting her up then waiting till I was over so that I could catch her on the other side.

'You are an expert when it comes to stiles!' I said.

'Oh, I love them!' she replied. 'Race you to the cottage!'

She was off like a rocket before I had a chance to lift the haversack so I carried it in my hands as all that was left was the empty plate, container and flask.

'Beat you!' Bonnie shouted.

The dogs began barking as we ran in the yard. 'C'mon lass, and boys!' I cried, and they ran circles round me as if I were a sheep. They were up for a bit of fun so I ran into the hayshed with all three tearing after me. Bonnie, not to be left out, followed in hot pursuit. Five minutes of frolic and tickling calmed the dogs down.

'What are you like?' Bonnie said, laughing heartily.

'I like that, and you'll find plenty of fun, if you don't succumb to the norm,' I said.

'It's true. If you are young at heart you will always remain so!'

'So I can call you my young Jamie then!' said Bonnie.

'That's me!'

Bess had followed me into the house, which wasn't allowed. Bonnie quickly and silently led her, putting her fingers on her lips as if to say shush to me. Then she pointed to Bess. I got the message and helped to lead her outside.

Bonnie said, 'She's a working dog and you're treating her like a pet.'

'Yes, I know. I find it difficult not to give her affection though.'

I gave her a hug and clapped. 'Go Bess!' and she ran off to the barn.

'Away you and get washed now!' said Bonnie.

A quick shower and change of attire and I was ready for the engagement party. I wore my kilt for the occasion, to the delight of Bonnie and Agnes.

'Aye, you'll not be out of place tonight!' said Agnes.

Bonnie had on a short kilt which drove me wild. 'What do you think, Jamie?' she said.

'Aye, not bad – maybe a little shorter would help!' I replied.

With that remark she came after me and I had to run outside. Obviously she had taken it to heart and believed what I was really saying was that the kilt was too short. She caught me easily and she scolded me greatly. 'Don't you like it?' she said.

'Like it! It drives me wild!' I replied with a grin. 'I just don't want anyone to see you in it.'

'That's all right then, I forgive you.' She kissed me and said that she would take it off.

'No, honest, I'll enjoy the night even more as I won't be able to take my eyes off your legs all night.' With that I made a dash for it as I knew she was going to thump me. I finally managed to quieten her down by saying how beautiful she looked.

'Aye, Jamie, I think you have a lot of Colin in you. You like to tease the lassies,' she said.

The coach arrived to take us to the venue and we all piled in, not forgetting the food hampers. Both Sandy and Gordon had adorned kilts, along with Agnes and Isobel in tartan. The guests, not wishing to be left out, were all decked out in some form of tartan or other.

'That's us, driver!' said Agnes.

The band was already set up for the evening with all their gear in place. I'm sure we must have been last to arrive as the hall could not allow any more guests to be seated. The community hall was nothing to write home about, but would serve the purpose for the event.

We made our way up to the table and without more ado Tom gave a speech welcoming Isobel and her family into the fold. The buffet was set out and a queue formed almost immediately. They had obviously heard of Agnes's baking.

'I thought they would have waited,' I said to Bonnie.

'Don't worry, Jamie, Agnes has held back half of the contents of the hampers. The rest of the food is in the kitchen.'

'Oh, that's excellent thinking!' I said.

'I knew that would please you,' said Bonnie.

The ceilidh was great and all of the guests were good dancers. Kilts were swirling in time to the music, bows and fiddles at top speed…

At the end of the evening I said to Bonnie, 'You must have a lot of experience at these reels.'

'Only when I come up north,' she replied.

'I never would have guessed that,' I said.

No one asked me to play a tune which I was glad of as it let me enjoy the dancing and gave me the opportunity for a slow dance with Bonnie. I think I would have resented someone else dancing with her if I had been part of the musicians providing the music. The evening closed with 'Auld Lang Syne' as we all made a circle. It was then hugs, kisses and tears all round as we said our goodbyes.

Morning came too soon and I found myself rushing to pack and wash before breakfast. Saying farewell to Agnes and Sandy was difficult, but I managed and I had to promise I would return very soon.

Bess came running out to greet me as I boarded the truck. Sensing I was going away the dog jumped up and made a fuss by licking me intensely before running off to its kennel.

It was waves of goodbye again. If I could change goodbyes I would do away with them; I always feel so tearful. Gordon then drove us to the ferry. We wished him and his future bride, Isobel, all the best for the future.

'I have the perfect girl, so I'm lucky!' said Gordon. 'I'll be sending you an invite to the wedding in late September. Now that the house is ready, Isobel wants to get married and settled into our home before the winter.'

'I'll look forward to the wedding; they are always good fun,' I replied.

'Isobel will make sure of that!' Gordon replied.

'Bye, Jamie. Bye, Bonnie. See you soon and have a good time,' said Gordon, smiling.

We boarded the ferry for Mallaig. I hadn't sailed this way before and words fail me to describe the view. Bonnie said to me, 'I love this trip to Skye. I'm so fortunate to have relations on this island.'

'You certainly are, Bonnie! I wish my great grandparents hadn't left the Highlands.'

I was pleased to accept Gordon's invitation to his wedding. It didn't make leaving so sad. Bonnie nodded agreement with me.

It was only a short sail across the Sound of Sleat with the ferry capable of holding a few cars and vans. We made our way to the train station which was only a short distance away. I remember Colin saying that this was the end of the West Highland line, or the start, whichever way you want to look at it.

There were plenty of seats as it was still early. Tourists would be making their way here. 'I hope we are able to see the views,' I said to Bonnie.

'Sometimes the trees along the track block the scenery,' Bonnie said.

Mallaig station is not far from the bustling port where an abundance of trawlers were unloading their vast catch. 'It makes me wonder, Bonnie, about the continuing catch of fish. Just look at what is being brought ashore here, and this is only one port. How the ocean is supposed to replenish itself with this haul being removed day in and day out I'll never know. I feel there will be a day of reckoning coming.'

'Maybe a programme of farming fish will come into being, Jamie.'

'I hope so for the sake of us all, and that includes all wildlife'

The train times were set to meet with the arrival and departure of the ferry so it was not long till we were under way. I began to tell Bonnie of one of my longest journeys on a train. 'Six years ago my mum took us all the way to Paignton in Devon. It was quite a journey by steam train at the time. We had part of a carriage with a door on both sides. The coach had no corridor so there was no ticket collector, only a check before and after the journey.

'It took almost fourteen hours to make the trip. I climbed on to the rack above which held suitcases and tried to have a sleep. The rack had steel brackets which held it to the wall with a net similar to ones used in football goals. It was very uncomfortable. However, I did manage a few hours' sleep.'

'Oh, that was a long journey. I have never been on one as long as that. I'm sure you were glad to get off,' said Bonnie.

'It was worth it though,' I said. 'I love Devon the way I love the north of Scotland. I hope to go even further next time and see Land's End.'

'Maybe you will have a car in a year or so, then you can drive yourself there,' said Bonnie.

'That's very optimistic of you, Bonnie!'

'Well, why not? They say if you can see it happening then it will happen.'

'Mmm...'

It was another wonderful train journey down to Fort William from Mallaig. One of the focal points is the famous Glenfinnan Viaduct which twists over the valley below.

'This is where Bonnie Prince Charlie met the clan chiefs to discuss his plans and fight for his throne,' said Bonnie, pointing to a monument built in commemoration of the rising.

'Aye,' said I, 'and ended up in Culloden Moor.'

'It was a sad time in Scottish history, Jamie.'

'I wonder how many Cameron relatives of mine were lost, Bonnie. Fathers, sons, cousins and uncles. Think of the poor women of the time losing all that was dear to them. It must have been heartbreaking for them. It's a wonder there were any of us left at all given the extent of the defeat.'

'Every clan was involved so it must have been the same for us all,' said Bonnie.

'I think we should lighten up a little, Bonnie!'

'Yes please!' she replied.

'Well, you know Colin called last night.'

'Yes,' said Bonnie.

'He was telling of his escapades after leaving the Kyle of Lochalsh. Do you want to hear?'

'I'll start tickling you if you start to tease again! You know full well I do.'

'All right then. He headed up to Gairloch in Wester Ross and set up tent for the night. Although it was a large site he was forced to pitch his tent close to the edge of the cliff as it was filled to capacity. The wind got up during the night and lifted the tent off him leaving him exposed to the elements with only a pair of flimsy underpants.'

'Ha-ha haa! That sounds hilarious!' said Bonnie.

'Of course, the tent next to him had four girls in residence, which was not surprising. Colin's tent landed on top of theirs and woke them up. When the girls popped out from the tent they were startled by a huge near-naked figure standing at the door of their tent.'

Colin's phone conversation:

'What do you think girls did in those sort of circumstances, Jamie?'

'Scream!'

'Yes, you're right, they started screaming! Boy did they scream! The whole campsite was now awake. I tried to point out my dilemma but all they did was point at my lower extremities. It turned out the girls were French, which I discovered once they had stopped screaming. They must have thought I was some sort of depraved maniac.

'Recovering my dignity with a pair of shorts I made signs of how the wind had blown my tent away. With my little knowledge of French I managed to bring on a relative calm and they began to titter among themselves. I salvaged my tent and went about trying to pin it to the ground to no avail. I pointed to my tent and rucksack and gestured that they sit on them till I return. They acknowledged with a nod.

'I then headed down to the beach to get some rocks. One of the girls decided to follow me to the beach, which was nothing unusual. Finding a stone to my requirements I put it under my arm. The girl, seeing what was needed, proceeded in doing the same.

'I went on further down the beach and became alarmed as the sand had gone over my knees. Whether it was my weight or quicksand I wasn't sure. Mustn't panic, I thought, ease back the way you came, boy.

'The girl had followed me and found herself in the same predicament, but being much lighter only sank to her calves. The girl easily lifted her legs more freely out of the sand, to my amazement. I knew then it was my weight that was pushing me further into the sand. I let myself fall forward and started to crawl on my hands and knees, to the delight of the young lady who was in hysterics at my antics.

'Reaching the bottom edge of the cliff I raised myself once more on to my feet. I beckoned the girl to me and pointed to various stones that were suitable for the purpose in hand. We carried as many as possible on each trip. It took two more trips to suffice.

'The girls gave a hand to put up my tent and placed the collection of stones around the base of the tent as well. I explained that it was the lack of space on the site that had forced me to the edge of the cliff which was open to the updrift of the wind. The girls had a larger and stronger tent but used some of the spare stones on their base as a precaution.

'Five o'clock in the morning, would you believe, was the time. Needless to say I went back to my tent and slept till lunch time.'

Colin continued:

'I met the girls that evening at the nearby hotel. It was real fun trying out my pidgin French on them. Every so often there were fits of laughter from them. I'm not sure why, but I guessed that they were taking sexual interpretations out of my explanations. I'll never know!

'One of them had a French to English dictionary which was produced later in the evening after we were all slightly intoxicated, which even added more fun to an enjoyable evening. I wish you were here with me, but I know you will be having fun yourself with Bonnie. Give her my regards and send her my love,' said Colin.

'I don't think so, pal! Regards, yes, love, no!' I told him.

'Is that what he said?' asked Bonnie.

'Yes! But that's Colin.'

'I hope you don't miss him too much,' said Bonnie.

'Not at all. I love being with you. I'll see plenty of him when I get back home.'

'That's OK then,' said Bonnie while kissing me.

'Do you want to hear more, Bonnie?'

'There's more?'

There's always more where Colin is concerned,' I said.

'Oh, go on then please! I love his stories.'

'Well, the girls asked him where he intended going the next day. Of course, Colin immediately answered the question with a question – a politician's ploy.'

This is how Colin told the story:

' "Where are you headed?" I asked them.

' "Oh we are heading up to Ullapool for two days then down to Inverness after that."

' "Why, that's exactly what I'm doing," I told them.

' "Have you got a car?" they asked me.

' "No," I replied.

'They told me they had a van but it would be a tight squeeze for me, and they made fun by gesturing to my size and bulk. By the way, Jamie, it took all evening to get this information using the dictionary. I could never have gleaned the whereabouts of where they were going, nor the lift in the car without it. I learnt their names, which seem so pretty when said in French. One petite blonde was called Emilie, the others, Liliane, Sylvie and

Jeanne. I mention the blonde who of course is my favourite.'

'Do you wish to learn more of Colin's exploits, Bonnie?'

'Oh, please keep going. His stories are fascinating,' said Bonnie.

Colin continues: 'I fell sound asleep that evening. Anything could be better than the previous night I had, no gales or heavy rain, only sweet dreams of French maids.

'In the morning the girls gave me a cooked breakfast and then asked if I would take down their tent and put it into their van. It was an old van but it suited their needs. I suspect they hadn't intended giving someone of my size and stature a lift. The girls were amazed how tightly I managed to pack in the tent and their bags.

' "We have so much room now!" Emilie said.

'I told them I was used to packing, so it wasn't a problem. It was about eleven o'clock before we were ready to go. You know how long it takes for women to get ready, Jamie. Unfortunately I was in the back of the van with the baggage, and the only view of the scenery was from the rear window, which was small. The girls decided on a stop halfway which I was relieved about. Oh good, they stopped at a hotel. I visualised a cold pint of beer and a bar meal.

'It was a relief to stretch my legs and wander down to the loch. Of course my entourage followed me and before long we were all having a paddle. I must say it's much more fun having four girls as companions rather than looking after you, Jamie boy.

'We piled back into the van. I felt like a sardine once more but we were only an hour from Ullapool so I contented myself with receiving the lift.

'After setting up camp we found a nice hotel on the outskirts of town. I felt like a celebrity taking four lovely girls out on my own. As the night wore on I felt more like a chaperone, as my female companions were besieged by the local lads, whose attempts, by the way, were pathetic in trying to woo them. The girls found it funny, though, with the signs they were making to try and make themselves understood.

'Oh, the last thing before I ring off. The bar closed at ten o'clock so it was an early bed – well, so I thought. One of the staff asked if we would like to buy tickets for the ceilidh which was starting at ten-thirty and continuing until 2 a.m. The girls snapped up the tickets and bought me one as well. Of course then the lights went out in the bar and we all tripped outside to wait in a large queue.

'Finally gaining entrance we made our way to the bar. As we entered the light came on and, lo and behold, the local lads were sitting on their stools drinking away in the dark. They burst out laughing when we appeared. They obviously knew the ropes, but couldn't let on else they might have found themselves on the street.

'Anyway it was a great night. I'm still aching from dancing with all the girls. I'll give my mum a call and tell her to get in touch with your folks.

'Bye for now, Jamie.'

'Oh, that was funny!' said Bonnie. 'Will Colin call your mum?'

'No. What he will do is call his mum and dad and they will contact mine. It saves us both money and they are happy with that.'

'Oh, that's us nearly there,' said Bonnie. 'Do you mind if we spend a few hours in Fort William? I would like to do a little shopping. The other reason is that I didn't want to sit all the way to Oban without a break, Jamie.'

'No problem. I can go down to the pier and see what's happening. I'll check when the next train is to Crianlarich before we leave the station.'

I reported back, 'The next service is not for two hours, Bonnie, which is a good break and gives you plenty of time for shopping.'

'Perfect! You don't mind, do you, Jamie?'

'No, I want a break myself.'

Chapter Thirty-four

The town was bustling with visitors; the weather had helped as coaches seemed to be coming through the centre of town from all directions.

'Will you be all right shopping on your own, Bonnie?' I asked.

'You go down to the loch and I'll buy us a snack and we can find a nice spot to eat it.'

'See you shortly, baby!'

I sauntered down to the harbour where two or three fishing boats had tied up. It was a day for the repairs by the look of it as noise seemed to be coming from all quarters. I couldn't see a soul so I concluded the maintenance must be being done on the engines and pumps without which the boat would sink.

There was a gentleman fishing off the pier so I wandered in his direction. As I was making my way along I noticed a sea cruiser in the distance. That boat looks strikingly familiar, I thought. It surely can't be the one Colin and I were abducted on, then dumped on the shores of Loch Ness.

Given the time lapse the cruiser could have sailed round the north of Scotland via the Pentland Firth, as the weather had been favourable. More likely it could have sailed back down using the canal as there was nothing to connect it to the robbery. Was I just daydreaming or letting my imagination run riot again? Time would tell.

I made my way further out along the pier and exchanged a few pleasantries with the lone fisherman. 'That boat!' said the man. 'Something strange about it – it has been circling for over an hour. Up to no good if you ask me!'

'Maybe it's waiting to pick someone up,' I said.

'Either that or something,' said the fisherman.

'It's definitely coming in now,' I said, 'look at the frothy wake it's leaving.'

'Aye, you're right!'

Just at that moment, I spotted two men running towards us along the pier. I turned to the fisherman at once and asked, 'May I borrow your rod?'

'Whatever for?' he enquired.

'Look, I know these two louts running along the pier. They are part of a gang that robbed a jeweller's over a week ago. I'm afraid they might recognise me as I informed the police of their whereabouts, but they managed to elude capture.'

Without saying a word he dug into his haversack and handed me a hat, one of those floppy type only a fisherman would wear. I quickly pulled it on and accepted the rod which was now being offered. The two robbers ran past without giving me a second glance, to my great relief.

'Looks like your pals are going for a boat trip,' said the fisherman, 'and they are acting suspiciously, with all their signals.'

'I think they still have the stolen loot on them and the cruiser is back here to collect it,' I said to him.

'It's a bit far-fetched for me but I suppose I'll have to take your word for it. What do you intend doing about it?' asked Andy (the fisherman, whose name I finally managed to secure).

'Once the boat berths in a couple of minutes I'll see what transpires. My hope is that they will stay on board and put to sea. That way I can inform the police where the boat is headed and that all the criminals are on board.'

We waited and waited but no sign of movement.

'Oh, I've got a tug on the line,' said Andy, 'feels like a big one.'

Our attention was now diverted to his catch rather the cruiser.

He reeled in the fish and exclaimed, 'It's a nice couple of mackerel on the hook. The tide's coming well in now, there must be a shoal in to feed.'

Just as he was putting his fish in his basket I saw Bonnie in the distance. I gave her a wave and she acknowledged me, blowing kisses.

'Your girl?' asked Andy.

'Sure is!' I said proudly.

She greeted me with a kiss and I introduced Andy to her.

'I have bought three pies. Would you like one, Andy? Jamie will eat two or even three if I leave them with him.'

'Thank you,' said Andy,' 'the fish can wait!'

We had only just finished our snack when I saw some movement on the boat. My two friends were disembarking, much to my disappointment. As they climbed on to the pier I told Bonnie that this was the cruiser that I was abducted on and the two robbers were now approaching us.

'Quickly, Bonnie, get out your camera and take a photo of Andy and me holding the fish. Wait till you have their heads in the frame then take the picture. It will give the police a mugshot of them and should help trace them.'

Bonnie did exactly as I said. 'Got them, Jamie!'

'Well done, darling,' I said.

'Oh, it's darling now is it,' said Bonnie, laughing loudly.

'Look!' said Andy. 'The cruiser is off now. They obviously have what they want now, else they would be staying.'

'You're right, Andy. It's time I phoned that number the detective gave me. He told me to contact him and let them take care of it. I will wait a couple of minutes though as I don't want those two to think I'm following them. I couldn't tackle them on my own.'

'Aye that'll no do you onny harm,' said Andy.

I thanked Andy for his help and wished him luck with his rod. 'Hope you get a good haul, Andy, and thank you for your assistance.'

'Glad to be of help. You and your girl have a good holiday; leave those thugs to the police.'

'Bye, Andy! Bye!'

I looked back as we reached the main road and I pointed towards Andy. 'Hey, Bonnie, he has got another catch. He's bringing them in now.'

'If Colin was here the pair of you would be out fishing and I would be on my own. Colin should think about marrying a fish,' said Bonnie.

Oh-oh, I thought, I had better not mention fish again.

'I have to find a phone, Bonnie.' Did you happen to see one in the high street when you were shopping?'

'Yes, I did actually. I called my mum to tell her that we were on our way to Oban now.'

'That's good. Do you remember exactly where it is?' I asked.

'Yes. It's in a small square in the centre of town. I think there are four of them altogether.'

'Even better. That means there is good chance of getting one working.'

Typical – when we arrived every box was occupied and we had only half an hour before our train left. 'Oh, I hope they are not too long, Bonnie!'

'Patience, Jamie, you won't have to wait long.'

'It's just that we have a fifteen-minute walk to the station, Bonnie.'

'Oh, I completely forgot that.'

Luckily a kiosk became vacant but a pushy woman barged in ahead of me saying she had been waiting much longer than me. I was caught unawares and let her go in. 'What was I to say, Bonnie? She looks to be in a hurry to make the call.'

'Always the charitable one, Jamie,' said Bonnie, giving me a kiss.

Moments after going into the kiosk the lady reappeared with a frown on her face. 'That one's useless!' she said. 'You'd better try some other one; I can't get it to take my coins!'

That did not deter me. 'Go in, Bonnie, I'll give it try.'

I put in two single shillings. One came back out as quickly as it went in. 'Have you another shilling, Bonnie?'

'Yes, I have plenty of change after shopping.'

'Give me that shiny one, it looks quite new.' I placed it in and, yes, it took it.

'Well done, Jamie!' said Bonnie.

I managed to get through to the inspector and told him that cruiser was heading down the loch towards the open sea. I also told him that the two thieves were at large and that I had taken a photo of them. He told me to hand the spool to the desk constable in Fort William. 'As soon as we have finished our conversation I'll inform them that you are coming.'

He went on to explain that he would call the coastguard at Oban and that there were many places that a ship of that sort could find anchorage. 'It could slip away under cover of darkness, but because you have told us he has just left port and has no suspicion of anyone following him, that gives us a ideal opportunity of catching him between Mull and Oban.'

I told the inspector where we would be staying in Oban and he wished us well.

'Let's get that train now, Bonnie!' I said.

We made the train just in time and found a good seat. 'I'm looking forward to this journey, Bonnie. It goes all the way through Rannoch Moor.'

'I think it will be a bit bleak if the weather is dull after we leave Roy Bridge,' said Bonnie.

'Have you been on this route then?'

'No, it's just I know what happens on the rail journey to Inverness. It's nearly always dark about forty miles from Aviemore when it passes through the mountains.'

As it turned out Bonnie was correct on this occasion and it was very misty as we stopped at Rannoch station. I hated to say she was right so decided to talk about the earlier incident.

'I'm just glad that I was able to pass on the whereabouts of those robbing thugs who beat me up. I can't wait to tell Colin. The police shouldn't be long in picking them up now, Bonnie.'

'The only things I care about are getting my spool with my photos of Skye and that we don't have any more to do with those clowns who hit you,' said Bonnie.

There wasn't much to add to that so I changed the subject once more. I began daydreaming of Skye as I lay on Bonnie's shoulder.

'What are you thinking about?' enquired Bonnie.

'Oh, how I'm going to miss Skye and my old girl Bess. She followed me everywhere and it broke my heart to leave her.'

'She certainly did take to you, maybe because you made such a fuss of her. Anyway, you can come up again in the autumn with me if you want.'

'Oh, I'll put that in my diary as a definite yes, then.'

'Goodness! I completely forgot to tell Aunt Agnes that Aunt Mary is coming down to pay her a visit. Remind me to phone her when we reach Oban, Jamie.'

'Will do,' I said. 'Oh, do you wish to hear a small poem that I wrote for you? Or will I tell it to you later?'

'Jamie, you don't tell women things later, we don't like suspense!'

'OK, you win! It's called:

Bonnie

From the first moment I met you
Your voice so sweet and tender, your heart so
Straight and true.
Your hair is dark as chestnut and glistens like
The morning dew.
Your eyes are deep with mystery, yet never hold
Their gaze.
Your touch is like the sun which sets my heart
Ablaze.
Your first signal lit a fire and set my world
Alight
You were mine from that moment and now my
World is bright.

Jamie Cameron

'Oh, that's for me, Jamie? How wonderful! Is that how you think of me?'

'Yes, my baby!'

Chapter Thirty-five

As we were now approaching Crianlarich I made my way to the cubicle rack for our luggage. This is where we were to change for Oban on the second leg of our train journey. I managed to dislodge both our packs after a bit of heaving and pulling. I can't understand how ours landed in the middle. I'm sure most travellers can relate to this.

The train came to a halt and I beckoned Bonnie to me. I lifted the rucksacks on to the platform, then Bonnie with outstretched arms next. She kissed me as I put her down,

'I'm sure you are going to make a habit of this. You seem too eager for a lift at every opportunity,' I said.

'Why shouldn't I!' she exclaimed.

I carried the sacks over to the other platform where the Oban train was waiting. We were fortunate to find a seat together on this occasion.

I said to Bonnie I wished to go to the toilet back on the platform as one cannot use the one on the train while it's stationary. 'You have to be in motion, and I feel I'm in motion.'

She burst out laughing. 'Hurry then, or it may not be trains we're changing.'

'I'll be as quick as I can.'

I located the gents at the south of the platform but found myself having to wait a few minutes as other passengers had found themselves in a similar position. Finally a booth became available. Thank God, I thought, I couldn't have held on much longer.

Halfway through my evacuation I heard the noise of a train on the track. Surely that must be the Glasgow train, I thought. I continued with my duties and washed my hands on completion.

I stepped out of the toilets and to my horror the Mallaig to Glasgow train was still in the station. My stomach began to churn as I turned to face the opposite platform.

The train had left. 'Oh no!' I cried.

A station worker hearing my wail approached and asked if I was all right. I explained what had happened and that my girl was on the Oban train. 'Look, don't panic,' he said. 'I'll phone Oban station and tell them you're OK.'

'What about Bonnie?'

'I'll tell them to inform her.'

'That's kind and reassuring of you,' I said.

'The next train to Oban isn't for four hours. You can catch a bus down the street in about ten minutes which will arrive half an hour later than the train you were supposed to be on. Have you enough money to pay the fare?'

'Yes, thanks. Let the station know I'm coming by bus and they can pass the message on to Bonnie.'

'I will! Best of luck then, son. I'm sure everything will work out.'

'Thanks again,' I said, and made a dash for the exit.

I reached the bus stop with two minutes to spare. The front seat was empty so I jumped in.

I had been so looking forward to this part of the journey on the train and this anticipation was now overshadowed by misfortune.

The bus came to a halt at Tyndrum. 'You have fifteen minutes,' said the driver. I had a quick cuppa and returned to the coach in plenty of time. I can't afford any more mishaps, I said to myself.

Depressed though I was I felt a calming uplift from the views along Loch Awe. I was pleasantly surprised that the road followed the route of the train mostly, which indeed was a bonus.

Having studied my map earlier I knew we would be in Oban an hour after we entered Benderloch. Further on came Connel Ferry, the old road link across the loch to Fort William. Falls of Lora is the name given to the flow from Loch Etive. It is best viewed at low tide and especially after heavy rainfall.

The old iron railway bridge is a marvellous piece of Scottish engineering. Unfortunately the train service to Ballachulish was never a success and was closed in 1954. It is now part of the main trunk road to Fort William.

I was now becoming desperate as we made the final approach in to Oban. Wow! The view reminded me of the film *Captain Horatio Hornblower*. I imagined a man o'war vessel in the bay, training its guns on the town.

The bus stage was next to the rail station. I was first off and sprinted towards the entrance. I expected to see Bonnie immediately, but as I searched I became more disconsolate that she was nowhere in sight.

Panic set in. Where was she? What had happened? Did she get off at the next station when I failed to return? I ran across to the ticket kiosk to try to find an answer.

As usual I was forced to wait as there were two people ahead of me in the queue. Now it was my turn. 'Has there been a young girl enquiring about a Jamie Cameron?' I asked.

'No, sir,' said the gentleman. 'Perhaps you should go and see the station manager,' he added, pointing in the direction of the office.

'Thank you, I will,' I said.

A fresh-faced elderly man with rosy cheeks opened the door. 'What can I do for you, young sir?'

'Did you receive a phone call from Crianlarich earlier today about me? I'm Jamie Cameron.'

'So you're Mr Cameron!'

'Yes, sir.'

'I did receive a call this afternoon telling me of your predicament and that your young lady had gone on without you. I'm sorry to tell you as far as I know she did not get off the train at Oban. I asked the guard on the train if any young lady had left the train with rucksacks at an earlier station. He informed me that this indeed took place at Tyndrum station near to Crianlarich.'

'Oh no!' I said.

'Don't worry, I truly believe that she will have taken the next train, which is due in a few hours. My guess is that she hoped you would be on that train and therefore was prepared to wait for it.'

'I'll just have to hang around then,' I said.

'No, you go for something to eat and then sit at the pier and enjoy the view. You will need to be patient. Don't forget her. She will be hungry, so get her a fish and chips or something for her arriving. I'm sure she will appreciate it.'

I sat and watched the boats come and go from the harbour which distracted my attention from the clock. I hardly tasted my fish and chips as I was really worried about Bonnie.

The ferry to the isles came and went again before the train arrived. I checked the clock; the train would be about due so I returned to the station carrying a fish supper for my love.

I could hardly contain myself as the train pulled to a halt. A mass of people emerged from the train, but still no sign of Bonnie. I ran up and down the carriages, jumping up and down in an effort to look in the windows. Still no Bonnie. I was beginning to get perplexed as negative thoughts were overtaking reality. Then she suddenly appeared with a rucksack on each hand trying to alight from the carriage.

'Bonnie! Bonnie!' I cried as I ran to the door.

She burst out crying at the sight of me. I lifted her into my arms and kissed all her tears.

'Did my baby miss me?' I asked.

'You don't know how much,' she replied, fighting back the tears.

I put her down and lifted the rucksacks from the train. I handed her a fish and chip bag.

'Oh, thank you, I'm really very hungry.'

I found a seat near to the Mull ferry harbour near to the shopping centre. She cuddled into me while eating and still sniffling. I told her that we would stay at the hostel for two nights, then I would find a B&B which would allow us to go dancing and have a late evening to finish off our holiday. 'Also I'll take you on a trip to Tobermory on the ferry.' I felt this was the least I could do after the trouble I had caused that day.

Finally she began to feel better at the thought of having me near. 'Oh, that sounds wonderful! I'll look forward to it. Are you able to afford all that?' Bonnie enquired.

'Yes. All the odd jobs Colin and I took on paid well. Believe it or not I have more money now than I left home with.'

She kissed me once more for reassurance and said, 'It must be time to go to the hostel.'

'Yes, it is. I'll carry the sacks and you too if you want.'

The beautiful smile returned and I knew she was fine.

As we made our way along the promenade I pointed to the cathedral. 'The hostel is not far from there. Colin told me, Bonnie.'

'That's good, for I'm tired!'

'We have certainly pushed a lot into one day,' I said.

'This is a beautiful walk, Jamie, I'm sure I will like promenading here all week.'

The hostel was exactly where Colin had said and we arrived in time before doors closing. I hoped I would have a good bunk. I didn't fancy one in the middle of the floor as I had had in Loch Lomond. Yes! I had been given a bunk in a small room at the rear of the hostel with only one other occupant. The room had only three sets of bunk beds so I was able to choose a lower one at the rear of the room.

I went to find Bonnie who I had arranged to meet in the large day room or lounge. 'How are you, baby?' I gave her a cuddle and she smiled.

'I'm fine now but I do want to go to bed if you don't mind.'

'No not at all. I was about to say the same thing. Oh, did you manage to get a lower bunk, Bonnie?'

'Yes, I'm in with some nice girls and they like quiet.'

'Oh, that's good, it makes such a difference.'

'Night, baby.'

'Night, Jamie.'

The next day Bonnie told me of her dilemma. 'I asked the ticket collector when the next train was for Oban. He informed me it would not be for another four hours. I tried hard to think what you might do in the circumstances. As Tyndrum was only a short distance from Crianlarich I decided to get off there. As you had four hours to spare I thought you would walk to Tyndrum and meet me to catch the train there.

'I gave up on that after an hour and a half and tried to occupy my mind in my book. I was alone and frightened for about two hours until other passengers appeared. I was so disappointed that we had not been on the same wavelength. It just never occurred to me that there was a bus service to Oban,' said Bonnie.

'Oh, my poor wee baby. I was devastated when I saw the platform empty and the train gone. I took the first thing that came along so that I would only be an hour or so behind you. It was the guard at Crianlarich that told me of the bus service to Oban.'

'It was the best feeling in the world when I saw you standing in the station at Oban, Jamie.'

'I'll second that,' I said.

To appreciate the beauty of Oban you need a day like this day. We walked into town at leisurely pace, passing the cathedral, the history of which I promised myself I would read up on.

'What a setting. If I were a priest I would seek this post if I was in this diocese.'

'I would give it to you I were the bishop,' said Bonnie, laughing.

We headed into town and Bonnie decided that she wanted to go up and see McCaig's Tower.

'I want to take pictures from the top. It's bound to have some fabulous views from up there, but I have no camera now you left it with the police at Fort William yesterday,' said Bonnie.

'I'll buy a new one for you. I noticed a photographer's shop at the corner in the main square, you can choose one there. If you don't mind I'll nip along to the police station and see if they managed to pick up the robbers.'

'Jamie, look, isn't that the boat we saw leaving Fort William coming into the pier?'

'Well spotted, Bonnie – and that's the coast guard vessel behind it. Yes they have got them, thanks to us. Thank goodness for that.'

As we passed all the small yachts moored in the bay a police car sped past and drew up at the hotel car park on the pier. As we approached the harbour we saw two men being taken off the vessel which had now berthed. They were hastily bundled into the back of the police car and then driven off, presumably to the nearest police station.

Just as we were about to walk away a voice called my name: 'Mr Cameron, is that you?'

I quickly turned round to see the detective who was in charge of the case. 'Yes, it is!' I said.

'I thought it was you, but I wasn't too sure. You will be pleased to know that we have found the rings on board plus a very expensive necklace. We have apprehended some men for questioning as a result of your call. The jewellers have offered £250 reward for the return of the stolen items, which means you and your friends, all three of you, are entitled to a share. I'm sure that will please you after all the trouble you have gone through.'

'Oh, that's wonderful, Jamie, we can stay in a big hotel for a few nights now.'

'Certainly can, baby,' I replied.

'Oh, the other matter,' said the detective. 'Here is your camera. I have removed your spool from it. I will post your photos to you at your home address. We haven't caught the two robbers yet, but it will be easier now that we have a picture of them. It won't be long till we catch up with them, but be careful meantime as they are dangerous. Bye now, enjoy the rest of your holiday.'

'Oh, we will!' said Bonnie. 'Bye.'

Bonnie was ecstatic at receiving part of the reward. 'He said I have to have a share in the reward money, Jamie. Is that all right with you and Colin?'

'Of course it is! It was you and I that put ourselves at risk in Fort William, and don't forget it was you who took their picture.'

'Yes it was! Weeeee!'

'I take it you're happy now then.'

'Oh, yes!' she said, hugging and kissing me all the while.

'Let's get a spool for the camera first then some food for a picnic on the tower.'

'I filled the flask with tea before leaving the hostel,' said Bonnie, 'so we are all prepared.'

We zigzagged all the way up the hill. 'It's pretty steep,' said Bonnie.

'I know your poor wee legs are hurting, but I'm sure you can make it,' I said.

The last 100 yards on the hill were extremely steep and I used my arm to push Bonnie's back forwards. 'Oh, that's good, Jamie, keep doing that. I feel as if I'm being propelled forward.'

'That's how it's supposed to feel! I wish someone would push me up the hill!'

We finally reached the path that led into the centre of the tower and Bonnie demanded to be carried as she was exhausted by the climb and the heat. 'Oh I can't go any further!' said Bonnie.

'Come on, baby, but I hope you're not leading me on.'

'No, Jamie, I feel faint.'

I swooped her up off her feet and into my arms and she hugged and kissed me.

'My strong hero,' said Bonnie.

'I hope you're not kidding, baby!'

'Oh no!'

'OK then I'll run up the path as quick as I can.'

Phew, I made it, but the sweat was dripping off me now. I laid her gently on the grass and collapsed beside her. A cup of water, then a snack with a cup of tea and Bonnie made a full recovery.

'I feel great now. I don't like going up steep hills,' said Bonnie.

'Perhaps big brother Angus knew that when he didn't want you with him.'

'You may be right, Jamie. Oh, I'm going to love being here with you, Jamie.'

'The views are stunning, aren't they, Bonnie?'

'Yes, my love!' she said, staring into my eyes.

'Are you taking the mickey out of me, Bonnie?'

'Am I not allowed to say what I see?'

'You win, my beautiful Bonnie!'

'You would think there would be an easier way to the top. It must difficult for older people to get up and down without a lift.'

'I think they should have a cliff railway for the tourists, with a restaurant and gift shop in the centre of the tower, especially for the middle-aged and elderly, as you say. It's usually more mature people like you that come on holiday here.'

I had to run after that remark! She found a new source of energy from somewhere. I tripped up and fell on the bank and the next thing I knew I was being tickled under my arms.

'I surrender! I didn't mean it, old girl!'

'Oh... Jamie Cameron, I'll... thump you! No... I'll tickle you to death for that.'

'Honest,' I cried, 'the wrong word slipped out!'

She wasn't satisfied till she had me almost licking her feet.

'Sorry, baby, pleasssssse stop tickling!'

'Well, all right!'

After our bit of fun, in which I lost, again, I went on to tell Bonnie that in Babbacombe just outside Torquay a cliff railway ferries people to and fro from the beach all day. I'm sure the bay would be deserted if it were not for the railway.

I think this building deserves recognition simply because of what the man stood for. If you read about the castles around Scotland they all have had work and extensions added throughout the centuries. The tower is a magnificent building; the leaflet I read told me Mr McCaig gave employment to the builders who were out of work. It was meant to be a large hotel with commanding views of the bay. However the money ran out and the worked ceased. I think it would be appropriate for my transport suggestion to be looked at, as this would create work and prosperity for the town – which was the intention of Mr McCaig.

'Why do you think it won't happen, Jamie?'

'Money first! The project would need government funding along with private investment. Then there is heritage, pure and simple. No one will want to put their name to any alteration for fear of criticism. That's only my view, passed on to me by my dad. I hope I'm wrong. We need to protect old buildings but we also need to move on.'

After relaxing for an hour Bonnie woke me. 'Are you going to sleep here all day?' she asked.

'Yes, if I don't get a kiss and cuddle.'

'Oh, come here then.'

I lifted her up on to one of the large openings on the tower. These were where the windows would have been fitted had the building been finished.

'You're as pretty as picture there, Bonnie, and you have been framed into the bargain.'

'I want one from all the frames, Jamie, and I want you in it along with me.'

'You be careful while I ask someone to take them. Don't want you falling down the cliff, so behave!'

'I promise, Jamie! Try those three girls over yonder. One will take them. They will probably want theirs taken anyway,' said Bonnie.

Finally Bonnie was satisfied with all the photos she had taken which I have to say were numerous.

'Well, my girl, are you happy now?' I asked.

'Oh yes! I have never seen a view as lovely as this before.'

'Yes, it is stunning I have to admit, and I can say "panoramic" as Colin is not here. I always come under fire from him when I try to portray the feeling I have for the scene I am witnessing before me.'

'The Americans would say it was awesome, Jamie.'

'From this vantage point we can look over the island of Kererra towards Mull, and with my eyesight I'm able to see the ferry which is a dot in the distance leaving Craignure to return to Oban.'

'I can't see it,' said Bonnie.

'It's only a speck on the horizon. Concentrate on your left away beyond the castle and you will see it.'

'I do now, Jamie! You have certainly got excellent vision. I am looking forward to our sail to Mull on the last day of the holiday.'

We could scan the whole town from this point and I pointed out the station. 'Do you see the rail station down there, Bonnie?'

'Yes, the blue building.'

'Well, I hope no one has a bright idea of keeping that relic. To me it is only a shelter and should be treated as such.'

Bonnie laughed and said, 'You certainly have a bee in your bonnet about buildings.'

We were reluctant to leave this beautiful setting so we lay down on the grass, still with a view of Mull through an aperture. As Bonnie lay my arms I told her about how I dreamed this town should have been.

'You know I like to daydream, Bonnie.'

'I certainly do.'

'Well, can you imagine if all our great-great-grandparents had stayed in Scotland how busy this town would be. I see it as a city with a bridge like the one in Sydney harbour. It would span over to Kererra from the hillside above the station. The island would have high rise like New York and ships would sail from all over the world into the sheltered horseshoe bay that is Oban. Behind the cathedral would be another bridge. A massive spanned bridge would carry a new rail network straight into Kererra, which would be the hub of the new city. I visualise this in 300 years' time for Oban City.'

'You are a daydreamer, Jamie, but I love you even more for it.'

Chapter Thirty-six

'Are you feeling fit now, Bonnie?'
'Why?'

'Well, do you see where I would build my bridge across to Kererra? That is what is called Pulpit Hill. I'm sure you can take a few more snaps from there. With a change of view you may catch one of the ferries coming through the narrow entrance to the bay.'

'Oh, you have convinced me. It looks very steep though, so I may need a carry,' said Bonnie. Which really meant she would insist on being carried the last 100 yards at least.

Bonnie enjoyed going downhill. She waited till I was a few yards in front and then ran into my arms.

'I hope you are frisky going up Pulpit Hill,' I said.

'I want to have my tea now before I do any more walking.'

'OK, Bonnie, that's fine by me. A fish tea will go down nicely.'

We found a cafe and took our time before attempting to try our next venture. A stroll along the harbour and then on to the hill was the intention, but Bonnie decided on a flat road leading along from the harbour which headed towards the yachts anchored in the sound. 'Oh, perfect,' said Bonnie, 'there are seats to view the bay and I can take all those snaps you mentioned earlier. Carry me to a seat, Jamie?'

How could I say no? If you saw her face then I'm sure you would agree. 'Come on then, my naughty baby.

'Listen, Bonnie, what do you hear?'

'Mm, the sound of the wind whistling through the trees.'

'Yes, what else?' I asked.

'Oh, a clinking sound.'

'You've got it! It's coming from the masts on the yachts and this will remind you of this afternoon for ever.'

'You are right, Jamie, I'll always remember being here with you.'

'If I'm ever rich I'll sail around here, I promise.'

'Then I'll be your galley cook,' said Bonnie. 'Oh, by the way, did you tell your mum and dad we are on holiday together?'

Silence…

'Didn't you tell them, Jamie?'

'Yes, I have Bonnie. What I haven't told them is that we are on holiday alone together.'

'So they think you are still with Colin, then?'

'Well, not exactly. I told them we split up after Fort Augustus and I headed towards Inverness. Whereas Colin was going to Ullapool all the way up the west coast.'

'Why didn't you tell them you were meeting me, then?'

'It's not easy. They are very strict and if they had met you before we left it might be different. She would have a fit if she knew I was going to stay with you in a hotel, even though it's in a different room. I will take you back home with me and let you meet them. That way I won't get a tongue-bashing.'

'Oh, I forgive you then, as long as you take me home to meet them.'

A quick change of subject required, I thought. 'By the way, Bonnie, did I tell you what happened to Colin after he left me at Invermoriston?'

'No! Please tell, I love Colin's stories.'

'Well, he got a lift soon after he left me at Invermoriston. A Land Rover pulled alongside and offered him a lift to the Kyle of Lochalsh.

Colin's story:

'The jeep began to overheat so I was forced to take a look under the bonnet. I found that one of the hosepipes was leaking so the radiator was running low on water. Forgetting about the pressure building up in the radiator, I turned the cap too quickly resulting in the cap whizzing past me and heading for the sky.

'I taped up the small fracture in the pipe the best I could, then the old gentleman asked, "Will you fetch water from the loch with a canister from the rear, if you don't mind, son? You are a lot fitter than me."

' "No problem!" I told him.

'I walked through what I would call a squelchy bog, down to

the water's edge. As I was filling the can I saw what appeared to be a dark cloud rising from the edge of the loch. What's that? I wondered. I had almost filled the can so I placed the cap on it and decided to make a hasty retreat to the car.

'Halfway to the car I was being attacked by a swarm of midges. They were all over me. I couldn't open my mouth. I tried my best to get them off my face and eyes. Finally I reached the car and threw myself in the seat. To the alarm of Bert, a multitude set about him. Hands were everywhere, swiping and hitting out. I had thought him frail and slow – however a new burst of energy was now being unleashed from this quiet, doleful person. He produced a cloth for both himself and me as we murdered them on the screen.

'The main swarm had now moved away so we were able to open the windows partially and rid ourselves of the remaining aliens. I was desperate to get outside but Bert insisted on waiting ten minutes so that we would have no further engagement with the enemy. Finally I got out and rid myself of any pestilence that was on me. I had lumps and bumps everywhere! I took my shirt off and shook it as best as I could.

'Taking the cap off the can I filled the radiator to capacity. "I hope I don't have to fetch any more water before we reach the Kyle, Bert."

' "Don't worry!" said Bert to me. "I won't ask you again. I wasn't too impressed with the friends you brought along this time." '

'It's hilarious the way you tell a story.' Bonnie was in stitches of laughter at my description and accompanying gestures of the tale related to me by Colin. 'Oh, I'm glad I wasn't there,' said Bonnie, 'I would have been screaming.'

'I don't think so,' I said, 'or you would have got a mouthful of midges.'

'Oh no, talk about something else, please!' Bonnie said, making a face.

'Bonnie! I have just thought – phone your uncle in Inverness and ask him if he will book a room for each of us in the Kererra View Hotel. If the booking is made then the question of my age should not come under scrutiny. He is a banker, after all.'

'I'll get in him on the phone when we reach the town centre,' said Bonnie.

We managed to find a phone box and Bonnie told Stephen I wished to speak with him. 'Hi, Stephen! We have been told we are entitled to a reward for helping in the recovery of the diamonds stolen in Glasgow.'

'That's good news,' said Stephen.

'Yes. I want to stay in a hotel with Bonnie for three nights. Can you help?'

'No problem, Jamie! I'll tell them I'll send a cheque, or I might send someone round from the branch in Oban to pay the bill. I'll tell them you have my authorisation to stay and I will tell your parents, which will keep matters right for you. You can pay me when you get your reward, Jamie.'

'Stephen, how can I ever thank you?'

'Just look after my wee girl.'

'Stephen's going to phone the hotel and book us in. He says there will be no problem, Bonnie.'

'Good old Uncle Stephen.'

Bonnie was almost skipping up the road to the hotel, 'Oh we can dance tonight, Jamie, isn't that wonderful?'

'Yes, everything seems to be working out for us now.'

Bonnie raced me to the hostel to collect our rucksacks; after gathering our items together we told the warden that we were now leaving and thanked him for his friendliness during our stay. We entered the hotel and asked if our rooms had been booked for us. The receptionist confirmed the booking and gave us the keys to our rooms, although somewhat surprised at our luggage.

I pressed my slacks and shirt on the room press which made them look like new once more. Bonnie had bought a nice light summer dress for the dinner dance and was still excited when she knocked on my door.

'We can go down for dinner now, Jamie.'

'I'll be there in a minute!' I said. I didn't want to open the door for fear she might want to come in. I would then probably panic in case someone saw her enter my room.

The view was stunning from my window; the hotel commanded a full view of the bay from its central position. My next view was of Bonnie in her new dress, with shining eyes, ivory teeth and silky brown hair. Not even the scene from my window could surpass this.

'My, you are so beautiful!' I said.

'Oh stop it! There are plenty of girls as pretty as me,' said Bonnie.

'Not in my eyes, Bonnie.'

She pulled me down and kissed me. 'Love you, Jamie.'

The meal was delicious and I felt like a prince being waited on, with my princess Bonnie beside me. With all the formidable setbacks since my hiking began I must admit I felt a sense of admiration within myself with what I had achieved along with Colin. Here I was dancing with the most beautiful creature I had ever laid eyes on and staying in a top-class hotel. I couldn't wait to tell Colin. I wondered what he would say when he heard about our windfall.

Before the evening ended I asked the band if I could sing a few numbers with them, to which they readily agreed. I sang 'Blue Moon' to Bonnie and then 'Catch a Falling Star', which went down well with everyone.

The band finished with one of those clinging numbers, which was Bonnie's favourite. The way she leaned on me made me feel I was carrying her.

'Love you, baby.'

'I love you too, Jamie, and I wish the night would never end!' said Bonnie.

Chapter Thirty-seven

After a hearty breakfast we decided to head for the beach.
'I'll go into town and get us some niceties for a picnic,' said Bonnie. 'I'll meet you out at the cathedral. You wanted to take a look inside, didn't you?'

'Yes I do! See you in a bit then.'

I managed to find a leaflet on the construction of the building before going on in. The cathedral was designed by architect Sir Giles Gilbert Scott and the foundation stone was laid in 1932. The building work was then completed in 1959. It was partially funded by money raised in Canada, America and Ireland. It is constructed from pink Peterhead and blue Inverawe granite. The original cathedral, on the Island of Lismore, now belongs to the Church of Scotland.

It wasn't long before Bonnie joined me inside the building. 'Oh, it's huge, and look at the massive pillars it has!' said Bonnie. 'And every word I say has an echo.'

The roof was all wood, with large structural beams, which added to the openness of the building.

'I'm glad we came in,' I said. 'I think we should say thanks for all our blessings, Bonnie.'

'I agree.'

We said a few prayers of thanksgiving then left for the beach.

Having walked only a few hundred yards Bonnie stopped at a small green park with seats facing the narrow part of the channel between the mainland and Kererra. 'I want to sit here, Jamie, and enjoy the stillness and the view for a few moments.'

I obliged by moving to the seat next to the small lighthouse. I was amazed how close the ferry came to the shoreline. I felt as if I could shake the passengers' hands. The tide was at low ebb and exposed the rocky coastline, which showed just how narrow the channel really was.

'I will call this place Peace Corner and always bring it to mind when I need calm.'

'That's a good name, Bonnie,' I said, 'but I'll call it Lord of the Isles Way, the highway to heaven.'

'Give me a kiss here so that I can remember the moment, and carry me back to the path, Jamie.'

'OK beautiful.'

We set out once more along the road to Ganavan, which was dangerous in places. Carefully we walked round a sharp bend, then jumped the fence into a small wood at the cliff edge, with Bonnie demanding to be lifted over as usual.

'I want to go as near to the sea as possible so that I can take a picture of the small island,' said Bonnie. She then ran ahead.

'Be careful!' I cried.

As I shouted two beautiful young girls sat up, slightly startled. They were sunbathing topless on a large flat rock, leaving nothing to the imagination. On seeing me they smiled without any embarrassment and simply lay back down once more.

Bonnie appeared from nowhere and dragged me away. 'You got more than an eyeful there, Jamie!'

'I certainly did, can't wait to tell Colin,' I said, laughing heartily.

I got a poke in the ribs for that, which was deserved, so I said no more of their near perfectly formed figures.

Taking the road once more we found a small deserted beach. 'I don't see any private signs, Bonnie, so we should be OK here.'

Quickly I took my top and shorts off and ran into the sea. I was desperate for a swim so I didn't wait for Bonnie, simply because I didn't want to put any pressure on her. Anyway, I wasn't sure whether she detested wet sand on her like some of my friends did.

I dived off a large rock into a deep pool with the surf breaking as I surfaced. Oh, this is magic! I thought to myself.

I looked to the shore and saw Bonnie running towards me in the water with what could only be described as a skimpy bikini. I swam to meet her and she screamed as I caught her in my arms. 'You are freezing, Jamie, let me go!'

'I love your choice of swimwear!' I said

'I put this on for you. I would never wear it on a crowded beach, Jamie.'

'Mmm, what a figure you have, Bonnie! Just as good as the ones I saw earlier,' I said. I got another belting for that, but she was laughing all the while.

We swam to the rock, dived in and surfaced together. 'You really are beautiful, Bonnie,' I said as we clung to each other in the water.

Sensing that I was feeling it difficult to control my emotions she broke off and swam to the shore. I followed her and before I could speak she took my hand and put the other on my lips.

'I'm a virgin, Jamie, the same as you, and that is the way I wish to remain till I marry.'

I managed to interrupt and say, 'Bonnie, I feel exactly the same way!'

'As long as you are happy with that,' said Bonnie.

'All I need to know, Bonnie, is that you love me.'

'Oh, I do, you must know I do, Jamie. I think of you first thing every morning and last thing at night.'

'So do I, my baby!'

We ran into the surf once more, splashing about like kids, and finished the day lying in each other's arms.

Chapter Thirty-eight

It was the final day of our holiday tomorrow so we had planned a sail to Mull on the big *Columba* ferry. We thought about taking one of the small boat trips but quickly dismissed it. I didn't fancy it, to be honest.

Next morning we made our way to the pier where a large queue had already gathered to board the mid-morning ferry. It took some time to board, however I managed to find two good seats on the top deck, out of the wind but with a perfect view of the town on the starboard side as we left port. I have to say I was caught up in all the excitement. People were feeding the birds; other people had their binoculars pointing to Duart castle far ahead to the left on the island of Mull.

On our right was the lighthouse on Lismore. As we passed by I commented to Bonnie, 'This place is really eerie. Look how the water is frothy right in the middle of the channel. This points to rock or parts of the island not too far below the surface.'

'It does look quite frightening!' said Bonnie.

On arrival at Craignure we had opted for a tour of the island which would take us to one of the many castles and then finally to Tobermory. I had seen so many castles that I had lost interest, so Bonnie and I went to the tea room and purchased a leaflet on its history rather than take the tour itself.

The driver was local and knew the places of interest. He stopped the bus at a tranquil spot and told us to sit quietly on the rocks. A few minutes later he pointed out a few hundred yards off. It was a family of otters, and Bonnie quickly snapped some photos with the new spool she had bought in Oban.

We carried on round the island and the bus quickly stopped. 'If you can get out speedily you will see a golden eagle flying above us!' the driver said excitedly. Cameras were out and Bonnie managed to snap one with a head shot of me in the foreground.

'Oh, I have a great one there!' Bonnie shouted. 'I hope it takes and comes out well.'

The driver continued and told us he would approach Tobermory from the north rather than the south. He went on to explain he could not attempt this on a windy day. Since it was still today he would take this route as long as conditions were favourable.

As we approached the area he built up enough speed on the coach to pass the dangerous point by now switching off the engine and putting it into neutral. It was plain to see why, as we passed huge rocks close to the road.

The driver had told us that the route was closed most of the time owing to the danger imposed by the crumbling rock which tumbles down the hillsides and over on to the road. I was quite pleased to hear the engine start up on the coach, which signalled that we were out of danger.

We drove down into Tobermory, which was a natural harbour filled with small craft and fishing boats. We had an hour to spare in the town so we opted to go for fish and chips and sit at the pier. The sun was shining brightly now, which lit up all the splendid colours on the buildings.

'I think we should get someone to take our photograph here, Bonnie,' I said. 'It will be a nice memento of our trip.'

There was no shortage of people so I got what I wanted. I got one photo of the pier and the town with Bonnie and me close together. It was a strange feeling after the photos were taken, which I was unable to explain.

The hour passed quickly and we had to run for the coach. Schedules must be kept on tours, especially when you have to catch a ferry.

'What a wonderful day, Jamie. It has been the highlight of the holiday. We have seen so much that one can only appreciate by seeing for oneself.'

'Indeed,' I replied.

As we boarded the ferry I thought I recognised two men in an old blue Morris van. It can't be them, surely. Anyway it's a different colour of van, I thought.

When we were aboard Bonnie kissed me and hugged me, then

said, 'I have something to tell you. Don't be alarmed!' she added, seeing the expression on my face.

I was a bit startled. What was so important? 'What is wrong?' I asked her.

She continued. 'I have passed all my higher exams with excellence.'

'That's wonderful!' I said excitedly.

'No, it's not that,' Bonnie replied.

'What then?' I was becoming anxious.

'It's that I have won a scholarship to go to university in America for four years. It's an opportunity of a lifetime and I have always wanted to see America. I feel I have to say yes, Jamie.'

I was stunned and lost for words.

'Say something, Jamie!' Bonnie said.

She was leaving for America. It would be impossible to turn down such an award. To say no to it would be a drastic measure; her career must come first. She would surely find another suitor over there, among all those giant footballers for instance. She is beautiful and I love her, but don't want her to go – all these thoughts were running through my head.

I feel totally gutted! What can I say to her? That I'm a selfish so-and-so? That I'm afraid I'll lose her? That I'm jealous? Oh, I feel ill!

'I have to go to the toilet, Bonnie, I won't be a minute.'

When I exited the toilet I made my way to the stern of the ship to view the Lismore lighthouse as we passed by. Trying to come to terms with what Bonnie had told me was difficult, but I had to try and convince myself it was for the best. I wished she had waited till after the holiday, though, as it had put a dampener on things.

I was about to turn on my foot but I was grabbed on both sides by the two clowns that had stolen our rucksacks. It was them I had spied earlier. I should have been more careful, I thought.

'Why, it's one of the hiker boys, Sam!' the burly one said.

'Do you think he would like a swim?' the other one asked.

'I'm sure he is feeling a little hot under the collar, Joe, and a cold bath will do him the world of good.'

'Don't be stupid!' I said. 'We are out at sea!'

'Oh, he's scared of the water, Joe!'

'Well, he'll just have to swim to the big lighthouse then, Sam.'

'My girl will tell the captain!' I said, in a panic.

'Oh, and we'll take care of your pretty girl too! Won't we, Joe?'

'Oh, we will!'

'Why, you pigs!' I shouted as I tried to struggle free, but it was no use. I was over the side and the next thing I knew I was in the cold, frothy water which gave me the creeps.

The things that went through my mind: What would happen to Bonnie? Would she think I had committed suicide? Would I ever see her again? Oh, it didn't bear thinking about.

I had phoned home the previous night and the news was not good at all. Colin was missing in the Cairngorm area. He had last been seen helping on the moors beating the heather. Three police forces had contacted my home and a girl called Katie was persistently calling, asking to speak to me. My mum had demanded to know what was going on.

Oh, I have to find a way to get on land, I thought. I'll swim as fast as I can so that I don't catch cramp. I have to find a spot to get on shore!

Will help come? Will Bonnie tell the captain before those thugs grab her? When all is lost one can either sink or swim!

Just a Memory

The heart that is open is the heart that is true,
The heart that was willing is now broken in two.
I gave everything, all the loving I had
To the one I most wanted, who left me so sad.
I'll treasure the moments, like the blossoms in spring,
All of the pleasure, the thoughts of happiness you
   bring.
A kiss in the moonlight, your sparkling eyes,
The flutter of birds in the evening skies,
To reach heights of rapture and then only to find
The one that you loved has left you behind.
So hard is the memory, so long is the day.

Now when I need you, you are far, far away.
I now shelter in shadows with a forgotten dream
Beside the still waters of a swift mountain stream.

Jamie Cameron

Oh, swim, Jamie! Swim! I mustn't give in! I will find a way! Bonnie! Bonnie! Please find help! She has to!

I'll keep telling myself, even if Bonnie is going away to America, it's not the end. I'll fight to keep her. She is mine and always will be. I can make it!

When in trouble, what would Colin do? The practical survivor. Yes, I have it! I've paid for three nights at a top hotel. There is no way I'm going to forfeit that without a fight. That's what he would tell himself.

That's just the spur I needed! I will make it now!

Acknowledgements

I acknowledge with gratitude the owners of the following websites, which I used to obtain the necessary records for this book. I have tried to be exact in all that is written. Any error has to be put down to the author and I apologise unreservedly beforehand should this prove to be the case. Sincere thanks to:

Aberfeldy: The Heart of Scotland:
http://www.fife.50megs.com/
http://tour-scotland.blogspot.com/
http://best-scottish-tours.blogspot.com/
A tranquil beauty spot set on the River Tay. Special thanks to Sandy Stevenson for the use of this website.

The Caledonian Canal:
www.britishwaterways.co.uk/scotland
Thanks to Alasdair Burns, Marketing Manager, British Waterways Scotland. For anyone wishing to see the Highlands, this is an ideal holiday destination. The Canal was an ingenious marvel of its era and has stood the test of time.

CalMac Ferries Ltd:
www.calmac.co.uk
Thanks to Stuart McLean, Marketing Development Officer. CalMac offer an excellent service to all destinations on the Clyde and the Western Isles of Scotland.

Sandy Ferguson (Photography):
www.fergusonphotos.co.uk
Sports, Public Relations, Press Photography.

Dunvegan Castle:
www.dunvegancastle.com
Thanks to Hugh MacLeod, Estate Manager. A visit to Skye is not complete without a tour of Dunvegan Castle.

Fort Augustus Abbey:
www.fortaugustusabbey.co.uk
Thanks to Tony Harmsworth for the use of this website and his assistance.

Inverary Castle:
www.inveraray-castle.com
Thanks to His Grace for the use of this website and to Jane Young, Manager. This is a magical castle in a beautiful setting and well worth a visit.

InCallander website:
www.incallander.co.uk
Thanks to Alistair Reid for accurate information on Loch Lomond and the Trossachs, a most wonderful place to visit.

SYHA:
www.syha.org.uk
Thanks to Louise Nowell, Sales and Marketing and also to John Martin, Archivist.

The National Wallace Monument website:
www.nationalwallacemonument.com
Thanks to Ken Thomson, Marketing Manager, Stirling District Tourism.

Stirling Castle:
www.historic-scotland.co.uk
Thanks to Peter Yeoman, Head of Cultural Resources. A special thank you to Historic Scotland for the use of their website on the history of Stirling Castle. The source of this material is CROWN COPYRIGHT, HISTORIC SCOTLAND.

For their general assistance, thanks to June Matchett and Aileen Stephen.

Note on SYHA: The Scottish Youth Hostels Association is a registered charity and operates as a not-for-profit organisation. It has a network of hostels of all types and sizes, taking in the stunning scenery of the mountains along with coastal, rural and city locations, and of course not forgetting our enchanted islands. Hostels are open to all and now cater for groups and families. The hostels have changed a lot since the early days and all are comfortable and welcoming with modern facilities and amenities. The Scottish Youth Hostels Association was also a founder member of the hostel grading scheme run by the Scottish Tourist Board, Visit Scotland, and most of the hostels have achieved awards in their Green Tourism grading programme. Hostelling is and inexpensive and enjoyable way to see Scotland's natural beauty.

Printed in the United Kingdom by
Lightning Source UK Ltd., Milton Keynes
139740UK00001B/6/P

9 781847 484543